JOHN GORDON SINCLAIR

---◆---

SEVENTY TIMES SEVEN

Complete and Unabridged

CHARNWOOD
Leicester

First published in Great Britain in 2012 by
Faber and Faber Limited
London

First Charnwood Edition
published 2013
by arrangement with
Faber and Faber
London

A catalogue record for this book is available
from the British Library.

ISBN 978–1–4448–1736–2

Published by
F. A. Thorpe (Publishing)
Anstey, Leicestershire

SPECIAL MESSAGE TO READERS

THE ULVERSCROFT FOUNDATION
(registered UK charity number 264873)
was established in 1972 to provide funds for
research, diagnosis and treatment of eye diseases.
Examples of major projects funded by
the Ulverscroft Foundation are:-

- The Children's Eye Unit at Moorfields Eye Hospital, London
- The Ulverscroft Children's Eye Unit at Great Ormond Street Hospital for Sick Children
- Funding research into eye diseases and treatment at the Department of Ophthalmology, University of Leicester
- The Ulverscroft Vision Research Group, Institute of Child Health
- Twin operating theatres at the Western Ophthalmic Hospital, London
- The Chair of Ophthalmology at the Royal Australian College of Ophthalmologists

You can help further the work of the Foundation
by making a donation or leaving a legacy.
Every contribution is gratefully received. If you
would like to help support the Foundation or
require further information, please contact:

THE ULVERSCROFT FOUNDATION
The Green, Bradgate Road, Anstey
Leicester LE7 7FU, England
Tel: (0116) 236 4325

website: www.foundation.ulverscroft.com

Born in Glasgow, John Gordon Sinclair moved to London in the early eighties and now lives in Surrey with his wife, Shauna, and their two children. He has had an extensive carrer in TV, stage and film, with starring roles in *Gregory's Girl*, *Local Hero*, and alongside Brad Pitt in the 2013 blockbuster *World War Z*. *Seventy Times Seven* is his first novel.

SEVENTY TIMES SEVEN

Danny McGuire doesn't like his job, but he's good at it. Since his brother's murder eight years earlier he has become a professional killer: a hit man for hire, bent on retribution. Danny's been contracted to eliminate the Thevshi — 'The Ghost' — the most elusive informant that has ever penetrated the Republican movement in Northern Ireland. But there's a problem: the Thevshi (A.K.A Finn O'Hanlon) claims to know who's responsible for his brother's death . . . When Finn is attacked in a bar he realises that the past has finally caught up with him. He embarks on a desperate journey to find Danny before it's too late. But they are up against someone who's spent years hiding a secret — a secret they'll go to any lengths to protect.

For Shauna, Eva and Anna

Then came Peter to him, and said, Lord, how oft shall my brother sin against me and I forgive him: till seven times?

Jesus saith unto him, I say not unto thee, Until seven times: but, Until seventy times seven.

Matthew 18:21–22

Acknowledgements

Over the course of the last few years I have learned that novel writing is a solo endeavour involving lots of people. With that in mind I would like to thank the following: John Rodgers for being a drinking buddy, travel companion, raconteur and unofficial adviser (but most of all for just being a pal); Robert Caskie at PFD and Michael Foster for their help and support; my editor Katherine Armstrong and Hannah Griffiths at Faber and Faber for their advice, support and sagacity; the Wotton Manor Hotel in Dorking, for offering sanctuary and limitless cups of tea and coffee; Ann McNulty of Bru An Tsosa in Camlough, County Armagh, for her hospitality and generosity; and Google Earth, without which I wouldn't know what Tuscaloosa looked like.

I would also like to offer one huge 'thanks' to my wife Shauna for her love, unerring belief, patience, uncanny editing skills and for selflessly creating the space for me to write.

Prologue

'Da. Come here an see this.'

The young teenager pushed her dark hair to one side and pressed her face hard against the cold pane of glass to get a better angle.

'Da!'

Her warm breath steamed the window and droplets of condensation raced each other in small rivulets down its smooth surface to collect in tear-shaped puddles on the sill below.

She shouted again, 'Da, look! There's some fella dragging a coffin up the middle of our street.'

Joe Fitzpatrick crossed from the kitchen doorway to stand with his daughter at the window of their small terraced house.

'Jesus Christ!' he muttered under his breath.

'There's stuff coming out of it,' said the girl.

'What the hell,' exclaimed Joe, making the sign of the cross. 'Come on you, away from the window.'

'But what's that? Look, it's all the way down the road.'

'Come away from the window,' snapped Joe.

'He's stopped,' said the girl.

Joe Fitzpatrick watched the young man lower the coffin to the ground and turn towards them, aware that he was being watched.

1

He stood in the middle of the street staring back at them, expressionless.

Joe grabbed his daughter by the arm and pulled her backwards out of view.

'Is it blood, Da?'

Joe Fitzpatrick didn't answer.

'D'you think he saw us?' she whispered, looking up at her father.

2

1

Tuscaloosa, Alabama, Maundy Thursday 1992, McHales Bar, lunchtime

'You figure it's him?'

'Yeah,' replied Vincent.

'Did you get a good look?'

'It's kinda dark back there, but it's him all right.'

'You seen a photograph?'

Vincent looked confused. 'There ain't no photograph.'

'So how you so sure it's him?' said Cola sharply. 'You don't want to turn round and check?'

'Don't have to. It's him,' said Vincent without raising his eyes from his beer. 'He's sitting there just like it was described.'

Cola Conrado drew smoke deep into his lungs and blew out a long thin jet of grey between his dry, cracked lips: the end of the exhalation punctuated by a perfect, rising smoke-ring.

His dark slicked-back hair was showing the first signs of grey around the temples and his voice clattered like a death rattle in his desiccated throat.

Sitting across the cityscape of empty beer bottles was Vincent Lee Croll; the perspiration on his dark-skinned forehead throwing off a sheen that accentuated his large, full lips — and

3

unfortunate lopsided features. His friends at school used to wisecrack that his mom was a Nigerian princess and his dad was a potato.

The barmaid was at the table.

'You want me to clear some of this for you?'

Cola stared at her from behind his black-glassed Aviators and made no attempt to disguise the fact that he was checking out her ass. He gave a small nod — like what he was looking at met with his approval — before adding dismissively, 'Yeah, and bring us two more beers.

'You see McCormack's drugstore across the street there?' rasped Cola, turning his attention back to Vincent.

'You'd better point, man, cause I can't read nothing cept my name,' replied Vincent idly.

Cola gave Vincent a sideways glance, then raised his finger and pointed across the street at a large green cross flashing outside a shop, with the words 'McCormack's Drugstore' written below in red neon.

'Can't write nothing but my name either,' continued Vincent.

Cola sucked air in through a gap in his crooked yellowed teeth and made a clicking noise with his tongue. 'You want to hear what I have to say, or you gonna pass some more gas bout how dumb you are?'

Vincent shrugged and gazed vacantly across the street to where Cola was pointing.

'You may not be able to read, but you know what a flashing-fuckin-green cross looks like,' continued Cola. 'First time I ever shot someone

4

dead was right over there, can you believe that? Kinda weird that we ended up here, eh? Don't you think? You figure that's significant?'

'What?'

'I haven't been back in Tuscaloosa in nearly fifteen years and we're about to do some business right across the street from where it all started for me. You don't think there's something freaky about that, or d'you think it's just a coincidence?'

'What, like an omen or something?' asked Vincent.

'Yeah! That's what I'm asking.'

Vincent considered it for a few moments then shrugged. 'Beats me.'

'Wasn't a drugstore then, was a convenience store. Wasn't too convenient for the Asian, caught the bullet with his forehead. The first thing everyone learns in a foreign language is how to swear, but to me that's fucked up. First thing you got to learn to say is 'Don't shoot.''

Cola stopped talking and stared out of the window.

Vincent wasn't sure if he'd finished or not so he nodded a few times before adding, 'That's a good story.'

* * *

It was as hot inside as it was out: well into the nineties. Cola shifted uncomfortably in his seat. The overhead fan was having little impact and the long-barrelled Magnum he had tucked into his belt was digging into his thigh, making his

5

teeth set against each other whenever he leant forward to pick up his beer.

'Where d'you leave the Fleetwood?' he asked.

'There's a lot the other side of the street,' replied Vincent.

'Next time we jack a car we got to make sure it has a few extras. That ride is a piece of shit, man,' said Cola as he drew down another lungful of smoke. 'When we're done here we ought to find the guy that owns it and run the son-of-a-bitch over. It's a goddamn disgrace.'

'You show up in a town like Tuscaloosa driving a car that's got all four doors, you in danger of getting pulled over by the cops,' replied Vincent.

'You show up *anywhere* in a Fleetwood you gonna have the whole neighbourhood watching anyway: few cops won't make any difference,' continued Cola. 'You couldn't have stolen something that had — at least — one window that wound down? Every goddamn one of them is jammed shut. I've had so much hot air blowing on my ass, my trousers don't fit me no more.'

The waitress arrived and placed two fresh glasses and a couple of bottles of beer on the table.

'That'll be four dollars.'

'For that kind of money you'd expect to have some air-con thrown in for free. I didn't leave for work this morning expecting to die of heatstroke in a goddamn bar.'

'You got to die of something,' replied the waitress, masking her irritation with a convincing smile.

Cola's face changed like a switch had been flipped.

'Too fucking right you got to die of something,' he growled. 'You want to bring me some ice and a towel, or you want to hang around here giving us lip then see how easy it is to 'die of something'?'

The waitress avoided Cola's hard stare and answered quietly, 'I'll go get you some ice.'

Vincent stared straight ahead. He knew for sure Cola was about to start in on him now. The guy was on a permanent short fuse. The least little thing would set him off. *Motherfucker should be in a secure wing*, Vincent was thinking, just as Cola poked him in the face with his finger.

'You cool?'

Vincent didn't respond.

'You listening to me nigga boy? . . . You know what I'm asking. You ready to go? . . . You cool?'

Vincent considered giving some of it back, but for now he just muttered under his breath, 'Jack Frost, brother.'

Cola crushed the lit end of the cigarette between his fingers and flicked the butt across the floor. 'Okay, here's the play. You go get the Fleetwood and park up at the end of the alley, runs up behind here. You see anyone come out the fire exit except me, you let him know you ain't pleased to see him . . . What'd you bring?'

Vincent pulled his jacket to one side and showed Cola.

'Glock-Compact.'

Cola shook his head. 'What the fuck you

thinking? You want something that's gonna make a big 'bam' noise. Like if you was to write it down, like in the comic books, it would have a big yellow flash with 'Bam' in the middle — make a noise that's going to discourage the other patrons from going for a bravery medal, you know what I'm saying. Let the target know you ain't fucking around.'

'This ain't my first time,' replied Vincent with a little edge creeping into his voice.

'Then why'd you bring a fucking pop-gun to the party, asshole?' Cola lit another cigarette. 'Pick me up in exactly three minutes. You think you can manage to count that high? If I ain't out in three then it's all fucked up an you's heading home on your own. C'mon, get off your skinny ass and let's get busy.'

Vincent lifted his awkward frame out of the chair and lumbered over to the large mottled-glass door at the entrance, his arms hanging limply at his side. He turned back briefly to Cola before leaving.

'See you in three.'

★　★　★

Cola tipped his chair back and tapped a drumbeat on the side of his beer bottle with his fingers. A table of noisy office workers nearby suddenly erupted in a burst of raucous laughter. Cola placed his beer slowly back on the table and turned to stare, willing one of them to catch his eye.

He checked his watch.

8

Time to go.

In one slick, easy movement he was on his feet with the Magnum in his hand and his finger squeezing the trigger.

'*Got a message from the boys back home, motherfucker!*' he shouted across the room.

The air exploded with a series of loud bangs.

BAM! BAM! BAM!

Just like in the comic books.

2

Danny McGuire had received the call just a few hours earlier. The thin, guttural voice on the other end of the phone sounded older than he remembered, but was easily recognisable: Lep McFarlane, one-time best friend of his elder brother Sean.

Danny's instinct on hearing the thick Newry brogue was to hang up, but Lep was the last person to have seen his brother alive.

'Wub? Weird I know, but . . . just listen.'

The phone call had taken Danny by surprise. He'd thought McFarlane was dead.

'Are you there, Wub?'

Danny didn't reply: he didn't know what to say. If the rumours were to be believed, it was because of Lep McFarlane that his brother had been killed.

'Wub, can you hear me?'

Lep sounded scared: speaking hurriedly, in barely audible whispers, struggling to compete with the din from the pub in the background.

'Wub, I've got hardly any coins left, c'mon, are you there?'

No one had called Danny 'Wub' in years: not since Sean's death. It was a nickname his brother used to taunt him with. Danny had no idea where it came from, but Sean and Lep would laugh every time they used it. They were the only two people who'd ever called him by it. Hearing it now after all this time reminded Danny how much it used to piss him off: still did.

Danny pushed the thick black-rimmed National Health glasses he was wearing further up on his nose and spoke. 'They putting telephones in coffins these days?'

'Jesus, I was just about to hang up.'

'What d'you want?'

'I need to see you. We have to meet. Don't believe anything The Farmer and his mob say about me Wub, it's a fucking stitch-up. If he tells you my name is on that list they stole he's talking out of his arse.'

'I don't know what you're talking about, Lep. What d'you want?' cut in Danny.

'Have it your way, Wub. Word travels fast — even to the dead. I know what you do for a living these days, so let's cut the coy crap.'

He wanted McFarlane off the phone before he said something that could land Danny in trouble. 'I can barely hear you. Why don't you try ringing back later,' he said.

'Give me two minutes Wub, you'll want to hear this. Something fishier than a trawler-man's dick about that break-in, don't you think? How was The Farmer able to stroll into Special Branch's offices in the middle of the night, and leave ten minutes later clutching a file that even the Prime Minister doesn't have the security clearance to read, tell me that? A file that's going to destroy the Brits' intelligence operation and get all those informers murdered — how does he

11

even know where to look? I'm telling you: dark politics at work. And you have to ask what the hell the Brits are up to. Finn O'Hanlon knows what I'm talking about. He's yer man: he knows the score.'

'Knows the score about the break-in?' asked Danny.

'Knows the score about me: about what happened.'

Danny heard Lep pause to take another slug of whatever it was he was drinking. 'The Farmer' was the codename for E. I. O'Leary: the commander in chief of the Irish Republican Army. He was also sometimes referred to as 'Old McDonald', but only by those who had known him from his days as a political prisoner in Long Kesh.

He owned a farm next to the border in South Armagh. Always came across on the news as a hard-done-by worker trying to eke out a living in what he called 'difficult times': just an ordinary farmer — doing an ordinary job — subjected to constant victimisation and witch-hunts by the Crown authorities.

But whenever his name was mentioned, the words murder, torture and death were usually tagged on to the end of the sentence.

'You ever heard of Finn O'Hanlon?' continued Lep.

'No,' replied Danny flatly. 'Don't call here again, Lep.'

'Wait, wait, wait, we need to get together. This is why I'm calling. I have to see you.'

Danny had stopped listening.

Lep was drunk: not making any sense. It was time to get off the phone. 'I have to go, Lep. If you're passing this way . . . keep going.'

'Wait!'

Lep's voice was raised in desperation. 'O'Hanlon says he knows who murdered Sean.'

Danny felt a kick in his stomach like peppered ice.

'Did you hear what I said?' asked Lep.

Suddenly Danny couldn't think straight.

Eventually in a low, quiet voice he managed to say, 'Where are you?'

'Purgatory,' replied Lep, 'but the Devil's got me by the ankles, you know what I'm saying? They're out to get me. That big fucker Owen O'Brien's been sniffing around Dundalk. He's here for me, I know it.'

'Meet me in Saint Pat's tomorrow morning after Mass,' said Danny.

'Hang on . . . '

Danny placed the receiver back in its cradle and leant his back against the wall.

He stretched his right hand out in front of him and tried to stop it from shaking.

★ ★ ★

Danny stood in front of the bathroom mirror — naked from the waist up — and ran his cold, bony fingers over the small sharp bristles that had started to grow like coarse velvet on his chin.

If he closed his eyes he heard his brother's screams, so he stared at his reflection without blinking.

13

Danny had experience of death from a very early age: his dad, his brother, Sean, friends at school caught up in the Troubles. Switch on the news any day of the week and some poor bastard had either been blown to bits or shot, or beaten to death. He had grown almost immune to it.

After his brother's murder Danny had been expected to join the IRA. He'd been approached several times to do so, but although he sympathised with their cause he didn't approve of their methods and on each occasion refused to become a member. Terrorism was too crude a method for conducting a war.

Instead he'd waged his own war: quietly taking revenge on those he held responsible for his brother's death.

He was selective. Any member of the security forces was a legitimate target: any member of the IRA who turned informer was a priority. Each killing was planned with precision and executed with an attention to detail that had — so far — kept him out of the clutches of the authorities.

Death was what Danny did for a living. He didn't like what he did, but he was good at it.

His glasses lay next to the soap on top of the sink; without them his face looked strangely naked.

His dark eyebrows and black, piercing eyes contrasted sharply with his pale, milky skin and gave the impression of a hawk hunting its prey as he tipped his head to one side and scanned his taut, scrawny features.

In the early days — before his brother was murdered — people would often stop him in the street, mistaking him for Sean. Danny could never figure out why. They were nowhere near the same build. Danny was three inches smaller and not as broad. Even from behind, Sean's hair was markedly lighter than the thick black mop of Danny's youth (he kept it short these days). Both had the same cheekbones and well-defined nose, the same easy smile, but Sean was considered the better looking of the two. In company people were instinctively drawn to him, leaving Danny to go largely unnoticed. It was a trait that Danny now saw as a strength.

Anonymity had become his credo, but it was a battle-cry to be whispered.

Danny flexed the lean, wiry muscles on his arms and shoulders and frowned.

'Jesus, you better start eating or you're going to fade away to nothing,' he said, tipping his head towards the mirror.

He slipped a fresh razor blade inside the metal holder and screwed it shut before lifting the small bone-handled shaver to his face and scraping it over his dry skin in slow deliberate movements. When the blade reached his hairline Danny didn't stop. He continued until all the hair on his head was lying in soft tufts — and short, matted clumps — at his feet.

After filling the sink with warm water he submerged his head and repeated the process until his face and scalp were completely smooth and free of hair.

Danny knew that each tiny follicle had the potential to turn informer were it to be collected as evidence at the scene of a crime.

15

The phone started ringing.

Danny stood in the doorway of the messy bathroom and listened.

After four rings the caller rang off, then the phone started ringing again. This time Danny made his way along the narrow hallway and picked up the receiver.

'Órlaith?'

'What about ye, Danny, everything all right?'

'Fine.'

'Sorry to call so late, yer ma's just been on the phone. There's something wrong with the lights in her kitchen. She wants to get an electrician in tomorrow.'

'Did you try the fuse box?' asked Danny.

Órlaith laughed. 'I wouldn't know what a fuse looked like if it crawled up my leg and bit me on the arse, never mind finding the box they're kept in.'

'Did you tell her I'd fix it?'

'No point! I'm taking her shopping for a few hours tomorrow afternoon. Why don't you nip round while she's out? If we finish early I'll ring the house and you can do a runner.'

'Aye, fine.'

'If you've no other plans why don't you head over here afterwards and I'll cook you your tea.'

'What's on the menu?' asked Danny.

'Whatever you're given,' replied Órlaith. 'You bring the alcohol, and your pyjamas if you're going to stay.'

'Aye, grand,' replied Danny.

'Are you all right? You sound a bit flat,' asked Órlaith.

'I just had Lep McFarlane on the phone.'

'Lep McFarlane! Jesus Christ, you are joking! I was convinced the little fucker must be dead,' said Órlaith. 'What the hell did the wee shite want?'

'He wants to meet.'

'Why?'

'Did Sean ever mention anyone called Finn O'Hanlon to you?' asked Danny.

Órlaith thought for a moment before answering. 'No, never heard of him.'

'Lep reckons this guy knows who killed our Sean.'

Órlaith was silent for a long time before she spoke again. 'You be careful now, you hear.'

3

Tuscaloosa, Maundy Thursday, McHales Bar, lunchtime

Even sheltering in the shade of the bar there was little relief from the stifling humidity outside. Finn O'Hanlon drew a hand across his brow as he made his way through the white shafts of sunlight that cut the lazy clouds of drifting cigarette smoke floating in front of him.

He was heading for a table next to the emergency exit at the far end of the tar-blackened, oak-panelled bar.

Finn sat with his back to the wall making sure he had a clear view of the entrance: force of habit from years of making quick get-aways.

Two things to know: who's coming in and the quickest way out.

He scratched at his beard and involuntarily licked his lips in anticipation of a cold beer.

The waitress headed over.

She was attractive; looked a little out of place serving in a local joint like McHales.

'Hi, my name's Marie. You wanna order from me or at the bar?'

'Who's serving at the bar?' asked Finn.

'Me,' she replied, 'but I make more on tips if I serve you at your table.'

'I'll get you at the bar then,' said Finn, making to stand up.

'Okay, sit down smart-ass. But be warned, 'no tip, no hurry'. It's an ancient Chinese proverb,' she said with a genuine smile that told Finn she hadn't been completely screwed over by life yet. 'What can I get you?'

'The coldest beer you have in your fridge and a razor please.'

'Is the razor for your face or your wrists?'

'My legs,' he replied.

Marie smiled again.

'Any preference of beer?'

'As long as it's cold and it doesn't have the letters B, U or D anywhere near the label, I don't care, Marie,' said Finn.

'Where's your accent from . . . Scotland?'

She had an easy laid-back manner that Finn liked.

'Ireland,' he replied.

'Shoot, I was going to say Ireland. I knew it was one or the other. It's just a slight twang, but it's still there. My great-grandparents were from Limavady in the north . . . The Mathisons?' she said as a question, like Finn should know them.

'Protestants?' he found himself saying.

It was dumb, but he hadn't bargained on getting into a conversation.

'Who knows?' replied Marie with a shrug.

'Over there, it's essential to know what side of the denominational border your name lies on or you could end up dead.'

'Sounds a scream,' she replied. 'My grandfather helped build the first Presbyterian church there: one of its founder members. So I guess that makes them . . . ' she paused, knowing she

19

was going for the gag, 'Muslims.'

'You living over here?'

'Sort of,' replied Finn.

'Sort of whereabouts?'

'Up near Cottondale,' said Finn, being deliberately vague.

'If New York's the city that never sleeps, Cottondale's the town that never woke up. You do something to offend someone in a past life?'

Finn didn't answer the question.

'You new here?' he asked.

'Been working here for just over six months,' replied Marie. 'You a regular? Can't say I've noticed you before.'

'Been in a few times, but not regularly.'

'I love your accent. 'Sort of' say something else.'

'I'm thirsty,' said Finn.

Marie caught that one square on.

'Oh sure! An ice-cold beer on its way. That's the first line of the Irish national anthem isn't it? Be back in a sec.' Marie threw the line over her shoulder as she headed back towards the cooler.

★ ★ ★

Finn liked McHales. He never went to the same bar on a regular basis and usually only ever stayed for one drink: two at the very most, but he was getting lax. The years spent looking over his shoulder were starting to give him neck ache.

There was a lot to be said for familiarity: it was much easier to spot something out of place. That's why Finn had broken his own rules and

20

been to McHales a few times.

It smelled of stale alcohol and had a perpetual haze of cigarette smoke: a boon to a reformed smoker like himself. The red leatherette booths were cracked at the edges and the long curving bar top looked like it had been covered in red Formica some time in the early Fifties. Spilling a drink in McHales only added to its character.

It was one of the few places Finn could relax.

He *needed* to relax.

A few regulars sat on tall stools, leaning over their drinks: heads cranked round to watch a re-run of some vintage baseball match on a television that hung precariously from the wall above them. The game was old enough to be in black and white, but that didn't stop them behaving like it was live. They banged the bar with their fists and muttered abuse at the screen every time the opposition scored a home run.

The usual office crowd sat near the front window making more noise than was necessary and having far more fun than the occasion warranted; happy to let everyone else in the bar know they were enjoying the 'Good Friday feeling'.

That's when Finn noticed the two guys sitting at the table next to them.

A skinny black guy and an ugly-looking dude with slicked-back hair, and shades too dark to be wearing indoors.

The black guy seemed uncomfortable: just staring at the floor or into his beer.

The pair looked out of place and anything out of place made Finn uneasy. He made a mental note to ask Marie if she'd seen them before, even though he suspected he already knew the answer.

Marie arrived with a beer and started to pour just as the office workers let out another raucous laugh. 'Same in every country,' she said, 'mix a suit with some alcohol, you get an asshole.'

Finn couldn't help smiling.

'They've been here since lunchtime, drinking Bahias,' she continued. 'I've stopped putting alcohol in them, but they're too stoked to notice.'

Finn's eyes were on his beer: Marie had the angle of the glass all wrong. Before he could stop her, a large frothy head had formed, leaving just an inch of golden liquid at the bottom.

'You live in Cottondale, this one's on me,' she said, looking at Finn like she felt sorry for him.

'Am I supposed to drink that or use it for shaving my legs?' said Finn.

Marie laughed out loud. 'Sorry. The college I graduated from didn't teach 'life skills'. I'll bring you a newspaper to read while it settles down — I'll bring you two, looks like it might take a while,' she continued. 'No razors either I'm afraid, but if you are contemplating suicide we've a shotgun behind the bar: it'd be messier, but it'd be over a lot quicker.'

'It's just an itchy beard.'

'Oh. Sure. Well if you change your mind let me know and I'll stick a couple in the barrel.'

'Don't look round when I ask you this, but the two guys sitting at the front door: they part of the furniture?'

'Never seen them before in my life, but the one with the Aviators thinks he's something: got a nasty bark. Kept staring at my ass like that's where I was speaking from. Didn't once look up to my face. First time ever, I considered talking out my ass could be a good thing. I could tell him what his chances were in a language he would understand.'

She was off again.

Finn followed her shapely, tanned legs as she headed towards the office workers' table with a tray full of impotent Happy Hour cocktails. In a way he could hardly blame the guy in the Aviators for staring too.

Finn watched the black guy stand up and shuffle out of the bar. The other guy stayed behind, leaning back in his seat giving the table of office workers a sideways glance.

Something wasn't right.

Finn tilted the glass slightly, poured in some more beer and waited patiently as the cool, golden rivulets ran down the inside, pulling some of the froth with it. He let it settle for a few more seconds before lifting it to his lips.

The first drink was always the best. Finn loved the cold fizz against the back of his throat: he looked forward to the initial wave of euphoria as the alcohol took hold and gently lulled the demons away.

But as Finn tilted his head back he caught a movement over to his left: the guy with the Aviators was on his feet pulling something from under his jacket.

Shouting now.

'Got a message from the boys back home, motherfucker!'

The guy was striding towards Finn, arm outstretched.

Finn was already on his feet: his wariness having given him a split-second advantage that could be the difference between living and dying.

Suddenly the air around him exploded.

Finn's glass of beer tumbled from his hand and caught on the edge of the table, flipping its contents in a large frothy arc over the booth.

He was halfway through the fire exit when the second shot slammed into the wall beside him.

Almost immediately another burst the door-frame just above his head and a fourth seared across the top of his shoulder.

The shots were so loud it was like the guy was holding the gun right next to Finn's head.

Finn sprinted down the alleyway at the rear of the building: his ears ringing, muting the everyday sounds of the street and turning the ordinary surreal.

A muzzle flash from up ahead sent him diving headlong over the bonnet of a parked car and crashing heavily to the ground on the other side.

The black guy he'd seen in the bar just a few minutes earlier was firing at him from the other end of the alley.

They must have been following him, watching his movements, waiting for him to drop his guard. But how could they have found him, how could they even know where to look, unless . . .

The windscreen above disintegrated, showering him in tiny shards of glass.

Finn was up on his feet heading back towards the fire exit when another bullet whistled past him and thudded into the wall, bursting the brickwork only inches from his face.

Just at that moment Cola appeared at the fire exit; his Magnum raised, ready to loose off another round.

Finn had nowhere to turn, nowhere to take cover.

He sprinted forward, covering the short distance to the fire exit in an instant, then launched himself at Cola's outstretched arm with a flying kick.

As Cola moved instinctively to block, Finn's foot caught him full in the chest, knocking him — winded — to the floor. Finn tried to scramble over him, but a large hand grabbed him by the ankle in a tight grip and started to pull him over: trying to topple him onto the ground.

Finn rained punches down on the guy's head as he struggled desperately to stay on his feet, but he couldn't break free. He was going down.

With a final desperate effort Finn lunged forward and grabbed hold of a fire extinguisher hanging from the wall.

As his legs buckled under him he managed to pull the extinguisher from its mounting and spin his upper body round, slamming the folded-steel base of the canister down with all his strength.

The hard rim struck Cola's face with a sickening thud.

Cola's grip relaxed instantly; enough for Finn to pull his leg free, but the fight wasn't over.

Finn scrambled back inside the bar and launched himself over the counter, leaving Cola struggling to his feet. Bottles and empty glasses

25

came crashing to the floor next to Marie who was cowering by the coolers, whimpering and sobbing, all her earlier confidence and self-assurance gone. 'Please don't hurt me. Please don't hurt me.'

Finn grabbed her by the shoulders — 'Where's the shotgun?' — but Marie was in shock, too terrified to answer.

She pleaded with him, 'Please don't hurt me, please don't hurt me.'

Finn was desperate. He shouted at her, 'Where is the fucking shotgun?'

Cola was back inside, blood pouring from what was left of his nose.

One of the office workers who had been cowering under a table stood up and tried to make a run for the exit.

'You leaving, motherfucker?' screamed Cola as he started firing wildly round the room. 'There you go.' The force of the impact blew the office worker out through the front window and onto the sidewalk. The television over the bar exploded above Finn's head, showering hot glass and splintered wood everywhere. The large glass-fronted cooler to Finn's right ruptured, spilling its contents all over the floor.

Finn shouted at Marie again. 'Where's the shotgun?'

Marie pointed a trembling finger at a shelf just below the till.

Finn saw the butt of a Mossberg 590 and pulled it out from under the counter.

There was no time to check if it was loaded: he racked it and stood up.

Cola Conrado was standing just a few feet away on the other side of the bar: the twisted gold frame of his Aviator sunglasses hanging limply to one side of his face. A large black fragment of lens protruded from the skin just below his left eye.

As he turned, Finn pulled the trigger.

The blast from the shotgun lifted Cola off his feet and slammed him against the wall; his chest ripped wide open.

Finn swiftly rounded the bar and made his way over to where Cola lay slumped against the back of one of the leatherette booths.

Without hesitating, he lifted the shotgun and fired another cartridge into Cola's head. Blood and tiny fragments of bone splattered up the wall.

Finn reached down and grabbed the Magnum from Cola's twitching hand.

The fire-exit door creaked behind him. Finn turned quickly and fired three times in rapid succession, all three shots penetrating the door at head height, leaving ragged holes the size of tennis balls.

Without waiting to see if any of the shots had hit their target Finn strode out of the bar. Pushing his way through the small crowd that had already started to gather on the sidewalk outside McHales, he crossed — as casually as possible — to the other side of the street.

He waited till he'd turned the corner into Seventh Avenue before breaking into a run. He headed east to Riverview Drive, then cut left into an alleyway behind a neat row of shops. The air

27

was thick and heavy in his lungs: stifling, choking, leaving him gasping for air.

He was blinking rapidly as streams of sweat ran down his forehead into his eyes.

It was only when he lifted his hand to wipe away the perspiration that he became aware of the pain in his shoulder.

Finn winced as he pulled his jacket aside. His shirt was already covered in a dark, glistening slick of blood.

Finn O'Hanlon had always known this day would come. What surprised him most was the overwhelming sense of relief he felt: finally something was happening.

They wouldn't stop until he was dead, but at least it would all be over.

Finn stared up at the cloudless blue sky. Over the years he'd come to realise that running to save your life was only worthwhile if you had a life worth saving.

4

Lep's face — etched with deep lines and covered in scraggy stubble — revealed little more than a faint smile of recognition as he crossed himself and slid along the pew to sit behind Danny McGuire.

McFarlane had aged a lot since Danny had seen him last. His eyes were sunken and lifeless, his dark gabardine suit stained and threadbare, its elbows and cuffs worn to a sheen. He looked more like a peasant worker in an old black-and-white photograph than a young man of just thirty-four — the same age Danny's brother Sean would have been were he still alive.

'I know what you're thinking,' said Lep as he shifted around uncomfortably on the hard wooden seat.

'If you knew what I was thinking you wouldn't have shown up,' replied Danny as he pushed his glasses up to the bridge of his nose.

'C'mon now, don't be like that Wub,' said Lep, acting offended. 'I'm the first to admit that this is an odd one, but when you've heard what I have to say you'll see there's no reason to be setting yourself against me right from the off. Hear me out, that's all I'm asking.'

Danny didn't like being called Wub, particularly by Lep. It was a reference back to a shared

29

past to which Lep McFarlane had given up all rights. If he said it one more time Danny would drag him out of the church and kick his skinny arse up and down Hill Street, but for now he let it pass.

They were sitting in St Patrick's Cathedral: a stained-glass sanctuary in the middle of Newry. Lep believed he'd be safe there, as though the prayer and incense-laden surroundings somehow provided him with protection. Despite everything that had happened, he was hoping that Danny wouldn't try anything stupid inside a church.

He was looking for an indication that everything was all right between them, but behind the glasses Danny's eyes were dead.

'The church is meant to be moving with the times,' continued Lep in a reverential whisper. 'You know, you're still not allowed to light up? I'm gasping here. Been trying to cut back, but as soon as I have a drink I'm screwed. For every fag I *don't* smoke I eat a bag of crisps,' he said, trying to defuse the tension between them. 'If the tar doesn't get me the saturated fat will.'

Lep was aware that — so far — he was doing most of the talking. He was doing his routine, firing off a few one-liners, but it wasn't working.

His hands were trembling. He tried to pull a cigarette out of its packet, but it flipped between his fingers and fell to the floor.

'What's this weather all about?' he said as he fumbled to pick the cigarette off the floor. 'It's like living in a Tupperware box, with the lid on.'

'Lep, just say what you have to say then be on your way,' said Danny, bringing him up short.

Lep sat in silence for a long while with his head tipped forward like he was praying, but he was waiting for the words to come.

Eventually he said, 'I want you to know I loved your brother like he was my own. You, your brother and your ma were like family to me . . . you *are* my family.'

Danny didn't make eye contact. He sat staring at the floor. 'If you're here to offer your condolences, Lep, you're eight years too late,' he said under his breath.

'I understand, Danny, fine. I understand,' replied Lep.

'You understand nothing,' snapped Danny. 'The night of the explosion, did you contact Órlaith or me and tell us what happened? Did you send flowers to Sean's funeral? Did you even bother to phone my ma to say you were sorry?' Lep felt Danny's dark eyes burrowing into him, searching his face: they both knew the answer to the questions.

'I got it all wrong, I know that Danny, but the situation was crazy. If I could swap places with Sean right now I'd do it in a heartbeat,' said Lep.

'I thought you were already dead. Where have you been hiding? Rumour was you cut a deal with the British and spent the last eight years in Long Kesh praying with the Protestants?'

Lep gave a wry smile.

'Worse. I've been living in Dundalk sur-rounded by fugitives and farmers that couldn't even spell the word 'Protestant'. I'd *rather* have been in Long Kesh, I tell ye. At least in there ye'd get decent books . . . food's better too.

Dundalk's like prison without the privileges,' said Lep. 'I know fine well what that big gobshite E. I. O'Leary's been sayin about me over the years, and I'm telling ye, he's way off the mark,' he continued. 'Spreading it round, that I'm an informer: that I was tipped off about the ambush that killed your Sean. Well, it's just not true! I'll be honest with you though, Danny: I don't know what is the truth any more. I have my own reasons for not being there the night your Sean was killed and it's got nothing to do with me being a tout for the Brits.'

Danny watched unmoved as the tears started to roll down Lep's cheek. As far as he was concerned it was an act, and not a very convincing one.

Lep leant forward and whispered, 'If I'd known what was going to happen that night I'd have been there, I swear. I'd never have left Sean to drive that car on his own. I loved your brother like he was my own.'

Danny had to stop himself from reaching behind and grabbing Lep by the throat. He wanted to throttle him, choke the life out of him for betraying his brother.

But at the back of his mind there was something troubling about McFarlane's sudden reappearance. Lep must have known the risks involved in showing his face back in Newry. As far as the IRA was concerned he was a 'Red Light': stop at all costs. A shoot-on-sight prospect. And yet here he was risking everything to meet with Danny.

'How did the SAS know which car was carrying the explosives, eh Lep? How did they know which car to start shooting at? You let Sean drive into an ambush and never said a word. You let my brother die.'

'I didn't know . . . ' protested Lep. 'For Christ's sake Danny, talk to O'Hanlon, he'll tell you. This guy says he knows who set your brother up. I swear on my mother's grave it wasn't me. He called me out of the blue, lives in the States. Says he knows what happened. I've got no idea who the fuck he is or how he tracked me down, but he said things; things that make me think he's the real deal. He mentioned people, places, things that have happened, that he could only know if he was a player.'

Lep reached inside his jacket.

'Hands out,' said Danny, in case Lep was reaching for a weapon.

Lep ignored him.

'Hands out yer jacket,' barked Danny again as he reached over the pew and grabbed him by the hair, but Lep twisted round and managed to break Danny's grip. He was strong for his size. As he pulled away Lep lost his balance and toppled backwards, catching his cheekbone on the edge of the bench.

'I'm trying to get a piece of paper Danny. For God's sake, what's got into you?' Lep was back on his feet.

Danny was taking no chances. He leapt over the pew and grabbed hold of Lep's arm. As he twisted it up Lep's back a Beretta fell onto the floor at Danny's feet.

Danny grabbed it up and held it to the back of Lep's head. Lep suddenly stopped struggling.

33

'Over the years I've murdered you in a million different ways, you treacherous little bastard. Give me one good reason why I shouldn't pull the fucking trigger right now.'

'It's for my own protection, Danny, I wasn't going to use it. I was reaching for a bit of paper I swear to God. Just let me get it, okay, please.'

Danny could hear the fear in Lep's voice: see it in his eyes. Whatever Lep said next would be the truth.

'Do you think I'd risk everything if I didn't think this was genuine? Talk to this guy. I'm wide open here, trying to make amends . . . please. I knew nobody would believe me: that's why I disappeared after they murdered your Sean, but this guy O'Hanlon can back me up. There's something else I need to tell you. This is why I wanted to see you. The security forces didn't tip me off about the ambush, I swear,' continued Lep. 'I don't know how he could have known, but . . . ' Before Lep could finish he was interrupted by a loud metallic clunk, ringing round the thick chapel walls.

Both men quickly sat down: acting as if nothing had happened.

Danny and Lep watched as a man wearing a green waxed jacket pushed open the large oak door and made his way down the aisle to sit in one of the rows towards the back of the church.

Everything about the guy was average: average height, average weight, average build. His hair was cropped short and he looked to be no more than thirty years old, but he'd already made a mistake.

34

Lep didn't seem to care that someone else was within earshot. 'Maybe someone tipped him off . . . ' he started to say, but Danny interrupted him.

'Shut up, Lep.'

Danny had noticed straight away that something wasn't right.

'Just let me finish,' continued Lep, but Danny stopped him again with an urgent whisper.

'Shut your mouth, Lep.'

The man in the green jacket sat with his hands clasped together deep in prayer.

Danny turned to Lep and said in a hushed tone, 'If you move from this seat I'll shoot you, understand!'

Danny then stood up and started to make his way to the back of the church.

★ ★ ★

Lep wasn't the only one wondering what Danny McGuire was up to.

Undercover agent Al Ballantine watched McGuire walk to the back of the church and disappear from view.

When he thought it was safe Al turned to look.

A thin metallic click from a hammer being cocked just to the side of his left ear made him spin back the other way. He couldn't see who was sitting behind, but he didn't have to. The hard, blunt end of a gun barrel was pressed roughly into the base of his neck.

Danny held his finger up to his lips.

'Shh! Here's something to think about. If you

35

want your future to be as long as your past you'd better not say a word: understand?'

Al Ballantine nodded.

Danny reached across, grabbed the green, waxy lapel of Ballantine's jacket and ripped it open. He pulled a length of cable and a tape recorder from the inside pocket and dropped it on the floor at his feet, then stamped down heavily, crushing it into pieces on the hard stone floor.

'You didn't cross yourself,' said Danny.

Al stared straight ahead and said nothing.

'You should always pay your respects to the big fella when you enter his house, but you just walked in and sat down. You walked in and sat down like it was your *own* house you were walking into. You didn't genuflect and cross yourself or even light a candle. How many self-respecting Catholics do you know would do such a thing?' continued Danny. 'Now, that lad over there and I are having a very important talk so why don't you head back to your pals in E4A and tell them how your lack of respect for God blew your cover. I know you're recording my every move at the moment, but this is a private conversation, so if you don't mind . . . '

A voice from the other end of the church stopped Danny.

'That's enough!'

Father Anthony strode down the aisle towards them. 'Please,' he continued. 'If you can't behave properly in here then you'll have to leave. Remember where you are.'

'My point exactly, Father,' said Danny as he

36

slipped the gun back into his pocket and stood up. 'Father Anthony, how you doin?'

Al Ballantine stood at the same time and pulled his jacket closed. The colour had drained from his face. He edged his way to the end of the pew and walked in silence towards the exit.

The priest was now standing level with Danny.

'I don't know what this is all about and I don't want to know, but not in here, d'you understand?'

'No problem, Father.'

'Was that a friend of yours you were threatening to shoot in the neck?'

'A member of the RUC on a close-surveillance outing.'

'Interesting!' replied the priest.

Danny heard the large church doors slam shut.

'My, my, everyone seems in a hurry to leave: a Protestant and a ghost from the past, not my usual congregation. Was that the wee shite Lep McFarlane scurrying out the door there too?' asked Father Anthony.

'It used to be,' replied Danny.

Danny bent over and picked the crumpled scrap of paper from the floor underneath Lep's pew.

On one side it read: 'Finn O'Hanlon, Apt B Four, The Glades, Cottondale 180218, Tuscaloosa, Alabama, USA.'

Danny turned the paper over and frowned.

'You all right?' asked the priest.

'No,' replied Danny.

On the other side Lep had scribbled:

SEAN WARNED ME ABOUT THE AMBUSH.

5

Tuscaloosa, Maundy Thursday

He'd waited long enough.

Vincent floored the gas pedal and simultaneously released the handbrake, sending the blue Fleetwood lurching in a tight arc as he sped off down the road.

The car turned left onto Black Warrior Drive and slowed as it moved past a crowd of onlookers spilling onto the road outside McHales bar. At the centre of the throng was a body lying motionless on the sidewalk and although Vincent couldn't see a face, he convinced himself it was Cola. If he hadn't been in such a hurry he would have noticed the regulation banker-grey suit and the polished shoes of the deceased.

Not that it mattered: Cola's limp corpse was just a few yards away inside the bar.

'Guess your career in crime ended right where it started, asshole,' Vincent muttered to himself. 'That I do call a coincidence.'

Vincent was trying to make himself feel better: saying — out loud — everything he'd been thinking in the bar. But the adrenalin was starting to wear off and the only thing that could really make him feel better was a saline drip and a shot of morphine.

His left arm was swollen and sore: the skin around his elbow felt tight, like it was about to split. Vincent had been standing directly behind the fire-exit door when the first shot blasted through and hit him in the arm.

It was an amateur's error on his part. He should have come at the door from one side like the cops did in the movies. Luckily for him the impact knocked him backwards out of the way of the other two shots, or he could have been sharing a body-bag with Cola.

Vincent could hear sirens wailing in the distance. It was time to get out of Tuscaloosa. He reached into his jacket and grabbed a pack of Lucky Strike, flipped the box open and using his good hand tapped out one of the sticks. Pulling the cigarette from the packet with his teeth he clicked the lighter on the dashboard into place, cursing as the traffic lights changed to red.

He was only a hundred feet further up the road and — in his rearview mirror — could still see the commotion surrounding the body lying on the sidewalk.

Vincent cursed again. Casually strolling down the opposite sidewalk, like he was out shopping for groceries, was O'Hanlon.

'Zippity-fucking-do-dah mister cool! Don't look like you got a care in the world.'

Vincent reached for his gun and looked over his shoulder to get a better view, but he was too late: O'Hanlon had already disappeared. There was no point in giving chase.

In his present state Vincent knew he'd never catch up with him, and even if he did, the streets were too crowded to start pinging lead. The whole area would soon be swarming with cops.

All along he'd argued with Cola that they should hit the guy in his own home: do it in the middle of the night when no one was around. But Cola had it in his big, thick, coked-up head that the bar would be better. Make a show of it. 'The guy lives in Cottondale man, he could be lying there dead for a couple of years before anyone would notice. Why make a show of it? We gonna put it on Broadway?' Vincent's argument was sound, but Cola wasn't having it: wanted to do it his way.

Except now it was all fucked up.

O'Hanlon was up and walking around. Cola was no more. And if that wasn't enough shit to clog up the sewer, Vincent was dripping blood all over his brand-new trousers.

'Ain't a show I'd buy a ticket for, bro,' he said to himself.

The lighter popped.

Vincent picked it out, pressed it to the tip of his cigarette and took a series of short puffs until the tobacco burst into a bright orange glow.

When the lights changed he jammed his foot to the floor again and looked in the mirror to see if there was any tyre-smoke as he pulled away, but there wasn't.

'Car can't even pull a goddamn wheel-spin, man. Cola got something right: this ride is a biscuit tin on wheels.'

Vincent hadn't travelled much further along the road when he came to a stop in a long queue of traffic waiting to turn right onto McFarlane Bridge. An early Easter rush of commuters heading for Highway Twenty, travelling north out of town. Now that he was on his own he figured he might as well go home and get cleaned up; maybe keep an eye on the news channels to make sure he wasn't one of the headlines.

He checked he had enough gas for the journey then took another deep drag on the cigarette: the last thing he wanted to do was have to stop at a gas station in the condition he was in.

Suddenly a thought struck him. *Shit*. He was going to have to stop anyway.

Vincent scanned the street ahead and a few seconds later pulled the Fleetwood over to the kerb and got out of the car. The sidewalk was busy, but despite the fact he was covered in blood, no one seemed to be paying him much attention.

He fumbled in his pocket for some coins and made his way over to a bank of call boxes sitting adjacent to a well-stocked newsstand. Vincent lifted one of the receivers and thumbed in a number.

It was answered straight away.

'Yeah.'

'Yo. It's Vincent.'

'Vincent who?'

'Vincent Lee Croll.'

'Who?'

'Cola Conrado's partner.'

'What you want? You finished already?'

'Yeah. All taken care of.'

'Then why the fuck are you ringing here?'

'Cola asked me to call see where he's supposed to pick up the money. We's still in Tuscaloosa, but we could swing by whenever's convenient.'

There was a silence at the other end of the phone.

'What d'you mean where's he pick up the money? We already paid half to the little coke-head, prick. You tell the drugged-up little asshole he's losing his fucking mind. Put him on.'

'He's not with me right now, he asked me to call and check on his behalf,' said Vincent.

'Well tell him on my 'behalf', he does any more 'shit' he's gonna change from an Italian into a fuckin Columbian.'

Vincent heard people on the other end of the phone laughing in the background.

'If he's holding out on you, Vincent: that's your problem. We paid him three thou, and that's all he's getting till we confirm for ourselves the job's done. He knows the routine. One other thing, Vincent.'

'Yeah.'

'Fuck off.'

The line went dead.

Vincent slammed the phone back on its lever.

Three thousand?

Six thousand altogether!

Cola had told Vincent two thousand in total.

When he'd asked the lying little asshole why it was such a small amount Cola started spinning Vincent all sorts of shit about the economy and how things were so bad it had even affected the price of whacking: told Vincent it was better to be working than sitting round playing with your dick all day.

'Half of something's better than half of nothing,' he'd said with that big thin-lipped grin that made Vincent want to smack him in the mouth.

'Yeah, and half of six thousand's a lot better

than half of two, you little fucking dick-squirt,' said Vincent out loud. A woman pushing a pram past him on the sidewalk gave him a look.

Vincent scowled back at her then hobbled painfully over to the car and clambered back in.

He pulled out into the stream of traffic and joined the queue again for Highway Twenty.

Cola was on his way to the morgue and Vincent had an idea where the little prick kept his cash. The more he mulled the situation over the better it looked. Vincent remembered a conversation he'd had with Cola when the two of them were stoned. Cola said he gave all his cash to his mom. Told Vincent it was perfect cause no one would ever think to look over at his mom's place, she being so old and frail and all. Said she was the only person on this earth he trusted. The deal was she kept it hidden somewhere even Cola didn't know: so he wouldn't go blow it all on drugs. Couple of times he'd flipped out on her when he was high: threatened her with all sorts, but she still wouldn't let on where the money was kept. That's why she'd stayed loyal, hadn't given up on her son, she knew that even in his worst, coke-fuelled rages he'd never lay a hand on her.

But Vincent was different.

He didn't give a shit about the old bitch: it wasn't *his* mom.

He smiled to himself. A plan was beginning to come together in his head. Vincent checked his gun: trying to remember how many shots he'd fired at O'Hanlon in the alleyway. He was using his fingers to count and steering at the same time.

One, two, three . . . so he should have seven left. Hopefully he wouldn't have to waste any of them on Mrs Conrado but if he had to, seven should be more than enough.

First thing he'd do when he got to her house was get cleaned up — that would save him having to go home. He could borrow some of Cola's clothes, maybe even lie low there for a few days. Act all dumb about where Cola might be. Make up some story about Cola telling him to wait there for him: make sure he remembered to unplug the television just in case the old bitch watched the news. It'd give him a chance to find out where the money was kept. Might even be a bonus in it for him on account of the extra running round he'd had to do. No point leaving any of it for the old lady. What'd she need money for at her age?

Once he had the cash he'd head back down to Cottondale and finish off the O'Hanlon guy, then go pick up another three thousand from De Garza's boys. All he had to do was remember where he'd put the piece of paper with O'Hanlon's address. Then he'd go do the job right. Whack him in his own home, the way it should have been done in the first place. He'd finish off Finn O'Hanlon: keep the money for himself, all six thousand of it. *Zippity-fucking-do-dah*.

Trouble was if O'Hanlon went on the run — which was the most likely scenario — that part of the plan would be 'my-oh-my, *not* such a wonderful day'. Also, if word got back to Hernando De Garza that the job hadn't been

44

finished properly then Vincent'd be in a whole lot of shit: he'd be better off whacking himself.

'Pheeew! There's a lot to consider, man,' mumbled Vincent as he headed up the ramp onto Highway Twenty.

As the traffic thinned out he started to pick up speed.

Maybe he wouldn't hang around too long at Cola's mom's. Probably best just shoot her straight off, find the money by himself, then drive back to Cottondale as quickly as possible before O'Hanlon took off.

Vincent nodded to himself: plan was sounding good. What did he need that sly little fucker Cola for anyway?

He'd have proved to De Garza he was capable of handling jobs on his own. He could tell the greasy Mexican fucker that from now on Vincent Lee Croll would be taking over Cola's workload. He'd be all set up.

'Yeah man.'

He reached over to wind the side window down before remembering it was jammed closed. The heat was unbearable and the smell of stale blood and sweat was starting to make him nauseous. He needed to get some air.

Vincent picked the gun off the passenger seat, screwed his eyes tight and pulled the trigger. The passenger window made a dull pop and filled the road behind him with thousands of tiny fragments of dancing glass.

It didn't feel any cooler.

Only six bullets now: that should still be enough.

He squeezed the trigger again.

Five bullets.

A hole the size of a cupcake appeared in the windscreen.

The rest of the screen had shattered, but it was still in one piece. The problem now: Vincent couldn't see a goddamn thing.

He raised his leg and kicked out, but nothing happened.

It took several attempts before the windscreen finally crashed onto the bonnet then slid onto the road and flopped haphazardly into the scrub.

It was noisy with the windscreen gone, but at least there was some airflow now and he could see where he was going again.

The faster he went the cooler the air felt on his clammy skin.

He wouldn't swear on the Bible, but he was sure he was starting to feel a bit better.

'Now we getting somewhere.'

Seconds later the Fleetwood veered across all three carriages of the highway and hit the central reservation at over a hundred miles an hour.

Vincent didn't feel the impact.

He wasn't aware of the three-hundred-and-sixty-degree spin, or the tyres bursting, or the car flipping onto its roof. He wasn't aware that when the car eventually came to a rest several hundred feet along the highway it was struck head-on by another vehicle, and that vehicle was struck by another, and it in turn by yet another.

★   ★   ★

Vincent was upside down; his head at a right angle to the rest of his body and his face caked with blood and dirt.

His eyes opened a slit.

'Now we getting somewhere,' he mumbled.

6

Belfast, Northern Ireland, Holy Tuesday

Chief Inspector Frank Thompson stood beside his desk, staring out of the window at the dank, overcast Belfast sky. Even on the rare occasions when the weather did clear there was no colour in the urban skyscape for the sun to illuminate: the most it could achieve was more shadows.

It had finally stopped raining: how long for was anybody's guess.

He'd just poured a cup of freshly brewed coffee and was contemplating having another cigarette: his third so far that morning.

Frank had given up smoking.

His dark-brown hair was longer than the regulations permitted, but as everyone on the front line in Northern Ireland knew, anything that marked you out as a member of the security forces marked you out as a target: that included the shine on your shoes, the crease in your trousers as well as the length of your hair and a hundred other nuances that had to be considered every day of your life if you wanted to survive. This attention to detail turned even the simplest of chores into a stressful endeavour.

Frank blew a circle in the thin film of fingerprint dust on top of the battleship-grey filing cabinet to his right, then placed his cup in the centre.

Frank had joined the Met in London as a cadet. He'd worked his way up through the ranks and was considered to be a good cop. He was a grafter: not one of the college boys who appeared on the scene every now and then with a firm grasp of the regulations and a head full of theory, but no common sense. Frank had gained his knowledge on the ground.

He'd made chief inspector before he was forty and was now — at the age of fifty-two — head of the intelligence-gathering unit in Northern Ireland known as Special Branch.

He had been groomed for the job in London and had made several trips to Northern Ireland over the years until one day he got the phone call offering him the post.

There was a lot to take into account before accepting the job. His wife and family were well established in their North London home. He had a good team around him that it had taken years of careful planning and meticulous vetting to put together: none of them would be coming with him. It wasn't an easy decision, but in the end his wife and his team told him to go — it was too good an opportunity to miss.

For the most part Frank enjoyed his job. But he'd had a lot of shitty times over the course of his career, and today was the pointy bit at the top of the steaming pile, as far as he was concerned.

Detective Inspector John Holden pushed through the door: hair matted to his forehead, a dripping wet coat flopped over his arm. Unusually for him, he was in uniform.

49

'Why do the big stories always break when it's pissing it down?' he said, loosening his tie. 'We should do press conferences indoors, like civilised people. Those photographers took pictures of everything but my arsehole,' he continued. 'When I left this morning there wasn't a cloud in the sky. I tell you, I've been rained on, hailed on, snowed on — it did everything but shit on me out there, it's unbelievable.'

'What did you tell them?' asked Frank, still staring out of the window.

'I said you'd be making a full statement on the six o'clock news and left it at that. I think it's pretty obvious we don't know what the hell is going on. The press are better informed than we are.'

John walked over to Frank's desk and was about to place a file on it when he stopped.

'Is this still a crime scene?'

'No, you're fine, but don't touch the filing cabinet, they haven't finished with it yet,' answered Frank.

John nodded.

'Smells like the bastards were smoking in here. Can you smell it? Disgusting.'

'That was me,' replied Frank flatly.

'Thought you'd given up?'

'That was when I was worried about dying of cancer. Right now . . . '

Frank didn't finish the sentence.

'Right,' said John, not sure where to take it next. He'd never seen Frank in such a foul mood.

He tried to change the subject. 'Gerry Clarke from Counter Surveillance called up to say the

50

sweep of the office was clear: the bastards didn't leave any listening devices behind so we're okay to go about our business. They've scanned everywhere except the toilets. I said to him, the IRA is not going to get much information out of there unless their microphones can pick up smells. Which reminds me.' John waved the file he was holding. 'The security guard that let the buggers in: this is his statement. If you want a laugh have a read. It stinks to high heaven. He's already got a claim in. Says he's too frightened to return to work, so he's been signed off on full pay. They must have beaten him with a bag of cotton wool; there isn't one mark on his entire body. The word 'collusion' is floating above his head in big, bright dayglo letters. I've got Sheena doing a background on him. Supposed to have been vetted before he started working here, but the security for this place is subcontracted out to a private firm. Can you believe that? Nobody even checks their bloody paperwork. Bet you a ten-spot there are some skeletons in his cupboard wearing black balaclavas and carrying Armalites.'

John paused for a second and stared over at Frank's coffee cup sitting in the circle of dust on the filing cabinet. 'I'm hoping the filing cabinet's not the only thing they've checked for prints?'

'Probably the only thing they would have touched,' replied Frank, retrieving his cup. 'The security guard let them through all the pass doors and into this room. They knew exactly where the list was kept. They weren't here for anything else.'

'How did they know it was here? There can't be that many people who even know it exists, let alone where it's kept. D'you think someone inside this unit's tipped them off?' asked John.

'It's got nothing to do with anyone in this unit, John. 'Something is rotten in the state of Denmark.' There's a bigger game in play: we just need someone to give us a peek at the rulebook.'

The phone on Frank's desk started ringing. He put a cigarette in his mouth, flicked his Zippo and picked up the receiver.

'Special Branch.'

The voice at the other end sounded calm: self-assured.

'Frank Thompson?'

'Speaking,' replied Frank as he eased himself into his chair.

'Robert Clancy, MI5.'

Frank covered the mouthpiece and indicated with a nod of the head for John to leave. 'I need to take this, John.'

'I hear those nasty terrorists have broken into your office and made off with a dirty-laundry list,' continued Clancy.

Frank interrupted him. 'We don't know for sure who it was yet . . . '

'We do know for sure, Frank,' said Clancy, talking over him. 'This is a 'for your information' call to say, don't lose too much sleep over the situation. No need to look too closely into this one, and no arrests without calling us first, d'you understand? As far as the press are concerned, you can make as much noise as you like — 'official inquiries', 'thorough investigations',

52

all that sort of nonsense — but keep the detail vague. Button up the sou'wester and ride the choppy seas, Frank, in a few days they'll be on to the next big story and those newspapers will be used to wipe their sorry Irish arses.'

'Thanks for the advice, Robert,' said Frank, making no attempt to hide the irritation in his voice, 'but it's more than just a dirty-laundry list. It's a list of informers we've invested a lot of time nurturing and bringing on, to the point where we get reliable and important information from them. When they start showing up with their heads blown off we'll need to do a lot more than make reassuring noises to the press.'

'It's not your problem, Frank. Ride the storm.'

'Our entire intelligence-gathering operation has just been flushed down the pan, Robert, so why don't — '

The line went dead.

As he replaced the receiver back in its cradle a piece of ash fell from Frank's cigarette, glanced off his tie and landed on his lap. It left behind a powdery grey trail just to the left of the razor-sharp crease.

The trousers had been picked up from the cleaners' that morning.

Frank took a long drag on what was left of the cigarette and sat for a moment in silence. He let the smoke escape slowly from his mouth and picked up a worn leather notebook from his desk, running his finger down the gold-edged pages until he reached the letter 'C'. Aside from 'Chrysaor Sa Runlifu', the only other thing written on the page was a telephone number.

'Chrysaor' was the codename for the Head of Intelligence and Anti-Terrorism, back in London: Frank's boss.

Frank had looked up 'Chrysaor' in the dictionary once: turned out it was a creature from Greek mythology. He wondered who the hell had the time to come up with these names, and couldn't be bothered trying to pronounce it, so called him 'Neil' instead. 'Sa Runlifu' was Frank's version of 'In Case Of Emergency'. It stood for 'Sound Alarm, Run Like Fuck'.

He picked the telephone receiver up and paused for a second . . . If this wasn't an occasion to sound the alarm, what was?

Frank punched in the number.

There was no answer.

He looked at his coffee mug and thought about taking a sip. The kind of day he was having, he knew — guaranteed — as soon as he lifted the coffee to his lips the person at the other end would pick up.

Frank drew the chipped mug across the desk, leant forward and sniffed: he loved the smell of fresh coffee. He picked the cup up and held it to his lips.

'Chief Inspector Thompson.'

The well-educated English accent betrayed no hint of surprise at receiving the call, but there was definitely a little irritation in the tone. 'Everything all right, Frank? I assume not, otherwise why the phone call? What seems to be the problem?'

Frank took another pull on the cigarette and tried not to boil over.

'I made the breakfast news this morning, Neil.

54

The press are all over the story of the break-in like flies that have just discovered shit comes from a cow's arse . . . I'm the cow's arse. They — like me — want to know how the Provos were able to stroll into my 'high security' offices like they had their own set of keys and make off with a list containing the names, addresses and fucking dick sizes of every informer we've ever used throughout the entire course of the conflict. And why the list included three of my own men who were working undercover until one of them was shot in the neck outside his house just a few hours ago. Also, how did the press get to know about this so bloody quickly? That's a bit of a problem too — I've just had a phone call from MI5 telling me to lay off anything but a cursory investigation, which is fine by me, but I'm the one left looking like I've got my dick in my hands, and a member of the IRA stroking my balls. So in answer to your question, Neil, yes, I do have a problem. I have several problems: one of the biggest being I have no idea what the fuck is going on.'

'I'm not really in a position to talk right now, Frank: meeting at Downing Street in five minutes. Why don't I call you back later this afternoon and I'll talk you through it.'

Frank could hear voices in the background: Chrysaor wasn't alone, but Frank didn't care, he needed answers now.

'I can't wait till this afternoon, Neil,' cut in Frank. 'The bodies are already starting to pile up. How about I ask the questions and you try your best?'

Without waiting for a reply he launched straight in. It was a standard Special Branch line of attack. Keep your subject on the tilt. Don't give them time to think.

'Did we know the list was going to go missing?'

'Possibly.'

'Possibly? For Chrissake Neil, c'mon, we either did or we didn't.'

'Is this line secure?' asked Chrysaor.

'Possibly,' replied Frank. 'Although the way things are going round here I can't bloody guarantee it.'

'We did know.'

It was the answer Frank least wanted to hear, but he didn't have time to let its implications sink in. 'Our entire intelligence-gathering operation is well and truly fucked now, Neil. We'll never be able to recruit another source again. If they know that we handed the IRA the list on a golden platter it's all over. The informers on this programme are supposed to be under our protection.'

'Not any more,' replied Chrysaor. 'The political situation has improved substantially over there: we're not under as much pressure as we once were, we needed to make some cutbacks. The resettlement programme to which you are alluding — with all that entails — is bloody expensive; we had to find a way of winding it down.'

Frank interrupted. 'We've just signed their death warrants, Neil, you know that.'

'If they can be found,' replied Chrysaor. 'I

56

don't imagine many sources will be hanging around to find out what fate awaits them . . . that's why we fed the press a few titbits this early on in the game. Publicise the theft of the list to give the buggers on it a chance to make their escape. It's the least we could do for them, but let's not get too sentimental, Frank. It's a little bit of housekeeping that needed to be done. What better way than to let those who created the mess in the first place tidy it up themselves? I admit that it's rather a crude method of saving money, and I did argue that we would be throwing away a lot of very useful and productive people, but there was no way of simply handing over the names of informers that were no longer of any use. It would have been too obvious what we were trying to do. Unfortunately it was an all-or-nothing play. I'm sorry you weren't told, Frank. That wasn't down to me, but it's done now.'

'The Thevshi's file is missing,' said Frank.

There was silence at the other end of the line.

'Did you hear me?' said Frank.

Chrysaor didn't sound too concerned. 'That's unfortunate. I would have thought his file might have been kept separate from all the others . . . in a safe, possibly.'

'This whole fucking building's a safe, Neil. If I'd known you were giving away the combination I'd have changed the bloody locks.'

'Yes, well. Nothing I can do about it, Frank, I'm afraid he's on his own now. And if anyone is well placed to get themselves out of the shit, it's him.'

Frank's secretary Sheena poked her head round the door and mouthed to Frank, 'I'll come back.'

Frank shook his head and waved her in.

'Got to go, Frank. I'll call you later. There's only a handful of us know anything about the Thevshi, and even less who he really is. Chances are the Provos won't know what the hell to make of it. I wouldn't worry. I'm sure he can handle himself.'

Chrysaor hung up.

Frank lowered the phone from his ear and turned.

'Sorry to interrupt, sir,' said Sheena.

'I was finished anyway. What's up?'

'Been a few sightings of Lep McFarlane cutting around his old haunts. Just thought you'd want to know.'

Frank looked surprised. 'Lep McFarlane! Really? I thought that little weasel was dead.'

7

Tuscaloosa, Maundy Thursday, late

Marie was standing at the main entrance of her two-storey Sixties apartment building using her foot to jam open the door. The small lobby behind her was in darkness and the concierge had clocked off for the night.

The cop standing on the step below was trying to act casual: hands on hips like he owned the place, still wearing his sunglasses even though it was dark.

Marie had hoped that Sheriff Bill Clay would drop her at the main gate, but he'd insisted on parking up and walking her all the way to her door.

She was staring at him with a vacant expression, not really paying attention any more. The guy sounded like he was reading from a book — like he was just out of cop academy. Wouldn't matter if he was telling you your grandmother had been hacked to death by a psycho or you'd just won the lotto, it'd all come out the same. He didn't listen either: liked the sound of his own voice too much, which she found odd as it only had one goddamn tone.

No matter how many times she'd corrected him, he still called her 'Mary' instead of 'Marie', so she decided to call him 'Ball' instead of 'Bill'. So far he hadn't noticed.

59

Marie was looking forward to a bath; she was tired and wanted to wash away the smell of institutions from her clothes. Must be the floor-polish they used or something, but the smell in the cop station reminded her of school. Local County probably had a contract with a cleaning firm that did all the municipal buildings, which would account for them all smelling the same.

She figured it was a good contract to have, then caught herself: Ball Clay was so dull he'd made her think about cleaning products?

Marie hadn't eaten anything since lunchtime and her stomach was beginning to hurt. If she didn't eat every couple of hours her blood sugar dropped and she got ratty.

The interview process had taken nearly eight hours and it was now well after eleven in the evening. At the station they'd offered to get her a burger brought in from across the street, but who the hell ate that shit any more? *Cops, obviously*, thought Marie.

They'd seemed genuinely disappointed when she turned it down. Even tried to persuade her that the burgers were the best in Tuscaloosa.

'The guy uses real beef.'

'As opposed to what?' she'd wanted to ask, but that would have meant getting involved in another conversation, so she'd kept her mouth shut.

Sheriff Ball Clay was still talking.

'Do you know any other tunes?' Marie heard herself say.

At least it stopped him.

'Excuse me?'

'I'm sorry my mind was elsewhere, which is really where I want to be too.'

'You sure you don't want me to see you up to your apartment, ma'am?'

'No really! Please! I'll be fine.'

'Sure, well if there's anything we can get for you, you just let me know.'

'Do you do deliveries?'

He looked up at her with no expression on his big dumb face.

Marie sighed, 'Do you do humour?'

'Excuse me, ma'am?'

Marie was finished with trying to be nice. 'Is this going to take much longer, Ball? We've been standing here so long my legs need waxing to get rid of the new growth.'

'No ma'am, I'm nearly through. Here's my card. Got all the numbers you'll ever need on it.' He handed a card to her that had his photograph on the front looking like he had someone's finger stuck up his ass. 'Just call the mobile, get straight to me. The whole force is carrying them these days. Makes you wonder how we managed before. We're gonna sit right over there, in that there vehicle for the rest of the evening, make sure you're okay.'

Just as Ball turned to point at the patrol car parked in one of the bays, someone came up behind him. The guy had to duck to avoid getting an elbow in his face.

'Excuse me, sir,' said Ball.

'Sure,' said the guy, flicking the cop a look.

Marie recognised the guy, but couldn't

61

remember his name; one of her neighbours from the floor below.

She smiled half-heartedly.

'Hi.'

The guy nodded to her and mumbled back at her. 'Hi.'

The guy didn't really look at Marie as he squeezed past her — through into the lobby. The brown takeaway bag he was carrying smelled good: something Asian, Indian food maybe?

There was just no stopping this cop. 'One of our Trauma team will be in to talk to you first thing in the morning. They'll take you through this whole situation; explain what happens if you need to go to court, make sure you're familiar with the procedure, and there's a couple of FBI agents driving down from Birmingham might want a word too, so don't book any holidays just yet.' He grinned like the finger had been taken out his ass . . . and something bigger put in its place. As he backed away he made a clicking sound with his tongue that made Marie want to reach out and strangle him.

It wasn't just the tiredness that was making her feel this way: it was the lack of food.

'You sleep safe, ma'am, you under the protection of the Tuscaloosa Sheriff's Department now.'

'Great,' she replied and made the same clicking sound right back at him. 'I was worried I'd have to take a sedative, but now I know you guys are looking out for me I'm sure I'll be fine . . . If I do have trouble sleeping I'll just run through everything you've just been saying: that should knock me out for a couple of days.'

Bill Clay smiled at her like she'd said 'Thank you.'

'You welcome, ma'am.'

Marie made sure the building's main door was securely locked then turned and walked wearily through the lobby. She thought about checking her mailbox, but she didn't even have the energy to do that.

The lingering smell of Indian food was making her mouth water. First thing she'd do was order some to be delivered, then mix herself a large whiskey sour and hope that the alcohol might blind her mind's eye enough to stop the flashbacks.

Every time she closed her eyes she could see the creepy guy in the shades flying through the air with his chest ripped open. The ringing in her ears seemed to grow louder with each replay. And the bitch of it all was that her mind kept playing the scene back in slow motion.

She would run a bath and change into some fresh clothes and get drunk.

Marie was still wearing the sweatshirt from work that said 'McHales' on the front: she'd only just noticed it was speckled with tiny spots of blood. Who the blood belonged to was a question for another time. Her hair looked like shit too.

She pushed through the double doors into the main stairwell and climbed to the first landing, then stopped for a moment. It was the first time she'd been on her own all day.

She wished there was someone waiting for her

in the apartment, someone she could offload to, tell everything she'd been through, how it had made her feel, how scared she'd been, then cuddle up and fall asleep, wrapped up safe.

Marie stood there in the dark empty stairwell with her head bowed and let a tear run down her face. She'd never seen violence like that before: for real, up close. The memory of it made her shudder.

It was much more brutal, much more savage than she could ever have imagined. And yet, at the same time there was something so matter-of-fact, so ordinary about it. That's what had taken her by surprise and left her feeling sick to the stomach. Alive one minute, dead the next.

She'd seen footage once of a Viet Cong prisoner being shot in the head — watched in disgust as blood spurted from the hole in the guy's skull while he sank slowly to the ground: his eyes still focused.

She had the same sense of repulsion now, but a hundred times worse.

The tears were falling freely.

★ ★ ★

Marie wasn't sure how long she'd been standing like that, when she was startled by a sudden noise echoing along the lobby.

Someone was pulling at the main door.

From the din they were making it was obvious they were eager to get in, but didn't have a key.

Marie tried to stay calm, but the day's events had left her feeling edgy and vulnerable.

They were rattling the door, kicking it, trying to force it open: the sound amplified and distorted by the marble floor and solid concrete walls.

She flipped the light switch on the landing, but there was no bulb so she had to clamber up two flights of stairs in darkness: her heart pumping like it was going to burst out of her chest and grab her by the throat.

When she reached the third floor she pushed her shoulder against the heavy inner door.

It opened on to a long, covered balcony overlooking a large inner courtyard that served all of the apartments. There was a lit pool and flat grassy lawn with uplighters illuminating some of the bigger plants.

Marie tried the light switch there too, but it wasn't working either.

She stopped.

There was a movement in the shadows halfway along the balcony.

Marie could make out the tall figure of a man standing outside her apartment door . . . standing there like he was waiting for her. It was difficult to tell — the light was so bad — but it looked like the guy from downstairs who had pushed past her at the main door a few minutes ago.

She wanted to turn and run, but whoever had been trying to get into the building had obviously succeeded and the sound of footsteps could be heard echoing noisily up the stairwell behind her.

Her only option was to move forward: meet

65

the guy head-on and ask him what the hell he was doing standing outside her front door.

She wished she could remember his name.

As she drew near he started speaking.

'What kept you?' he asked.

Marie stared at him for a moment.

'I was having a little 'me time' in the lobby,' she replied. 'And I couldn't find the off button for the sheriff.'

The guy held up the brown paper bag.

'You hungry?'

His voice was familiar, but somehow didn't match the face.

'Is it Indian?' asked Marie.

'Thai.'

It was only then that Marie realised.

'Do you know how to mix a whiskey sour?' she asked.

'No,' he replied. 'Do you know how to pour a beer?'

Marie started to get the keys out of her bag.

'You've had a shave. Makes you look . . . ' She paused for a second and smiled. 'Older.'

8

Newry, early hours of Maundy Thursday

Four intruders.

Danny knew they were coming long before he felt the cold, hard barrel of a Browning L9A1 pressed firmly into his cheek.

He'd been expecting a response. Holding a gun to the head of an E4A operative in the church — even if he'd had no intention of pulling the trigger — wasn't the smartest thing he'd ever done. It was bound to provoke a reaction.

Seeing Lep McFarlane again had thrown him; made him drop his guard and act like an idiot. He'd lost control and that wasn't good.

Not only would there be a reprisal, but it opened him up to the possibility of charges: 'possession of a firearm,' 'threatening a member of Her Majesty's security forces', any other shit they wanted to throw in the mix. But Danny knew that's not how it worked in the real world: he was fairly certain the security forces — particularly the covert ones — preferred hand-to-hand in the street, rather than face-to-face in a law court. Prosecuting him would take too long, with no guarantee of a conviction, and the E4A operative — the guy in the church — wouldn't want to make an appearance in court. Not only would it be an admission that they were conducting close-surveillance operations, but the officer's cover would be blown, and that was not an option. Far better to send in a team: deliver an unofficial response in person and let him know the security forces weren't to be messed with.

Danny reckoned that's what was happening now. It was confirmation that he was under surveillance — otherwise, how did they know he was staying the night at Órlaith's?

He heard the front door crack open, and the sound of footsteps as they padded swiftly up the stairs. He heard the warning creak from the top step as each of them passed over it.

The bedroom door eased open and three of the men entered the room. The fourth he guessed had gone to the bedroom next door where his sister-in-law lay sleeping with her seven-year-old daughter Niamh.

Through half-closed eyes he could just make out their shadowy outlines as they moved quickly to take up positions, strategically placing themselves so as to prevent any means of escape: one by the window, one by the door, and one holding the Browning against his cheek.

On an invisible signal, the two others raised their weapons and pointed them at Danny.

His 9 mm was just a few inches away under his pillow, easily within reach — but Danny knew if he made even the slightest movement they would shoot him.

The three men had Heckler sub-machine guns fitted with suppressors clipped over their shoulders; all were wearing balaclavas pulled down over their faces and none of them was in uniform.

If — as Danny suspected — they were SAS, he was in the shit. E4A were police: what the hell were the army here for?

He'd been arrested plenty of times over the years, always in the middle of the night: questioned well into the early hours, and always released without charge. Special Branch in particular were determined to get something on him, but never could. The authorities had very little to go on except their own suspicions. The reason for the arrests had changed from pragmatism to harassment, with no specific purpose other than to intimidate him — but Danny knew instinctively that tonight was different.

The shouting started.

'Rise and shine fuckwit. C'mon you dirty Irish cunt. Up. Up. Up. Move it or get a bullet in the head.' The one holding the gun in his face grabbed Danny round the back of his neck and started to pull him up out of bed.

'C'mon move it! Get your dirty Fenian arse into gear.'

Danny let himself be hauled to a standing position.

He reached over to pick his glasses off the bedside table, but his arm was quickly smacked down with the butt of the Browning.

Danny was naked except for his jockey-shorts.

Having no shoes on — for him — was like having two weapons less: he couldn't do much damage with his bare feet. At some point he would have to fight back: retaliation was inevitable, but the last thing he wanted was for the fight to start in the bedroom where there was no room to manoeuvre.

'Under the Geneva Convention I'm allowed to get myself dressed,' said Danny, 'and put on my glasses.'

'Get your murdering Irish arse down the fuckin stairs now,' was the reply.

Órlaith appeared just outside the bedroom door with sheets gathered around her and a gun pressed against her back.

'For God's sake! What the hell is going on?'

'Phone John McGovern, Órlaith, tell him something bad is about to happen.'

'It's three in the morning,' mumbled Órlaith, still half asleep. 'Lawyers are not nocturnal: I'm sure he'd love to help, but only during daylight hours.'

Danny would have argued the point, but there was no time.

'Yer man here is trying to deny me my human rights,' he said, leaning over to pick up his shoes.

'Up straight, fucker,' barked the soldier holding the Browning. 'Human rights are for human beings, c'mon get a fuckin move on.'

Suddenly Danny's head was yanked up and he was pushed towards the door. One of the other soldiers stepped in front of him and caught him hard in the stomach with his elbow.

Danny fell winded to the floor: he hadn't landed a punch and already he was down. As he struggled to catch his breath Danny felt another crack on the side of his cheek from the heel of the soldier's boot. Almost instantly he could taste the metallic saltiness of fresh blood in his mouth. Another onslaught of punches and kicks left him curled in a tight foetal ball.

He heard Órlaith screaming: 'Leave him alone you fucking animals.'

Danny was being pulled to his feet.

'Okay, okay, I surrender. Take it easy for Christ's sake, I surrender,' he said, trying to stall the soldiers long enough to get his breath back.

He was hurt, but not too badly.

Once they got him outside there would be no witnesses; they could do what they liked. If he was going to make a move, now was the time — while he still had some strength left.

Outnumbered and with the odds heavily stacked against him there was no chance of winning the battle, but at least he wouldn't be the only one with a headache in the morning.

Danny glanced over his shoulder and bowed his head slightly to Órlaith.

'For Sean.'

Órlaith knew by the tone of his voice what was about to happen and tried her best to smile back at him. 'Do your worst, Danny,' she said with a rueful smile.

Suddenly Danny feinted to the right, spun quickly on the balls of his feet and smacked one of the soldiers on the side of the head with the knuckles of his tightly clenched fist. As the soldier recoiled Danny brought his knee up with a sudden jerk and caught the guy hard in the groin, at the same time flicking his head forward. There was a dull crack as the top of his forehead connected with the bridge of the soldier's nose and sent him crashing to the floor.

The speed of the attack had taken the others by surprise and given Danny a small advantage, but it wouldn't last. He had to throw everything he had at them as quickly as possible.

One of the other soldiers was already on him. Danny flicked his elbow up to parry a blow and caught the soldier square on the jaw with a well-timed right hook. The soldier was knocked backwards against the bedroom wall.

There was a sudden explosion of violence as the remaining two soldiers retaliated. Danny managed to sidestep a machine gun swung in a tight arc, avoiding the full impact. But it still caught him a glancing blow on his left cheek. He could feel someone kicking at his legs trying to knock them away from under him.

He managed to get a couple more jabs in before another blow to the side of his face sent him crashing heavily to his knees.

Órlaith was trying to pull one of the soldiers off him. Danny heard the sickening thud as she was punched full on the face, the force of the blow knocking her unconscious to the floor.

A sudden burst of rage helped Danny to rally momentarily. He struggled to his feet and lashed out at the soldier standing immediately in front of him, but with little effect.

He was aware of the soldier's forehead lurching towards him, but could do little to stop the impact.

A flash of white light exploded inside Danny's head as their two skulls cracked together. He staggered backwards unsteadily for a few paces before falling dazed to the floor.

The dull rhythmic pounding in his ears obscured any other sounds in the room. Niamh stood beside her mother with tears streaming down her face. Through a hazy prism Danny saw his hand reaching out to her. He could just make out the figure of a soldier heading towards her. Danny heaved and groaned like a wounded animal.

'*Leave her alone.*'

But a dark abyss had opened beneath him. He could feel himself slowly pitching forward, and tumbling in.

★ ★ ★

Danny was aware of an uncomfortable sensation in his wrists. He tried raising his hands, but a sudden stab of pain made him stop. His hands were tied behind his back with a thin nylon cord: bound so tightly that even the smallest movement made it cut deeper into his flesh. Trickles of warm blood seeped from the raw wound, down between his fingers and onto the ridged steel floor below.

His eyes were wide open, but he could see nothing. No chinks of light penetrated the darkness. A black hood tied securely round his throat was making his breathing choked and difficult. Danny writhed around the floor and kicked his legs out in an effort to free himself from the bindings, but it only made the pain worse and he soon stopped.

He had to concentrate: bring his breathing under control, try to work out where the hell he was.

He knew he was in the back of a truck or van, but where they were heading was anyone's guess. Whoever was driving seemed to be deliberately aiming for every bump and pothole in the road.

Several times Danny tried to sit upright: but the rocking motion and sudden jolts made it impossible for him to keep his balance.

The image of Niamh standing beside Órlaith with tears streaming down her cheeks flashed into his mind. The expression of fear on her young face made Danny feel ashamed. He realised in that moment that he was tired of it all, tired of the beatings, and the killings and the bombings and the shootings. He was tired of the effect it had on his family. He knew how much stress it was putting on Órlaith. The strain of not knowing where he was, or who he was with, or if she'd ever see him alive again, showed clearly: she looked much older than her years. Her eyes used to sparkle and gleam, but now they were dull and lifeless . . . like his mother's. Danny couldn't recall the last time he'd made either of them smile or laugh.

He thought of his mum's face when she'd heard that Sean — her eldest boy, her first-born — was dead. Even now, eight years later, Danny couldn't bear to let the image form in his mind. His mother's life had crumbled to ash: her spirit and soul were buried in the same grave as Sean. She had pleaded with Danny not to get involved. She'd begged him, on bended knee, but Danny was set on revenge. The only promise he had made was not to join the IRA. That didn't exclude him from associating with them, working for them, killing for them. As far as she was concerned her pleading had counted for nothing: now she could barely bring herself to speak to him. When he called her she'd hang up without saying a word, as if the thought of losing another son was too much to bear and it was easier, somehow, to pretend that he'd never existed in the first place.

But she didn't understand: no one did. Danny blamed himself for Sean's death.

★   ★   ★

He had been paying football in the street with his pals the night that Sean was murdered.

Sean had pulled up in a stolen car, wound down the window and shouted for Danny to come over, but Danny's mind was on the game. He'd run over to the car, but barely listened to what Sean was saying.

'Promise you'll look after Ma and Órlaith for me.'

'Do it yourself.'

'I'm serious, Wub, promise me.'

'Whatever you're up to just don't get caught, then I won't have to.'

'Swear to me.'

'I swear.'

Sean grabbed a handful of Danny's sweatshirt and pulled his head through the window of the car. 'Take care, our lad!' he said as he kissed

75

Danny on the forehead.

Danny broke free and pushed back from the car.

'Hands off, you'll get me lynched.'

'What's the score?'

'Five nil, but we're a man down.'

'Five nil! Is it girls youse are playing?'

'Aye, very funny,' shouted Danny over his shoulder as he headed back to the game. 'Just don't get caught.'

★　★　★

He hadn't picked up on the clues. Sean never came looking for him, so why had he done so that night? In retrospect Danny realised Sean was there to say goodbye. He must have known something was wrong and that he wasn't coming back. The question was: who else knew?

Danny felt guilty that he hadn't said goodbye properly. He felt guilty that he hadn't tried to stop Sean from driving off. He felt guilty that somehow all of it was his fault.

Once he'd tied up the loose ends surrounding his brother's murder, it would be time to make things different.

All he had to do was survive this.

Without warning, the van suddenly slewed off to the right and skidded to a halt. Danny could feel the skin on his elbows chafe and burn as he slid along the ridged metal floor and crashed into the far wall.

For a few minutes everything was quiet. Then an icy blast of cold air swept over Danny as the van's rear doors were thrown wide open. He was grabbed roughly by the arms and dragged out onto the road where he stood trembling, not with fear, but with cold and exhaustion. The hood was ripped from his head. Two men stood in front of him, one of them fixing a suppressor to the end of a 9 mm.

'We're in the middle of nowhere so nobody's going to hear this thing pop anyway, it's just that my friend and I don't like loud bangs,' said the one holding the gun.

Danny could hear the sound of babbling water from a nearby stream and could smell the fresh air of the countryside. As he looked around it struck him that these might be the last things he'd ever see, or hear, or smell.

'Down on your knees and face the ditch,' said the soldier holding the gun.

Danny didn't move.

The guy walked behind him and kicked the back of his knees, knocking him to the ground.

'You want to see your Órlaith's lipstick on my cock before you die, or would you rather see his?' said the soldier, nodding towards his comrade.

The two men laughed.

'C'mon, cheer up fuckwit, we're just giving you something to think about for the rest of eternity.'

Danny stared defiantly into the soldier's face as the gun was lifted and placed against his forehead.

'While you were having a wee snooze in the van we went back inside and made her happy. She said it was the first time she'd ever had an orgasm.'

Danny kept his gaze steady, determined not to give them the satisfaction of showing any emotion.

'Any last requests?' said the soldier.

For a moment the wind buffeting against Danny's naked body seemed to subside; the branches of the trees fell quiet, the long grass in the field beyond the hedgerow stood still. Then . . .

. . . Nothing . . .

. . . A long silence as if time itself was holding its breath . . .

. . . The three short clicks followed one after the other: click, click, click.

The soldier squeezed the trigger again for a fourth time then bent over and whispered in Danny's ear. 'That's how easy it would be. Now you're wondering how we know their names? We know everything. Where you live, where Órlaith works, what number bus she gets, where Niamh goes to school, how many times a day your mother takes a shit. We could take you out any time we like, you dirty Irish fuck. You ever point a gun at one of our comrades again and you're dead. We're watching you, McGuire.' With that the two men turned and walked casually back to the van, climbed in and drove away.

Danny watched the van disappear from view then smiled faintly.

KIB 1024.

9

Tuscaloosa, Maundy Thursday, late

Vincent could hear voices in his head: he didn't recognise them as the ones he usually heard, the imaginary ones. These voices were real, using words he didn't understand, like they were talking in code: obviously educated . . . white. Right now he didn't care: the pain in his arm had gone.

Vincent tried to open his eyes. He couldn't understand why his goddamn eyelids wouldn't work, why such a small movement — one that happened involuntarily a thousand times a day — had become such a pain in the ass to do. Vincent tried to speak — ask what the hell was going on — but he was so heavily sedated his mouth wouldn't open either. The best he could manage was a long moan lasting the length of a full sentence.

'Looks like he's coming round.'

'Top him up with some more anaesthetic; we don't want him awake before they get here, but no more morphine until we establish who's picking up the tab.'

'Nice,' thought Vincent. 'Whatever happened to the Hippocratic fuckin oath?'

The voices continued. 'He gonna be okay?'

'Concussion, and a few bruises but nothing more serious as far as the crash is concerned. Miraculous!'

79

'And his arm?'

'Gunshot wound, no denying. Lost a lot of blood due to that, but he's been topped up so he should be fine. Go ask the front desk what's happened to Sheriff Beasley and tell them to get a member of the security team down here as quickly as possible. If he does regain consciousness and wants to go home I don't want to be the one to tell him 'no'. Maybe give him another squirt of the pentobarbital, but take it easy . . . we do want him to wake up eventually.'

Vincent was confused: on the one hand he was enjoying the vibe: he'd never been a fan of the heavier narcotics — preferred a 'smoke to a coke' — but if the shit made you feel this good, he could be persuaded otherwise. Trouble was the word 'sheriff' had set an alarm bell ringing in Vincent's head. His dilemma was this: should he keep his eyes closed a little longer and see if he could figure out what the hell these guys were talking about, maybe get another hit of the pentobarb-shit, or should he get himself together and get the hell out of wherever the hell he was?

The effects of the drugs were making it hard to think straight. The last thing he could remember with any clarity was the crowd on the sidewalk outside McHales. Everything after that was a blur.

He needed to focus: get a handle on what was going on. A blood-pressure monitor just to his left was beeping and whirring: every so often it would burst into life and the collar wrapped round his arm would inflate and tighten automatically. It was only after it had inflated for the third or fourth time that Vincent realised he was in a hospital: the carbolic scent and clean antiseptic smells suddenly made sense.

He tried to concentrate on the noise of the machine in the hope that it would help him to stay conscious. All his instincts were telling him to get out of there as quickly as possible.

Someone was standing next to the bed. Vincent realised too late that it was a nurse, increasing the flow of anaesthetic. He let out another moan — 'No. No more shit till I can figure out what's going on.' — but the effects were immediate: he was falling, floating, comfortable, happy, warm, relaxed, carefree and well and truly fucked all in the same instant.

★   ★   ★

When Vincent eventually floated to the surface again he found he could open his eyes. His lopsided gaze slowly focused on a large round face hovering just inches above his own.

'Cock-a-doodle-do, brother! That sound good to you?' said Sheriff Beasley.

'Shit. I've died an gone to hell?' replied Vincent, still slurring his words slightly from the effects of the drugs.

'Vincent Lee Croll?' asked the sheriff.

A deputy standing by the door had his arms crossed behind his back like he was on guard duty. Vincent stared at him and smiled, 'S'that you?'

The deputy shook his head: had the deadpan look on, like he wasn't going to take any shit.

81

'Then, as we is the only three in the room and you two's way too ugly to be named Vincent, I guess it must be me.'

The sheriff pushed his face even closer to Vincent's.

'You aware the vehicle you were driving at the time of your incident was stolen, Mr Croll?'

'I wasn't even aware I was in a *vehicle*. How would I know whether it was stolen or not . . . I is suffering from amnesia, officer: got it so bad I can't even remember what colour I am. Hope to fuck it ain't the same as you,' replied Vincent.

Sheriff Beasley ignored the comment and pressed on. 'We also recovered an unregistered weapon from the vehicle. You got anything to say about that?'

Vincent screwed up his face. 'Man, you been eatin way too much red meat. You mind stepping back a bit? If you got private medical you should ask if one of the doctors in here got anything to help you out . . . but as my ole grandma used to say, 'halitosis is better than no breath at all'. Although in your case: not much better.'

The sheriff tried again.

'You able to explain why you got a gunshot wound in your arm, Mr Croll?'

'Seems to me like you got amnesia too, Sheriff. Seems to me like you've forgotten the *co-rrect* procedure. How long you been in the law, Sheriff Beasley?' asked Vincent, reading his badge. 'You smell like you been doin it for long enough to know I ain't answering one fuckin thing you gonna ask me, so why don't you get your big, fat, ugly face outta my way and do

82

things the way they supposed to be done. That means I can keep you on my Christmas-card list and I don't sue you and your department for all sorts of shit. Cause the way I'm reading this story in the newspaper is, you an your boyfriend over there came in here an threatened to beat the shit out of me cause I'm a poor nigger-boy . . . Least that's the version of the complaint my lawyer will be workin from.'

Sheriff Beasley raised his hand and struck Vincent hard across the mouth. The force of the blow split Vincent's lip on the crease and spattered dark red blood over the clean, white walls and ceiling.

'Oh, man. What'd you have to do that for, Mr Beasley?' spluttered Vincent, playing it all hangdog. 'I just got topped up, on account I lost so much blood in my accident and there you are going and spillin it again all over my nice clean pillowcase.'

'You sustained all sorts of injuries in your motor vehicle, Mr Croll. You think anyone's gonna raise an eyebrow if I do beat the shit out of you?'

Sheriff Beasley aimed another blow: this time at Vincent's arm. It caught him just above the elbow, where the bullet had torn away the flesh. Even with the help of the medication the pain was excruciating.

Vincent let out a yelp.

'Mr Beasley: the first one I could have put down to a lapse in judgement, but now I'm beginning to think you don't like me. What I ever done to you?' Vincent moaned, his face all

83

screwed up with pain.

'My fellow officer and me are just waiting for your discharge papers then we gonna take you over to our place and ask you these questions again. See what smart-ass answers you can think of there, see how chirpy you are when the medication wears off.'

Vincent smiled up at the sheriff. ''Chirpy'? . . . 'Chirpy'? What school you go to teaches you words like 'Chirpy'? You got a good right hook for a fat-boy sheriff, but you got to get a bit more street with your chit-chat, man.'

Sheriff Beasley looked like he was about to punch Vincent again. As he drew his hand back, Vincent suddenly reached up and grabbed him by the throat. He still had enough strength in his good arm to hold the sheriff up. In the same movement he'd unclipped the sheriff's gun from its holster. Despite the searing pain Vincent managed to swing the pistol in a tight arc and smash it into the underside of Sheriff Beasley's chin. The sheriff stumbled backwards and fell to the floor, blood pouring from a gaping wound just below his mouth.

The speed of the attack caught the deputy off guard. As he fumbled to draw his weapon, Vincent shot him twice: once in the chest, and once in the throat.

The deputy stared at Vincent with a look of disbelief as he clutched at his throat, but thirty seconds later his eyes lost focus and he was dead.

Vincent tore the blood pressure cuff from his arm and unhooked himself from the various monitors he was attached to. Alarms started sounding. He tried to pull the power cords from the wall but that only made matters worse. Vincent kicked out, sending the monitors crashing to the floor.

Sheriff Beasley sat up suddenly and threw a punch, catching Vincent hard in the groin. Vincent winced and stumbled backwards. As the sheriff tried to pull himself up on the side of the bed Vincent started kicking. The first blow caught the sheriff on the side of the face, snapping his head back violently. There was a cracking sound as his skull glanced off the metal bed-frame.

'Mr Beasley, you gotta stop fuckin hitting me man,' said Vincent as he stamped down heavily on the officer's face. Sheriff Beasley's arms flailed around in a vain attempt to hit back at Vincent, but he was starting to lose consciousness. Only the sound of people banging at the door stopped Vincent from kicking him to death.

The deputy's body was slumped against the door, preventing it from being opened. Vincent pointed the gun at the door and fired off a couple of rounds.

There were screams from the corridor.

No one was trying to get in any more.

It was time to leave.

His clothes were on a table just under the window, folded neatly in a clear polythene bag. Vincent tried to pull on his trousers as quickly as possible, but they were so soaked through with blood they kept sticking to his legs. His shirt wasn't any easier, but he had no choice: there was nothing else to wear.

Vincent looked out of the window and was relieved to find that he was on the ground floor.

'Something going my way at last.'

He took a step back and fired again.

Glass exploded onto the lawn outside.

As he started to clamber through the broken window a hand reached up and caught hold of his foot.

'Shit, man, you don't know when you is whipped.'

Sheriff Beasley's blood-drenched face was staring up at him, his arm outstretched as he gripped Vincent's leg like a vice.

'Let go of my fuckin leg, man, you messing up my strides,' said Vincent with a scowl.

'You got a couple of bullets left in your gun, Mr Beasley . . . you want em back?'

Two loud bangs marked the end of Sheriff Beasley's life.

10

*Armagh, Northern Ireland, Maundy
Thursday, dawn*

To the south of him lay Chimney Rock Mountain and to the north he could just make out the small coastal town of Newcastle mirrored on the shimmering waters of Dundrum Bay. If he was right, he was on Kilkeel Road, some way north of Bloody Bridge: An Area of Outstanding Natural Beauty.

His lips cracked a thin smile.

It was small consolation, but at least he knew where he was.

Danny had barely enough strength left to stay upright. Each faltering step left him struggling to balance and several times his legs buckled underneath him: like a drunk, but without any of the fun. The exertion of reaching the main road had used up the last of his reserves.

He knew of a safe-house nearby: a cottage used by volunteers to lie low after carrying out what were referred to as 'military operations'. The cottage was only a few miles north from where he was standing: a thirty-minute walk if he was fit. But in his present condition, he'd never make it that far. It had taken almost half an hour to travel less than fifty yards. At this pace it would take him nearly three days to reach the cottage. If he didn't find shelter soon he'd be lucky to survive three more minutes. There was no option but to keep walking in the direction of the nearest town . . . and pray.

The sound of a car engine in the distance made Danny turn sharply, his hand already in the air in a pitiful attempt to wave it down, even though the car was still hidden from view by the bend in the road. The sudden exertion made him lose his balance and he stumbled backwards against the sea wall. By the time Danny had scrambled back to his feet it was too late. The car sped past and continued on into the dim, grey mist rolling down off the hills. Danny thought he glimpsed the driver's eyes in the rear-view mirror staring back at him, but he could hardly blame the guy for not stopping. If he'd been behind the wheel he wouldn't have stopped. Picking up strangers in these parts wasn't recommended at the best of times. No one with any sense would pull over for a half-naked guy covered in blood and stumbling around like a drunkard.

The possibility of rescue had lifted his spirits momentarily and galvanised him against the sharp-toothed breeze that had started to blow in off the Irish Sea. However, the sense of elation quickly turned to disappointment, then from disappointment to an overwhelming feeling of desolation, as he tried once again to move forward.

Danny was in real danger of dying and there was nothing he could do to stop it.

After three more steps he collapsed heavily to his knees.

Being surrounded by death from an early age

88

was one thing, but Danny had never once imagined how his own life would end.

Certainly not like this.

A strange noise — a loud, distressed screech, like the sound of a baby crying — echoed off the hills. Danny twisted round and scanned the surrounding countryside. There was nothing to see but the shadows of gorse bushes jostling each other as they set themselves against the stiff breeze. The sound came again, this time much closer. Danny's eyes strained for signs of movement, but still nothing. Suddenly there was a commotion of rushing wind above Danny's head, followed by another harrowing squeal. Danny threw his arms up instinctively to protect himself from the invisible attacker and felt a series of blows smacking off his raised forearms. A moment later a large black crow landed in a flurry of beating wings on the verge just a few yards ahead.

'You fucker!' cursed Danny breathlessly. 'What the hell are you doing? You scared the shit out of me.' Danny stared at the bird: his mind scrabbling to make sense of what he was seeing. 'What the hell d'you want with me, Morrigan? Tired of 'guarding my death'?'

The bird's nicotine-yellow beak opened wide and let out a loud squawk as if it were answering him back.

Danny had been fascinated by the story of the Morrigan ever since he'd read about it in school. In Irish mythology the Morrigan was the goddess of slaughter who took the earthly form of a crow. She was a harbinger of death: when she appeared on the battlefield she was said to be waiting to devour the souls of the dead.

'If you think I'm going to just lie here and let you watch me die, you're wrong,' said Danny. He pressed his knuckles onto the ground and pushed himself into a squat. From there — after a lung-searing effort — he raised himself up to a standing position and faced the crow. With arms spread wide open in a grand gesture of defiance, Danny summoned every ounce of energy he had left.

'Come ahead, ya bastard, c'mon. I am Danny McGuire and I'll have the fuckin lot of ye. Those that killed my brother are going to die. I'll kill every goddamn one of them, Sean, then stand beside you. I am Danny McGuire and I have not yet fallen.' In his delirious state he imagined that all Ireland had turned to listen as his words echoed from Black Hill to Knockdore and Carnabanagh to Carncormick and off the peak of Trostan out across the Atlantic Ocean.

When he had finished he lunged towards the crow, screaming at the top of his voice, 'C'mon ya bastard, do your worst.'

But the crow was gone.

Standing in its place was a young woman with dark eyes and raven-coloured hair.

'You all right there, mister?' she asked.

Danny was certain now that he was hallucinating. 'You look good in human form,' he said.

'Thank you,' replied the girl, looking confused. 'Are you all right?'

Danny was staring straight at her, frightened to close his eyes in case she disappeared.

'Do I look all right?' he replied, his voice little more than a whisper.

'I was being polite: you look like shite. I was wondering if you needed a lift somewhere?' she continued.

It was Danny's turn to look confused. The line between what was real and what was the product of his imagination had become too blurred. Eventually he replied, 'You going anywhere near a bus stop?'

The girl suddenly smiled. 'I was thinking more like a hospital or something.'

'I'll mess up your car,' said Danny.

'Well don't be worrying about that,' she replied. 'It isn't exactly a limo.'

Danny swayed unsteadily as he glanced across the road at the old Ford Escort parked on the verge.

'Well? You after a written invitation?' asked the young woman.

'Are you the Morrigan?'

'The what?'

'The Phantom Queen . . . the Terror?'

'Sure, I don't know what you're talking about,' replied the woman.

'What's your name?' asked Danny.

'Is that going to make your mind up whether to accept a lift or not?'

'My ma told me never to accept lifts from strangers.'

The girl smiled again. 'My name's Angela.'

'Aren't you scared?'

'Of you?' Angela shook her head. 'If I sneezed right now I could knock you over. Now why don't you get in the car before I lose one of my legs to frostbite.'

Danny wanted to move towards her, but the darkness was closing in around him.

★ ★ ★

When he opened his eyes again he was sitting in the passenger seat of Angela's car with her warm coat laid over the top of him. He had no idea how he'd got there.

'Are you from heaven or hell?' mumbled Danny quietly.

'Newry,' replied the girl.

Danny's eyes struggled to focus on her, 'Near enough,' he said. 'If I die will you tell Órlaith . . . I forgot to get Easter eggs?'

'If I knew who Órlaith was then I would, but it's probably better if you live long enough to tell her yourself. You don't want 'I forgot the Easter eggs' to be your epitaph.'

Danny smiled faintly as the gentle motion of the car cruising along the twisting country roads lulled him back to sleep.

★ ★ ★

Someone was standing over him.

He could feel hot water stinging the cuts in his feet and arms, then a deep, rich, warmth enveloped his body.

Did he ask the angel if she knew Órlaith, or had he only thought about asking?

Cool cotton sheets pressed against his face

and the musky scent of his mother's hair filled his nose.

The pain was gone, but he could feel himself sinking deeper and deeper into the darkness.

★   ★   ★

The air around Danny was still. No sound penetrated the delicate membrane surrounding the vision playing itself out before his unfocused gaze. Nothing existed in his present but the past: a memory.

Cailleach Berra's Lough stretched out frozen before him. It was covered in a sheet of burnished ice that creaked and groaned under the weight of the young boy lying in the middle, his face shrouded and obscured by the white clouds of breath billowing from between his chattering teeth.

Danny couldn't see the boy's face clearly, but he knew he was staring at his younger self.

'He's passed out,' said a voice.

Danny's mind was filling in the blanks, presenting him with a perspective he couldn't possibly have seen for himself.

Sean was trying to lift Danny off the ice, but the area surrounding the two boys started to crack and give way. The more Sean struggled, the more they were in danger of crashing through to the freezing waters below. Lep MacFarlane shouted words of encouragement from the far shore, but did little else to help his friends. Eventually — heaving with the exertion — Sean managed to drag Danny to safety. He made it to the embankment and collapsed in a heap on the crisp gorse.

⋆ ⋆ ⋆

Danny opened his eyes.

Sean was standing at the foot of the bed. 'You'll be all right, our lad, don't you worry now.'

Danny scowled. 'I never thanked you for saving my life.'

Sean raised his finger to his lip. 'Shh!'

⋆ ⋆ ⋆

Danny tried to focus. He didn't know where he was. He tried sitting upright, but found the effort too much. Sharp, debilitating pains stabbed and hacked at the inside of his skull and made him moan out loud.

The room was dark but for a few chinks of daylight at the edge of the curtains. Slowly the objects surrounding him became more familiar. He was in his flat . . . but had no idea how he'd got there.

Danny freed his right hand from underneath the covers and held it up in front of his face. How had it come to be bandaged? He turned his head slowly, wondering if Órlaith had been in the room. He tried to call her name, but the best he could manage was a hoarse whisper.

There was a noise outside the bedroom door: a loud creak that sparked a surge of adrenalin as he instantly recalled the events of the previous night. Danny pressed his head deeper into the

94

pillow and realised his Glock wasn't there. He'd left it at Órlaith's.

The handle on the bedroom door turned slowly anticlockwise and clicked open. A young woman was standing in the doorway.

'You've got me for about another half an hour, then I have to be getting back to work, I just thought I'd check you were okay an see if there's anything else you needed.' She walked over and placed a glass of water and some painkillers on the table beside the bed.

Danny stared at her for a few moments, 'Órlaith?'

'No. Nor Sean, nor the Morrigan nor your ma neither,' she replied. 'You were mumbling all sorts of nonsense in your sleep. How're you feeling?'

It was only when the girl smiled that Danny remembered. 'Have you ever had a hedgehog shoved down your throat and pulled out your arse?'

'Not that I remember,' replied Angela.

'How did we end up here?'

'You told me the address.'

It was clear from the look on Danny's face that he couldn't remember anything.

'You were pretty adamant you didn't want to go to the hospital,' continued Angela, 'so I brought you here.'

'How did we get in?'

'A key . . . and before you ask: it was under the doormat. You're not in great shape, you should really see a doctor. If I was you I'd take up another sport — rambling's too dangerous.'

Danny smiled weakly. 'I was sightseeing,' he said, not wanting to have to explain the real reason for the state he was in. 'Visiting old haunts. My brother and I used to play on the beach in Newcastle when we were lads.'

'Naked?' she asked.

'Always,' he replied. 'You're the angel, aren't ye?'

'Sort of,' she replied. 'It's Angela.'

Danny gave a slight nod. It was starting to come back to him.

'You're Danny McGuire,' she said quietly, as if someone might be listening.

Danny took his time answering.

'Bits of me.'

'I've seen you before.'

Danny turned his head to get a better look at her.

'I used to live in Clanrye Avenue.' Angela paused for a moment. 'My da was Joe Fitzpatrick, he knew your da, I think.'

'Aye, that's right,' said Danny. 'I think I remember your da. He was a RA man, is that right? So, you're a girl from the Meadah?'

Angela nodded. 'I watched you from my living-room window once, carrying your brother's coffin up the road.'

'I didn't carry it,' interrupted Danny, 'I dragged it.'

'Why?'

'It was too heavy to carry.'

'No, I mean, did you not consider using a hearse?'

'There wasn't enough of my brother left to bury. I was trying to make a point.'

'What was in the coffin?'

'Blood . . . from the abattoir. I dragged it past every RUC officer and soldier I could find on my way to the cemetery.'

'The story became a bit of a legend on the estate,' continued Angela in the same quiet tone. 'My da said you were off your head. He heard you refused to let the RA give your brother a proper send-off.'

Danny interrupted her again. 'He heard wrong. My ma . . . she wouldn't have them anywhere near the funeral. I don't mean to be rude, but what the hell does this have to do with anything, Angel?' asked Danny with a little edge creeping into his voice.

There was silence in the room.

Danny's head was throbbing. Even the smallest of movements caused pain in some part of his body. He was aware that he'd been short with her, but right now he didn't care: everything was hurting.

Eventually Angela leant over, picked up a glass of water and held it to Danny's lips. 'If you drink some water, you'll feel a lot better a lot quicker.'

'Is there nothing stronger?' asked Danny.

'PG Tips,' she replied.

'I'm sorry, Angel. I feel like I was run over by a truck and got my sleeve caught on the bumper. You know what I mean?'

Angela pursed her lips. 'It's all right,' she said. 'I don't know when to keep my mouth shut.'

'Will you help me get dressed, Angel?' Angela wasn't sure if he was deliberately calling her Angel or if he had made a genuine mistake. She thought about correcting him, but if she was being honest, she liked it.

'Not if you're thinking of getting up,' she replied.

'Where d'you live now? Are you still in Clanrye Avenue?' asked Danny.

'Why d'you want to know?'

'Send you a thank-you card.'

'You were well brought up.'

'I like to say thanks.'

'Just say it then. You don't need to be sending me anything.'

'Fair enough,' said Danny. 'Thank you for helping me out.'

'Are you going to drink this or will I use it on the plants?'

Danny raised his head as far as he could and took a sip of water. The cold, flat liquid tasted good.

'See if you look out the window, is there a white Transit van across the street?' he asked.

Angela put the glass down and crossed to the window. She pulled the curtain aside and looked out. There was nothing parked directly opposite the house, but about a hundred yards to the left she could see a white van. Angela turned as she heard Danny painfully manoeuvring himself into a more upright position: his battered body was a pitiful sight, sitting there slumped on the edge of the bed.

'There's a white van a little way up the road, doesn't look like there's anyone in it,' she said.

'I need you to do me one more favour before you go, Angel,' said Danny. 'Have you time to go buy me some Easter eggs?'

11

Tuscaloosa, Maundy Thursday, late

Finn sat down heavily on the faded, brown-leather, button-fronted sofa and savoured every mouthful of the cold beer. The painkillers had started to kick in and the dull nagging ache — where the bullet had grazed his shoulder — was beginning to ease. He wanted to lay his head down on one of the large cotton cushions flopped over either end of the couch and close his eyes, but he knew he'd have to drink a lot more beer and swallow the rest of the painkillers to have any hope of switching off the static buzzing inside his head. At least for now the volume was turned down.

Red Headed Stranger was spinning at 33 rpm on the battered old Panasonic sitting on the floor just in front of the window. Finn was trying to focus on the words of 'Blue Eyes Crying in the Rain' crackling gently through the stereo speakers. But his eyes were getting heavy. His head dropped forward as he lost the struggle to stay conscious. The sudden jolt made him sit bolt upright, staring round the room — for a brief second — wondering where he was.

Marie was standing next to the bedroom door. 'Too much excitement for you?' She was barefoot, wearing a pair of worn-out sweatpants and a loose oversized T-shirt that looked like a guy's. 'I've fallen asleep listening to Willie Nelson a few times too, but never in a stranger's house.'

'It's not Willie Nelson, it's the painkillers: they're pretty strong,' replied Finn slowly.

She'd washed off all her make-up and her wet hair hung loosely about her face. Standing there framed in the doorway she appeared small and vulnerable: younger-looking, but somehow more attractive.

The smell of Patchouli-scented-soap and freshly laundered clothes drifted towards Finn and reminded him how badly he needed to get cleaned up.

'I don't know whether to thank you or kick your ass,' said Marie as she crossed to the counter and refilled her glass from a jug of whiskey sour sitting inside the fridge door. 'I can't figure out if you saved my life today, or if it's because of you McHales is now closed for refurbishment and I've got a horror movie playing in my head every time I close my eyes.'

Trying to act casual now: putting on a good show. But Finn could tell she was still uneasy, maybe even scared. The door to her bedroom had been locked and bolted when she'd gone off to get showered. But here she was now, with a couple of sours in her, playing it cool.

'Apparently you've done the community-at-large a big favour by shooting that guy. So far the cops have got you down as the reluctant hero,' she continued. 'The guy killed for a living, if that doesn't sound like a contradiction. Had a rap sheet it'd take you a couple of days to read through. Culo's his real name: Cola to his friends.' She looked at Finn to see if there was any reaction to the name, but Finn just sat there drinking his beer, looking sleepy.

'They're trying to figure out if it was you he was there to 'deliver the message to', or the guy in the suit who took the short-haul flight onto the sidewalk. Asshole worked for the bank across the street; was in McHales with his mistress who also worked in the bank as his secretary. That's not a scenario you come across very often, is it? Honestly! If I was a guy, and I wanted to have an affair, the last person in the world I'd pick would be my secretary. Too obvious! Anyway, the cops are working on the wife to see if she'd found out about the affair and arranged to have her husband hit.'

Marie was heading back to Finn with a fresh beer. Ever the professional barmaid: never leave them with an empty glass.

'I'll pour if you don't mind,' said Finn, reaching up to take the bottle from her.

'I told the cops, I was going to ask the banker guy to leave anyway: he was upsetting the other customers with all his gold Rolex bullshit and financial blah, blah. Although I did add I'd have preferred it if he'd used the front door.'

'What else did you tell them?'

This stopped Marie for a second. She looked straight at Finn: serious now.

'I told them you never paid for your drink.'

'That all?'

'Pretty much . . . they really want to believe the banker's wife did it. It'd make their lives a lot easier.'

'What do you believe?'

'I saw the wife being brought into the station. If she was *acting* upset she should be given an Oscar: didn't look like crocodile tears to me. My hunch is this all has something to do with you. The FBI are hardly likely to pay much attention to a bank employee who's screwing around.'

There she was, still coming at him. Smiling as she said the next bit. 'Looked to me like the 'asshole' was aiming at you when he pulled the trigger. D'you know what 'Culo' means in Italian? 'Ass'! Cops were laughing their heads off when they found out . . . Not exactly street, is it? A hit man called 'Ass'. His partner's name is Vincent Lee Croll. Cops put him down as Vincent Lee Hole. Even I smiled at that . . . Have you come here to 'pop' me, seeing as I'm the main witness?' Playing with him now the third sour was kicking in. 'I have to warn you I'm allergic to pain: brings me out in tears,' she continued, 'so if you could 'pop' me in the least painful way you know, that'd be great.' She couldn't help the flirtatious grin, adding, 'If you know what I mean.'

Finn didn't speak. He just stared at his beer.

A serious look crossed Marie's face.

'Have you come to pop me?'

'Maybe,' he replied. 'I thought a Thai takeaway first though, sort of a last supper, y'know?'

'Be warned, there's a cop car outside. If anything goes wrong I've to flash the lights three times . . . Can you imagine? You're being attacked, the last thing you're going to be looking for is a goddamn light switch.' She smirked to herself. 'When I was in the shower there I thought, 'I'll flash it *four* times' just to see what they do.'

She took another hit of her sour. 'I was also standing there waiting for the screechy music to start and the big knife to slash through the shower curtain.'

'How d'you know it won't?' said Finn, going for the deadpan look.

She saw through him straight away.

'I don't have a shower curtain. This food smells great, d'you mind if I help myself?'

Finn nodded. 'Sure. D'you want me to taste it first; be on the safe side? It'd be very easy to disguise the taste of poison in a red duck curry.'

Marie looked from the food up to Finn. 'Good idea. Are we expecting company?' she asked as she moved over and sat down cross-legged on the floor just in front of him.

'I wasn't sure what you eat, so I got a bit of everything.'

'Must have cost a fortune.'

'Everything I've got,' said Finn.

Marie didn't have to look at him to know he wasn't joking.

'How'd you find out where I live?'

'I waited in a burger bar across from the police station until they brought you out, then followed you home.'

'How d'you get through the gates here?'

'Drove in right behind you.'

'That easy, huh?'

Marie emptied the brown paper bag's contents onto the coffee table and tutted.

103

'D'you mind eating it from the cartons? The dishes are all packed away.'

'I'm fine . . . I'm not really that hungry,' replied Finn.

Marie looked at him, then down at the food.

'Maybe you *should* have the first mouthful.'

Finn saw her watching as he leant forward and ate a few of the noodles. It crossed his mind to grab his throat and fall to the floor, writhing in agony, but he decided against it. 'Mmm, tasty! Maybe I will have some,' he said.

As Marie spooned some rice from one carton into another Finn looked around the apartment. There were brown cardboard packing boxes everywhere. Some with old newspaper and bubble-wrap spilling out, but most still taped shut. On one side of the room there was a wall of boxes, five wide by four high. Aside from the loose packing material the place was clean and tidy, if a little sparse. The only other furniture was the beaten-up leather sofa he was sitting on, a matching metal-framed lounger and an old television that looked like it had seen better days.

'Moving in or out?' he asked.

'In,' she replied, leaning over to pick up her drink from the floor, bending just enough that Finn could see down the open neck of her T-shirt to the cup of her bare breasts. 'I left my husband about eighteen months ago and moved in here . . . haven't quite got round to unpacking yet. Actually he left me. Died of a heart attack at forty-two.'

'Sorry to hear that,' said Finn.

'Don't get your hanky out just yet. If he hadn't

died of natural causes, I'd have killed the asshole anyway. Smoked so much dope he thought the *National Enquirer* was the *New York Times*. Couldn't understand why none of it was reported on NBC. And — hand on heart — I couldn't tell you why I married him in the first place. He had no money, no personality and he was a lousy lay . . . his dick used to get hard once a year and it was usually when I was out at the shops or fast asleep. Trained as a chef, but preferred to stay home and get high. Used to rub my tits like he was kneading dough. You can tell I miss him.'

There was an awkward silence.

Finn and Marie caught each other's look. It was over in an instant, but it was enough to give Finn the feeling.

'Thai is just the thing after a gunfight,' said Marie, breaking the spell. 'Don't you think?'

'Yeah. I used to prefer Chinese, but I hardly ever eat it now. Keeps me awake at night,' replied Finn.

'Let's face it, when you've blown someone all over a wall with a shotgun you need to get your sleep,' she said, without looking at him.

Finn didn't reply.

He was trying to gauge where she was coming from now, but he was struggling to stay sharp: a combination of tiredness, painkillers and alcohol.

He was enjoying her company. Finn could imagine things working out between them, but not now. He needed to find out what had been said at the police station and leave her to get on with her life.

She leant forward to put the glass back on the floor and there they were again. Finn could see a line where her bikini top must have been and the sun had browned her skin.

As she sat up she caught him looking and raised an eyebrow.

'I flick that switch three times and this place will be swarming with cops.'

'You keep bending over like that I'm going to flick the switch myself,' said Finn, standing up. 'Mind if I get myself another beer?'

'Help yourself,' replied Marie.

Finn was struggling to keep his balance.

'What else d'you do for a living?' he asked, as he opened the fridge door and grabbed a bottle of Sierra Nevada.

'What d'you mean? I'm a barmaid,' said Marie.

'You don't do anything else? You don't look like a barmaid,' replied Finn, crossing back to the sofa.

'What do barmaids look like?' replied Marie.

'Not like you,' said Finn. 'You always worked in bars?'

'Feels like it,' said Marie.

'Okay. I'll come at it from a different angle . . . what did you want to do when you left school?'

'I wanted to be a lawyer and save the poor.'

'From what,' asked Finn?

'The law,' replied Marie. 'What did you want to be when you grew up . . . a marksman?'

Finn cracked a smile. 'I've never killed a man yet I could sit down and reason with.'

106

As soon as he said it he realised he'd gone too far. Marie's gaze dropped to the floor and the atmosphere in the room suddenly turned: as if a storm cloud had passed in front of the sun.

'Every now and then you say something that scares the shit out of me,' said Marie. 'It's all a bit too casual, you know. We're sitting here like we meet for Thai every Friday night . . . but we don't . . . I'm actually . . . ' She didn't finish the sentence. Finn could see her eyes filling as she struggled to hold back the tears. 'Y'know what I mean. It may look like I'm okay with everything that's happened, but I've only ever seen this sort of shit on the telly, where it's sanitised: far enough away from reality to make it harmless. But when you see it for real, your mind . . . it's so confusing because your mind is still trying to figure out when the ad breaks are coming and everything can return to normal, but — at the same time — it knows that's not going to happen.' Marie paused for a second and looked up at Finn, trying to smile. 'I don't even usually use words like 'shit'.'

The tears were now streaming down her cheeks. 'It's not me,' she continued. 'Suddenly I feel like I'm living somebody else's life.'

Finn didn't know what to say. She was right. Killing that asshole had come too easily to him. He didn't feel any remorse: in fact, he didn't feel anything. It *was* all too casual; too easy. This girl didn't belong in his world.

'Do you think if I'd asked him nicely he'd have sat down and talked it out?' said Finn eventually. 'I had no option. He wasn't aiming at my shoulder . . . he was 'missing' my head.'

Marie wiped her cheek with the back of her hand.

'So it *was* you he was there for,' she said.

12

'D'you have a copy of yesterday's *Irish Times* please?'

That's what she'd been told to say, so she'd said it. The guy behind the counter stared at her, the friendly smile nowhere to be seen now she'd said the code words.

'Are you lookin for a particular story?' he asked hesitantly.

It was the right question, so she answered.

'Danny McGuire: any stories about him?'

The guy looked her up and down. 'Is that right? And would you be wantin it delivered anywhere in particular?'

Danny had told her that the newsagent would be suspicious, but if she said exactly what he'd told her she'd be fine.

'To Old McDonald,' replied Angela.

The guy still looked tense, but he nodded as if he was satisfied.

'What's the message?'

'Mr McGuire wants to send his apologies, but he's going to be a bit late for the meeting. He says he'll explain it all when he gets there.'

The guy nodded again. 'You'd better wait in case there's an answer.'

As he turned to go Angela said, 'Oh. Sorry, one other thing, do you have any Easter eggs?'

The guy paused for a second. 'Is that part of the message?'

'No. Mr McGuire asked me to get him a couple of Easter eggs.'

The shopkeeper pointed behind her. 'Over in the far corner, there's Cadbury's, Galaxy, the lot. He usually goes for the most expensive rather than the biggest.'

'Thanks,' said Angela as she headed off down one of the aisles.

It was only a small newsagent's, but there was a larger than average selection of eggs. She chose what looked to her like a couple of upmarket boxes and headed back to the counter.

What was she thinking, running errands for Danny McGuire: getting involved in God only knows what? She'd already worked out that 'Old McDonald' must be E. I. O'Leary, the commander in chief of the IRA. 'Old McDonald had a farm, E. I. E. I. O'Leary.' It wasn't the hardest code to crack.

As Angela stood waiting for the shopkeeper to return she glanced out of the window. Suddenly her stomach churned over. A guy in a black leather jacket was staring at her from across the street. He made no attempt to disguise what he was doing: didn't drop to his knees and start tying his shoelaces or pretend to be looking in a shop window, or even turn away: none of the usual. He didn't seem to care that he'd been spotted: just stood there, making sure she got the message that he was watching her.

Angela's heart started pounding in her chest. The guy was pointing something at the window that looked like a gun.

She was about to duck down when she noticed the small set of headphones and the cable connected to whatever it was he was holding. Not a gun, but a microphone.

Had he been listening in on the conversation? Angela started replaying in her mind everything she'd said. She'd done exactly what Danny had told her to: if anything went wrong it wasn't her fault.

Angela wasn't sure what to do. Danny hadn't mentioned anything about guys with goddamn microphones. There was no script to work off.

The shopkeeper was taking his time. It wasn't that long a message. 'What are you doing, sending it in Morse code?' she murmured under her breath.

She wanted out of there.

'Calm down, calm down,' she said to herself.

The door to the back room flew open with a bang, making her jump.

'Christ!'

The shopkeeper was behind the counter again. 'You all right?'

'Yeah, fine,' said Angela. 'I was looking at the guy across the street pointing the bloody microphone at us.'

'What guy?' asked the shopkeeper.

Angela looked out of the window again, but no one was there. The man had disappeared. 'I swear on my mother's life there was a — ' Angela stopped herself. 'Doesn't matter! My mind was running away with me,' she continued. 'I haven't slept for nearly thirty hours. I'm imagining things.'

The shopkeeper's face remained impassive: he didn't seem to care.

'You've to tell yer man not to worry. They know all about last night and he's to make his way over when he can. Old McDonald still wants to see him though, but there's no rush.'

Angela thanked him and headed for the door.

The shopkeeper called after her, 'Are you going to take the eggs?'

'Jeez, I'm going off my head here,' said Angela returning to the counter. 'How much do I owe?'

The newsagent shook his head and gave a wry smile. 'Yer all right, there's no charge.'

As Angela reached across the counter to pick up the bag of eggs the shopkeeper suddenly reached out and caught her by the arm. 'You mind how ye go there, all right? Don't get too involved.' He let go of her arm, and started busying himself with the cigarettes stacked in rows on the wall behind: acting like nothing had happened, ignoring Angela now, as though she had already left the shop.

Angela wanted to ask, 'Don't get too involved in what?' but she knew he wouldn't answer. Danny McGuire had tilted her world up on its end: everything she recognised as familiar was still there, but it had all slid into a messy bundle in a corner of the room that was her life.

Back out on the rain-splattered street Angela looked for signs of the man in the leather jacket, but he was nowhere to be seen. Aside from a few scraps of soggy paper floating along the gutter, the street was empty.

As Angela set off, she felt certain that she was being watched.

The heavy rain had soaked through her thin jumper making her blouse cling uncomfortably to her skin and causing her to shiver. The shop was only a short distance from Danny's house. He'd laughed when she'd suggested taking her car, but Angela was wishing she'd ignored him.

'By the time you've opened the door and turned on the ignition you'd be on your way back,' he'd said.

She had another look over her shoulder before breaking into a run.

Angela reached the corner of Derrybeg Lane and stopped. The white van was gone, but standing on the pavement next to where it had been parked stood the guy she'd seen outside the shop.

She considered running back the way she had just come: but where would she run to? In the brief moment's hesitation the guy had spotted her. He pushed himself off the metal railings and started towards her.

Angela decided her only option was to keep going, try and pass the guy: get as close to Danny's house as possible and if he tried anything, scream the goddamn place down. But fear had left her paralysed, frozen to the spot, unable to move in any direction.

When the guy was only yards away Angela suddenly came to her senses: she lashed out, swinging the bag of Easter eggs in a wide arc and catching the guy full in the face. It was never going to stop him, but at least she was moving now: taking some action. She let go of the bag and launched herself between the parked cars that lined the whole of the street.

She didn't see the dark-blue car, or hear the tyres squealing as it skidded to a halt, but she was aware of her legs being knocked from under her: aware of her breath being punched from her lungs as she bounced off the bonnet and landed heavily on the ground. She was winded, but before the driver of the car had even opened his door she was up and running, breathing heavily as she struggled to get her lungs working again. Her only objective now was to get to the end of Derrybeg Lane and the safety of Danny's house.

When Angela reached the front door she realised she had no idea which key fitted the lock. She looked over her shoulder and saw the guy running across the road towards her: he was less than a hundred yards away, shouting something she couldn't make out.

The small clump of keys Danny had given her slipped from her grasp and fell to the ground. She quickly scooped them up, fumbled for another key and tried again. On her third attempt the key eventually slipped in. Angela stumbled into the hallway and slammed the door hard behind her.

'Danny! Danny,' she shouted. 'Are you there?'

As she stood in the narrow hallway listening to the sound of her own breathing she became aware of the stinging sensation in her legs. Angela looked down and saw blood trickling down her shins from ragged gashes on both of her knees.

'Danny!'

The knuckles on her right hand were skinned as well, and her wrist was throbbing painfully.

Angela made her way cautiously upstairs to the bedroom.

'Danny, you there?'

Angela winced with pain as she pressed her damaged hand against the bedroom door and eased it open. The cup of tea she'd made earlier was still sitting on the bedside table: the half-eaten piece of toast on the plate beside it. Everything was exactly as she'd left it, but somehow — Angela knew — the whole world was different. The house seemed to reverberate with empty silence.

A realisation struck her with such intensity it made her reach out to steady herself. There was a moment where she thought she was going to collapse. She'd been in such a state of fear when she'd run up the driveway that she failed to register her surroundings fully, but subliminally she must have taken the information in. Angela reluctantly made her way over to the window and pulled aside one of the curtains. She was right . . . the space outside Danny's garage was empty: her car was gone.

The guy in the leather jacket was standing across the street staring up at her impassively: leaning against the railings again, letting her know he wasn't going away.

Angela stepped back from the window.

Another thought struck her. Danny had used

115

her to lure the guy away from the front of the house so that he could leave without being seen.

'You're a sneaky son-of-a-bitch, Danny McGuire,' she said to herself as she looked around the empty room.

Suddenly her whole body seemed to ache.

13

Tuscaloosa, Good Friday, mid morning

'Do you think if you saw him again you would recognise him?'

'Which one — the black guy shooting up the alleyway or the guy from Cottondale with the funny accent who saved everyone's lives and knows how to handle a shotgun?' She saw the two FBI agents exchange a glance, but thought nothing of it.

'The guy with the funny accent,' replied the grumpier of the two.

The image of Finn lying on the sofa snoring as Marie snuck out the door earlier that morning flashed through her mind. 'Yeah, I'm pretty sure I would recognise him again,' she said. 'Why, do you have photographs or photofits or whatever they're called?'

'Not yet, but we're getting there. Most people in the bar were watching the asshole doing the shooting rather than paying attention to who or what he was shooting at.'

Marie's attention was drifting again. There was something about these guys that pushed all her 'off' buttons simultaneously.

She'd been surprised at the amount of media attention the story was attracting. When she'd arrived at the police station earlier she'd had to push her way through a crowd of journalists and

117

news cameras to get up the steps. It wasn't until she was safely inside the building that she'd fully registered why they were all there: the shootings at McHales and at the hospital were front-page material. It got her thinking: made her realise that she really didn't want to be a part of all this.

The two agents who'd travelled down from Birmingham had kept her waiting for nearly an hour. She was cold and not in the best of moods. Marie had been sitting in the air-conditioned interview room for too long answering dumb questions: the same dumb questions she'd been asked the day before, the only difference being, the two dumb nuts doing the asking were the FBI instead of 'Ball' and his local deputies. They'd introduced themselves as Agent Joe Evelyn and Agent Jeff Kneller with a silent 'K'. Kneller looked like he smoked sixty a day, two at a time. The centre of his grey moustache was stained nicotine-brown, as were the middle and index fingers of his right hand. Marie supposed he was grumpy because he'd run out. She couldn't figure out why the other one — Evelyn — kept staring at her chest.

Marie felt her stomach cramp and realised she'd need some painkillers pretty soon. No wonder she'd been feeling a bit cranky the past few days; she'd put it down to the circumstances, but she knew now that wasn't the only reason. About half an hour into the interview Marie had caught sight of her reflection in the glass. Her shoulders were tense, sitting high, and she was making no attempt to disguise the bored expression. It suddenly struck her as odd that

118

she was wearing a suit: she never wore a suit. Why had she gone to the bother of dressing up? Was she trying look more respectable? What did she care if the FBI thought she'd come too casually dressed?

The jacket was a light-grey serge material tailored to fit her slim waist. The skirt came down to just below her knees and was fitted too, although — there was no denying it — since Alfredo had died she'd gained a few pounds and the skirt looked lumpy in all the wrong places, especially when she was sitting down. She was even wearing a pair of sensible shoes: a two-inch heel that was easy to walk in. Between that and the white fitted blouse, she figured she looked like she was going for a job in a bank.

'Mrs Weir?'

Her focus was back on the grumpy one, Kneller.

'What?'

'You're the only one so far who seems to have had a good look at him . . . or spoken to him. Do you think you could give us some more detail on what he looked like? Fill in some of the blanks?'

There he was again: staring into her eyes like he was going to ask her out on a date.

'Well, other than what I told the guys yesterday, I don't know what else to say. Everything about him was average: his hair, his height, his clothes . . . his teeth, just . . . average.'

'When you say 'funny accent' where d'you think he was from?' continued Kneller.

Up to this point everything she'd told them had been the truth, but Marie knew she was about to cross the line. She was deliberately going to lie and she wasn't even sure why.

'Poland maybe . . . I don't know, all he asked me for was a beer — 'Beer', you know. It tastes the same in any language . . . sounds the same too.' The last comment got the other one — Evelyn — smiling, but it earned him a look from Grumpy Kneller.

'I know this has been a traumatic experience for you, Mrs Weir — '

Marie interrupted him. 'Actually it's Bain. Weir was my married name, and as the sorry loser who was my husband is now leading the life he really deserved all along, I'm just plain old Marie Bain again . . . If that's okay? And before you go on, let me just say, you have no goddamn idea how traumatic the last few hours have been, so don't even try and empathise, it's fucking patronising. Most of the trauma I've suffered has been from freezing my tits off in here answering the same dumb questions over and over again like somehow the whole goddamn thing was my fault. So please let's just get finished so that I can go home and try to find the rewind button — or better still the erase button — and maybe forget about the fucking nightmare that has become my life.'

'I understand and I am really sorry, we just wanted to hear it from you instead of reading through second-hand notes, but that's fine. I understand . . . I really do . . . Let's wrap it up. I have to ask you one last question, even though I think I already know the answer.'

Grumpy leant back in his chair and took off

his glasses. 'Are you willing to go to court when we eventually make some arrests?'

'Can I say no?' asked Marie.

'Sure,' he replied.

'What happens then?'

'We subpoena you and you have to go to court.'

'So why ask?'

Marie put her head in her hand and drew her thumb and forefinger together till they met on the bridge of her nose. 'I thought it was all sewn up: the banker's wife did it?' said Marie eventually.

'The guy who was killed in the bar yesterday was a professional hit man: he only fired two shots in the direction of the banker's table, and I think it was just unfortunate that the banker's head was in the way of one of them ... he certainly wasn't the target. All the other shots — eight in total — were fired at your 'Polish' friend. There's no doubt that Culo Conrado was aiming at him. Now his partner who was waiting in the alley is also a professional, by the name of Vincent Lee Croll. The guy's a dope-head with the mental capacity of a battery hen, but that hasn't stopped him from killing two police officers last night and the chances are he's not going to stop until the Polish guy is dead too. If Lee Croll doesn't finish the job, he doesn't get paid and if he doesn't get paid he doesn't get his drugs and so on and so on. We are talking about a guy who put the 'wreck' in 'recreational drugs'. So you'll forgive my partner and me for wanting to find out as much as possible first-hand. We want to catch this asshole before he kills another few innocents in his pursuit of his own wealth and happiness. If you find it a little inconvenient to be here answering a few silly fucking questions then I apologise, but as I've said, the situation has gotten a whole lot worse since you left here last night and we'd be very grateful if you'd bear with us just a little longer.'

Grumpy pushed his chair back and stood up.

Marie could see that he was angry, but she gave him credit for trying to contain it: maybe he wasn't such an asshole after all.

'There are a lot of other places we'd rather be right now too — Miss Bain — than in here investigating who killed Culo Conrado and the subsequent death of two of our colleagues, but you know what they say: 'When there's shit flying around watch out for the asshole.' Unfortunately for me, today I have to be the asshole.'

Marie smiled faintly at the image, but Kneller's face didn't crack.

'I'm not making jokes here, Miss Bain,' he continued. 'The quicker we can get Vincent Lee Croll off the street the quicker we'll know why he was trying to hit the Polish guy and hopefully find out who the hell the Polish guy is. But until then, there is a very real risk that the Polish guy is gonna want you dead too. You witnessed him commit a murder. Mr Lee Croll would probably like a word with you as well. And if all that isn't bad enough there's a Mr Hernando De Garza skulking around in the background. You ever heard of him?'

'No.'

'Well let's hope things stay that way, cause he is the nastiest little piece of shit that ain't already in hell . . . and that's because hell refused him entry. He deals drugs, he deals arms, he deals hookers and he has people murdered for looking at him the wrong way. Unfortunately he also pays his taxes so a lot of powerful people have him over to their house for dinner.'

'Why you telling me all this: he invited us round for drinks?'

'No. He employs lowlifes like Croll and Conrado to do his dirty work. And if De Garza is behind all of this then God help you. There you have it. Anything smartass you'd like to add?'

Marie said nothing. She wanted to get up and walk out, but she knew the guy was right. She was in a situation that was completely beyond her realm of experience and if she was being honest she was scared as hell. Marie's first line of defence was a sarcastic comment, or a cutting remark, but these guys weren't going to take any shit from her. For once she didn't have a comeback.

'If you're trying to frighten me, Agent Kneller: congratulations.' Marie felt her cheeks burn crimson and her stomach cramp again. There was a squealing noise as the legs of the chair scraped along the polished stone floor. Marie stood abruptly and bent over to pick up her bag.

'I have to go.'

The other agent who had barely said a word suddenly jumped in.

'Wait, please. Let's just rewind for a second . . . '

But Marie didn't let him finish. 'I'm sorry, I really need to go. I'm trying to help you, I really am, but this whole situation is just too goddamn surreal. You're talking to me like I was the one who pulled the trigger. You guys might have seen lots of people killed right in front of you, but it's never happened to me. If you need me for anything else you can contact me through my lawyer or get your goddamn fucking subpoena.' She started to falter. 'And I'm . . . you know . . . I just want to get the hell out of here.'

Kneller was backtracking now, aware that he'd come on too strong. 'If you want to wait for five minutes we'll arrange for someone to take you home.'

'I can make my own way,' said Marie as she headed for the exit.

Kneller was on his feet now, holding his hand up to stop her.

'Miss Bain, I'd like to apologise. We are all feeling the pressure at the moment. I didn't mean to get so het up. Obviously you're free to do what you like, but I'd warn you that all my instincts are telling me this is a nasty situation we got on our hands here. Why don't you let one of our guys give you a lift and we'll arrange to talk to you later. Take the rest of the weekend, but we will need you here first thing on Monday morning. Sure, we can do that through a lawyer, but I'd rather we kept it informal and stayed friends. Now, the front of the building is swarming with press and it really wouldn't be a good idea to get your photograph in the papers or on television right now in case Lee Croll or the Polish guy or De Garza see it. Then, who knows what sort of trouble you could find yourself in.'

He was standing right in front of her, blocking her way.

Marie stared at the floor. 'I just want to go home,' she said in a quiet voice.

Agent Kneller took a step to the side and held open the door for her.

As she walked out into the corridor Marie heard him call after her, but she'd stopped listening, something about leaving by the back entrance.

The door slammed shut before he'd finished.

★ ★ ★

'Did you hear that?'

'Yeah.'

'She didn't realise what she said, but she will. Probably hit her first thing in the morning. That's when all my revelations come to me: soon as I wake up.'

'You see her eyes switch direction when she mentioned the guy was Polish?'

'Yeah.'

'What you thinking?'

'I'm thinking there's no way in the world the guy is Polish . . . I mean, she blushed too. But why would she lie? I'm also thinking I hope some dickhead doesn't 'accidentally' reveal Miss Bain's identity to the press. Lee Croll and the Polish guy who isn't Polish would have no option but to look her up.'

'D'you think De Garza's involved?'

'Conrado and Croll don't work for anyone else.'

'Feeding her to the press is too risky. She's the only real witness we've got.'

'It won't take them long to figure out who she is anyway. All they got to do is ask a few of the regular drinkers who the hot barmaid is. Might as well earn fifty bucks for passing on the information. She's smartass enough to look after herself, don't you think?'

'I could be that dickhead for fifty bucks.'

'You don't need the fifty bucks.'

'Cheap.'

Agent Kneller's face almost cracked a smile. 'Need to keep an extra-close eye on her then; make damn sure we're there if Lee Croll or anyone else does show. It's a gamble, but how else are we going to flush them out? You cold?'

'Not as cold as she was,' replied Evelyn. 'You see her nipples sticking out her blouse?'

'I was watching her eyes the whole time.'

'Yeah, right.'

'Turn the thermostat back up . . . dickhead.'

14

'Well bless my hole. If it isn't the man himself!
What happened to you? You look like I feel
. . . and I feel like shite.'

Danny's thin-lipped smile made his face hurt.

E.I. held a finger to his lips — 'Shh' — then
gestured Danny to take a seat opposite him at his
large oak desk.

O'Leary's study had an elevated view out over
the fields of his extensive farm. On the horizon a
large, green Massey Ferguson tractor was pulling
a tanker behind it, spreading slurry.

Danny moved awkwardly to the edge of the
desk, but stayed standing. He was still in a lot of
pain.

E.I. scribbled a note on a piece of scrap paper
and pushed it across the worn leather surface of
the desk. Danny adjusted his glasses and picked
up the note. '*Were you followed?*'

He shrugged and raised his eyebrows as if to
say 'Who knows?'

E.I. pulled the scrap of paper back with his big
farmer hands and scribbled again.

'*Tape on, then follow me.*'

Danny nodded: it had been a long time since
he'd visited the old farmhouse, but he still
remembered the routine.

E.I. raised his large bulk from the fragile,

127

oak-framed chair and turned to a tape machine sitting on the bookshelves behind. He flicked the 'on' button and listened for a moment as the opening strains of Wagner's *Lohengrin* eased through the speakers. The tape had been mixed amateurishly with E.I.'s gruff, Capstan-Full-Strength voice, reading aloud a randomly chosen passage about striking dustbin men from the previous day's *Irish Times*. The overall effect was a strange, uneasy marriage of sounds.

With a nod of the head E.I. gestured to Danny to help him lift the rug Danny was standing on. Danny slid the rug to one side with his foot then E.I. pulled open a trapdoor in the floor. They both made their way down a set of rough wooden steps to a narrow tunnel just wide enough for E.I.'s large frame, but not quite tall enough for either of them to stand upright. The tunnel was lit by a string of worker lamps threaded along one side of the timber-framed structure that lined the walls and ceiling, and stretched for some fifty feet along its entire length.

E.I. closed the trapdoor behind him and dropped down the last few steps until he was standing behind Danny.

'That'll keep the bastards guessing, eh? C'mon, let's get a beer.'

As the men made their way along the tunnel E.I. continued, 'Sometimes I read the *Beano* or the *Dandy* instead of the *Times*, depends on my mood. There's a van full of microphones pointing at the house parked in the field across the back there. I'm sure they know it's a tape, but who gives a fuck eh? I can't have a shit without some bugger recording the event. But I'm getting fed up with it, I tell ye. I'm negotiating to buy the land they're parked on from the old bastard that owns it; then I'm going to sue the Brits for trespass. Made him a fair offer for it, that he turned down, so I told him he has to give it to me for nothing now, or I'll kill his family.' E.I. let loose a thick, coarse laugh. 'Sent a couple of the lads over to the old bugger's house to tell him to his face. You would have thought someone was standing behind him giving him a round of applause, the noise the bastard's sphincter was making.'

At the end of the underground passage, another set of steps led up to a trapdoor that opened out into a large barn. The barn was lined with rectangular bales of hay three deep and stacked from the floor all the way up to its corrugated roof, some thirty feet above. In one corner sat a full-size snooker table with a game in progress. Six onlookers sat on benches, drinking and waiting their turn to play. One of the men looked familiar to Danny, but he couldn't remember his name. Danny nodded over, but for some reason the guy didn't look too happy to see him and turned away.

A couple of E.I.'s armed bodyguards were seated at a large rectangular drawing table drinking beer and reading the sports section of the newspaper. The drawing table was set in the middle of the cavernous hall of hay next to a fridge full of alcohol, and was surrounded by a few old sofas and armchairs. The low-level lighting and the sound of *Diamond Dogs* blasting from the large

129

speakers hanging precariously from the metal rafters above gave the place the feeling of a seedy nightclub on the brink of financial ruin. At the far end there was a mountain of stolen goods, everything from televisions and computers to bicycles and curling tongs, all stacked in neat rows.

E.I. caught Danny's gaze. 'Need a new telly?' he asked. 'After we've had our wee chat you can do a bit of shopping.' His bloated, pugnacious face tried to smile, but it looked more like a scowl. 'Don't look so worried, Danny, we'll do you a discount.'

He grabbed a beer from the fridge.

'Welcome to the republican remedial club, shelter to the needy, the greedy and the criminally insane,' he continued. 'This is what you're missing out on when you're sitting there in your ivory tower pretending you work alone. These are your comrades-in-arms.'

Danny thought he detected a little warning note in E.I.'s voice, but he didn't care: he knew he was regarded as an outsider and he was happy to keep it that way.

Despite its size, the lack of doors and windows made the barn feel claustrophobic. Danny looked for an exit but it seemed the only way in and out was back through the tunnel.

'Is there somewhere more private we can go?' he asked.

'Relax, our lad,' said E.I., putting his arm round Danny's shoulder and causing him to wince. 'We're all on the same side. These people are your friends. Grab yourself a beer an let's have a wee chat.'

Danny helped himself to a can of Coke from the fridge, then lowered himself slowly onto the sofa next to E.I. 'Has Órlaith been in touch?'

'Sure, she called here first thing this morning asking if we knew what the hell was going on. I told her we didn't know a bloody thing.'

'Did she say where she was?'

'She's at yer ma's. Says she's not going back to her house, 'till you stop doin whatever it is you're doin',' answered E.I. 'She sounded in a bad way, Danny. Told us what had happened last night. Bastards, eh? D'you know who they were?'

'SAS without a doubt,' answered Danny.

'D'you think they're on to you?'

'No. I've got a close-surveillance team on my hole. Caught one of them in church the other day with a microphone up his sleeve on a fishing trip: putting pressure on me, hoping I'll do something stupid — which I duly did, of course. I pulled a gun on him. I think they were letting me know it wasn't a smart thing to do. I need to lay low for a bit.'

'E4A?' asked E.I.

'I think so,' replied Danny.

'What are they up to?' asked E.I. 'E4A are police, not army. D'you think they're getting the SAS to do their dirty work for them these days?'

'Possibly,' replied Danny. 'Since that list went missing they're expecting me to get busy . . . could be that as well.'

'How did you suss him out?'

'He forgot to cross himself.'

'Aye, it's always the silly things that fuck you up, am I right, Danny?'

131

E.I. was sly: he liked to unsettle people by making them think he knew more than he was letting on. His small, dark eyes were difficult to read and reminded Danny of a shark. Let your guard down for a second and he'd bite. But Danny was ready for him.

'I don't do silly things,' he said, adding 'generally.'

'What were you doing in church?' asked E.I.

It crossed his mind that Órlaith might have mentioned to E.I. about the meeting with Lep McFarlane, but Danny was fairly sure she hadn't. Either way he wasn't going to be the one to bring it up. 'Confessing my sins,' was all that he said. 'Priest said if you ever fancy going, he'd get the *Guinness Book of Records* there to time it.'

E.I. only ever laughed at his own jokes, but he did give Danny a smile. ''Pure as the driven snow', our lad. 'Pure as the driven snow'.'

He banged his hand on the arm of the sofa, signalling the end of the small talk.

'I have a wee proposition for you, Danny, that could suit all parties involved: get you out of Northern Ireland for a while, away from the Snoops, the SAS, and give me an enormous amount of satisfaction.' E.I. was staring at him now. 'Before I start: did you happen to get a look at the list?'

Danny shook his head.

'You sure?' pressed E.I.

'I never even touched it. Eamon dropped round to my place for a beer after the operation, but as far as I'm aware he'd already passed it on to Quig. Why?'

132

'Are you sure?'

Danny wondered why E.I. was asking. 'Positive,' he replied.

'Did Eamon look at it, or Quig, d'you think?'

'Possibly, I've no idea,' said Danny, pushing his glasses further up on his nose. 'I never spoke to Quig. They might have had a look to check it was the right thing, but that's about it, I really don't know. Is there a problem?'

E.I. deflected him with another question.

'How's yer ma, Danny? You looking after her all right?'

Danny wasn't interested in talking about his mother: he wanted to find out why E.I. had asked to see him, then get the hell out of there.

'She's fine.'

'I know how she feels about us, Danny, but you tell her the door here is always open if she needs anything.'

'I will.'

E.I. lowered his voice. 'I tell you, and I've never said this to anyone, but I have nightmares about what happened to your Sean. The explosion was the size of a fuckin mountain in my rear-view mirror; I can still feel the heat on the back of my neck. I've had people swear they saw it light up the sky as far away as Dublin. There's no consolation in it, but your Sean wouldn't have felt a thing.' E.I.'s monotone voice betrayed no emotion as he spoke. 'If we'd detonated that bomb where we'd intended: not only would it have taken out the Prime Minister, but half of Belfast as well . . . Aye, your Sean wasn't a soldier, he was an army, our lad. A terrible loss.'

133

E.I. paused and took a drink of beer before continuing. 'Anyway, the reason I bring it up is, we've had a few sightings of Lep McFarlane cutting around his old haunts. Would you believe the fuckin cheek of the dirty little tout: daring to show his face in Newry again?'

Danny wasn't sure if he was being paranoid or just over-sensitive, but once again it looked like E.I. was watching him for a reaction.

'Anyway I thought you'd want to know Danny . . . He's a kill-on-sight job.'

'Is that what you wanted to see me about?' asked Danny.

E.I. looked like he was expecting more of a reaction from Danny: his eyes narrowed, but Danny was giving nothing away. 'It was one of the things, the support act if you like, but here's the main event,' said E.I. 'While we're on the subject of treacherous little bastards who deserve to die, there's something I want to ask you. I know you like to set your own agenda, Danny, but how d'you fancy a wee trip to the States courtesy of the Irish Republican Army?'

Danny looked at him and shrugged. 'Work or pleasure?'

'Depends how you look at it, our lad,' replied E.I. with a crooked grin. He leant towards Danny and whispered under his breath, 'Would giving the Thevshi an OBE be regarded as work or pleasure?'

'One Behind the Ear': Jam a gun behind some poor fucker's ear and pull the trigger. It was a traitor's death, an informer's fate . . . an OBE.

Danny let the question settle before answering.

'Have you found him?'

E.I. nodded. 'We have his name: the one they gave him when they changed his identity, that is, the address they relocated him to and would you believe it . . . a bloody telephone number. I don't have to tell you, Danny, what it would mean to the republican movement to have the bastard's head on a spike. You'd be a hero, I tell ye.' E.I. had something else to say that he didn't want anyone else to hear. He leant forward again. 'I'll be honest with you, Danny. It's not a question of who has the biggest army, or the best weapons or the just cause: information is the key. We've been infiltrated up to our bloody necks: if we lose this war that'll be the reason. They have all the information. You don't know who to trust these days. We have to make an example of the Thevshi to show any other fucker thinking of grassing on us that — no matter how long it takes — we'll find them, and execute them without mercy. It's essential to our survival. And all those bastards who have informed on us in the past are now shitting themselves in case they're on that list. I know you're not an active member, Danny, but I'm sure even you can see what a coup it would be for us.'

E.I. suddenly sat back and smiled. 'And if all that's not enough, the job's worth a quite a few doubloons too. Shooting that dirty piece of shit in the head could be worth nearly twenty grand . . . enough to retire on.'

E.I. was staring at Danny again with the same intensity as before: scrutinising him, no doubt about it.

Danny fixed his eyes on the floor. 'So 'The Ghost' really does exist?'

'He sure does,' replied E.I. 'Hopefully not for too much longer. But as you know, nothing is ever straightforward on this tiny island of ours. We have one small problem. We were a bit too eager to kill the cunt: so we asked a favour of a friend out in Alabama — guy called Hernando De Garza. He's a big player: into arms, drugs, vice, you name it. Won't touch anything that doesn't carry a hefty jail sentence: likes risk. He goes and employs a couple of local tradesmen, who — of course — fuck it up. Missed their target. Stupid fuckers tried to hit the Thevshi in a bar. The guy lives on his own in the middle of nowhere and these eejits try and take him out in a crowded bar. Can you believe that?'

'So he knows we're on to him?' interjected Danny.

E.I. nodded again. 'Aye, course he does. If you were up for it we'd want to get you out there as soon as possible. We want it done right, Danny, and we want it done right now. You're the man for the job. What d'you say?'

Danny didn't have to think. 'I've a few things to sort out beforehand, but I'm ready to go anytime you like,' he replied.

'Grand, Danny, that's just grand. We've got a tug-of-war team flying out to Boston the day after next. It's a bit of a pain in the arse cause you'll have to make your way cross-country from there, but at least you'll have some craic on the plane. They're a good bunch of lads, and it's a half-decent cover story. Owen O'Brien's going, d'you know him?'

136

'I know who he is,' replied Danny. He realised then that the man he thought looked familiar a few minutes earlier was O'Brien.

Owen O'Brien used to hang around with Sean at school, but no one liked him: too argumentative. Too eager with his fists if he didn't get what he wanted or you looked at him the wrong way. He'd fought his way through the ranks of the Republican Army to become head of their internal security, responsible for interrogating suspected informers and disciplining the younger members of the organisation if they stepped out of line. If you were up before O'Brien it was already too late. Very few survived the ordeal. In many ways O'Brien and Danny did similar jobs, but Danny regarded himself as a professional and O'Brien as nothing more than a gangster.

'Nasty fucker,' continued E.I. 'Don't go near him if he has a drink in him. It was O'Brien poured a kettle of boiling water over that young lad O'Patrick's girlfriend. Sure enough it made the boy talk, but the girl was scarred for life and O'Patrick ended up dead anyway — but what was I saying? Oh aye. Looks like we've qualified for the tug-of-war world championships in Oshkosh, can you believe that? We'll get things set up for you: sort you out with some cash and a passport and so on. Whatever you need, just let us know.'

'Any chance of getting hold of a MSG90?'

'You going to take the Thevshi out long-distance?' asked E.I.

Danny didn't answer.

'I'll get it for you, no bother,' continued E.I.

137

'The guy I was talking about earlier — Hernando De Garza — he'll sort you out. We owe him for the hit on the Thevshi, and even though he fucked it up we're gonna pay him. The guy can get his hands on all sorts of US military hardware, so we need to keep him sweet. I'd like you to take him some cash, maybe place an order if you don't mind. De Garza reckons he can get his hands on a couple of Stingers the CIA are sending to the Mujahideen in Afghanistan. You wouldn't have to bring anything back, just check it's legit, give him the deposit and leave the rest to us. Would you be okay with that?'

'No problem,' replied Danny.

'But, in terms of your own personal weaponry, you can have whatever you like, Danny, as long as you bring home the Thevshi's scalp.'

'Were the Thevshi's details on the list then?' asked Danny.

'Page one,' replied E.I.

'Unbelievable! So where's he been hiding?'

'The beginning, middle and end of nowhere: ever heard of Tuscaloosa, Alabama?' asked E.I.

Even though he had, Danny shook his head.

Danny was sure he knew the answer to the next question, but he asked it anyway. 'What's he call himself?'

'Finn O'Hanlon,' replied E.I.

Danny didn't know why he decided not to tell E.I. that it was the second time in as many days that he had heard of Tuscaloosa, and the second time he'd heard of Finn O'Hanlon. Danny wasn't sure either why he didn't mention the meeting with Lep McFarlane.

He just had a feeling.

'You want a lift home, Danny?'

The meeting was over.

Danny eased himself painfully up from the sofa. 'I'm fine E.I. I've got a car.'

'I'm surprised you can bloody walk, never mind drive a car. You sure you're all right?'

'Fine. Really. One last thing, E.I. Does Bap still work at the DVLA?

'That bollock has never done a day's work in his life, but that's who pays his wages.'

'Could he check out a number plate for me?'

'Sure, if the vehicle's in Northern Ireland he'll find it for you. Fire away.'

'KIB 1024.'

15

'That greasy, back-stabbing little bollock doing the interview was getting my blood up,' said Frank. 'When he asked if the break-in was 'down to the Special Branch's incompetence or the IRA's cunning' I seriously considered knocking him out. Cheeky bastard. If only he knew the bloody truth!'

Detective Inspector Holden, Detective Sergeant Warren and Frank Thompson were walking past the large sweeping reception desk in the lobby of UTV — the local television station — heading for the exit. Frank had just recorded an interview for the evening news and was in a sombre mood.

'How did that come across?'

'Better than the six o'clock the other night: not so much on the back foot. Are we really launching an official inquiry?'

'Are we fuck,' replied Frank.

The three men pushed through the revolving door and headed out across the car park. The rain had eased but the cold April wind buffeted and blustered around them as they walked towards their car.

Frank pulled his heavy black woollen coat tight.

'Got a call from Sheena, Chief,' said DI Holden. 'Lep McFarlane's body's been found on the Omeath Road with a bullet in the back of the head. At least they think it's him . . . there's not much left of his face: difficult to make a positive ID.'

'Christ, he didn't last long, did he?' replied Frank. 'Poor bugger's only been back in town for a few days.'

'That's not the best bit, sir. You'll never guess who was the last person to see McFarlane alive — spotted leaving St Patrick's in Newry just a few minutes after McFarlane — on Tuesday morning.'

'If I'll never guess,' replied Frank, 'just bloody tell me.'

'Have a go.'

Frank was in no mood for playing guessing games. 'The Pope,' he replied flatly.

'Too holy: we're talking the other end of the spectrum here,' continued Holden. 'Closer to the gates of Hades than St Peter's; guess again.' Holden raised his eyebrows, pausing a moment to give the imminent revelation more drama. 'Danny McGuire.'

Frank's mood picked up a little. 'Danny McGuire: you sure?'

'Couldn't be more so,' replied DI Holden.

'Any witnesses willing to back that up?' asked Frank.

'Better than that, Chief,' replied John, grinning. 'We've had an E4A close-surveillance team running an op on McGuire from a few weeks before the list was stolen: more a stroke of luck

141

on our part than forward planning, but it could prove to be very useful. If anyone's going to get busy round about now it'll be him. They've got snaps of him leaving the church.'

'Let's get a hold of those as soon as possible,' said Frank.

'Should be arriving back at HQ any minute,' replied DI Holden. 'A couple of the E4A team are heading over for a debrief. I told Sheena to send them straight up.'

Frank nodded. 'Good. We don't want to screw this up because we're not communicating within our own departments.'

The men had reached the dark-blue unmarked police car. Warren extended a thin telescopic pole with a mirror on the end and made a cursory check under the vehicle for explosives, then held the rear door open. Holden and Frank shuffled in, then Warren made his way round to the driver's door and climbed in as well.

'Turn the heater up full, David, would you, it's like a bloody fridge in here — I've got a couple of hairy ice-cubes where my balls should be,' said Frank, shuddering as if he had to illustrate the point further. 'Danny McGuire, eh?' Frank kept it flat. 'And the two men were definitely meeting each other, they didn't just happen to be attending the same prayer group?'

'They were the only two in the church apart from the priest, Father Anthony,' said David Warren. 'We've already had a chat with him, but he's one of *them*, so he's not confirming anything one way or the other. Apparently he turned a shaky shade of green when he heard

142

that McFarlane was dead,' continued DI Holden. 'Danny McGuire got a call from McFarlane the night before asking for the meet. E4A have a tap on his phone. They're transcribing the conversation.'

'I wonder what brought McFarlane back to Northern Ireland after all this time; I haven't heard of the little fucker for a good few years,' said Frank. 'In fact, I thought he was already dead.'

'Who knows,' replied Holden. 'The last intelligence we had on him, he was trying to kill the Prime Minister with a car bomb, then he vanished off the radar. But that was quite a while ago. I bet he's wishing he'd stayed put, eh?'

'A murder victim, executed like a tout, and a top hit man together in the same church just hours before his killing. It doesn't get much better than that,' said Holden.

'Why would McGuire want McFarlane dead?' asked Warren.

DI Holden leant forward. 'McFarlane is an informer. Not only that, but McFarlane was supposed to be the driver the night Danny McGuire's brother ended up getting blown to pieces.'

'I wasn't around when all that shit was going on,' said Warren, looking back at Holden in his rear-view mirror.

'Yeah. Sean McGuire drove straight into an ambush the SAS had set up,' replied Holden. 'Two hundred rounds fired at a car full of Semtex. Car, Semtex, Sean McGuire, *kaboom!* Shame, eh?' he added unsympathetically. 'But

143

Lep McFarlane was supposed to be in the car as well. The SAS claimed they had nothing to do with it, but how many times have we heard that?'

Frank Thompson wasn't one for letting his enthusiasm show. He'd had plenty of near-misses over the years so knew not to get carried away. However, this scenario seemed to play out surprisingly well. 'Let's not get too excited just yet,' he said. 'It's not like Danny McGuire to be this sloppy. There's no way he would allow himself to be seen with a target just hours before he was going to shoot the bugger in the back of the head.'

Frank was beginning to warm up. 'Get a forensic team down to St Patrick's and give the place a thorough going-over.'

'Sheena sorted that this morning, Chief,' said DI Holden, interrupting. 'They should be there right now.'

'Great,' continued Frank. 'Get them to look over McFarlane's clothing specifically for traces of McGuire. I want as much concrete evidence as possible.'

'Why don't we have McGuire picked up right now, let a few of his comrades know we're questioning him . . . maybe let slip that he's being 'very co-operative',' said DI Holden. 'Start tipping the bastard off balance.'

Frank gave Holden a look: it was a bad idea.

'Nobody in the IRA would believe for one minute that he was co-operating with us. And my inclination is to do the opposite: back off, wait to see what his next move is. If he knows we're watching he'll do nothing at all.'

144

'Might be too late, Chief,' said Holden. 'Al Ballantine was caught with his pants down in the church. McGuire confronted him: pulled a weapon on him.'

'Ballantine pulled a weapon on McGuire?' asked Frank.

'No, McGuire pulled a weapon on Al.'

'Jesus Christ,' exclaimed Frank. 'So McGuire knows for sure there's a team on him.'

Frank caught DS Warren and Holden exchanging a glance.

'If there's more you better tell me.'

'Four men entered McGuire's sister-in-law's house the other night in the early hours of last night and drove off with him in a van; E4A were parked across the street, they confirmed it was an SAS unit. I get the impression the four guys weren't dropping round for a cup of tea, that's for sure.'

'What the fuck are the SAS doing there? Who in God's name sanctioned that?'

'Cosmo Cullen's leading the E4A operation: he's ex-army,' replied Holden. 'He called in a favour to put the frighteners on McGuire.'

Frank banged his fist against the side of the car door in frustration. 'For fuck's sake! When we get back I want Cullen and Ballantine in my office as soon as possible. Those stupid bastards may well have blown our best chance yet of chopping McGuire off at the knees.'

DS Warren started to say, 'But if he killed McFarlane — ?'

Frank interrupted him. 'And if he didn't, what then?'

'He threatened Ballantine with a gun.'

'Prove it,' replied Frank. 'One of your witnesses is already dead and the other is a goddamn priest who's a card-carrying member.' Frank cleared a small circle of condensation from the rear passenger window.

'Jesus Christ!'

He stared out at the fresh downpour of rain.

'Don't anyone say another word, okay. I need to think.'

16

*The outskirts of Newry, early hours of
Good Friday*

Corporal Tony Lynch sat up in bed and pulled
his 9 mm Beretta from the holster hanging on
the bedpost next to his head: it was an instinctive
reaction. He wasn't sure if the dull sounds he'd
heard were part of his dream, or just the wind
tugging at the gaps in the rotten window frames,
making them rattle — but something had woken
him up.

His eyes took time to adjust to the smothering
darkness. Even then he could only make out a
thin slither of moonlight pushing between the
drab curtains hanging above his bed. It was
impossible to pick out any other detail in the
small bedroom.

He sat quietly for a few moments filtering
through the familiar creaks and groans of the
derelict farm cottage, listening for any sound
— however small — that didn't belong. Every
house had its own way of talking: a language of
cracking floorboards and creaking doors with
which Tony liked to familiarise himself as quickly
as possible whenever he arrived somewhere new.

The cottage sat at the end of a long dirt track
close to the border with the South. If Tony and
his team were compromised they could easily
slip across to the relative safety of the Republic

147

of Ireland. The cottage was also far enough away from the nearest village for the team's comings and goings — they hoped — to go unnoticed.

Tony listened intently for a few more minutes before concluding that tonight — aside from the usual groans and moans — the house had nothing new to say.

He pressed the 'glow' button on his Suunto wristwatch: another ten minutes before he'd have to get out of bed. It would be his turn to sleep in the van tonight, so he was happy to savour every last minute inside the warm comfort of his sleeping bag.

Rainwater poured noisily from the broken gutter outside the bedroom window into a large puddle that had formed on the saturated ground below.

He smiled to himself as he thought of Jacko sitting up all night in what they'd nicknamed 'the Drum'. It hadn't stopped raining since they'd arrived in Northern Ireland and the van they used as a lookout post reverberated noisily to the rain's incessant beat. It turned an ordinary picket into four hours of mind-numbing monotony.

The SAS team had been late back from last night's op and Jacko had tried bribing the others in the unit with the promise of 'free beer for the rest of their lives' if one of them would take his place on watch. Stevie and Spider had told him to piss off straight away. Tony considered it, briefly, but he was too knackered. Every member of the team was exhausted, so it was only fair that Jacko took his turn.

The team's tour of duty was nearly over; it had been long and intense. The ops themselves were stressful enough; mostly reconnaissance and intelligence-gathering with the occasional 'intervention' — like the other night when they'd done a favour for one of Tony's old colleagues from his days in the regular army — but all the sneaking around they had to do before and after was what really cranked up the pressure. Even the short walk across the mud-caked yard was beginning to piss them off: it was impossible to get to and from the cottage without getting rained on, or covered in mud. Every operation either started or ended with wet kit.

They arrived in the dark and left in the dark. If whoever owned the cottage was aware that there were four men living there, it wouldn't take long for that information to get back to the IRA.

The brief had warned them to treat everybody in the area as the enemy: 'Every farm truck's a rocket launcher, every parked car's a roadside bomb, every postman's a spy . . . If you see a dog sniffing round the van, shoot it in the fuckin head. If you don't it'll turn you in!'

Everything they did would be construed as suspicious, which is why they went to such lengths to cover their arses: one of them in the van parked near the end of the drive, one downstairs, both on watch. That way the other two could sleep upstairs: guaranteed some much-needed rest.

Days were mostly spent in the smaller of the two bedrooms with the curtains drawn: talking in whispers, planning for that evening's mission.

No radio.

149

No television.

No down-time.

It was a bit of a head fuck, and the tours could last anything up to six months, but thankfully this one was nearly over.

It was Tony's fifth visit to Northern Ireland in charge of these lads. They were tight.

Tony's wristwatch started to vibrate.

'Wakey wakey, rise and shine; shave, shit and shower,' Tony whispered under his breath.

He swung his legs out of bed and slipped his feet into his damp twelve-button Doc Marten boots. Even though he'd slept fully clothed, Tony couldn't stop himself from shivering as the cold musty air hit his tired body.

Discovering the cottage still had a power supply had been a welcome bonus. They'd managed to rig up the boiler to provide them with hot water, but it was temperamental and took most of the day to heat enough for all four of them. If he was sharp he could get to the shower ahead of the others, use up all the hot water before they did. Jacko had managed to do it three days in a row — the bastard — but the others were starting to get pissed off with it now.

It was still worth a try. Tony grabbed a dry towel from his kit bag and made his way along the short corridor to the bathroom.

He leant over the bath and turned the lever on the mixer tap from 'Bath' to 'Shower'. The showerhead immediately spluttered into life, catching him on the top of the head with a flush of cold water. 'Bastard!' he exclaimed.

He held his hand under the spray and waited

for the warm water to flow through, then reached down to pick his towel off the floor.

Tony froze.

The noises again!

A sudden rush and he was on: all trace of tiredness gone in an instant.

In that moment Tony knew that the sounds he'd heard earlier were not part of a dream; they were real. The unmistakable sound of muzzled gunfire, and it had come from somewhere inside the cottage.

Tony left the shower spitting and hissing hot water into the bathtub, and made his way quickly back to his bedroom. He snapped on his gun belt, checked that the Beretta was loaded, slotted a fresh magazine into his Heckler MP5 and took a defensive position by the door. When he was certain the corridor was clear he headed towards Spider's bedroom.

There was no longer any light spilling out of the kitchen on the ground floor. It had been switched off.

But by whom?

The upstairs hall was now in total darkness.

Tony slipped quietly into Spider's bedroom.

Over to his right, in the small single bed squashed against the wall, he could just make out the rumpled silhouette of Spider's slumbering body.

'Spider!'

In less than three steps he'd covered the distance between the door and the top end of the bed. 'Spider, wake up you fucker, we have a situation.'

Keeping his attention focused on the door, he reached down and gave Spider a shake.

'C'mon . . . wake up, we've got visitors.'

As he touched the duvet he pulled his hand away sharply.

'Shit!'

Tony rubbed his fingers together and cursed under his breath.

He pulled the curtain aside to let in more light and winced as he caught sight of the gaping hole in the side of Spider's head. The wound glistened in the dark and oozed blood from a gory well created by a single shot to the skull.

Tony picked up Spider's walkie-talkie from the floor beside his bed.

'Stevie, are you there? If you can't talk, give me a couple of clicks to let me know you're all right . . . Stevie?'

He flipped the small rubber-clad lever to a different channel and tried again.

'Jacko, you there pal . . . C'mon?'

Tony listened for a few seconds, then tried again.

'Jacko, for fucksake! You there?'

He was about to put the walkie-talkie down when it crackled into life.

'He's here . . . but not for long.'

Suddenly there was a loud whoosh outside that sent a fireball mushrooming into the sky. There then followed a brief instant where it seemed as if nothing else was going to happen. But Tony knew the pause was just the blast gathering itself together before ripping the building in two. Suddenly the windows burst from their frames, sending glass and splinters of wood crashing to the ground. Doors slammed against walls or flew off their hinges as the force of the blast tore through the small cottage. The walls of the bedroom erupted in a frenzy of searing flames. Tony shielded himself from the worst of the explosion then scrambled to his feet and stared out at the Drum.

The flames engulfing the van railed and flicked furiously at the night sky.

Out of the corner of his eye he saw a figure in the shadows moving back across the yard towards the cottage. He raised the Heckler to the window and fired off a burst, but the figure had already disappeared.

Tony listened hard to the crackle of blistering paint and the hollow rush of air as the tyres exploded in the intense heat, but there was no sound coming from inside the van.

Tony's mind switched to combat mode.

The first two shots he'd heard must have been for Spider.

With Stevie dead in the kitchen and Jacko in the van it was all down to him.

He had to act quickly.

No time to hesitate.

Tony cleared the remaining shards of glass from the window frame and sprayed the rear end of the van with bullets; clipped in another Mag. and emptied it too. If there was even the remotest chance that Jacko had survived the explosion, he wasn't going to let him suffer for one moment longer. He knew if the positions were reversed Jacko would have done the same.

153

The walkie-talkie hissed into life again.

'Your turn, soldier.'

Tony didn't respond. Instead he knelt down and pulled three more clips of ammunition from Spider's gun-belt, then made his way over to the door and back out into the corridor. With his weapon raised, elbows tucked and finger resting lightly on the trigger he crept slowly towards the head of the stairwell.

He had no idea who or how many he was up against.

The only thing he knew for certain: he wasn't going down without a fight.

Tony stood motionless at the head of the stairs, straining for the faintest sound.

'Talk to me, house, c'mon, talk to me,' he said to himself.

The noise of the shower spraying redundantly into the empty bath wasn't helping.

Tony turned as the petrol tank in the van outside suddenly exploded, scorching every wall in the house with a burst of bright light. It briefly illuminated the silhouette of a man standing — unseen — in the doorway behind him.

Thump!

The first bullet hit him in the shoulder and sent him twisting violently to the floor.

He squeezed the trigger on the Heckler, spraying bullets randomly over the walls and ceiling.

Thump!

The second bullet ripped through his forearm and shattered his elbow into tiny fragments, the force of the impact pushing his arm out at an awkward angle, but that was all . . . there was no pain.

Clinging to the banister for support, Tony managed to pull himself up to a standing position. He wanted to get to his feet and face his enemy.

Thump!

The third bullet punched him in the chest, expelling all the air from his lungs and knocking him backwards onto the floor.

As he lay there motionless, he realised the strange sound he could hear was the blood gurgling in his throat as he struggled to breathe.

Tony recognised him straight away: he recognised the dispassionate face and the dead eyes. Standing there, making sure Tony got a good look; letting him see the face of his killer.

Tony tried to squeeze the trigger one last time, but there was not enough strength left in his hand.

Still no pain.

Then a voice.

'The woman you punched in the face was my brother's wife; the young girl you scared the shit out of is my niece. When you murdered my brother I swore to protect them: keep them safe. That's what I'm doing now . . . Any last requests?'

Thump!

★   ★   ★

A haze of heat from the burning wreckage blurred the figure's outline as it moved quickly

155

away from the flame-coloured night.

Through the blaze and the blistering paint Danny could still make out the embossed letters of the van's registration plate.

KIB 1024.

17

Angela's mother turned down the volume on the radio before looking over at Angela with a puzzled expression on her face. The two women sat staring across the kitchen table at each other until the sound of knocking came again.

'Is that someone at the front door?' asked her mother, stating the obvious: a habit that Angela found increasingly irritating. 'It's too early in the morning to be calling on folk, is it not? The birds are still singing.' She stayed seated and nodded in the direction of the hallway. 'Well, you'd better go and see who it is.'

Reluctantly, Angela made her way out into the hall and headed towards the front door, racking her brains as to who it could be. Her encounter with the guy in the leather jacket outside Danny's had left her feeling nervous and vulnerable, scared even.

She had called for a cab to come and pick her up from his house: an expense she could ill afford. When it eventually arrived, the taxi driver gave her a curious glance as she looked around for the guy in the leather jacket, but he was nowhere to be seen. Even though she was certain the taxi wasn't being followed she'd asked the driver to take a different route home just in case.

157

The longer route had added to the cost.

Angela slipped the brass chain between the stays, then opened the door a few inches.

'Who is it?' shouted her mum from the kitchenette.

Angela felt her cheeks burn.

'It's the fella who stole my car, Ma,' she replied.

'What's he doing calling at this time in the morning? I hope the cur's here to give it back?'

'My ma wants to know if you've come to give me my car back?'

Danny's breath puffed in grey transparent swirls as he stood shivering on the doorstep of the small pebble-dashed bungalow. He shifted his weight uncomfortably before replying, 'Sort of . . . D'you mind if I come in for a minute?'

'Do we mind if he comes in for a minute, Ma?'

'Get the keys off him and close the door, Angela, you're letting all the heat out.'

'How did you know I lived in Dunnaval?'

'Got a pal works for the DVLA, ran your plate through for me. Came up: Greencastle Road, Dunnaval.'

'Is that allowed?'

'As long as you don't tell anyone in the RUC you're doing it,' replied Danny.

Angela shook her head slowly then unclipped the latch and opened the door fully. 'You'd better come in before my ma has a stroke. But don't plan on staying long: I've got to get to work this morning . . . can't afford to take any more time off.' Angela peered over Danny's shoulder at her car parked alongside the kerb. 'I hope you've put

158

petrol in it. The tank was nearly full when you stole it,' she said as Danny edged past her into the hallway.

'I only borrowed it,' he replied.

'You 'only' used me to lure those men in the white van away from your house and then stole it. I don't remember handing you the keys.'

Angela was giving him a bit of a ride, but he didn't mind — he couldn't explain why, but it was good to see her again. 'You don't need keys for those old Fords. You can get into them and start them up with a penny.'

'Only someone who steals cars would know something like that.'

In truth, Angela didn't care about the car: if anything, she was disappointed to get it back. What was troubling her more was the fact she was wearing her nurse's uniform. She'd had the seams round the waist adjusted to make her stomach look flatter, but the alterations had made the skirt flare out at the back. Her bottom looked huge — or so she thought. Why hadn't he brought the car back yesterday when she was wearing her black slacks and fitted jumper: an outfit that showed off her slim figure to its best advantage?

Worse still, Angela didn't put her face on in the morning until she was heading out the door so she was standing there with no lippy, no concealer and worst of all, no mascara. *Jesus. Catch yourself on, girl. The guy's married with a child and he nicked your car.*

Angela closed the door behind Danny and ushered him into the living room. There was a strong smell of petrol on his clothes.

'What's the scent . . . Eau de BP?'

She could tell he didn't get it.

'You smell like a leaky jerry-can.'

'Do I? Christ, so I do,' replied Danny, finally catching on. 'Aye, it's a new fragrance from Fabergé: one pound fifty a gallon. I must have spilled some when I was filling up your car.'

'Aye right,' said Angela with an expression on her face that told him she didn't believe him.

'Check for yourself: cost me nearly fifteen quid,' said Danny earnestly. 'To be honest, it'd have been cheaper getting a taxi.'

Angela's eyes narrowed. 'Well next time why don't you do that? Then I won't have to take the two-hour bus ride to work, because there is no direct service from here into Belfast so I have to change buses and they don't operate on anything even remotely resembling a timetable. Nor would I have to sit up all night wondering what to tell my insurance company or whether or not I should call the RUC, because if I don't tell them it's been stolen the insurance won't pay out and that'd mean getting the bus to work for the next few years until I could save up enough to buy a new car and even then I wouldn't know where to start because I'm not a big fan of cars; another brain-ache. Which make, which colour, how many doors? Should I get one that has better locks? And I know what would have happened. I'd give up and take the bus. I worked out if I did that for the next ten years I'd have wasted over a year of that waiting for, or travelling on, public-bloody-transport. So the next time you're

160

thinking 'Should I nick that car or take a taxi?' my advice would be take the goddamn taxi.' Angela paused and smiled.

'You've given it a lot of thought,' said Danny.

'Your mind starts to wander, sitting in a bus shelter for so long. Take a seat — but, don't get too close to that fire, you'll go up in a ball of flames.'

Danny made his way round the garish floral-patterned sofa and sat down.

'The number twenty-three goes from here into Belfast.'

Angela let that one pass. 'D'you feel like tea?'

'Aye, that'd be grand,' replied Danny.

'Hungry?'

'Right now, I'd eat shit if it had salad cream on it.'

'We only do bacon and salad cream, but if you hang on I'll ask my ma to nip down to the Co-op.'

Angela headed back to the kitchen, leaving Danny staring at a small pile of coal in the ash-dusted hearth. He didn't really want a cup of tea. He'd said yes so that he could be in her company for a little longer.

Little fissures of orange glow were still visible in what remained of last night's fire. He gave a small shudder as the image of a van engulfed in flames flashed through his mind.

Angela was back, standing in the doorway.

'Ma says we're fresh out of shit. How about some bacon?'

'Bacon'll do fine, but I don't want to make you late for work.'

She felt her cheeks burning again.

'You all right?' asked Danny.

'Fine,' she replied.

There was an awkward silence, then Angela said, 'I didn't realise you wore glasses.'

Danny pushed them up on his nose. It was an action that had developed into a nervous habit — they were never in any danger of falling off. 'Well, you haven't known me for very long, I suppose. I only wear them on special occasions.'

'Does returning stolen goods count as a special occasion?'

'If you're the one getting the goods back then I suppose it does,' replied Danny. 'How much did your car cost you?'

'Why you asking?'

'I want to buy it off you.'

It was blunt, but it answered her question.

'You want to buy it off me?' repeated Angela, raising her eyebrows. 'I don't remember putting a 'for sale' sign in the window.'

'I'll give you five grand for it.'

Angela raised her eyebrows even higher. 'Are you off your head? It's not worth five quid . . . plus, it's not for sale.'

Danny pulled a fat bundle of notes from inside his jacket and placed them on the small wooden coffee table that sat between the sofa and hearth. 'I didn't expect to have to bargain with you, but if that's how you want to play it, five-and-a-half grand and not a penny more.'

'I'm not bargaining, Danny, it's not for sale.'

'You're a tough negotiator.'

'I'm not negotiating.'

'Six grand.'

'No.'

'Seven?'

'Jesus! No.'

'Seven-and-a-half?'

'Stop it, Danny.'

'Eight?'

'Stop it,' she said more firmly.

'Okay you win. Ten grand, take it or leave it?'

Angela was staring at him. It was more money than she had ever seen in her life. If she worked for another twenty years she knew she would never have that much in her bank account, but she also knew she couldn't take it. She was trying to read Danny's face, find out what he was thinking, but the mask was on — as always.

Angela was resolute. 'Thanks for the offer, but I'll leave it.'

Her mother entered the living room and placed a hot mug of tea on the coffee table. 'There's no bacon left, you drink that up and be on your way, son.'

'Ma, that's enough,' said Angela, interrupting.

'I'm just saying. I've gone through enough trouble when your father was alive and I don't want any more. Not for me, not for you. Drink your tea, and then I'd be grateful if you left my daughter and me in peace. And you can take your money too. We won't be needing it.'

Angela got to her feet and shepherded her mother back towards the door. 'That's enough, Ma, please. There's no need to be rude. Go back to the kitchen and make me some toast, would you? I'll be with you in a minute.'

Danny got to his feet as well. 'I'm sorry, Mrs

Fitzpatrick, I just want to say a few words to Angela then I promise I'll leave you alone.'

'Finish your tea then out!' continued Mrs Fitzpatrick, hardening her tone.

'Enough,' said Angela, matching her mother.

She waited for her mum to go into the hall then closed the door behind her.

'I'm sorry about that . . . ' she started to say as she gathered the cash off the table.

'Yer all right.'

'I'm all she's got. She can be a bit over-protective.'

'Honestly, it's fine,' said Danny.

When Angela had gathered up each of the thousand-pound bundles she held them towards him, but Danny kept his hands by his sides. 'If the car means that much to you, you can have it,' she said. 'I don't want your money, Danny, okay. Please take this back.'

She lifted her eyes and caught Danny's stare burrowing deep inside her, catching and holding her; connected.

'The car means fuck-all to me,' said Danny quietly under his breath. 'You're the only person, in a long time, that's done anything good for me, and for that, I owe you.' He saw Angela make to interrupt him and held his hand up to stop her. 'Don't say another word; just wait till I'm finished, okay? If you hadn't stopped and picked me up the other day I wouldn't be here now . . . for that I owe you. Decency doesn't drink in the same bars as me these days: you reminded me that it still exists and for that I owe you as well. I want you to accept this money as my way

164

of saying thank you: I'll be offended if you don't. Now, I have one last favour to ask. If you don't want to do it, if you want to say no, I'll understand, but right now you're the only person I know I can trust.' Danny pulled another thick envelope from his pocket and handed it to Angela. 'There's another ten grand in here I'd like you to deliver to Órlaith.'

Angela felt her stomach turn over at the mention of his wife: she struggled not to let her emotions show on her face.

She nodded.

'The address is on the front and there's a letter in there for my ma, I'd be very grateful if you made sure she got it. There's other stuff I want to tell you, but it can wait.' With that Danny moved closer to the door.

'Why can't you take it yourself?' asked Angela.

'I have to be getting on my way, places to go, things to do, a tug-of-war to be won.' Danny was already in the hall. 'That, and Órlaith's staying round at my ma's house and my ma hasn't spoken a word to me for over five years. It's complicated, but as I say: it can wait.'

'I won't get a chance until the weekend. Will that be okay?' asked Angela.

'Sure there's no hurry,' replied Danny. 'By the way, what happened to the Easter eggs you went to buy for me?'

Angela could feel a tear burning its way to the surface. She didn't know why, but she wanted to cry. 'I used them as an offensive weapon to ward off an attacker, but I'll tell you about that later. 'It can wait', too.'

'You'll have to take that up with Órlaith and Niamh, the eggs were for them. Don't go getting upset now, Angel, there's plenty more in the shop.' With that he bent over and kissed Angela softly on the lips: it was quick and tender and before she could respond it was over.

'What time do you finish at the hospital tonight?'

'I start early-shift tomorrow so I'll be finished by about four today.'

'I've got a lot I need to sort out before my flight tomorrow, but I can take care of that this afternoon. I'm free for a drink tonight.'

'Good for you! If that's your way of asking me out, you old charmer, I'm afraid I don't date married men.'

'Good for you!' replied Danny. 'Who said anything about a date? We're just going for a drink. I'll pick you up here at six, is that too early?'

'No,' she heard herself say.

'I'll park round the corner so that you don't have to explain anything to your ma. See you later, Angel.'

Angela felt her face flush again.

18

Finn O'Hanlon's forehead creased as he rolled onto his side and felt a stabbing pain from the three-inch strip of grazed flesh Culo Conrado's bullet had left behind on his shoulder. His eyes felt like two hard-boiled eggs that had been cracked open using a blunt steak knife.

Finn swung his legs down over the edge of the sofa and manoeuvred himself — with some effort — into a sitting position. His blood-stained shirt had dried onto his skin and he was still wearing the clothes from the previous night, including his tatty Converse.

He had no recollection of asking to stay over, so could only assume that he had passed out on the sofa and been left where he'd 'fallen'.

Half-eaten cartons of food lay scattered on top of the small coffee table and even his empty beer glass was still sitting where he'd left it, tucked under the sofa. The only thing that had changed was that sunlight was now glaring through the curtainless windows instead of orange sodium.

Apart from his shoulder — and the thud of a dehydrated headache — he felt reasonably okay. The crushing tiredness from the previous day was gone and he felt ready.

Ready for what, was a question he'd try

167

answering after he'd showered and made himself a coffee.

Finn sat still for a few moments listening for any other sounds of life.

Marie's bedroom door was slightly ajar, but he was pretty sure she wasn't in there: the apartment felt empty.

Finn stood up and shuffled over to the sink, filled the kettle and searched the cupboards for a packet of fresh coffee. It wasn't difficult to find. There was nothing else except coffee and Oreos.

As he waited for the kettle to come to the boil he headed towards Marie's bedroom and stuck his head cautiously round the doorframe.

There was a clean folded towel, sitting on the end of Marie's crumpled bed with a note resting on top of it, but no sign of her.

Finn picked up the note.

Dear Mr O'Hanlon,

Feel free to use the shower and any soapy things, but no rummaging in my drawers . . . I'll know!!! I'm guessing you've nowhere else to go so I've left you a set of keys and fifty bucks (nothing smaller in my purse) on the floor by the front door. If you turn right out the main gate and walk along a few blocks you'll see a diner called Carlo's on the corner. The décor's all wrong, but the breakfast is the best in Tuscaloosa. Washing machine and dryer under the sink! No offence, but I didn't open the window in the lounge to let the fresh air in: I opened it to let the bad air out. Off to the sheriff's to meet a couple of FBI agents, come all the way down from Birmingham to talk to 'lil ole me'. They must think I know something. Thank you for not murdering me in my sleep.

M x

PS Please destroy this after reading: aiding and abetting a felon is a hangable offence in Alabama. Worse than sitting on a bus with the white folk.

PPS Are you a felon?

Finn looked across at the tall dresser on the opposite side of the room and figured that the long thin drawer at the top was probably the one to go for first. It would never have occurred to him to go rummaging, but now that she'd put the notion in his head what was he supposed to do? He walked over and slid open the top drawer. There in front of him was a jumbled mess of Marie's underwear. Mostly thongs, and lacy strings with embroidered panels, nearly all of them black. Finn smiled: she'd left another note in the drawer which read, 'Shame on you.'

Finn picked up a piece of sheer, triangular gossamer, with straps no thicker than a pencil. A thin whistle escaped between his teeth.

'Holy Mother of God!'

Finn dropped the piece of lingerie back onto the pile and was about to close the drawer when he noticed the handle of a Snub Nose .38 sticking out from under an unopened packet of stockings. Finn pulled the drawer out further. There was a full box of .38 millimetre shells sitting alongside.

169

The sound of the kettle clicking in the other room made him jump.

He carefully put everything back the way he'd found it and headed through to the kitchen.

'Thank you for not murdering me in my sleep,' he muttered, placing Marie's note on the worktop. He lifted the kettle and poured the hot, steaming water over a tablespoonful of coffee he'd tipped into a paper filter. As he waited for the dark brown liquid to percolate through Finn stripped off.

Everything went into the washing machine, socks, underpants, jeans, T-shirt and Converse: the sum total of his possessions. Whatever else he owned he'd have to leave behind in his apartment in Cottondale: everything except the cornflake packet. He wondered if the two assholes that had tried to hit him in McHales had gone there first. If they had, and they'd found the cornflake packet, then Finn's escape plan would be null and void.

It was risky, but Finn knew he had to go back.

The coffee was ready. He sipped it as he walked back through Marie's bedroom into the en-suite bathroom. He pulled the shower curtain to one side and turned on the taps. Before stepping into the shower he examined the cut on his shoulder in the full-length mirror on the back of the bathroom door. It didn't look as bad as it felt.

Generally he kept himself fit, but the last few months he'd been getting sloppy: skipping the morning run, not doing the push-ups or sit-ups. It was beginning to show. The time had come to start running for real. His past wasn't snapping at his heels any more, it was standing right in front of him, baring its teeth.

How did they find him? They must have followed him to McHales. Or had they been watching him for months? Why there? Why not hit him at home where it would have been a lot quieter: no witnesses? Unless they still didn't know where he lived and just got lucky finding him in the bar.

Finn tried rolling his head around to relieve the tension in his neck, but he felt the skin around his wound tighten, so he stopped.

The large crucifix tattooed across his back was beginning to look smudged around the edges: definitely not as sharp as it was when it had first been done, just a week after he had arrived in America. A seraph nailed to a cross: her six wings spread out — covering most of Finn's back — with intricately detailed feathers. The upright post, latticed with Celtic banding, ran from the nape of his neck to the base of his spine, and the crossbar stretched from shoulder to shoulder. In the twisted ribbon near the bottom of the cross the words 'Sanctify yourself' were written in black Celtic scroll. He'd had it done to remind himself of the burden of guilt he would bear for the rest of his life.

'Not looking quite so sharp. You sure you're ready for a fight?' Finn asked the seraph.

He stepped over the edge of the bath and squeezed his eyes shut as the warm water hit his wound. A bottle of shower gel hung on the stem of the hot tap by its plastic hoop. Finn unscrewed the bottle top and held it to his nose. The smell was instantly recognisable: the delicate musky aroma that had wafted ahead of Marie when she'd appeared at her bedroom door last night. It was a scent full of promises: the promise of intimacy and sensual pleasure. The promise of warm, wet kisses and dark, passionate sex.

But Finn couldn't allow himself to go there. There were too many other things to think about; things to focus on . . . like how to stay alive.

He reached down and turned the hot tap anticlockwise.

Finn stayed under the freezing cold spray for as long as he could bear, then turned off the water, stepped out of the bath and dried himself. He fixed the towel round his waist and headed back through to the lounge.

The dial on the washing machine had barely moved. His clothes wouldn't be ready for at least another hour.

Finn picked up the phone sitting on top of an unopened packing box, freed a length of cable and made his way across to the window.

The sun felt warm on his skin and there was a balmy flow of air blowing through the four-inch gap between the sill and the bottom edge of the window. The patrol car that had been parked in the lot just inside the main gate was gone. The street beyond the perimeter fence was quiet, with only a few parked cars dotted along on the grass verges that ran adjacent.

Flanking the parking lot on either side were two small squares of grass — with benches set around wooden picnic tables — for the residents of the apartment block. One of the tables was host to three or four crows pecking at a discarded cardboard lunch box, left curling at the edges, in the full glare of the sun. Large flowerbeds bulging with mature perennials and colourful springtime flowers surrounded both the grass squares and acted as a screen from the world outside. To anyone else it might have seemed like an idyllic scene, but Finn had a dark shadow clouding his thoughts: an uneasy feeling he couldn't shake off.

He lifted the receiver and dialled.

Three thousand miles away a telephone rang unanswered for several rings until there was a click followed by a long silence, then a beeping noise that was Finn's cue to speak.

'Mr McFarlane . . . I need to talk to you.' His tone was slow and deliberate — more American than it had sounded before — whispering each word as though he was trying to disguise his voice. 'If you're there, pick up, I need to ask you something.'

Finn waited, but there was no response.

'I need to know who you've been talking to, Mr McFarlane. Two assholes have just tried to get funny with me in a bar. I'd just like to confirm you got the information to the right person. Call me back as soon as possible on the number I gave you before. I'll be there at nine o'clock your time, all right?'

Finn slowly replaced the receiver. He knew he was taking a risk leaving the message, but there was nothing else he could do. If Lep

173

McFarlane had delivered his message to Danny McGuire, then Finn was certain that McGuire would come looking for him. The problem for Finn was that he could no longer hang around in Cottondale waiting for him.

He stood staring out of the window for a long time before he became aware that he wasn't the only person in the room.

19

Angela rounded the corner near her house and saw her car parked on the pavement.

It crossed her mind that almost everything that had happened since she'd met Danny McGuire had been unusual. She was about to be driven in a car — that ten hours ago had belonged to her — by a man she barely knew who only a day earlier she'd found stumbling around on a deserted country road after being almost beaten to death. Danny McGuire was married. He had a child. His brother — a prominent figure in the IRA — had been murdered. If she called any one of her friends and asked them what she should do, every one of them would tell her to turn heel and run. If the situation were reversed that's the advice she would give.

Angela paused for a moment and considered going back home.

★   ★   ★

Danny caught a movement in the rear-view mirror and immediately got out of the car with the intention of opening the passenger door for Angela, but the sight of her standing at the corner of the street made him pause.

175

She was wearing a long grey coat that had a dark fur collar and was tied at the waist with a thick belt. Her black hair framed her face in long wavy curls and her eyes — with nothing more than a little mascara — looked twice as big as he remembered them. Her lips looked soft and natural. She'd worn heels that made her appear taller, and sheer stockings that defined the outline of her shapely legs. She looked amazing.

Danny was still wearing the same clothes he'd had on when visiting her house earlier that morning. His face was badly swollen on one side and the bruising around his right eye had turned from a deep purple to black. He looked down at his dirty top and faded jeans then held his arms wide, shrugging his shoulders by way of an apology. She got it immediately and shook her head in a silent rebuke.

Danny made his way round to the passenger side and held the door open.

As she drew near he adjusted his glasses and smiled.

Angela fixed him with a steady gaze.

As she bent down to get into the car Danny said, 'You might have made a bit more of an effort.'

★   ★   ★

The Mourne Arms was set into the hillside overlooking the seaside town of Newcastle on the south-east coast of Northern Ireland. The early-evening light had faded by the time they reached the pub, and the bay in which the town sat twinkled and shimmered in the fresh

176

darkness. When Angela questioned him on why they were travelling away from Newry he made the lame excuse that he wanted to test-drive her car. Danny made his mind up in that moment, that — even though it was a joke — it would be the one and only time he'd ever deceive her.

The route took them along the Kilkeel Road, past the exact spot where Angela had stopped to pick him up. Neither of them spoke much until they were a few miles further on, when Danny turned to her and said, 'Thanks again.'

Danny had chosen the Mourne because no one he knew drank there. They could spend a few hours with no interruptions.

Several times on the journey he'd checked to make sure they were not being followed, and only when he was satisfied that was the case did he turn off the main road and head up the narrow country lane leading to the pub.

* * *

At the Mourne, they found themselves a table tucked away in the corner by the fire and ordered some food, even though neither of them felt very hungry.

Their conversation flowed freely. They were at ease in each other's company. The only pauses came when they caught one another's eye and momentarily lost the thread of what they were saying.

Angela was soon on her third gin and tonic and starting to feel it. Danny was on his second Guinness. He pushed his spectacles up on his nose and took a sip from his pint.

'Is that just a nervous habit?' asked Angela.

'What?' replied Danny.

'You keep adjusting your specs. Either they don't fit or it's just a habit you've got into. Are they for reading or distance?' she asked.

Danny thought about what he was going to say before answering, 'Neither.'

' 'Neither'?'

'I don't need them at all. I'm not long- or short-sighted, I'm just sighted . . . normally.'

'Why do you wear them then?' she asked with a puzzled expression on her face. 'They make you look like a bit of an eejit.'

'Which bit of an eejit?' asked Danny, coming back at her.

'There's no bit of an eejit that looks good, so take your pick,' replied Angela. 'Are you trying to look intelligent?'

Danny smiled. The reason he wore glasses was to give himself a split-second advantage in a fight. Most people were still unwilling to throw the first punch if their opponent was wearing glasses. It gave Danny that momentary opportunity to strike the first blow, which was usually all he needed to win. But he was reluctant to start a conversation that focused on the topic of violence.

'I think they make me look quite intellectual, yes,' he answered with a big silly grin on his face. 'Now, there's a word you couldn't even spell, I bet.'

' 'Intellectual', sure I can spell it,' said Angela. 'E-E-J-I-T.'

Danny took his glasses off and placed them gently on the bridge of Angela's nose. 'Here, you need these more than I do. That's not how you spell it at all,' he said.

Angela gave an awkward little half-smile.

'You all right?' asked Danny.

'Fine.'

'Something wrong? You look all worried.'

'She's very pretty,' said Angela before she could stop herself.

'Who?' replied Danny.

'Your wife.'

'D'you think so? And how would you know that?'

'I'm just saying. I saw the photograph you have in your room. She's a beautiful-looking girl.'

'And I'm just saying, how would you know?' Danny let it hang. Angela placed her empty glass on the low table in front of them. 'I've never dated a married man,' she said.

'Neither have I,' interrupted Danny.

'I'm serious. I don't know that I feel that comfortable with it.'

'I'm not married.'

'All right, your girlfriend then.'

'I don't have a girlfriend.'

These were not the answers she was expecting: Angela sat staring at him in silence.

Danny stared back.

It occurred to him that Angela was the most beautiful girl he'd ever seen. He wondered if he should tell her right there and then, but he had to let her off the hook first. He took another sup of his drink before continuing.

'Órlaith is married to my brother Sean. When he was murdered I promised I'd look after her and her wee girl. I go over there whenever I can, or she comes to me. I make sure she's all right. Quite often I stay. I sleep in her bed — and she sleeps with her daughter. And on my mother's life, I've never laid a finger on her, nor would I ever want to. As far as I'm concerned she's still my brother's wife and always will be. She's my big sister . . . ' He paused for a moment then added, ' . . . -in-law.'

There was no response.

Eventually Danny asked, 'Do you believe me?'

Angela's tone was subdued. 'Yeah,' she answered.

'And there is one other thing it's very important you should know,' continued Danny. 'I think you are the most beautiful girl I've ever met in my life.'

This conversation was not going at all the way she had imagined. Suddenly she couldn't think of one thing to say.

'What are you thinking now?' asked Danny.

Angela was staring into his eyes.

'I'm thinking I wish I hadn't ordered so much food.'

'Do you want me to go up to the bar and see if they'll change it?' asked Danny.

'No, I want you to finish your drink and take me home.'

Danny looked concerned. Maybe he had played it all wrong.

'Sure. Are you okay?' he asked.

'I don't mean to my house, you Bog-Irish eejit. I meant to yours.'

Danny couldn't disguise the look of relief. 'Jeez, I thought you'd taken a turn for the worse there.'

'Maybe I have,' replied Angela.

'I'm pretty beaten up. Everything hurts. I'm not sure I'll be fit for much.'

'I'm a nurse,' replied Angela. 'I know ways of relieving pain that'll make your hair stand on end.'

20

Tuscaloosa, Good Friday, late morning

It crossed her mind as she stood in the doorway that it wouldn't be so bad if the towel accidentally unwrapped itself and dropped to the floor.

Finn wasn't overdeveloped, but the muscles — especially on his arms and shoulders — were toned, well defined: his stomach still flat and firm. She thought of her late husband's stomach and smiled. If Finn's was a six-pack, Alfredo's was a beer keg.

She was surprised at the tattoo. Not the fact that he had one, but the size of it. An angel on a cross, covering the whole of his back.

Marie was just on the point of feeling embarrassed at how long she had been watching when he suddenly turned round.

'I hope you don't mind,' said Finn holding up the phone.

'As long as it wasn't long-distance,' Marie replied, kicking off her shoes and heading into the bedroom.

'Been standing there long?'

'Just in,' she lied, shouting back to him, 'It's not as hot as it looks out there, if you're planning to go sunbathing?'

She was referring to the fact that he was naked except for the towel.

182

'Everything I own is in the washing machine,' replied Finn, 'even my shoes. I thought about wearing some of your stuff, but none of it fitted.'

Finn followed her and stood in the doorway of her bedroom. Marie was looking right at him.

'You get my note?' she asked.

'Yeah!' replied Finn.

'Both of them?'

'Were there two?' said Finn, holding her stare.

Marie was studying his face, looking to see if he was messing with her.

'What?' asked Finn, his voice a little higher than he'd have liked.

'You didn't get the second note?'

'No.'

'You didn't have a rummage around in my top drawer?' said Marie, holding his gaze. 'I'll know.'

'I certainly did not,' said Finn, trying to get the indignation level just right.

'Yeah, yeah!' said Marie, taking off her jacket and throwing it on the bed. 'It's the first thing everyone does when they're left alone in a stranger's apartment. Sniff their underwear and check for porn.'

Finn changed the subject.

'Did they make you go to court?'

Marie looked round at him. 'How d'you mean?'

'Where I come from you only ever wear a suit if you're up in court.'

Marie screwed up her face. 'I know! What was I thinking? I've still got it in my head that you need to dress up for authority. I look like I work in a bank, don't I?'

183

'Or the Salvation Army.'

'That bad?' she frowned. 'No point putting it back in the wardrobe then. Next time you see this suit I'll be polishing the silverware with it.'

Marie sat on the end of the bed and slipped her skirt over her hips, then stooped to pick her jeans up from the floor. As she bent over Finn couldn't help but stare at her perfectly formed bottom. She was wearing a more sensible pair of cotton briefs than the ones he'd seen in her drawer, but the effect on him was the same. There was nothing overtly sexual in her actions. If anything, it was the casualness that Finn found so arousing. As she sat back on the bed and started to pull her jeans over her slim brown legs Finn wished he had more than just a thin towel hanging between him and the rest of the world.

He turned away and headed back into the lounge.

'You hungry?' called Marie.

'Yeah,' replied Finn, trying to think of anything other than her arse. 'What about Granny's?'

'Eh?'

'Carlo's, I was thinking of Carlo's,' he said, correcting himself. 'I hear they do the best breakfast in Tuscaloosa.'

Marie came into the room dressed in a pair of jeans and a black fitted T-shirt. On her feet she wore a pair of battered old trainers. Even dressed down she looked great.

'Now I look like I rob banks. We're too late for breakfast, but their brunch is even better. You going like that?'

'Sure! Why, is there a dress code?' replied Finn.

'Towels are fine, just not in that colour.'

'You know, it's probably not a good idea for us to be seen together. Maybe we should just have something here, then . . . ' — he hesitated, not really wanting to say the next bit — ' . . . I'll leave you to get on with your life.'

'Oh! Sure!' said Marie, unable to disguise the disappointment in her voice. She hadn't really considered he'd have to leave. 'Sure! I wasn't thinking. Why don't I run across the road and get some stuff from the deli?'

'Fine, yeah,' said Finn.

Marie bent over to pick up the fifty dollars she'd left on the floor earlier in the day, then turned as she opened the front door. 'I don't know what you like.'

'I'll just have a bit of whatever you're eating and a double espresso,' said Finn.

Just as she reached the door Finn had a thought.

'Marie.'

'Yeah?'

'No granola.'

She smiled and left the room.

Finn made his way over to the window and waited for Marie to leave the apartment block. He watched her walk across the parking lot and out through the large wrought-iron security gate at the far end. She strolled across the street like a catwalk model, her movements full of subtle grace, natural and elegant: very feminine. When she reached the far side of the road she turned

185

and looked up: almost as if she knew Finn would be watching.

She didn't do anything dumb, like wave, but even at this distance Finn could make out the smile on her face. He saw her mouthing something. He couldn't be sure, but it looked like 'Shame on you.'

Finn hoped she could see him smiling too.

★ ★ ★

When the washing machine finished its spin cycle Finn transferred his clothes into the drier, then made his way back to the window.

As he waited for Marie to emerge from the delicatessen he noticed the car. It was parked right outside the front gates. The two men sitting up front were staring up at the window. Finn ducked out of the way, but it was too late. They'd seen him.

The sound of the car doors slamming shut echoed across the lot. Finn could hear muffled voices, then the whirring and clanking of the main gate sliding open. Finn glanced out of the window and caught sight of both men's heads disappearing under the sandstone ridge that ran the full length of the apartment's façade. A moment later the buzzer by the front door of the apartment let out a shrill, metallic squawk. Finn could see Marie: outside the deli now, waiting to cross the road.

He prayed that she would look up.

The buzzer sounded again.

Marie was waiting for a car to pass before

crossing the narrow road: she hadn't noticed the guys at the entrance to the building. Finn wanted to open the window and shout, tell her to stay where she was, but he couldn't.

He needed to get dressed and out of there.

Whoever was downstairs had their finger pressed firmly on the buzzer, determined to keep it there till someone answered.

Finn saw Marie set off across the road then suddenly stop and turn back on herself. She was on the grassy verge staring anxiously up at the window.

Finn held his hand up to the side of his face and mimed a telephone.

Marie nodded and quickly headed back into the deli.

A few seconds later the telephone started ringing.

Finn snatched it up.

Marie sounded scared. 'Who are they?'

'I don't know,' replied Finn urgently. 'They're not the Feds you talked to this morning?'

'No!'

'Where's your car?'

'There's an underground car park,' replied Marie. 'Take the stairwell at the other end of the balcony.'

'You got the keys with you?'

'They're next to the lamp on the bedside table . . . or on the bed maybe. Who are they, Finn?'

The buzzing stopped.

'The front door's open,' said Marie, struggling to control the fear in her voice. 'I can see them. They're in. Finn, they're inside.'

'Go to your car, I'll see you there in a minute.'

Finn slammed down the phone and ran through to the bedroom. He wrenched open the top drawer of the dresser and pulled out Marie's Colt and the box of cartridges. A second later he was back in the lounge tugging at the door of the drier, but the door wouldn't open. He tried forcing it, but it wouldn't budge.

'Shit!'

Finn had no option: he had to get out of the apartment.

★ ★ ★

The door to the apartment slammed closed behind him as he ran along the balcony towards the fire exit. He was naked except for the towel wrapped around his waist.

The landing doors at the far end of the balcony clanked open and the two guys were in the hall.

'Hey!'

One of them was already sprinting towards him.

Finn reached the other end of the balcony and burst through the fire-escape door.

He had barely cleared the first landing when he heard the door above crash against the wall.

The two men were leaping the stairs three at a time, catching up fast.

In desperation Finn leapt the last remaining set of steps, but as soon as he jumped he knew he wasn't going to make it. His foot caught the edge of the bottom step and he tumbled painfully onto his ankle, hitting the concrete floor hard. The impact knocked the gun from his hand and sent it spinning along the ground out of reach. There was blood seeping from cuts in his knees and elbows.

The two guys were now less than six feet away. Finn scrambled over and grabbed the gun. In one swift movement he was back on his feet.

'One more step and I'll blow your fuckin heads off.'

It was a risky strategy: he had no idea if it was loaded or not.

There was such ferocity in Finn's tone that — even if he hadn't been holding a gun — neither of the men would have dared move.

'I swear to God, I'll shoot *you* in the head . . . and *you* in the fuckin heart.'

Finn got the reaction he was hoping for, the flash of fear in their eyes. It was slight, but Finn had been in enough scraps in his life to know that — for the moment at least — he was in charge.

'I'm going through this door: if either of you feels brave enough or stupid enough to follow me, that's fine, cause I don't give a shit if I kill you here or through there. It's up to you.'

Finn fumbled behind his back until he found the door handle then slowly backed out into the car park.

Just as the door closed Finn saw the unopened box of shells he'd been carrying lying at the foot of the stairs. He had sixty seconds before they realised the gun wasn't loaded.

The rolled-metal shutters started cranking

open on the other side of the underground car park. Marie was running down the ramp.

'Jesus, Finn, who the hell are they?'

As Finn approached he tossed her the car keys.

'You'd better drive.'

Marie got in first and turned the key in the ignition, but the two guys were already through the door and sprinting towards them.

Suddenly the car spluttered into life.

Marie flipped the gearshift into reverse and jammed her foot hard to the floor. She had to fight to control the car for a few seconds as it screeched backwards, only narrowly missing a concrete support pillar. Marie pushed it into drive and shot forward in a cloud of blue exhaust fumes. The sump crunched hard against the ground as the car sped up the ramp, out into the bright Alabama sunshine.

Neither of them spoke until they reached the Black Warrior River on the outskirts of town.

'Where we going?' asked Marie, staring straight ahead. 'I'd suggest my mom's, but she hasn't seen a naked man in over twenty years, the shock would kill her.'

Finn didn't look round. 'Yeah, better stop at a mall and buy some clothes first.'

'You okay?' asked Marie.

Finn was staring straight ahead, lost in thought.

'They weren't carrying.'

'What?' asked Marie.

'The guys, they weren't armed,' said Finn, like he'd just figured something out. He turned to

Marie, 'I don't think they were looking for me.'

Marie stared back at him. 'What, you think they'd come for me?' she asked, looking scared.

Finn didn't answer.

'More cops?' asked Marie.

'No,' replied Finn. 'I don't think so. They'd have side arms.'

'What are you talking about? You're scaring the shit out of me, Finn. Who do you think they were, then?'

'I don't know. If they'd come for me I'd probably be dead right now: I was wide open there, but all they did was chase me.'

'So who were they?'

Finn shrugged his shoulders. 'The press, maybe?'

'How would they know where I lived?'

'Some asshole at the cop station.'

Marie had no idea where they were headed or where they'd end up, but she didn't care: she wanted as to get far away from Tuscaloosa as possible.

'What do we do?'

'Better find somewhere to lay low for a few days until we can figure out what's going on.'

★   ★   ★

After travelling in silence for another twenty or so miles Marie eventually turned to Finn.

'How did you know where to find my gun?'

'A lucky guess,' replied Finn, unconvincingly.

'Shame on you,' said Marie, raising an eyebrow.

191

'It wouldn't have even crossed my mind to look if you hadn't suggested it in the note.'

Another silence.

'There's a road map in the glove box,' said Marie.

Finn reached forward and flipped it open. 'Where we going?'

'The nearest mall,' replied Marie. 'The map's to cover yourself with.'

21

*Belfast International Airport, Holy
Saturday, early*

'There must be something big goin down, half the British army's turned up to see us off,' whispered Owen O'Brien under his breath.

'And the other half are outside on the checkpoints. I thought I was going to miss the flight, I tell ye,' replied Tony-O as he used his feet to shuffle a half-empty holdall a few steps further along the marble floor of the terminal building. 'I've never been stopped and searched so many times in my life.'

'Something must have happened, this place is usually deserted,' continued Owen.

'Did you not hear?' replied Tony-O. 'Four soldiers shot up near Aghmakane.'

'Jesus Christ,' scowled Owen, raising his eyebrows. 'I hope it doesn't mean our flights are delayed.'

'That's if we even get on the flights,' said Tony-O. 'I got lifted here once before and they kept me in a holding cell until the flight left. About a minute after it had gone they released me: no charge. They knew fine well what they were doing. So don't be thinking about giving these bastards any lip, just keep your mouths shut and let's get on the plane. It's not worth it.'

Danny reached up involuntarily and pulled his

193

peaked cap a little further over his eyes.

Tony-O was still talking. 'I called E.I. and asked him what the story was, but he swore he knew nothing about it except that it happened yesterday morning. He thinks they were SAS though, not your common or garden squaddie. It's a bastard: if we'd known all this shite would be going on we could have travelled another time.'

Crazy-Pete joined in, his breath reeking of alcohol. 'As long as we get through in time for a couple of pints, cause there is no way I'm getting on a plane without getting pished first.'

'What you on about, Pete? You're pished already. Just make sure you take it handy when they're checking our tickets, we don't want any trouble,' said Tony-O, firing off a warning in Crazy-Pete's direction.

'No intention of causing any trouble,' replied Crazy-Pete. 'I'm just saying I could do with a pint.'

The men fell silent as two soldiers walked past with Thompson sub-machine guns clamped across their chests.

'Whoever thought of calling something at an airport 'terminal'? I mean that's just wrong,' said Owen O'Brien.

★ ★ ★

Danny was standing in line for check-in feeling very conspicuous alongside eleven members of the Newry tug-of-war team. His face was still a mess. Angela had attempted to cover the

194

bruising on his face, but there was nothing she could do to mask the swelling round his left eye.

They'd woken up in Danny's flat and had breakfast together before Angela headed off to work. They'd made love into the early hours of the morning then slept soundly until Danny's alarm went off at 7 a.m.

The love-making had been tender and passionate, and real. There was an ease and honesty between them that neither of them had ever experienced before: a strange sense that they'd known each other for ever.

When Angela left for work she had tears in her eyes.

As he waited in line, Danny wished he could go to her now. He wanted to turn round and walk away.

The check-in area was teeming with members of the security forces. Danny had already identified two undercover Special Branch officers mingling with the crowds of passengers.

A sharp pain in his right hand made Danny wince. He was trying to keep his hands hidden inside his jacket pockets, but it was a painful process: they were covered in cuts, and his knuckles were badly swollen.

RUC officers with flak jackets and sub-machine guns were striding up and down the queues picking people at random, checking their passports and travel documents. Soldiers stood sentry at all the exits and entrances scanning the faces of passers-by.

Danny was uneasy. He hadn't been expecting such a large security presence. He was travelling with a false passport supplied by E.I. O'Leary, which normally wouldn't bother him, but there had been no time to check it over properly and today wasn't the day to test the forger's workmanship.

Danny looked out of place amongst the other team members. He wasn't small, but in comparison to them he was the shortest by at least six inches. Not one of them weighed less than two hundred and fifty pounds, most of the weight being carried in their barrel-shaped bellies. They were all ex-wrestlers or heavyweight boxers, and from the number of broken noses and scarred faces it didn't look like many of them had ever won a fight.

The words 'NEWRY TUG-OF-WAR '92' were emblazoned in arching gold lettering across the front of the black baseball cap he was wearing. The outline of two men pulling at either end of a rope was embroidered on the back of his matching black bomber-jacket with the additional wording 'WORLD CHAMPIONSHIPS OSHKOSH '92' written underneath.

Danny would have preferred to travel alone: even now he was still thinking about making his own way over to the States. A boat to the west of Scotland, drive to Newcastle on the east coast of England and catch a ferry to Holland: from there he could fly anywhere in the world. It would take longer, but there was little or no threat of being lifted. The problem was time: if he was to have any chance of finding O'Hanlon, Danny had to get to the States as quickly as possible.

'If they ask, don't say you're a 'puller', you

196

better say you're the coach.'

Danny turned to find Owen O'Brien standing next to him.

'What?' asked Danny in response.

'You'd better say you're our coach, cause you don't look like you could tug a snotter out of your nose.'

Those of the team in earshot started laughing. Danny tried to smile, but two RUC officers had turned round and were heading towards them.

'Passports, papers and tickets, please.'

Danny handed his documents to one of the officers and put his hands back inside his pocket.

'Would you mind keeping your hands where I can see them?' said the officer, making it sound like a command rather then a question.

'Feeling the cold a bit there, officer,' replied Danny impassively.

'I don't care if you're feeling your dick, get your hands out of your pockets where I can see them,' replied the officer, giving Danny the stare now.

Danny did what he was told. The officer had clocked the swelling and bruising on his face and Danny could see him glancing down at his knuckles.

'Where you travelling to?'

'Oshkosh,' replied Danny.

The officer looked up from Danny's passport like he'd misheard.

'Where?'

'Oshkosh: somewhere in the USA, but don't ask me for directions, you know what I mean?'

The officer cut in before Danny had finished:

'Take off your hat and your glasses.' He was looking at the passport again.

Normally Danny would have given the officer some of it back, but he couldn't afford to get involved in any trouble so, once again, he did what he was told.

Out of the corner of his eye Danny could see Crazy-Pete scowling and flexing his shoulders. He grunted something inaudible at the RUC officer.

'This your passport?' continued the officer.

'Yes,' replied Danny.

'Any other ID, Mr Leonard?'

'No.' Danny kept his gaze steady.

The officer was examining the passport more closely, like he'd noticed something out of place. He flicked through a few pages before getting to Danny's photograph at the back.

'This supposed to be you?'

Danny shrugged his shoulders: it might not have been the best photograph ever taken, it looked more like his brother Sean, but it was definitely him.

'It is me, yeah,' he replied.

'What happened to the side of your face?'

Crazy-Pete answered for him. 'He got fed up answering stupid questions and battered the shite out of the wanker doing the asking. Why don't you ask him a few more and he'll show you?'

Tony-O tried to jam himself between the officer and Crazy-Pete. 'That's enough now, Peter.' But it was too late: the switch had flicked and Crazy-Pete was on. He stuck his face right in

198

front of the RUC officer and let out a loud, ripping belch. 'Excuse me.'

The officer didn't flinch. 'Get your big ugly face out of my way or I'll have you for breach of the peace.'

The other officer who had been quietly standing by stepped in.

'Move back there, big fella, and let's see your passport and tickets.'

'Youse don't look like you work for the airline,' replied Crazy-Pete, squaring up to both officers. 'Let's see your ID cards and I might show you mine. Otherwise you're getting fuck-all unless you've got a warrant.'

The group had started to attract the attention of other officers who were now making their way towards them. Tony-O tried to intervene again. 'For Christ's sake Peter shut up and show the cunt your passport.'

'Right, that's enough of the language, pal.' The first officer handed Danny his papers and pushed Tony-O back, away from the rest of the group. 'Just step to the side and keep your big mouth shut, you.'

Tony-O turned to Danny and winked. Danny wasn't sure, but it looked like Tony-O was signalling for him to move up the line, closer to the check-in desk: it was a subtle flick of the head, but Danny caught it straight away. He slipped round the back of Crazy-Pete and was quickly swallowed up by the rest of the team. Owen O'Brien appeared over his shoulder and said under his breath, 'Here we go.'

Crazy-Pete tried to move up the line of

passengers as well, but the two RUC officers were blocking his way.

'Get your passport and travel documents out now or you're not flying anywhere today, do you hear me?' said the first officer, grabbing Crazy-Pete by the arm.

'Take your dirty Proddy hands off me or you'll have to learn to type using your toes,' said Crazy-Pete, wrenching his arm free from the officer's grip.

'Here, slow down Peter, for God's sake,' said Tony-O, still trying to stop the situation getting out of hand. 'Show the man what he wants to see and let's be on our way. Sorry, officer, he's had a few too many. We're on our way to represent Northern Ireland in the Tug-of-War World Championships and we don't want any trouble, we really don't. Need every man we've got, you know what I'm saying — even the pished ones. We were having a wee celebration. The pair of us had a few too many lagers when we heard about those four SAS lads that never made it for breakfast yesterday.'

★   ★   ★

Danny had reached the check-in desk. He could see Crazy-Pete and Tony-O in the middle of the terminal surrounded by RUC officers and at least two or three soldiers. As he handed over his tickets to the girl behind the desk he heard Crazy-Pete let out a roar.

Danny turned to look over his shoulder just as one of the RUC officers went reeling backwards,

200

blood pouring from his nose. Suddenly the tall, corrugated roof of the terminal building was echoing with the dull, sickening thud of flesh on flesh. Screams and shouts bounced off the grey brick walls as the remaining officers weighed in to restrain Tony-O and Crazy-Pete.

The girl at the check-in desk tore off a section of Danny's ticket and handed back his passport and boarding pass. 'There you go, Mr Leonard, that's you all checked in.' She looked past Danny to where the fight was now well under way. 'Friends of yours?'

'Never met them before in my life,' replied Danny. 'You any good at tug-of-war? Looks like we're going to be a few men short.'

The girl raised her eyebrows. 'Is that what you call 'men'?'

★ ★ ★

Danny tried the telephone number again. He let it ring for over a minute before hanging up and putting the scrap of paper that E.I. had given him back in his pocket.

He dialled another number.

'Hello, 752416, can I help you?'

'Angela?'

'No, she's just left for work, son. Can I take a message?'

'It's all right, I'll try her again later, thanks.'

Danny was about to hang up.

'Who will I say called?' asked her mother.

If Mrs Fitzpatrick knew it was Danny she wouldn't be too pleased.

'If you could just tell her that the Legend called.'

'No worries, son.'

The phone went dead.

Danny looked around the departure lounge and made his way over to a quiet table in the corner with a view overlooking the runway.

'Sure I can't get you a pint of something, big fella?'

Danny looked round as Owen O'Brien placed two pints of Guinness on the table and sat down beside him.

'No thanks, I don't drink and fly.'

Owen raised his eyebrows, but made no further comment. 'D'you have a pen and a piece of paper handy?'

'What for?' asked Danny.

'I'm going to give you the number of the hotel the boys and me are staying at in Oshkosh. E.I. doesn't want you phoning him from the States, for obvious reasons, so you can contact me when you've done what you have to do. All you have to do is let me know 'It's sorted' and I'll tell E.I. when I get back. Does that make sense?'

Danny nodded.

He was sure E.I. would have discussed the reasons for his trip with O'Brien, but nevertheless the conversation unsettled Danny.

'Terrible news about Eamon Ò Ruairc, eh. Did you hear?'

'Hear what?' asked Danny.

'It was just on the telly there,' continued Owen. 'Shot dead on his front doorstep. Tragic, eh? Says on the news he had three kids under five. Is that not bloody awful?'

Eamon was one of the two volunteers involved in the operation to steal the list from the headquarters of Special Branch — the other being a schoolfriend of Danny's called Quig McGuigan. Danny had seen Eamon briefly on the night of the break-in, but hadn't heard from Quig in a while.

'When did it happen?'

'Yesterday morning,' replied Owen, picking up his Guinness and taking a sip. 'I just heard it on the news when I was at the bar there. Two in two days: where's it going to end?'

'Two?'

'Aye sure, Lep McFarlane too.'

'Lep McFarlane?' Danny tried not to sound surprised.

'They found his body up the Omeath Road with an OBE.'

That was the reason Danny had been unable to contact him the night before. The poor bastard was lying in a ditch with a bullet in the back of his head.

O'Brien was staring at him.

'What're you looking at me for? It wasn't me that did it.'

'Here, relax, Danny, I know it wasn't you. Sure I caught the wee fucker myself, didn't I? Got a call from someone saw him drinking in the Mountain Bar in Camlough. Started crying like a fuckin baby when I walked in. Took him out the back and shot him there and then.'

'What was he doing back in Newry?' asked Danny, wondering if Lep had said anything to

O'Brien about their meeting.

'Exactly what I asked him: 'What the fuck are you doing back here?' D'you know what he said?' O'Brien looked at Danny as if he was expecting a reply, but Danny just shrugged. 'He said he'd come back to say sorry to his family. I mean, what's all that about, eh? I know for a fact the wee shite was brought up by his grand-mother. Sure his ma and da died when he was still in primary school and his granny was buried about twenty years ago. Lep McFarlane RIP . . . 'Rest In Piss' more like, eh?'

Danny stared out at the rain lashing the runway and said nothing for a few minutes. When he turned round again Owen was well into his second pint.

'I thought you'd be more pleased,' said O'Brien, looking over at Danny.

'Pleased? Why would I be pleased? I couldn't give a shit.'

'Sure he's the wee tout that got your brother killed, isn't that right?'

Danny didn't answer. It was time to change the subject.

'What happens to your chances in Oshkosh now that Crazy-Pete and Tony-O have got themselves arrested?' asked Danny.

Owen smiled and took a sip of beer before answering. 'Do you know how many 'pullers' there are in a tug-of-war team?'

'No idea,' replied Danny.

'There's eight pullers and one extra: usually the coach.'

'Don't you need subs?' asked Danny.

'What for?' replied Owen. 'All you're doing is pulling a bit of fuckin rope. E.I. told us to get you on the plane no matter what. That was just a wee diversion we had planned in case you were spotted. Crazy-Pete and Tony-O didn't even have plane tickets.'

22

The girl with too much make-up on working behind the front desk of the Lakeshore Hotel didn't look up at the unassuming figure walking past and into the elevator. She heard the collapsible gate clunk into place and the electric motor whirr into life, but paid little attention. The drive cables clattered around in the lift shaft and the counterweights dropped noisily as the Twenties birdseye-maple elevator cabin lifted to the second floor. When it stopped the man made his way down the long stale corridor that stretched out in front of him, coming to a stop outside room 260. A small set of Wiggler Rakes — thin, flexible wires — was produced and after careful consideration, the chosen 'rake' was inserted into the lock. With a few deft twists and turns the various cylinders clicked into place and the door swung open.

Danny stood motionless, taking in the dimly lit room. The contrasting decor had a tired, grubby feel about it: none of it quite matched up to the promise offered by the picture postcards of the hotel on sale in the lobby. The bed looked deep and comfortable with large sky-blue satin pillows resting against its tall, pink-velvet, button-fronted headrest: all of it uncomfortably at odds with the pale mustard paper that covered

206

nearly every wall in the building.

In the far corner sat a faux-Victorian bureau, just as it had been described to him. Danny crossed the room and knelt in front of it. He pulled the bottom drawer clear and laid it to one side before reaching in and feeling around the bureau's carcass. After a few seconds he pulled out a small parcel wrapped in white polythene and placed it in his holdall. He then retrieved two boxes of cartridges before sliding the drawer back into place and leaving the room.

The elevator clanked its way back to the ground floor and Danny crossed the lobby to the check-in desk. He had to wait for the girl to finish whatever she was doing before she looked up and acknowledged him.

'I'm sorry, sir, I didn't see you standing there. Can I help?'

Danny pushed his glasses up on his nose.

'I have a reservation under the name of Leonard.'

The girl handed Danny a form.

'I have an envelope here for you, Mr Leonard. Someone left the keys to your car for you. If you could fill in this registration form and let me swipe your credit card. You're in room 260, at the front of the building on the second floor.'

'I'll pay cash.'

'I need to take a two-hundred-dollar deposit, I'm afraid.'

'Don't be afraid, that's fine. Is the room across the corridor available?'

Danny was instinctively wary. Room 260 had been booked for him, but he didn't want to sleep in there. If anything went wrong it would be the first place they'd look. He was being over-cautious, but that's how he worked.

'Let me just have a look. 261's free but it's not as nice. It does overlook the pool though.'

'Perfect,' replied Danny.

'Sure. I'll just grab you the key.'

The girl handed Danny a bulging envelope and a room key with an eight-inch rectangular piece of wood attached to it by a small brass chain.

'You use this on muggers?' asked Danny, wrapping his fist round the fob and holding it like a truncheon.

The girl's face was blank. 'It makes the key a little more difficult to lose,' she said.

'Could you get a porter to help me carry it up to my room?'

It was obvious from her expression that checking people in and out of the Lakeshore Hotel, Tuscaloosa, didn't require too many qualifications. Danny was too tired and hungry to explain that he was joking.

'What time does the restaurant open?' he asked.

'Breakfast is at 7.30 a.m.'

'Breakfast?' replied Danny. 'It's only 9 p.m. I have to wait until breakfast?'

'The main restaurant closes early over the Easter weekend.'

'The bar?'

'Closed too.'

'Anywhere local?' asked Danny.

'Nowhere till Monday night. But, there's a minibar in your room.'

208

'Is there a telephone in my room?'

'Sure.'

'Am I allowed to use it?' asked Danny, only half kidding.

'Sure,' replied the girl earnestly. 'If you ring room service they'll maybe rustle you up a sandwich . . . but nothing hot.'

'Is Alabama a cold state over Easter too?' said Danny, giving it one last try.

This time the girl smiled, but she still answered, 'No, I don't think so.'

* * *

Danny sat on the edge of the bed in the darkened room and stared out through the open glass doors at the palm fronds swaying gently in the warm evening breeze, their long spindly leaves masking the light from the pool, and the uplighters of the inner courtyard. The quiet rustling sound and concerted trills of cicadas reminded Danny that he was in a foreign country. An immaculate-looking sandwich lay half eaten on a plate next to him. Just like the postcards of the hotel, it promised more than it delivered. The cheese should have been called something else. It was bright orange and had a consistency that Danny had never experienced in his mouth before: like flavoured lard. The ham was 'wafer-thin,' with a taste to match, and the coleslaw so sweet that each mouthful gave him a sugar rush. There was so much food on the plate it had become unappetising. Despite his hunger, Danny managed only a few mouthfuls before giving up.

He'd been travelling for most of the day, and the long hours spent sitting motionless on the plane combined with the after-effects of the beating had finally caught up with him. Everything ached: his arms, legs, eyes, head — even his fingers.

After mixing himself a convincing vodka martini from the limited stock of alcohol in the minibar, Danny found he barely had the energy to drink it. His head kept tipping forward and several times the highball glass he was holding slipped from his grasp. Taking another sip, he placed the martini on the table next to his bed and picked up the phone. He tried O'Hanlon's home number again, letting it ring for over a minute before hanging up. He wasn't expecting anyone to pick up and even if they had, what was he going to say? 'Wait there, I'm coming to get you'?

★　★　★

Danny pulled one of the large pillows under his head and lay back. It was still too early to go to sleep, but he couldn't keep his eyes open. He thought about calling Angela, but wasn't sure what he'd say to her, either. All he knew was, he wanted to hear her voice.

Outside in the corridor a door slammed closed. Danny awoke to the sound of a couple's muffled arguing, drifting off towards the elevator. He glanced at his watch, it was now 2 a.m. He must have nodded off.

He couldn't remember if Ireland was five or

210

six hours ahead. If it was six hours Angela might have already left for work. He dialled anyway.

'Seven-five-two-four-one-six, hello!'

The voice at the other end was warm and friendly: there was no doubt it was her this time and not her mother.

'Angel?'

There was a moment's silence before she responded.

'Leg End?'

'Eh?'

Danny heard her laugh.

'My ma left me a note saying that someone called Leg End called to talk to me. It was the way she'd written it down. She'd split 'Legend' into two words. I was wetting myself when I worked it out.'

'Aye, well, Leg End's probably about right,' replied Danny.

'Are you all right? You sound tired. Where are you?'

Straight into nursing mode! 'I'm grand,' he replied. 'A bit knackered, but I feel fine.' He ignored the last part of her question.

'I delivered the letter to your ma and gave Órlaith your envelope, she said if I talked to you to say thank you. She was overwhelmed. We both got a bit emotional: no idea why. You should give them a call, Danny.'

'Don't use my name over the phone.'

He hadn't meant to sound so abrupt, but he could tell by the silence that's how it had come across. 'Sorry Angel,' Danny continued. 'You never know if some sad-arse might be listening

211

in. Phone tapping is illegal, but it doesn't stop them having a go, y'know what I'm saying?'

'I think so. I'll stick with Leg End,' said Angela. 'Sorry. All I was going to say was they're worried sick, you should give them a call.'

'Aye maybe! How was my ma?'

'Quiet,' said Angela.

Danny wasn't surprised.

'Have you found anyone called Decency to go have a drink with?' asked Angela.

'What d'you mean?' replied Danny

'You told me you'd fallen out with some fella called Decency and he wouldn't meet you for a drink any more.'

'I was being poetic.'

'Is that what you call it?' said Angela.

'Are you taking the piss?'

'Yes,' replied Angela.

'Next time I see you I'm going to skelp your arse.'

'Mmm! Sounds good. I think that's about the only thing we didn't try.'

'You looked amazing,' said Danny.

Angela wasn't used to getting compliments: she wasn't quite sure how to respond. 'Thank you,' she said eventually.

'I wanted to keep telling you, but . . . I don't know . . . I was just a bit overwhelmed.'

'Stop it now, you're making me blush.'

An odd silence followed. There was much more to say, but it was obvious neither of them wanted to go first: scared they might reveal too much of themselves and frighten the other off.

Eventually Danny broke the silence. 'I'd better

get cracking. Call you tomorrow, eh?'

'My ma's just come in with my breakfast, I'd better go anyway.'

'I'll never lie to you, Angela,' said Danny.

'Why are you saying that?'

'I don't know, I just thought I should tell you.'

'Where did the money come from?'

'I said I'd never lie: I didn't say I'd tell you everything you wanted to know.'

'Relax! I was just testing you. I have no interest in where the money came from. Better go before Ma starts complaining about my toast getting cold. Call me when you can.'

'Will do, Angel.'

Danny held the button on the phone down for a few seconds then released it and dialled another number. It was a while before anyone answered.

'Hello.'

'It's me. Sorry to call so early.'

'Jesus, where are you? Are you all right? I really thought that was it this time. You didn't even call us to let us know you were all right. I had to phone E. I. O'Leary to find out what the hell had happened to you.'

'I'm sorry it all got a bit out of hand, but I'm fine. Don't worry. Did Ma get my note?'

'She did, but she doesn't believe you.'

Danny had written to his mother to tell her he was intending to leave Northern Ireland. He wanted to get away from his life there: away from the Troubles. He wanted to leave his past behind and start again. He hoped that she understood and that once he had established himself she would join him. He explained in the letter that there was one more thing he had to do, before it would all be over. He also wrote that he loved her.

'What are we supposed to do with all that money?' asked Órlaith. 'I haven't told your ma yet. She'll only trouble herself over where it came from.'

'Tell her she should trouble herself about where it's going instead. The money's for you and Niamh and Ma. Tell her you had a big win at the bingo. You can do what you like with it. I'll be away for a while . . . on business . . . so that's to tide you over. But don't take it to the bank or you'll have the Special Branch at the door before the ink's dried on the pay-in slip.'

'Where am I supposed to hide twenty grand . . . under the mattress?'

'Twenty?'

Danny had to think for a minute.

'Is there a problem?'

'Jesus! It was only supposed to be ten. She's given you her half as well.'

'Whose half?'

'Angela's! She was supposed to give you ten and keep ten for herself.'

'Well I won't touch a penny of it till you've sorted it out. I don't know what you're up to, but keep yourself safe, all right?'

'Tell Ma I meant every word of what I wrote.'

'I will. And you look after that Angela. She seemed lovely: don't be mucking her about. D'you hear me?'

Sometimes Órlaith sounded like she was his

big sister. It was a role that she had adopted quite naturally, and one that Danny didn't mind her having.

'I'd better go,' said Danny.

'I want you to promise me you'll look after this one.'

'I promise,' replied Danny. 'I'd better go. You take care.'

'You take care,' replied Órlaith.

Danny replaced the receiver. He wanted to call Angela back straight away and ask her why she'd given her share of the money to Órlaith, but it could wait till the morning. He lay back on the pillow and closed his eyes.

★ ★ ★

When he next looked at his watch, it was just after 7 a.m. The shadows had been replaced by flickering sunshine. He could have sworn he'd only closed his eyes for a second, but he'd been asleep for almost five hours. Danny sat up and caught sight of the perfectly preserved sandwich at the bottom of the bed. He knew if he left it there for a month it would still look exactly the same.

The telephone beside the bed started ringing. Danny picked it up, but waited for whoever was calling to speak.

'Mr Leonard?'

'Who is this?' said Danny, trawling his memory to place the voice.

'You shifted rooms! We thought for a minute you hadn't made it. You get the delivery?'

'Who is it?' repeated Danny, letting the suspicion in his voice show.

'Relax, big fella, it's O'Brien, just checking you've got everything you need.'

There was something about Owen O'Brien that Danny didn't like: he wanted to get off the phone as quickly as possible.

'Your special request is in the boot of the car.' O'Brien was talking about the Heckler & Koch MSG90 Danny had asked for. It was a sniper rifle that had its faults, but it was light and accurate. 'Unfortunately it was too conspicuous to carry in to the hotel so we had to leave it in the boot. Don't wait too long before you deliver De Garza's money to him, he's an impatient fucker and The Farmer wants to keep him sweet. Anyway, did you get the car keys?'

'Yeah. Where is the car?'

'Fuck knows,' laughed Owen. 'The valet parked it. It's a black Cadillac. I thought it was just those big stretch things they made, but no, it's a wee one. I didn't know they made normal cars as well. Give the valet the keys and he'll bring it round to you. Anyway, Mr Leonard, better get on: qualifiers today and I don't mind telling you, we've got no chance. You should see the size of some of these American fuckers. I think we're the only tug-of-war team using alcohol instead of steroids. If you need anything else let us know . . . Happy hunting.'

Danny put the phone down. He leant forward and dragged his holdall across the bed. After pulling out the plastic bag he'd retrieved from inside the bureau he lifted a tightly wrapped

216

bundle the size of a bag of sugar onto the bed. He carefully removed the various layers of tissue and held up a dull-silver Walther PPK. He dropped the clip out the bottom of the butt, filled it with bullets, then slotted it back in and screwed on the suppressor.

Danny stood side-on to the mirror and raised the gun at his reflection.

'You have been tried by the Army Council and found guilty of treason and betraying the republican cause. In your absence you have been sentenced to death. I'm here to execute you.'

Danny dropped the gun to his side.

'Happy hunting.'

23

Tuscaloosa, Easter Sunday, evening

'Says here the Preserve is quite a special place.'

'Bits of it are,' replied Marie. 'Stays green all year round except for autumn, when it gets even more beautiful. We used to drive up to the Cherokee Falls near Fort Payne when we were kids. Do some kayaking down the river — if the water was high enough. Maybe we could go there tomorrow?'

She was halfway through a bottle of Californian Blanc and pouring herself another glass.

Finn tossed the dog-eared tourist pamphlet back on top of the Sixties-style coffee table and pulled aside a piece of material passing itself off as a curtain.

The sky was growing steadily darker and the air inside the room felt heavy and oppressive.

'What's happened to the weather?' asked Finn.

'It'll blow over in an hour. If you're worried you're sweating up your new clothes you can always take them off,' replied Marie, raising an eyebrow like she was suggesting something else.

Marie was lying on one of the two single beds with her bare feet dangling off the end. 'This is the nicest motel I've ever stayed in.'

Finn looked up at the cigarette-stained ceiling. The wallpaper was peeling off the walls in several

218

places and the beds were covered with dank
bri-nylon throws. Finn would have put money on
the television in the corner being a black-and-
white.

'Really?' he replied.

'It's the *only* motel I've ever stayed in, so
maybe it doesn't count.'

Marie pushed herself up onto her elbows.
'What happens now? Is there sort of a manual or
something, tells you what to do? I've never gone
on the run before. I mean, what are you
supposed to pack?'

Finn shrugged his shoulders.

'You hungry?' asked Marie.

Finn shook his head. 'Not really.'

'Me neither,' said Marie.

'How'd it go with the Feds on Friday?' asked
Finn. 'You never said.'

'God, that seems like it was about two weeks
ago,' replied Marie. 'It's hard to believe that was
only two days ago.' She let out a long sigh. 'They
just went over the same old crap as the cops did.
Wanted to hear it for themselves — too lazy to
read the notes.'

'They were checking you out. See if you'd be a
reliable witness.'

Marie was sitting up now.

'How d'you mean?'

'They ask you lots of inane questions then
throw in one or two curve balls,' replied Finn.
'Staring at you like they were taking in every
word, when in fact they weren't listening — they
were watching.'

'Yeah. One of them couldn't take his eyes off

219

my tits. But it was the other one who was really freaking me out. I thought any minute he's going to ask me on a date. Didn't stop staring into my eyes.'

'They were checking you out,' continued Finn. 'Behavioural psychology. They're looking for your lying zone.'

Marie was staring at Finn in disbelief.

'Did you tell them any lies?' he asked.

Marie thought for a moment before answering.

'I told them I thought you sounded Polish, but that was about it.'

'Polish?'

'It was the only other Catholic nation I could think of.'

'So now they know that I'm not Polish, and that you are capable of lying.'

'Are you kidding me?' said Marie, her face serious now.

Finn crossed the room and sat on the single bed opposite her.

'Turn this way.'

Marie swung her legs round so that she was sitting facing Finn.

He was staring into her eyes just like the cop had.

'You're much better at it than the FBI,' she said.

'What's your name?'

'Guess.'

'C'mon, play the game. I want to show you — What's your name?'

'Marie Bain.'

220

'Where d'you live?'

'Tuscaloosa.'

'You married?'

'Not any more.'

'What did your husband die of?'

'Heart attack.'

'You seeing anyone else?'

'No.'

'You scared?'

'Kinda.'

'Did you lock your bedroom door on Thursday night because you thought I was going to kill you?'

'Yeah, or worse.'

'What else did the FBI ask you?'

'If I'd be able to recognise you again,' replied Marie, flicking through her mind for anything else.

'What did you say?'

'I said, 'Who, the black guy in the alley or the guy from Cottondale who knows how to handle a gun?''

'What'd the agents say to that?'

'Nothing.'

'Okay, we're done.'

'So did you find my lying zone?'

'Everything you said was true except the bit about seeing someone else.'

Marie let out a snort. 'Pah. You're making this crap up. You nearly had me there.'

Marie reached over and grabbed her glass of wine from the bedside table. There was a guy she met occasionally, used to come into McHales. They'd meet up and have sex, but that was it.

They had nothing in common: no emotional attachment.

'Bullshit,' said Marie, puffing out her cheeks. 'Just . . . bullshit.'

Finn got up from the bed and grabbed another bottle of beer from the brown paper bag sitting on the low-rise coffee table.

'Okay. How does it work?' asked Marie.

'What?'

'The lying zone.'

'When you answered the other questions you looked up to the right, but when I asked you if you were seeing someone you looked down to the left — chances are that's your lying zone,' said Finn, moving back to the bed. 'I ask you lots of questions I know the answer to — things I know are true — then slip in the occasional question where I don't.'

Marie lifted the glass to her lips and took a sip, looking at Finn like she still wasn't sure.

'Okay, let me try you.'

'I've been trained to counter it, so there's no point.'

'Why would you need training in how to avoid answering questions honestly?'

'Is that your first question?'

'I'm serious.'

'Let's play something else,' said Finn.

'No sit down, c'mon, let me have a go. See what I come up with.' Marie didn't wait for Finn's approval.

'Are you Finn O'Hanlon?'

Finn stared straight at her, but didn't reply.

Marie tried again.

222

'Are you Irish?'

Again Finn said nothing.

'*Did* you come to my apartment the other night to kill me? The Feds think that's what you're going to do.'

Still no response.

'Well, it's not much of a game if you just sit there saying nothing. These are the easy questions — I've still got the curve ball to come.'

'The whole idea is to say nothing,' said Finn. 'If you admit to anything, even something as simple as your name, you're engaging with them. They'll twist it round and come at you from all sorts of angles. Before you know it they've got you by the bollocks and you're heading off to jail for the rest of your life for a crime you didn't commit. It's hard, but the rule is say nothing.'

Marie poured some more wine into her glass. 'See, now I've got loads of questions like: who are 'they'? Who are *you*? Who am *I*? What the hell is this all about? Are you a goddamn spy or something?'

Marie was watching Finn closely for some sort of reaction, but nothing was coming back at her. 'Okay, let's assume that you're not going to jail if you answer *my* questions,' continued Marie. 'And let's also assume that I'm not interested in finding your lying zone. Can we just have a normal conversation? I won't even look at you if that helps.'

'Okay,' replied Finn.

Marie turned to face the wall.

'What's with the big angel on your back? You got a Travis Bickle thing going?'

223

'Who's Travis Bickle?' replied Finn.

'You remember in *Taxi Driver*? Travis Bickle is De Niro's character. He plays the screwed-up Vietnam vet with all the jail tats.'

'I never saw it.'

'What's yours?'

'It's the seraph that appeared to St Francis of Assisi in a vision on Mount Alverna: marked him with the stigmata. He used to drag a cross around with him everywhere he went as an act of penance.'

'The seraph dragged it?'

'St Francis.'

'So is it a symbolic act of penance?'

'You could say that,' replied Finn.

'Did you go through my underwear drawer?'

Finn tried not to smile. 'Is that one of your curve balls?'

'No.'

'Why don't you turn round now?'

'I'm checking if it's possible to *hear* your lying zone.'

'No. I didn't go through your underwear drawer,' replied Finn.

'I don't even need to see your eyes to know you're a lying son-of-a-bitch,' said Marie. 'I've got a system too: smalls with string to the right, lacies beside them, cottons next to them and bras over on the left. When I came home to get changed they were all mixed up.'

'You see! I'm engaging with you in a conversation and you've got me tried and convicted already.'

'Were you checking my ass out this morning when I was getting dressed?'

'Curve ball?' asked Finn.

'No.'

'Of course . . . I wasn't checking out your ass.'

Marie turned back to face him.

'Liar,' continued Marie. 'I watched your reflection in the mirror, you were staring at it like you'd never seen an ass before.'

'You were sticking it in my face. I had no option. And to be honest I haven't seen an ass quite like that before.'

Marie liked that.

'Do you want to kiss me?' she said.

Here was the curve ball, flying towards him at a hundred miles an hour.

Marie was staring straight at him, taking him on.

Finn hesitated before saying, 'Yes . . . but not on the mouth.'

Marie liked that one too. She let it sink in. The atmosphere in the room had changed: it was still hot and sticky, but suddenly that didn't seem so bad.

Finn and Marie were just inches apart.

'Do you want to lick me?'

'No.'

'Liar. Do you want to fuck me?'

'No,' replied Finn, looking deep into her eyes.

'Liar,' said Marie.

Their lips were almost touching.

Suddenly Finn pulled away.

'I thought you told them I'd asked for a beer?'

Marie's brow furrowed. 'Are you fucking serious?' she asked. 'I'm just about to get naked here. What the hell does beer have to do with anything?'

'You told them, the only thing I did was to ask you for a beer.'

'Are we still playing the game?' asked Marie, 'because I don't know what the hell is going on now.'

'No,' said Finn, aware that the tone of his voice was freaking her out.

'I said to them the only conversation we had was you asking for a beer . . . Jesus, Finn.'

'How do you know I lived in Cottondale?'

The last question caught Marie in the stomach, knocking the air out of her. She'd thrown Finn a curve ball, but he'd hit it straight back at her. Suddenly she understood why the cops had exchanged a look. It was right around the time she'd said 'Who, the black guy in the alley or the guy from Cottondale who knows how to handle a gun?' How could she possibly have known he was from Cottondale unless they'd had more of a conversation?

'Well, I'll tell them I forgot that bit in all the excitement of people getting fucking shot. Why does it matter?'

'It matters because it's inconsistent. To their way of thinking it looks like you're holding out on them. They're going to pick through everything you tell them from now on with a fine-toothed comb.'

'Well, I won't be telling them anything else now that we're on the run, so don't worry about it.'

Finn stood up and walked over to the window. 'It's not a game, Marie. You're the innocent party in all this and you're in danger of ending up in some very deep shit.'

'So what d'you want me to do? Drive back to Tuscaloosa and hand myself in? Tell them the guy they're looking for has been staying in my apartment?'

'Yes.'

Marie was staring up at Finn in disbelief. 'Are you fucking serious? What about the press guys who saw us leaving together in the same car . . . how do I explain that?'

'Tell them I'd threatened to kill you and you were scared.'

'Jesus, Finn, when you throw a curve ball . . . Whoa! It's not a ball, it's more like a goddamn hand grenade.'

'I don't know what's coming my way, but it's not going to be good. I don't want you getting caught in the crossfire. It's real — you could end up dead.'

Marie watched Finn turn and look out the window.

'Doesn't mean we can't fuck.'

Finn stood with his back to her and didn't answer.

'You still there?'

'Yeah, I'm thinking I need to go to the apartment.'

'Now? Why don't we wait: go tomorrow evening?'

'I should probably go alone.'

'Oh yeah?

Finn heard her jangling the car keys.

'And how you going to get there . . . you planning to walk?'

24

Cottondale, Alabama, Easter Sunday, evening

The storm clouds had passed swiftly over the low-rise buildings of Cottondale, giving way to a bruised-blue evening sky and light drizzling rain.

Danny was parked in a side street across from Finn O'Hanlon's apartment.

The three-storey red-brick building opposite had graffiti covering the walls of the ground floor, and the majority of the windows looked like they'd been boarded up for some time. The entire neighbourhood looked like it had been boarded up along with it.

A Victorian-style balcony ran the full length of the building on the first and second floors, with heavy glass panels acting as dividers between each of the apartments. The white paint on the balustrade had crackled and peeled in the humid atmosphere: the exposed wood underneath was grey and rotten.

Danny had planned to drive around for most of the day to familiarise himself with the area, but there wasn't a lot to see: he was all done within less than an hour. Cottondale was not the sort of place you'd take a tour bus to: even after sundown, when the appearance of every other small town in America improved under the soft glow of orange sodium, it still looked bleak. If O'Hanlon *was* the Thevshi then he must have been really desperate not to be found, to put up with living here. It was a good place to hide, but a shit place to live.

Danny had been sitting in the car long enough to get himself noticed, but not long enough to know for certain if there was anyone inside O'Hanlon's apartment. Aside from an old Mercedes that had circled the block two or three times — like the driver was lost — the street was deserted. However, even odd places have their own normality: a rhythm of life imperceptible to the casual passer-by. A guy sitting in a car on his own for most of the afternoon would be sure to attract attention: a beat out of time. It was time to make a move.

Danny pulled the MSG90's scope from its soft leather pouch and sited it on O'Hanlon's front room. The magnified image told him nothing that he didn't already know: the flat was empty.

Situated directly opposite the shabby apartment block sat a small glass-fronted coffee shop with high stools facing out onto the street. From there he'd have a clear view of the first-floor balcony and the front door to the building: it would be easier to see who was entering and leaving. Maybe he'd go in and have a Coke, wait around for another twenty minutes or so to see if anyone showed up: or alternatively he could head into 'Jo's Bar' on the far corner and get a beer. Or maybe he'd just walk across the street and ring the bloody doorbell: the chances of O'Hanlon still being around were nil.

Danny wanted to have a nose around, get a feel for who this guy was: hopefully find a photograph so that at the very least he would know what the guy looked like. He flipped the handle on the glove box and lifted out the Walther PPK to check it was loaded. He'd already checked it ten times, but it was something to do. Danny liked the feel of the PPK in his hand. It was a good weight; comfortable grip too. He tucked it in his belt, pulled on his leather jacket and got out of the car. Immediately Danny wished he'd worn his light cotton Harrington instead. This late at night — even with the light rainfall — the temperature was still in the eighties. Before he'd reached the other side of the street he was covered in sweat. The heat was fine; it was the humidity that made it unbearable. Danny never imagined he'd long for the cold grey Newry drizzle, but anything was better than this.

There was a light on in the apartment next to O'Hanlon's. Whoever was in there was playing gospel music too loud for the time of night, but it sounded good echoing down the deserted street.

Of the twenty or so rectangular slots in the brass-framed plate screwed to the sidewall at the entrance, only three had names written in them. Flat B Four — O'Hanlon's — was one of the blanks. The other names looked like they were Polish or Russian — something Eastern European.

Danny pressed the buzzer and waited.

Nothing.

Earlier on he'd driven down the alleyway at the rear of the building. It ran north to south along the back of the block. Danny decided to head round there and look for a way inside.

As he turned to walk away the lock on the main door suddenly buzzed and clicked open. The noise startled him. He hadn't expected a response.

He peered from underneath the overhang to see if anyone was looking down at him from the balcony of O'Hanlon's flat, but there was no one there.

Danny hadn't really thought this through: he'd been so sure O'Hanlon was gone.

Reading off one of the other nameplates he leant forward and pressed O'Hanlon's buzzer again. 'Mr Slovensky, parcel for you. You want me to bring it up?' Danny said, trying an American accent.

There was still no answer, but the lock buzzed again. The tall main door creaked and groaned loudly as Danny pushed against it, the sound reverberating down the hollow corridors. If O'Hanlon was upstairs waiting for him then he would know for certain that Danny was inside the building.

The place looked derelict. The only evidence that anything had ever lived there was the overpowering smell of piss and dog shit. And the temperature inside was worse than outside.

Halfway along the unlit corridor sat two doors, adjacent to one another; wooden battens were nailed across their frames, barring entry. At the far end was a stairwell leading to the upper floors.

Danny wiped the sweat from his forehead and

stood for a moment, taking in his surroundings. The foul smell made him want to retch.

It struck Danny that this was a suitable place for a tout to live: hiding out in a shithole like a fucking rat. Served O'Hanlon right.

He turned back towards the entrance and took a big gulp of fresh air, then quickly made his way to the other end of the hallway. When he reached the stairwell he checked there was no one looking down on him before silently climbing the stairs to the first floor.

Danny was soon standing outside the door to O'Hanlon's apartment: listening for any signs of movement. But it was difficult to hear anything over the din of the gospel music.

He stood for two or three minutes before creeping back along the corridor towards the stairwell and up to the next floor. As he suspected, the apartment directly above also had a piece of two-by-two nailed across the doorframe. In a matter of seconds he had ripped the timber off, and — using his Wiggler Rakes and a heavy shoulder — managed to force open the door.

The air inside the apartment was dry and musty, and particles of dust, disturbed by Danny's intrusion, swirled in front of him, catching what little light there was spilling in through the windows.

In the middle of the room sat the carcass of an old sofa and next to it the remains of an upright piano. It looked as if the previous occupants had tried to strip it down in order to transport it elsewhere, then given up.

Danny tried the doors leading to the balcony

and was surprised to find that they weren't locked. He stepped out into the warm night air and peered over the edge of the wooden balustrade. Beneath him he could see the irregular pulse of Cathode-ray blue illuminating the balcony adjacent to O'Hanlon's and he could hear the soaring voices of the gospel choir as their song reached its hallowed conclusion. Danny didn't mind the music, but he wished they'd turn the volume down.

The drop to the balcony below looked no more than six or seven feet. After checking that the street was still empty, Danny climbed over the railings and started to lower himself down.

He realised too late that he'd underestimated: even at full stretch he couldn't feel the top rail of the balustrade below. The only option he had was to drop lower and hold on to the concrete lip that ran around the bottom edge of the balcony, but there was no way of pulling himself back up.

The palms of his hands were covered in sweat and he could feel his grip starting to slip. If O'Hanlon looked out of his lounge window right now, it would be all over for Danny.

'You breaking in or breaking out?'

The voice startled Danny so much that his right hand lost its grip on the wooden balustrade, leaving only his left to take his weight. As he scrambled desperately to regain a hold, the voice came again.

'There ain't nothing to steal round here so I'm guessing you musta forgot your keys or something.'

Danny managed to grab on and twist his head

round. His instinct was to reach for his gun, but there was no way he could do that without falling thirty feet onto the sidewalk.

A small, skinny black kid was leaning out over the balcony next to O'Hanlon's. He had a joint the size of an Esplendido hanging from his bottom lip.

'Hey, Mr O, balcony lights is still bust which is why I didn't recognise you. Can't see for shit. And you had your fuzzy face took off too. You okay? Ardel an me's been in session all day; not quite on the moon yet, but we is on a rocket ship heading in that direction. We're so out of it, we is listening to goddamn gospel music . . . and it's soundin good! Ardel says to me, 'Okay Hud, the lyrics is white-supremacist Christian, but the music is all black.' And the way the sisters sing it, man, specially the Mississippi Mass Choir. Man, those bitches can soar. It's got the hairs on my neck tingling like I'm plugged into the mains.'

Hud turned and shouted over his shoulder.

'Hey, Ardel, turn the goddamn music down, man, I'm talking to Mr O . . . Come see. He's hangin from the upstairs balcony like Batman. Where you been, Mr O, we ain't heard you bangin around for a few days now? You been away getting yourself shaved?'

Before Danny could answer, Ardel joined Hud at the railings.

'Mr O, where you been?' asked Ardel. 'What you doin hangin off the balcony? You should've taken the stairs. They smell of shit, but they's much more convenient.'

Hud started laughing hard. 'Convenient.

Where'd you learn a word like 'convenient', man? You crack me up, Ardel.'

'Convenient as in 'convenient store',' replied Ardel, laughing too.

'It's 'convenience store'. You's Grade A, man. 'A' for asshole. Convenience is wid an 'S' not a 'T', man.'

Danny's strength was starting to give.

'Any chance you boys could give me a hand here?'

'You fine, Mr O. If you fall there ain't nothing on the sidewalk you gonna hit, but the sidewalk itself.'

'Seriously Mr O,' said Hud. 'You fine. Drop your feet another inch and you're there.'

The overhang was obstructing Danny's view. He had to trust that Hud was right, but if they were stoned enough to think that he was O'Hanlon, they were stoned enough to misjudge the distance between his feet and the top of the railings. But Danny's arms were aching; he wouldn't be able to hold on much longer.

Danny closed his eyes and let his hands slip from the wooden railings. Almost immediately he found himself balancing on top of the handrail below. He quickly steadied himself by bracing both arms on the underside of the overhang, then jumped down to the safety of O'Hanlon's balcony.

'You hidin from that big black dude's been round lookin for you? That why you're all shaved . . . you trying to look like you is someone else?' asked Ardel. 'That explain why you's pushing our buzzer and asking for Mr Slovensky? It

235

cracked us up. I said to Hud it's like a code or something. 'You want me to bring the parcel up?'' continued Ardel, mimicking Danny's tone. 'Man, we were on the floor.'

Ardel started laughing again, but Hud stayed serious. 'What happened to your face, Mr O? That lopsided motherfucker caught up with you already? Consolation is, your face is going to get better: his face, there ain't no cure for. Asshole gave us fifty bucks, said there was another fifty if we call him soon as you show up.'

'Yeah, he's been hangin out over at Jo's,' said Ardel. 'Drinkin margaritas and tryin to look mean. Jo's upset cause the dude don't eat nothing. Just drinks fancy cocktails and sits there arguing with his reflection in the window. Ah says to Jo, you don't want to upset him by makin him eat your food, but Jo don't get the joke . . . She thinks she's pretty good in the kitchen, but she ain't. Big, ugly motherfucker don't look too well either . . . Him I mean, not Jo. Looks kinda pale for a black man. Says he has some business wid you, but if you ask me he's not the kind you want to be doin business with, Mr O. Had a big nine-mil. stickin out his coat, was the only business he had about him. You know what I mean. What he don't know is, Jo's keeping a check on him for us. She don't like the look of him either and she got an eye for that kind of thing.'

'We goin back to the choir now, Mr O, catch you later,' continued Hud as though he'd just remembered the music was still playing. 'We see that big motherfucker hangin round we'll bang

236

on the wall; give you some warning. Won't cost you fifty dollars either, for you it's free . . . Say amen, somebody.'

Ardel was laughing again. ' 'Say amen.' Man you crack me up.'

The two of them disappeared behind the opaque glass screen separating the two balconies.

Just as Danny turned away Ardel's face appeared again round the edge of the glass. 'We'll throw you over a bag, Mr O. It's mellow enough, but don't smoke it all at once — it can sneak up and fuck you in the ass. Catch you later.'

Danny shouted after him. 'Ardel.'

'Yeah.'

'Did the guy give a name?'

'Yeah. Vincent.'

'Thanks.'

Danny shouted after him again.

'Ardel.'

'Yeah.'

'Turn the fuckin music down, would ye?'

There was another burst of laughter.

Danny turned to face the sliding glass doors. He checked to see if they were unlocked before pressing his face against the glass to look inside. That's when he heard the scream.

Suddenly the balcony was flooded with light. There was a woman inside, standing in the corner of the lounge, holding a Snub Nose. One hand on the light switch, the other pointing the gun straight at him. All of a sudden the balcony was plunged back into darkness.

Danny didn't have time to jump out of the

way before there was a flash and the first bullet exploded through the balcony door. Long slivers of glass hurtled out over the railings and down onto the street below. The woman fired a second and third shot in quick succession, both bullets fizzing past close to Danny's head.

She'd emptied the weapon in less than ten seconds and hit nothing but the scenery. Whoever she was, she was no pro, but even amateurs can get lucky. Danny dropped to the floor. He had already fired back twice, but he was shooting into the darkness: aiming to miss.

The next instant she was gone. Danny heard her footsteps retreating into the dingy shadows of the apartment, and she screamed as he fired another round.

He didn't want to hit her. He needed to talk to her, find out what she was doing there; ask if she knew where O'Hanlon was.

He punched the remainder of the glass out of the aluminium doorframe and crawled inside, on all fours, to the far side of the room where he sat with his back pressed against the wall.

Danny raised his hand and wiped something wet from his cheek. Several small lacerations on his face and forehead were oozing blood that collected at the end of his chin and dripped onto his shirt. 'Jesus, what a bollock,' muttered Danny under his breath.

'Listen!' he shouted. 'I need to talk to Finn O'Hanlon. I don't mean him or you any harm. I've come to help. I know there are people trying to kill him, but I promise you, I just need to talk to him. You're out of bullets so I'm going to put

238

the hall light on and throw my gun down to you. That way you're in charge, okay?'

Danny dropped the clip out the handle of his Walther PPK and slid the empty gun along the wooden floor.

'I'm unarmed, and you're the boss. If you want to talk, I'll be in the kitchen looking for something to drink.'

25

Marie pulled up alongside the overflowing trashcans in the unlit alleyway at the back of Finn's apartment, and pushed the stick into neutral. She left the engine running to keep the air conditioning on.

The storm clouds Finn had seen from the window of the motel had travelled with them on their journey back to Tuscaloosa, keeping pace with the car as it sped along the freeway. The heavy rain had now eased to a light drizzle, leaving the ground glistening and the air stifling and humid.

'I think we're here,' she said, talking to herself in a quiet voice. 'Nice neighbourhood, if you're into shabby.' She was trying to reassure herself everything was okay, but when she checked her lipstick in the rear-view mirror, she noticed that her hand had a slight tremor. Marie wasn't even sure it mattered a damn what her lipstick looked like: all she was going to do was pick a few things up from Finn's apartment and drive straight back to the motel.

Marie once told her friends that she felt life wasn't so much passing her by as ignoring her altogether; exciting things always happened to *other* people. But here she was taking a Colt Snub Nose .38 Detective Special from her purse

240

and unclipping the magazine like she knew what she was doing.

'There's as much chance of me shooting someone as there is of finding all four wheels on my car when I get back.'

As she moved her purse over to the passenger's seat a hand reached across from behind and grabbed her forearm.

Marie jumped and let out a squeal. 'Jesus Christ. I nearly shot out the goddamn windshield.'

'Sorry,' said Finn from the floor in the back of the car. 'Listen, if you don't feel good about this we can turn round and head back. I don't want you to go in if you're not happy.'

'Are you kidding? All I ever do is sit and *watch* the news: you think I'm going to pass up an opportunity to *be* the news? I'm shitting myself, but in an excited sort of a way. I'll be fine,' she replied. 'In and out, grab the cornflake box, grab your gun, and hold my breath on the stairwell,' she said, recapping everything Finn had told her on the journey from the motel. 'Why don't I leave this with you?' she continued as she held the Snub Nose between her thumb and forefinger and pushed it towards Finn. 'I'll get your gun from under the pillow and use *that*. If I'm attacked on the way in, I'll smack the son of a bitch over the head with these.' Marie picked up the clump of keys Finn had given her and passed them back to him. 'Which one's which again?'

Finn had been lying on the floor of the car for almost the entire journey: his neck felt like it was about to break and the wounds on his shoulder and knees were giving him hell. He took the keys

241

awkwardly, trying not to raise his head above the level of the door, then pointed them out to Marie one at a time. 'This one's for the back entrance to the building' — Finn held it up — 'and this one's the door to the apartment. If you get in there and think anything looks out of place or doesn't feel right then get the hell out of there, okay?'

'Okay.'

'You see the window just to the left of the fire escape on the first floor?' said Finn.

'Yeah.'

'That's the bedroom: as soon as you're in, come to the window and flash the torch, so I know everything's all right.'

'How many times? I'm just thinking, we should have a code in case something's wrong, you know, like someone's inside waiting, then I can flash a certain number of times and you'll know. But make it an easy code. If it's too complicated I'll mess up.'

Finn let out a snort.

'What're you laughing at?'

'You,' he replied. ''A code'? What, like Morse code? You think you'll have time to spell out 'Someone's beating the shit out of me. Help'?'

'Sure. And where he lives; where he likes to shop — you can tell a lot about someone from what they're wearing,' replied Marie, joining in.

'Take the gun. If anything kicks off, start firing, and don't stop until they stop breathing.'

Once again Finn had stopped Marie in her tracks.

'That what they teach you back in Ireland?' she said.

'No, it's what you learn when someone's trying to kill you. If you don't stop them — they'll stop you. They're going to keep coming at you until you're dead, by which point it's too late to say, 'Shit, maybe I should have shot first.' Believe me, if you've ever had someone point a gun at you it's the fastest lesson you'll learn in your life. And if you do start shooting you'd better mean it, because they're not going to give you a second chance. What they teach you in Northern Ireland is, 'Don't give them *any* fuckin chance.''

The atmosphere was sober again.

Finn didn't mean to give her a hard time, but she was treating it like it was all a joke. He needed to remind her that this was a grave situation with serious consequences. It wasn't fair on her, but Finn didn't know what else to do; she was beginning to matter to him.

They both sat in silence: the connection between them momentarily lost.

'Doesn't feel right, does it?' said Marie, eventually.

Finn felt his stomach churn. He knew he was asking too much of her. He'd got her involved in a screwed-up situation that was nothing to do with her and here he was giving her attitude for putting her life in danger.

'You're right! I don't even know what I'm thinking, asking you to go in. Let's drive round the front again and if it looks quiet, I'll run in and grab the stuff myself,' he replied.

'That's not what I mean. I've been trying to work out why this feels so odd,' she continued. 'I

243

think it's because there's no music: makes it all seem a bit ordinary — flat, you know? It needs a bit of music to set the tone. We need a soundtrack.'

Finn smiled. 'We need to get out of here as quick as we can, before someone notices the car and the soundtrack's for a car chase. Let's drive around the front, then I'll run in.'

'What if they're watching the apartment?'

'I'll be in and out so quick they won't know what to do . . . plus, I know where everything is. It'll be much easier.'

Marie put everything she needed in her purse and opened the car door. 'Wooh! It's sticky out here!'

'Where are you going?' asked Finn.

'If they spot you going into the building it's all over. If they see a woman they don't know they're not going to bat an eye. It makes more sense. Will I leave the engine running? If I take the car keys, it'll get hot in here, but then, I don't want someone driving off with you in the back.'

'Get back in the car and drive round the front.'

Marie flung the door wide and stepped out into the warm air. The sound of gospel music could be heard, pumping out of one of the other apartments in the block. She popped her head back inside. 'I was thinking more Run-DMC than the Mississippi Mass Choir, but at least it's music. Be careful what you wish for, eh?'

'It's my neighbours, Ardel and Hud. When you get into the flat, bang on the wall and they'll turn it down.'

'I like it loud.' And with that she was gone.

Finn propped himself up high enough to see over the top of the door and watched as Marie's shapely figure disappeared into the blackness. He hadn't noticed it until Marie pointed it out, but the music was loud: even with the car door closed, Finn could still make out the lyrics — 'Say amen, somebody.'

*   *   *

The first thing that hit Marie as she pushed open the fire-escape door was the smell. Finn had warned her, but it was far worse than she was expecting. She covered her nose and mouth and made her way — as quickly as possible — past the bags of rotting litter and household waste till she was standing outside Finn's front door.

Marie let herself into the apartment and hurriedly locked the door behind her. The stale atmosphere inside was a lot more appealing than the stench out in the hallway, so she stood for a moment in the darkness letting the foul air clear from her lungs and wondering what had happened in Finn's life to bring him to this shithole.

Marie didn't want to hang about. She started running through Finn's description of how the apartment was laid out. The lounge was to the right of the front door and had a kitchen leading off it, and a large glass door that ran the length of the balcony. Both bedrooms were left down the corridor and had a small bathroom sandwiched between them.

'Don't put the light on, don't use the torch

except to signal, grab the cornflakes, grab Finn's gun, get the hell out' — that was it.

Marie's eyes were now accustomed to the dark, but she could still only make out vague shapes and outlines as she made her way down the short corridor.

She moved slowly through into Finn's bedroom, heading for the window, then pulled back the curtains. The car looked much more conspicuous parked in the alleyway than she'd imagined. She flashed the torch three times to let Finn know that she was inside, but it was too dark down there to tell if he'd seen her.

The bedroom was small: most of the floor space taken up by a messy double bed and a large chest of drawers covered with books. Finn told her not to bother picking up any clothes: it was better to buy new.

Marie moved away from the window and opened the top drawer of the chest. She was surprised to find it empty; the second and third drawer, the same — empty except for some faded sheets of wallpaper used to line the bases. Maybe he kept his stuff in the other room.

There was an unexpected lull in the music from next door: a brief pause.

Suddenly a floorboard creaked nearby. Marie stood frozen to the spot trying to hold her breath, but her heart was pounding, demanding oxygen. She tightened her grip on the Snub Nose and listened more intently. It was difficult to tell if the noise had come from inside the flat or from one of the other apartments. The noise came again, but this time she got a fix on it. She was certain it had come from the apartment above. Marie's shoulders sagged and she started to breathe again. 'Just grab what you came for and get to hell out of there, come on.'

Moments later she was heading back along the corridor towards the lounge. Without thinking, she reached up for the light switch. It was an instinctive reaction, but Marie knew instantly that it was too late.

The light had been on only for a split second, but that was enough for Marie to see the guy's face pressed against the balcony door.

She screamed and tried to lift the Snub Nose, but it felt like it had suddenly gained two hundred pounds. The muscles in her arms had drained of all their strength and her fingers refused to work. It was only when she saw the figure out on the balcony reach for *his* gun that she managed to pull the trigger.

There were two loud explosions and the room was instantly filled with acrid smoke. She could hear Finn's words echoing in her mind: 'Start firing, and don't stop until they stop breathing.'

Before Marie knew what had happened, she'd emptied the gun and the trigger was clicking lamely in her hand.

Another two loud cracks reverberated round the walls of the small lounge.

The guy was firing back.

Marie turned and ran.

Yet another shot. This time the bullet fizzed overhead and burst into the ceiling just above her head, showering her in fine white plaster dust.

247

She could hear the guy crashing through the balcony doors. He was in the apartment.

Marie pulled frantically at the front door, her hands trembling with fear.

She was sobbing.

She knew that the door was locked, but what had she done with the goddamn keys?

Suddenly it hit her. They were sitting on top of the chest of drawers in Finn's bedroom, where she'd left them alongside his gun.

26

Vincent Lee Croll lifted the bell-bottomed glass and sucked margarita through two twisted pink straws till it made a sound like a coffee percolator. The woman behind the counter might have a face on her like a bulldog's ass, but she knew how to mix a drink. Vincent was on his fourth. The painkillers had stopped working a long time ago and various parts of his body were beginning to hurt. The alcohol was helping, but he needed more. It was only when he stood up and tried to walk over to the bar that it hit him just how strong the margaritas were. The toe of Vincent's shoe caught an uneven floorboard and he nearly went over. Jo behind the bar flashed a look when she heard him cussing, but he didn't give a shit. It wasn't as if he was upsetting a packed house — in fact, apart from one other guy sitting at the bar and an old couple over in the corner, Vincent was the only one there. He knew the old bulldog wasn't going to throw out a fee-paying customer, even if the look on her face said she wanted to.

'Be easier if you did service at the tables,' he dribbled as he placed his glass on the counter.

'Who fur,' she replied with a heavy southern drawl, 'me or you?'

Vincent checked his pockets: he had fifteen

249

dollars left, which meant another three drinks, or two drinks and a couple of packets of Marlboros. Either way he was nearly out of cash. 'Any chance of a 'good customer' discount, seeing as I'm keeping the place going all by myself here?' he said, giving it his best toothy grin.

Bulldog Jo didn't lift her head from the newspaper she was leaning over.

'Sure. How about I refuse to serve you another margarita. That way you get a discount of five bucks.'

Vincent's big dopey eyes stared back at her for a few seconds while he decided which way to take it.

'Why you chewing on my ass, sis? You been nibbling at it ever since I got here. So much so that I got no ass left to sit on that seat over there. Gonna need a cushion to rest the bare knuckle of my butt on. All I'm suggesting is that I buy three drinks at a reduced rate to save me getting up and down every couple of minutes and you throw in a packet of smokes as an all-inclusive deal.'

'How about I serve you one more drink for the road and you can have one of my cigarettes as a going-away present?' she replied, still reading the newspaper. 'That way you'll have enough money to call a cab.'

Vincent kept up the dumb smile. He thought about shooting her right between the fucking eyes, but he would then have to kill everyone else in the bar and that might turn his luck the wrong way. Vincent sucked air in through his teeth and tried again.

250

'C'mon, sis, I'm asking you nice now. You standing there looking so sweet you're rotting my teeth. Okay, I will buy one more drink, but I'd like it to be a pitcher of margaritas and if you could possibly include a packet of smokes I'll give you fifteen bucks, and that is everything I own.'

Bulldog Jo was peering at him now, over the thin metallic rim of her glasses. 'Well seeing as how you asked so nice,' she said, making no attempt to hide the sarcasm.

Vincent watched as she threw together the ingredients of his drink and poured the mixture into a glass jug. She put the jug down on the bar and pulled a packet of cigarettes from a display stand just behind her.

'You need a fresh glass?'

'Shit, for fifteen bucks I'm expectin a goddamn butler to carry me *and* the drink to my table,' replied Vincent, even though his cheeks were beginning to hurt with all the smiling he was doing.

He fished in his trouser pocket for his last three bills and slapped them down just far enough out of reach to make Bulldog have to stretch across the counter top.

Vincent pushed himself away from the bar and slouched back to the window. After lighting another cigarette he climbed unsteadily onto a tall wooden bar stool and stared out at a blanket of cloud that had pushed in from the south, making the evening seem darker than usual. Through the dirty window of the bar Vincent could also see a dim blue glow lighting up the

251

balcony of the two skinny dopeheads that lived next to O'Hanlon. Vincent had sat at the window for over an hour watching people come and go from their apartment. Within minutes of arriving each visitor would appear on the balcony for a smoke, which confirmed what Vincent already suspected. The guys across the street were dealers: the visitors were trying out the merchandise.

Now that the margaritas were hitting home runs unopposed Vincent was starting to get ideas again. If O'Hanlon didn't show up soon, he'd go over and bust the dope dealers. It'd be an easy hit. Knock on the door like he wanted to ask them some more about O'Hanlon, then as soon as they opened up ... whack. Knock one of them out straight away. Let the other one know he was serious and not to fuck him about. It hadn't occurred to Vincent when he'd been over earlier that they were stoned, but now he'd figured it out, it made sense. Only problem he could see was if Mr De Garza had them on his books. If that were the case they would be off limits. But in all his years of smoking dope he had never heard of anyone dealing out of Cottondale. Vincent smiled. What had started off as a fairly ordinary day was turning out to be a rollercoaster ride with a shitload of opportunities opening up for him. When the cops had come into his hospital room Vincent thought that was it, game over. But as soon as they had been removed from the equation, everything had started to turn around.

The first bit of luck: the room he'd jumped

out of at the hospital was right next to the parking lot. Within seconds he had the driver's door of an Oldsmobile Cutlass sedan open and was heading to his sister's house for a shower and a change of clothes with WTXT blasting out some classic Country on the radio. The plan to go to Cola's mum's house and sort the old bitch out would have to wait.

The second bit of luck: when he'd turned into his sister's street he'd seen the Black and White sitting out front, in her drive. Vincent had driven straight past just as the cops were getting out of the car and crossing the street. They didn't even look his way. Vincent drove on to a friend's house instead and got fixed up there.

The third bit of luck: finding the two wasters across the street, Ardel and Hud. There for the taking was a big bag of weed and a cash bonus for the minimum of effort.

Vincent tipped the jug of margaritas and filled his glass to the brim. A thought struck him and he turned to shout over at Bulldog Jo.

'Hey sis, how many drinks in a jug?'

Jo looked over at him and frowned.

'What?'

'How many glasses d'you get in a jug?'

Bulldog Jo knew straight away where this was heading. 'Four!'

'How much does it cost?'

'Twelve bucks for a pitcher.'

Vincent's smile was gone.

'So how come I've been paying tourist rates — buying them individually for five bucks each — and you never says?'

Bulldog Jo shrugged her shoulders. 'You never asked.'

'Plus you owe me three,' said Vincent.

Jo shook her head. 'No, you got a pack of smokes.'

'Okay, but they is only two-fifty a pack, or are you charging me tourist on them as well?' said Vincent, beginning to get a rise. 'You took three bucks off me.'

'So I owe you fifty cents — you can collect it on your way out. Now relax your bony ass and stop shouting your mouth off all over the place. You annoying the other customers.'

Vincent was about to start on her again when something caught his eye.

Someone was climbing over the railings on the balcony above O'Hanlon's apartment. The guy was trying to drop down but his feet were a few inches short of the railing below: dangling there like he was about to fall. Next thing Ardel and Hud were out on their balcony making conversation with the guy like they were all best of friends.

Vincent couldn't believe what he was seeing.

'Sheeeit . . . O'Hanlon!'

Vincent smiled to himself and muttered under his breath. 'You see tha's why I didn't shoot this place up . . . cause I knew it would turn my luck in the wrong direction. Vincent — looks to me like you staring at the double jackpot.'

Vincent picked up the jug of margaritas and carried it back over to the bar, taking care not to let any of it spill.

'What time you close?'

Jo was reading her newspaper again.

'Usually round midnight, but I'm thinking I might close up early tonight.'

'Closing early for the tourists?' Vincent shrugged like he wasn't bothered. 'You keep this in the cooler till I get back. Got some work to do, but it won't take long. You can hang on to the fifty cents you owe me too. Call it a tip.'

'Gee, you sure?' said Jo, out loud so the other drinkers could hear. Got the two old folk in the corner smiling till Vincent stared them down.

When he was finished across the road Vincent would come back and pistol-whip the bitch, but for now he'd settle for hitting her with an exit line.

'Lady, we used to have a dog looked like you when I was growing up. Bitch was so ugly we tied the leash to its hind legs, shaved its ass, and walked it backwards.' Vincent looked over at the old couple again and scowled. 'Why ain't you smiling now, for fuck's sake? That's a good line.'

If he'd waited a few seconds he'd have seen Jo pouring the jug of margaritas down the sink and picking up the telephone, but Vincent was already out onto the street. He kept tight to the edge of the building, skirting the shadows as he made his way quickly along the sidewalk opposite O'Hanlon's.

He figured this guy O'Hanlon was scared to go in through his front door, in case someone was waiting for him on the other side. From where Vincent was standing now it looked as if the guy had his face pressed up against the balcony doors trying to see in.

Suddenly the guy was in silhouette. For a split second there was light flooding onto the balcony from inside the apartment.

Vincent had to duck down as the balcony doors suddenly erupted with a loud crack and a bullet ripped through the air, embedding itself into the wall beside him. '*Sheeeit.*'

Vincent had to stay low as two more bullets whizzed past.

When he looked up again the light was off and the guy had disappeared.

Vincent wasn't sure what was happening: maybe someone else had been hired to finish the hit, and had been waiting inside the apartment just like O'Hanlon had feared. But jumping in on someone else's contract was against the rules. If another asshole was trying to prevent Vincent claiming the prize money then they would get a goddamn bullet too.

Right now, though, he didn't give a shit. O'Hanlon was back and that meant Vincent was still in the frame to collect.

As he crossed the road Vincent pulled the 9 mm from his belt and flipped the safety off.

'Tomorrow you is heading straight to the track to bet on some nags, you lucky hound-dog,' he said to himself. The big toothy grin was back.

He lifted the gun to his lips and kissed it. 'Okay doll, you ready to spit some nasties.'

27

Cottondale, Easter Sunday, evening

'Listen!' she heard him say. 'I'm unarmed, and you're the boss. If you want to talk, I'll be in the kitchen looking for something to drink.'

Considering she'd just tried to shoot him, he sounded pretty calm.

Marie heard some movement, then a thump as the guy's gun hit the floor and slid along the hallway. It was just out of reach, but there it was, just as he'd said.

There was always the chance that he might be carrying another weapon, but — for whatever reason — her instinct was to trust him.

Marie stood in the darkness for a few moments wondering what to do next.

She had the front-door key now, but her hand was trembling so much that she'd never get the key in the lock.

The guy was rummaging around for something in the kitchen.

What the hell, she thought. Marie walked back into the lounge.

The guy was sitting in one of Finn's old leather armchairs in the corner of the room with a beer in his hand like the place was his. The music was still booming away next door and it sounded like the neighbours were playing ball against the dividing wall.

'Sorry about the mess: I haven't had a chance to tidy up,' he said casually, referring to the bits of glass from the balcony door strewn across the floor. 'You want one?' He was holding out a bottle of Skeeter Bite towards her.

Marie's mouth was too dry to speak so she nodded instead.

The guy got up and went over to the fridge. 'What do I call you?'

Marie stared right at him, conscious that she might reveal her 'lying zone' like she'd done with the Feds. The first name that came to her was:

'Delores.'

The guy pulled out a beer from the fridge and opened it, set it on the counter and went back to his seat. His face was quite badly swollen on one side and he had blood dripping down his chin from a collection of little scratches on his face.

'You got any Germolene . . . 'Delores'?'

She knew by the way he pronounced her name that she might as well have told him her real name.

The neighbours were banging on the wall again.

Marie kept the gun pointing at him as she moved further into the kitchen and lifted the beer. She'd never been a big fan of beer, but she took a long slow drink before answering.

'What's Germolene?'

'What d'you call it over here?'

'Call what?'

'I don't know. Antiseptic cream, I suppose.'

'We call it Foille.'

'Do you have any Foille I could borrow?'

asked Danny, wiping a droplet of blood from his cheek with the back of his hand.

'It's not my apartment,' she replied, trying her best to sound in control, 'so I wouldn't know.'

'What did you do with my gun?'

'Left it in the bedroom.'

'You can put yours down if you like,' said Danny. 'I know you're all out.'

Marie squeezed the trigger.

The recoil jarred her wrist as the .45 ACP hollow-point blasted a three-inch hole in the floor beside Danny's foot.

The loud percussion made both of them jump.

Marie struggled to keep her voice steady as she said, 'Different gun.'

'Okay,' replied Danny. 'Well, that'll teach me.'

Danny was annoyed with himself for not noticing that she'd switched from the Snub Nose.

'Where did the Glock come from?'

'The bedroom. Belongs to the guy who owns the apartment.'

'Is he here?' asked Danny.

'No.'

Marie slugged at the Skeeter Bite till she'd nearly finished the bottle.

'D'you mind if I ask you some questions?' continued Danny.

'Seems like that's all anyone wants to do these days,' replied Marie. 'How about I ask you some first?'

'Well as you're the one with the gun, I suppose it's only fair.'

'Let's start with some easy ones and then I'll

throw in a few curve balls,' said Marie, aware that her hand was still trembling and her heart rate was pounding way above normal.

There was more banging on the wall.

'Where you from?'

'Northern Ireland,' replied Danny.

'What were you doing on the balcony?'

'Looking for a guy called Finn O'Hanlon. I was told this was where he lives.'

'Why didn't you try the front door?'

'I did, but there was no answer.'

'So you thought you'd climb onto the balcony?'

Danny didn't have an answer for that one, so he shrugged instead.

Marie said, 'Why'd you start shooting at me?'

'You started shooting at me,' replied Danny. 'I was returning fire. At least I was aiming to miss.'

'I thought the rule was to keep firing till the other guy stops breathing?'

'Did O'Hanlon tell you that?'

It was Marie's turn to shrug.

'If you check you'll see I was firing at the ceiling,' continued Danny, pointing behind her.

Marie stopped herself from turning to look. She'd seen enough movies not to fall for the sucker punch. 'It's okay, I believe you,' she said. 'Are you here to kill Finn O'Hanlon?'

'I'm here to ask him what he knows about my brother. I was given his name by a guy in Ireland called Lep McFarlane, told me O'Hanlon could help.'

'And you've travelled all this way just to *talk* to him?'

'Listen, I don't even know who the hell you are. The only reason I'm answering these questions is because you're holding the weapon and I'm hoping that — at the very least — you might take a message to O'Hanlon for me, or better still, take me to see him in person. My brother was murdered and I'm told *he* knows something about it; that's why I'm here. Yes, I want to talk to him.'

If Finn's story about behavioural science was right, so far the guy seemed to be telling the truth.

Marie took her time before asking the next question . . . 'You think O'Hanlon murdered your brother?'

She was hoping the answer would be no.

'I didn't say that. I said he knows something about what happened.'

'What's your name?'

Danny's eyes flicked down to the left before he answered. 'Mr Leonard.'

Marie decided to pick him up on it straight away. 'You don't want to tell me your real name?' she asked.

Danny looked up; maybe he'd underestimated her, but for now it was the only name he was going to give. 'Do you know the Lakeshore Hotel . . . 'Delores'?'

'The one on Coker that's nowhere near a lake?' replied Marie.

'As far as I know, it's the only hotel in Tuscaloosa called 'Lakeshore',' replied Danny. 'I'm in room 261.'

'Why you telling me?' asked Marie.

'I'm guessing the chances of you taking me to

261

O'Hanlon right now are pretty slim, so if it's all the same to you I'd like to head back to the hotel and pick the glass out of my face: get myself cleaned up. You can tell O'Hanlon where I'm staying and if he's interested he can get in touch: if he's not, then no harm done and all I'll have wasted is the price of a plane ticket. If you tell him it was Lep who passed on the message to me, he'll know that I'm genuine. It was O'Hanlon who contacted me in the first place.'

'Lip?' said Marie, finding the guy's accent difficult.

'Lep,' replied Danny. 'Short for Leprechaun.'

Danny made to stand up.

Marie's voice sounded strangely hollow to her. 'Just stay right where you are, Mr 'Leonard'. You seem like an okay guy, but I'm twitchy as hell right now. I'd hate to shoot you by mistake.'

The music coming from next door stopped. The sudden silence seemed to heighten the air of tension in the room.

'Now,' she continued, 'I have a couple of things to pick up, then I'm going to leave — *before* you. So you might as well sit back and enjoy your beer.'

Danny kept his eyes on her while he took another slug of beer and sat back down in the armchair.

Marie walked over and lifted a family-size box of cornflakes down from one of the shelves in the kitchen. She was surprised at how heavy it felt.

As she started backing out of the room she could hear more thumping noises on the wall, this time louder, more urgent. Suddenly, Danny was back on his feet, moving towards her.

'Give me the gun, Delores.'

Marie pointed it straight at the middle of his chest, but he was still coming.

'Give me the fucking gun.' He was shouting at her now. 'Someone's coming for Christ's sake, *give me the gun.*'

★   ★   ★

Danny had only just realised that the banging noises were Ardel and Hud trying to warn him someone was coming, but it was too late.

Suddenly there was a noise like a cannon going off and a ragged hole the size of a watermelon appeared in the front door. Marie screamed and almost lost her grip on the Glock 21 as she lunged forward out of the line of fire.

The lock on the front door exploded across the corridor and slammed into the wall opposite. The whole room seemed to shudder and shake.

Marie screamed again: someone was kicking hard against the front door. Danny made a grab for Marie's hand but she anticipated the move and pulled the gun out of reach. The Glock caught him on the forearm knocking it from her grasp. As it bounced along the corridor out of reach there was one final splintering crack and the front door flew open.

Danny ran back to the kitchen and grabbed a large carving knife from one of the drawers, slid it up the sleeve of his jacket and quickly sat back in the armchair.

When he looked up a tall skinny black guy was

standing exactly where Marie had been just a few seconds earlier. In one hand he was holding a 9 mm, in the other, the Glock 21. The guy's left arm looked stiff and swollen and his face appeared to have taken a few bad beatings in its time. Even before he spoke, Danny could tell from the lazy eye movements and the stench of alcohol that he was drunk.

Danny glanced over the guy's shoulder looking for signs of Marie, but she was nowhere to be seen.

'Mr O'Hanlon, you sittin there all cool like you was expecting me. You alone?'

'Just me,' said Danny.

'I heard a woman's voice. She the one shooting at you a minute ago and doing all the screaming, or was that you acting all pussy?'

Danny let the question sit for a moment before answering. No point arguing with a drunk pointing a couple of shooters at you, he reasoned. The guy was tall, six foot two at least, carrying no excess weight, more like an underfed horse than an athlete. Looked like he had a brain the size of a walnut too.

'Where'd she go?'

'Who?' asked Danny.

'You throw the bitch out for taking a few pops at you, huh? Or is she the one went running into the bedroom just as I made my entrance? You got to show them your knuckles every now and then, Mr O'Hanlon. Teach them they get a smack, they start shooting at you in your own home. Just ain't correct. Once I've delivered the message you got coming I'll go and sort her out

264

for you. She pretty?'

Danny didn't answer — he was watching the guy struggle to stay focused, figuring out if there was enough time to throw the knife before the guy could get a shot in.

'My name's Vincent Lee Croll, I'll be your Whackster for today. You lookin at me like you weighing up your odds on something, Mr O'Hanlon,' said Vincent as he stood there swaying back and forward. 'Unless you is Matt Helm and you got a cigarette lighter fires missiles or something, I'd say you is well and truly screwed, so don't even consider it. There anyone else in here I should know about cept you and your girlfriend?'

Danny shook his head.

'What I can't figure is why you'd want to come back. If I had someone after shooting my ass in a bar, I don't think I'd go home . . . Unless I'd left something of value I needed to pick up. You got anything of value you want to give me, Mr O'Hanlon? If you tell me where it is I might just turn round and walk out what's left of the front door.'

'I'm not O'Hanlon,' replied Danny.

Vincent cackled sarcastically. 'Yeah, and I'm not going to shoot you in the fucking head in a minute. You think just cause you shaved your beard and got your face beat up a little you become a whole different person?' Vincent lowered his voice. 'To be honest I don't care if you're O'Hanlon or not,' he continued. 'I been through so much shit the past few days I'm gonna kill you anyways — although before I do, I would like to thank you for showing my partner Culo where the big golden stairway is, cause he was messing my head to the point I couldn't think straight. But now he's gone I got a whole world of opportunities opening up in front of me. If you bump into Culo Conrado on your travels be sure and tell him I'm doin good. Tell him I always thought he was an asshole. You do that for me, Mr O'Hanlon, and I'll make sure I get you with the first bullet.'

Danny felt the blade jab into the palm of his hand as he let the knife slip from his sleeve in readiness. He sat waiting, hoping the right moment would present itself before Croll did something stupid like pull the trigger. He needed Croll to lower the guns so that they weren't pointing straight at him: that way — even if Vincent fired back — he'd have less chance of hitting anything.

'You want one?' Danny held up the bottle of beer. He wanted to keep Vincent talking. 'Skeeter Bite! Got a bit of a kick: brewed locally.'

'Thanks, but I got a busy night ahead. Got a visit planned with your neighbours, and a big jug of margaritas across the street ain't getting any cooler. So — much as I'm sure we've got plenty to talk about — I can't hang about.'

Out of the corner of his eye Danny noticed a movement on the balcony, but Vincent had caught it too. Suddenly Croll turned and started firing with both guns at whatever was out there. In the same instant Danny raised his arm in a small, but powerful upward movement and flicked his hand forward, releasing his grip on the knife. The dark

266

bone handle spun through the air and delivered the blade deep into Vincent's throat. It struck him with such force that the shiny steel passed clean through his windpipe and out the other side.

Vincent lurched backwards, clawing at his throat. He immediately started retching and coughing as his airways filled with blood.

In the same moment Danny heard a loud, mechanical, rasping noise coming from the balcony.

Vincent started juddering and shaking in a grotesque dancing movement as his body lifted off the ground, and slammed backward against the wall, blood spurting from a cluster of small holes that had suddenly appeared all over his torso.

Hud ducked in through the balcony doors holding an Ingram M10 sub-machine gun. He walked over to Vincent and fired another burst into his head.

'Hope this motherfucker wasn't a friend of yours, Mr O.'

'He was the pizza delivery guy,' said Danny dryly.

Hud turned and stared at Danny.

It took him a few seconds, then he started laughing hard. 'You crack me up man. 'Pizza delivery guy'! I was looking at you all serious too,' said Hud, picking the two guns from the floor that Vincent had been holding and passing them over to Danny. 'You hear us banging? We were hitting so hard we nearly knocked a hole in the goddamn wall.'

'I was a bit slow on the uptake,' said Danny. 'I didn't realise until it was too late.'

'Ardel be here in a minute; help us clear up. He was coming along the fire escape — the two of us was gonna do a pincer movement on the big motherfucker — but Ardel met your girl climbing out the window: she was so scared. She lucky she's alive, cause all Ardel saw was a head poking out and he nearly starts flicking his trigger finger . . . Was a close thing. He's acting like he's her own personal bodyguard now: making sure she gets to her car safe, then he'll be right up. Said to tell you she'll meet you down there. You got Jo to thank for this; she called us, told us Lee Croll was heading over. She's good that way: looks out for us. Says his mug shot's on ABC News: got the headline slot. Man, I told you he was givin off bad vibes. Asshole killed two cops. Jo said to tell you there's a black-and-white of you too, Mr O' Hanlon. Is only a drawing, but she says it's definitely you: you and a girl, who I presume to be the one Ardel is escorting right now. You got to get your skinny white butt in a taxi and cross the state line.'

Hud stepped over Vincent's body and flipped the light switch. 'Man, this dude's got a lot of blood in him for a skinny guy.'

He started laughing again. ''Pizza delivery guy' . . . You crack me up.'

Hud looked round, shaking his head and smiling.

Suddenly he lifted the M10 and pointed it straight at Danny. The wide-mouthed grin was gone, and the frown was back.

'Wait a minute. Who the fuck are you, motherfucker? You ain't Mr O.'

28

The Hawaiian-style poolside bar they were sitting at looked unconvincing and out of place during daylight hours, but at this time of night — with lines of coloured bulbs strung along its dried-grass roofline and the soft glow from the glass-covered candles that flickered on the wooden counter — 'Chi Chi's' felt almost authentic: the atmosphere was warm and relaxed.

Palm trees and pots of trailing jasmine helped soften the look of the paved area next to the pool that sat adjacent to the bar. Sinuous patterns, thrown up by the underwater pool lights, flitted and danced along the walls and balconies overlooking the inner courtyard. A few of the small round tables sheltering in the shade of the large palms were occupied by the last of the evening's drinkers.

In another time, and under different circumstances, Marie could imagine this to be one of those nights that left an imprint. The recollection of which — at some point in the future — would be triggered by a smell or taste, or piece of music that would bring with it a wistful smile: a ghost of a memory in muted shades rather than a vision in glorious Technicolor, but still a night to remember.

269

As she sipped from the rim of her salted cocktail glass, however, Marie knew she would remember this evening for very different reasons.

Finn took a thick bundle of folded dollars from his pocket and peeled off two bills.

'Cornflake cash?' asked Marie.

'Sure is,' he replied.

'How much had you saved up?'

Finn gave her a sideways glance.

'I'm curious to know how much a cornflake box can hold,' she said defensively. 'I'm not sitting here working out my share.'

'About thirty,' replied Finn.

Marie raised her eyebrows. 'Really. Thirty thou? And, do you have it with milk or fruit juice in the morning?'

Finn smiled, but Marie could tell he was still distracted.

'That a family-size box?' she persisted.

'Sure,' replied Finn. 'There's a diary in there too, takes up a bit of room.'

'You keep records?' said Marie sounding surprised.

'Not like a daily diary, more just a collection of notes; stuff I don't want to forget.'

Marie stared into her glass, mulling something over in her mind.

After a while Finn caught the look and asked, 'What you thinking?'

'I'm thinking why does a guy like you have thirty thousand dollars hidden in a cornflake box?'

Finn shifted awkwardly in his seat and shrugged his shoulders. 'I was saving for a rainy

270

day,' was all he said in reply.

Marie was hoping Finn would open up, give her a little more, but it looked like that was all she was going to get. She turned and smiled and tried to make light of it. 'You're picking me up all wrong. Why did you hide the money in a cornflake box instead of a Krunchy-Bugs box? You'd get more into the Krunchy-Bugs.'

'Yeah . . . but then you've got to eat Krunchy-Bugs.'

'Good point,' nodded Marie. 'But they are 'full of oaty goodness'.'

Finn sensed he was being evasive and relented slightly. 'Would you believe me if I told you Ardel and Hud gave it to me?'

'Ardel and Hud?'

'I can tell by your eyebrows kissing your fringe you're having difficulty swallowing that one.'

'Ardel and Hud gave you thirty thousand dollars?'

'Not all at once . . . and not for nothing. We look out for each other, and every now and then they give me a kickback. I don't have much to spend it on, so I save. Over the years it's mounted up.'

'Do you deal for them?

Finn smiled. She didn't mind coming at it head-on. Finn admired her for that. 'No, I cover their backs every now and then — that's it.'

'You never consider sticking it in the bank: earn some interest at least?'

'Can't use a bank.'

' 'Can't' as in you don't know how, or 'can't' because you're not allowed?'

'Not allowed,' replied Finn. 'How am I doing?'

'So far your eyes have stayed focused on me. Haven't strayed over to the left once, so I'm going to say . . . I believe you,' answered Marie as she took another sip of sour. 'One last question: is this a rainy day?'

'This is a monsoon — and chances are high, there's a storm-front coming in right behind,' he replied. Finn wanted to change the subject now. 'You ready to go again?'

'In the time it takes you to order another I'll be finished the rest of this,' replied Marie, lifting her glass. 'This guy really knows how to mix a sour. The ones I serve in McHales don't taste anything like this. It's like a whole different cocktail.'

Finn caught the barman's attention and indicated 'same again' with a wave of his hands. The guy nodded and started mixing the ingredients for another two whiskey sours in a silver shaker.

'I think he uses eggs,' said Finn, 'to smooth out the taste.'

'Eggs. You sure?'

'Maybe just the whites,' said Finn.

'What does he do with the yolks?'

Finn looked at Marie and smiled. 'You getting high already?'

'Why are you saying that?'

'How do I know what he does with the yolks? Who cares?'

Marie cracked a smile. 'I care.' She put her empty glass down and smacked her lips. 'Damn, these are good.'

Marie leant in closer. She was staring into Finn's eyes, giving him that feeling like floating in warm, still shallows.

'What?' he said, giving her some of it back.

'Let's just get in the car and drive up to Cherokee Falls like we planned. I've got a bad feeling about all this.'

All Finn said was, 'It'll be fine,' then turned to look up at the balcony again.

Finn and Marie had been sitting at Chi-Chi's waiting for 'Mr Leonard' for over an hour. The barman had pointed out room 261 to them, and from where they were sitting they had a reasonable view of his balcony.

Finn lifted the house-phone from the bar and dialled the room again: there was still no reply.

'Maybe Vincent Lee Croll got him,' said Marie, pronouncing his name 'Vinshent'.

Finn gave her another look.

'I know I said Vinshent, I was just fooling,' she said, looking right back at him.

'Vincent didn't get him,' said Finn.

'You seem pretty sure.'

'I am sure,' said Finn. 'Did he say anything else, other than tell you he was staying here at the Lakeshore?'

'Said a leprechaun had given him your message and that was why he was here,' said Marie: she'd already told him all this. 'He was very laid-back considering I'd just sprayed a barrel-full of bullets all over the place, even if none of them hit the target. His face was pretty beat up too: like he'd been in a fight, and the other guy was bigger.' Marie paused for a second

273

while she thought, then, 'He said you know who murdered his brother and he wanted to talk.'

Finn sat nodding his head as if this all made sense.

'What you thinking?'

'I'm thinking when Ardel brought you down to the car I should have gone up to the apartment. The guy was right there.'

'But Lee Croll was there too. It would have been suicide. Coming here is bad enough. How do you know you can trust this guy 'Mr Leonard' — not his real name. I found his lying zone too.'

'If it's who I think it is then I can trust him.'

Marie stared at her drink in silence for a few moments. 'Do you know who killed his brother?' she asked eventually.

'I know a lot about what happened,' replied Finn.

'Couldn't you just call this 'Mr Leonard' and tell him over the phone?' asked Marie, a serious tone entering her voice now.

'There's things I need to show him . . . in person.'

'What, like evidence?'

Finn didn't get a chance to answer. The barman slipped a couple of fresh coasters in front of them and placed their drinks on top. 'This for the sours?' he asked, lifting two ten-dollar bills.

Finn nodded, 'Keep the change.'

'Thank you,' said the barman, turning his attention to Marie. 'Excuse me, do we know each other?'

Marie screwed up her face like she was trying to remember and replied, 'I don't think so.'

'You look familiar,' continued the barman. 'You ever lived in Montgomery, or got family there?'

'Is that where you're from?' asked Marie.

'Not originally, but I've lived there for a long time,' he replied. 'You go to high school there maybe?'

'No,' replied Marie. 'I've only ever been there once to visit the Rosa Parks memorial. I was ten years old.'

The barman said, 'My memory don't stretch back ten minutes, so it ain't that. Never mind. Sorry to trouble you.'

'If it comes back to you, let me know,' said Marie, smiling up at him. 'I'm hoping we weren't lovers.'

The barman laughed as he headed off to serve another customer.

Marie turned back to Finn and could tell immediately that something was wrong. He'd pushed his chair back and was standing with his back to her, his body ridged and tensed.

'You okay?'

She followed his line of vision up through the palm trees, past the overhanging Victorian wall-lamps, to room 261.

The light was on and there was a figure moving around in the room.

'Let's just get in the car,' said Marie. 'We haven't heard from Hud or Ardel yet. It might be Lee Croll up there.'

* * *

Danny threw his holdall onto the bed and headed into the bathroom to wash his face. He really needed to shower, but there was no time.

Hud had stood in the apartment giving him the stare — the M10 pointed at the middle of his chest — while Danny tried to convince him he wasn't a threat to O'Hanlon. It was fairly easy to tell something close to the truth; from Lep's message about Finn, to landing in Boston, flying to Birmingham, then the train journey to Tuscaloosa. The only detail he left out was the contract with E. I. O'Leary to kill O'Hanlon. When Ardel appeared from the hallway a few minutes later holding Danny's gun he had to go over it all again. If it hadn't been for the police sirens squealing in the distance he reckoned he'd still be there. It was only when Hud asked him if he'd cleared his prints from the knife sticking out of Croll's throat that Danny knew for certain they believed him, and he was allowed to leave.

Danny checked himself in the mirror. The cuts on his face were largely superficial, but there were still some small slivers of glass left that he had to remove.

Back in the bedroom Danny slid the balcony doors open to let in some air. If he'd looked down at the Hawaiian-style shack in the far corner of the courtyard, he'd have seen the woman calling herself 'Delores' sitting there on her own, staring anxiously up at the window, but he was too preoccupied.

He moved over to the bed and loaded twelve

276

shells into the staggered-line clip of his Walther before sliding it back into the handle. Ardel had thrown it to him just as he was leaving. 'This piece is hot now, bro. Better take it with you,' he'd said.

Danny grabbed a couple of beers from the minibar and left the room.

He crossed the corridor to room 260 and let himself in.

He flipped the tops off the beers and placed them on the carpet by the door, then pulled over a chair from beside the small writing desk in the corner and sat down.

All he could do now was wait.

★ ★ ★

The first beer was still half full when he heard the now-familiar hum of electric motors from the elevator at the other end of the hall. There was a single chime as its doors rattled open.

Danny flipped the safety off, stood up and pressed his eye to the spyhole in the centre of the door.

★ ★ ★

Finn moved warily along the corridor checking the room numbers as he went. He held Marie's Snub Nose loosely by his side. When he got to room 261 he stopped.

The door had been left open: inviting him in. But it was an invitation he was suddenly reluctant to accept. Finn looked up and down the empty corridor then knocked on the door.

There was no answer.

After a few seconds he tried again, but there was still no response. Warily Finn pushed the door ajar, and entered the room.

The light was on in the bathroom and there was a grubby-looking holdall lying on the bed: aside from that, there were no other signs of life.

Finn picked up the holdall and looked inside: empty except for a plastic bag and some bubble wrap. He checked the wardrobes . . . empty too. The sink in the bathroom had some blood smeared around the bowl and the towel hanging over the bath was stained red, but where was 'Mr Leonard'?

Finn walked out onto the balcony. He looked down through the dimly lit trees and saw Marie taking a sip of cocktail. When she saw him she stood, and held up her thumb as if to say 'Everything okay?' Finn shrugged his shoulders: everything fine so far.

The sky was a deep void of purple and black. The warm night air smelled clean and fragrant after the rain, but something wasn't right.

As Finn turned to go back inside he felt the gun digging hard into the back of his neck.

'You have been found guilty of treason against the republican cause and sentenced to death in your absence. I'm here to carry out the will of the Republican Army council and execute you.'

Finn tried to turn, but the gun was pressed even harder. 'Keep facing the front, you dirty fuckin tout, and let your gun drop onto the floor. The only reason you're still alive is because you know something about my brother. It's the likes of you that got him murdered in the first place; so don't even think about fucking me about. This weapon I've got pointing at your skull has a hair trigger.' Danny could feel his anger rising. He stabbed the end of the barrel into Finn's neck again, this time with so much force that it broke through the skin.

A small circle of blood appeared at the base of Finn's skull.

'I've got twelve rounds loaded in here and I'll pump every single one into you if you even think of fucking with me, d'you understand?'

Finn muttered an acknowledgement under his breath.

'Here's what's going to happen,' said Danny through gritted teeth. 'We're going to walk inside and have a wee chat . . . and depending on what you have to say for yourself, you might walk out again. But I warn you, O'Hanlon, it better be fucking good, because I'm your last chance. I'm all that's standing between this life and the next . . . . C'mon, move.'

As he was backed in through the balcony doors Finn glanced down and saw that the bar stool where Marie had been sitting was empty: he hoped she wasn't on her way up.

Suddenly Finn's head snapped backwards. Danny had grabbed him by the hair and pulled him off balance. In the same movement he'd struck Finn hard on the side of his face with the stubby end of the Walther's ridged handle. The sharp, stabbing pain made Finn's legs give way underneath him and he collapsed backwards into

279

the armchair. 'Jesus!' He folded his arms over his head to shield his face from any further blows . . . but for now the assault seemed to be over.

Finn could see that the Walther was no longer pointing at his forehead, but dangling limply by Danny McGuire's side. If he lunged forward now he could easily grab it and twist it from his grasp.

Finn slowly lowered his arms and looked up. Danny was staring back at him, his face blank, lacking any expression whatsoever. It was as if he had suddenly been struck dumb. His breathing was short and laboured and the hand holding his gun had started to shake and tremble. The only sounds that could be heard inside the room were the palm fronds, brushing against each other in the gentle breeze outside, and the occasional incomprehensible murmur wafting up from the poolside bar.

Danny tried to speak, but the words seemed to catch in his throat, like they were too difficult. There was a question he wanted answered. It was the reason he'd made the journey to find O'Hanlon. It was the reason his hand was now shaking uncontrollably. But Danny could barely breathe. He had tears streaming down his face.

Sitting in front of him was the man who could give him the answer to the question that had plagued his every waking hour for the last eight years, but now, suddenly, there was no reason to ask it.

Danny recognised the man sitting in the chair, but his name was not Finn O'Hanlon.

Suddenly Finn bowed his head forward and

mumbled quietly, 'I'm sorry for everything I've done, Danny, but I had no choice.' He paused for a few moments before slowly rising to his feet and taking a step forward. 'I'm sorry, Wub.'

There were only two people in the world who called Danny by his nickname, and one of them — Lep McFarlane — was dead: the other was his brother, Sean McGuire, who now stood before Danny with his arms outstretched.

He was speaking again. 'I have no right to ask, Wub, but I need all the forgiveness you have in you.'

'Are you the Thevshi?' asked Danny through his sobs.

Sean's eyes were focused: staring straight back at him, letting him know that this was the truth. 'No.'

Only then did Danny open his arms and accept his brother's embrace. The only thought going through his mind at that moment was to hold on and never let go.

29

Marie had a recurring nightmare. She was a lawyer defending a major criminal. The judge would ask questions she didn't know the answer to. When her client was in the dock, she couldn't remember his name and constantly had to refer to her notes, but the pages in front of her were always blank. She'd been given the case by mistake, but there was no one to tell. When she woke up she was always left with the vague sense that she didn't really know what the hell was going on in her life.

It was the same feeling she had now: only this wasn't a dream.

Marie was frowning. She couldn't figure out what was bothering her more: the rising body count and the fact that Vincent Lee Croll had found them so easily, or what had happened earlier in the motel room, when Finn had avoided making love to her.

He wanted her, no doubt about it, but something was holding him back. They'd started to kiss, the attraction and intensity definitely there, but suddenly Finn had pulled away, saying, 'No, this is not what you want.' She had to stop herself from shouting at him, 'It is what I want, please just fuck me.' Maybe she was reading too

282

much into it all, not seeing the situation as it really was. But Marie was certain of one thing: she was falling in love with this man.

On the journey from Finn's apartment he'd wanted to hear every detail of what happened with Croll and the other guy calling himself Mr Leonard. When she mentioned Lep's name Finn's whole demeanour suddenly changed. He had smiled and nodded to himself like somehow he'd been expecting this news. The idea had been to head for Cherokee Falls — lie low for a few days before crossing the state line — but straight away he'd asked her to turn the car round and head back to Tuscaloosa. He didn't say why, in fact he didn't say another word for the rest of the journey.

She'd tried to ask him what the hell was going on: why were they heading back? But it was like Finn disappeared right in front of her: no longer available, his mind switched on to something else. Eventually she'd given up.

He didn't come alive again until they were sitting at the bar.

'Just to let you know, we getting to last orders. You still got some in here.' The barman was holding the silver shaker in his right hand and Marie's glass in his left. 'You want to finish it off and order another, or you all done?'

'I'll just finish what's in there,' she replied.

'You live in Tuscaloosa?'

'I think so. I'm not sure any more.'

'You want me to call your mommy: get her to come pick you up? You're looking like you is lost.'

Marie smiled. 'You're very perceptive, but I'm fine, thank you.'

'You here on a visit?'

'Sort of.'

'What you work at?'

'I used to be a barmaid.'

'No kidding.'

The guy was short and heavy-set with dark shiny hair and a moustache: his accent was either Mexican or Spanish. The way he pronounced 'kidding' like 'keeding' gave Marie a kick.

'If I was kidding I'd come up with a better vocation than barmaid. No offence,' said Marie.

'Ees okay,' replied the barman. 'I trained as an accountant, but for some reason no one in America wants a Mexican looking after their money.'

Marie didn't feel much like talking, but the guy seemed okay and she knew herself how tedious serving drinks could be.

'I didn't think you were from Montgomery,' said Marie, giving the guy an opening.

'Lived there from when I was thirteen. I'm from Chimalhuacán in Mexico originally: right bang in the middle. It's so hot there in the summer you climb into the oven to cool off. Your husband looks like he got something big weighing him down. Making his head sag.'

'He's not my husband,' said Marie.

'Your boyfriend?'

'I don't know how you would describe him. I don't think there's a category for what he is.'

'So long as he treats you okay, ees the main thing.'

'You still got the accent pretty strong.'

'My wife's from there too. We speak Spanish to each other every day is probably why.'

'That where you learned to mix such great sours?' she said.

'Thank you! It's the egg-white finishes them off. My grandma showed me how to do it. She used to travel to the coast every day and make them on the beach for the tourists.'

'What did she do with the yolk?'

'You're the first person's ever asked me that. Hangover cure: very popular. In Chimalhuacán everybody likes to drink: round here's the same, but *here* everyone pretends they don't.'

'So you punish them with egg-yolks?'

'Mix a shot of brandy, some honey and a couple of egg-yolks in the blender for ten seconds, with a little tomato juice and hot paprika. My grandma called it a 'Bloody Headache' . . . Actually it's not so bad.'

Marie screwed her face up. 'Sounds disgusting.'

'It works. Guaranteed. Twenty minutes later you're all set to start boozing again.'

'How much of it you supposed to drink?'

'You don't drink it. It's a chest-rub. Ees only in Alabama they drink it.'

Marie stared at the barman.

'No, I is just keeding with you.'

Marie laughed out loud, then noticed the barman glance over her shoulder towards the reception area. Next thing he was leaning in towards her — a bit too close — his face suddenly serious. 'Listen, I don't want to get caught up in any trouble or nothing,' he said under his breath. 'Seems to me like you're a nice lady, but there are cops in the lobby and I'm pretty sure they ain't here to check in. Don't turn round, cause they're looking this way right now,' he continued, keeping his face straight like they were discussing the weather.

Marie felt a sudden rush of anxiety and had to fight to stop herself from pushing back and running.

'I just remember where I know you from. You're the barmaid from McHales right? You been on the news.'

Marie couldn't hide the look of shock: she didn't know what to say.

The barman stopped whispering and started talking in his normal voice: answering a question she hadn't asked.

'The ladies' restroom: sure. It's over the other side of the pool in the far corner. If you head for the red exit sign you can't miss it.'

A guy she didn't even know was telling her where the exit was, sticking his neck out for her. Marie pulled a fifty from her purse and put it down on the counter.

'Thank you,' she said.

'Hey lady, the drinks have already been paid for.' He picked the fifty-dollar note up and handed it back to her. 'Thank you, but I don't want your money. Seems to me like you going to need it more than me. And just so you know: it wasn't me who called the cops.'

He reached to wipe his cloth over the bar.

Marie made her way round the pool towards

the exit sign. She looked up and saw Finn standing on the balcony with his head bowed forward like he was staring at something on the floor below his feet. Marie was praying he'd look towards her — see her leaving so she could signal to him that something was wrong — but if she waved up at him it would draw attention.

It was difficult to tell because of the foliage obscuring her view, but the way Finn was standing, something about his posture, didn't look right.

Suddenly his head tipped forward violently as though he'd been struck from behind. She wanted to call up to him, check he was okay, but two sheriff's deputies were marching towards the bar followed closely by another couple of guys she recognised as Kneller and his sidekick Evelyn. That's when she noticed 'Mr Leonard' standing behind Finn holding a gun to his head.

Until now it had all seemed like a bit of fun, an exciting, weird, distraction from her mundane life, but as Marie scrambled up the stairs to the second floor she couldn't decide if it was the sours or the situation, or both, but something was making her feel like throwing up.

The corridor in front of her swept round in a long dark curve. Marie focused on the ever-decreasing door numbers as she ran past: odds to her right, evens to her left. 267, 265, 263, 261.

For the first time in her life she didn't need someone to tell her what to do. Without hesitating she stepped backwards, then lunged at the door with the full weight of her body.

The door slammed back on its hinges and crashed against the wall.

She'd been certain she was going to find Finn lying in a pool of blood, with Mr Leonard standing over him and smoke trailing out of his gun. But the scene that greeted her was very different.

The two men were standing holding each other, locked in a tight embrace.

She could see glints of light reflected off the steady stream of tears trickling down Finn's face.

As Marie edged further into the room Finn lifted his head and stared at her, but said nothing. She was suddenly aware that she was intruding on an intensely private moment.

It was Marie who broke the silence. She had no choice. In a hushed but urgent tone she said, 'There are cops everywhere. We've got to get the hell out of here, right now. They're in the lobby.'

The 'Leonard' guy suddenly pulled away from Finn and bent down to pick up his gun.

★   ★   ★

Joe Evelyn was waiting patiently at the top of the main stairwell for Jeff Kneller to come up in the elevator. Kneller's lungs were so shot through with tar he couldn't make it up a flight of stairs without having to rest. The last two years he'd only just made it through the annual medical, and he'd been warned to quit or face an early retirement notice.

The only way to get Kneller to quit smoking would be to shoot him in the heart. His family

288

doctor had done just that, according to Kneller. He'd told him he had terminal cancer. Kneller had known the guy from school: asked him not to share the information with anyone. Begged the guy not to write it up, and to pretend that Kneller hadn't made it to the appointment. The doctor had agreed, but only if he quit smoking and applied for early retirement.

The lift doors chimed open and Kneller emerged through a swirl of grey-blue smoke.

'You ain't supposed to be smoking in the elevator,' said Evelyn.

'Says who?' replied Kneller.

'The sign there says 'no smoking'.'

'That's for the guests. I'm just passing through.'

'So are the guests,' said Evelyn, unclipping his standard-issue Walther from its holster and checking it was good to go. 'You ain't supposed to be smoking at all.'

'We really should get married, you and me,' said Kneller, doing the same with his gun. 'Formalise the nagging.'

The two deputies Kneller had sent up the back stairwell were waiting patiently outside room 261. One either side of the door: both with their weapons drawn.

Kneller and Evelyn lowered their voices as they approached.

'We got a game plan?' asked Evelyn.

'Sure,' replied Kneller, stepping up to the door and kicking it open. *FBI. Nobody fucking move.*

The two deputies jumped in behind Kneller

289

and took up firing positions. Evelyn edged in beside them with his arms outstretched, clutching his weapon, finger on the trigger, sweeping the room.

'You sure it was 261?' asked Kneller, lowering his gun.

'S'what the girl on reception said,' replied Evelyn.

'So where the fuck is everyone?'

★   ★   ★

In the pale green glow from the dashboard, Danny's face looked tense and drawn. He felt like he was drowning and didn't know which way was up: didn't know what direction to swim in to break the surface.

The blue shield on the overhead gantry said 'Route 82: Greenwood, Tupelo', and 'Route 20/59: Birmingham'. The nearest state was Mississippi, just west of Tuscaloosa on the 82, but Danny turned right, heading north-east to the state of Georgia — which was much further. He'd travel through Birmingham as far as Anniston then leave the highway in favour of the smaller, less obvious back roads: hopefully cross the state line before daybreak then head straight for Atlanta. He needed a town big enough to disappear in for a few days, while he figured out what to do.

There wasn't much traffic on the freeway. It meant he could make better time, but the drawback was that the Cadillac would be easier to spot.

The car surged forward as Danny pressed his foot against the soft, yielding accelerator pedal. He was anxious to put some distance between himself and Tuscaloosa.

The first thing he had to do was find somewhere quiet and get Finn and Marie out of the boot.

30

Birmingham, Alabama, Easter Monday, early

The tall glass office block sat on the corner of Third Avenue and Highway Sixty-five, with a view north-east all the way up to the international airport. Every so often a plane on its final approach would fly in low, making a noise like it was going to land on the roof.

The Birmingham skyline twinkled and shimmered in the hazy dawn light. Streams of red brake lights and rivers of white headlamps meandered and criss-crossed in the busy streets below as the people of Alabama headed into work.

A television in the corner of the office was throwing shadows mutely around the otherwise dimly lit room on the top floor.

Hernando De Garza checked his fingernails — the girl who usually gave him a manicure wouldn't be in for a few days and it looked like one of them was chipped. He frowned, and continued what he was saying. His voice was soft, with a barely detectable sibilance.

'All I'm saying is it's turning into a very different scenario. We'd have to think real hard about helping you any further. It's getting hot out there even in the shade. We got two dead cops, and a couple of junkie hitmen fucking us in the ass from beyond the grave. Alabama is crawling with officers of the law.' Hernando smoothed his eyebrow over with his middle finger before continuing in his heavy southern drawl. 'There's talk it's gone Federal. The FBI all cleaning their noses ready to have a good sniff around.'

Hernando looked over for a reaction. 'Culo Conrado and Vincent Lee Croll were sub-contractors. They wouldn't have been our first choice so whether they is alive or dead don't matter a fuck. But what is of concern is your employee — Danny McGuire. So far he has failed to deliver . . . on all fronts. I'm sitting here with two Stinger missiles I put a lot of effort into procuring for you and all I got to show for it is a Federal fucking headache and an empty wallet. McGuire hasn't shown up with our money, which is discourteous at best. And the word I'm hearing is that the target, your guy O'Hanlon, is still slinking around Tuscaloosa. The hit on O'Hanlon was a favour. The money for the Surface-to-Airs is non-negotiable and is now owing.'

The guy sitting opposite De Garza in the faded blue jeans and worn-out bomber jacket didn't look too happy. He wanted to tell Hernando to fuck off. He wanted to tell the queenie little asshole that if he had employed professionals instead of a couple of ex-junkie fuck-ups like Conrado and Croll then there would be nothing to discuss, there would be no situation. But he was under orders. Owen O'Brien had been on his way to the finals of the tug-of-war in Oshkosh when E.I. had called to say De Garza wasn't happy. 'You're the most senior man out there and the closest,' E.I. had told him. 'Get on a plane and find out what the fuck's happened to Danny, and do whatever it takes to keep De Garza sweet before this turns into an international incident.'

He'd left plenty of messages at the hotel asking Danny to get in touch, but there had been no response.

When E.I. had mentioned to him that he had given Danny the contract to hit O'Hanlon, Owen had voiced his concerns. He'd had a bad feeling about McGuire's involvement and now things were beginning to unravel it looked like he'd been right.

O'Brien stared right back at De Garza: orders or not, he wasn't going to take any shit from him. 'We didn't realise we were paying for sub-contractors,' he replied. 'We thought — the amount of money it was costing — we were getting pros. And as far as the Stingers are concerned we were only ever going to pay up once we'd checked they were legit.'

Hernando stopped studying his fingers and looked up: deciding whether or not to pull the Magnum out from the desk drawer and shoot the ugly Irish fucker where he sat. He waited for a few moments wrestling with the impulse to kill him, right here in his office.

'You got what you paid for,' said Sly from the other side of the room, picking up on the expression on Hernando's face. 'And you heard what Mr De Garza just said. So far you have paid us fuck-all, so you got nothing to bitch about. We've done everything you asked.' Sly pointed at the open wooden crate sitting on the floor in the middle of the room. What d'you think that is? You don't think that big green gun in there with FIM-92 painted on the side is fucking legit? You want me to make it live and fire one up your ass so you can decide for yourself if it's gonna explode or not?' Sly shook his head before continuing. 'D'you use your head for cleaning the floor in Ireland — cause you got nothing in there but a fuckin vacuum?'

Hernando De Garza held up his hand like a cop stopping the traffic. 'Hold on, here comes the news. This is why I got the television on: I want you to see this. I mean it's the fucking headlines, you know? Turn it up, Sly.'

Sly pushed himself off the picture window he'd been leaning against and walked over to the television. His black cotton trousers were stretched to the limit over his well-defined thigh muscles. He wiggled his hips like a dancer and made a big thing of bending over to turn the volume up. Showing his ass to De Garza, he flicked a cheeky glance at O'Brien, who turned and looked out the window.

'Sly, get your whore's ass out of the way, and go sit down: I can't see a fucking thing,' snapped Hernando.

'The way Mr O'Brien been staring at me I figure he wants to make a deposit in my prison wallet. I'm just giving him a preview,' replied Sly.

The lady on television with the white polished teeth and phoney smile was talking to camera: playing it straight. Normally she did the lighter items: how to make your butt look good in a bikini, how to make your face ten years younger using only cold cream and aloe vera, how to cook the perfect sponge cake: aspirational nonsense for housewives, or the long-term unemployed. But here she was now, with the same puffed-up hairstyle, struggling to sell the serious stuff. The graphic behind her read WANTED FOR MURDER in bright red Courier, stamped across a mugshot of Marie Bain and an identikit photograph of Finn O'Hanlon.

'The hunt for two-time cop killer Vincent Lee Croll came to a gruesome end last night when his body was discovered at an apartment in Cottondale. In a statement issued by the Sheriff's Department it was revealed that officers also attended the Lakeshore Hotel in Tuscaloosa in connection with the ongoing investigation. No arrests were made, but it is believed that Finn O'Hanlon and barmaid Marie Bain — both now suspects in the fatal shooting at McHales Bar in downtown Tuscaloosa last Thursday — are also linked to the incident involving Lee Croll in Cottondale. The couple were spotted at the Lakeshore Hotel, but managed to evade capture despite a large police presence. FBI agent Jeff Kneller, leading the investigation, told ASN that O'Hanlon is considered dangerous and should not be approached by members of the public. Marie Bain, formerly a witness, became a suspect when a letter linking her to O'Hanlon was discovered at her apartment. Detective Kneller appealed for any witnesses to come forward . . .'

Hernando De Garza had stopped listening.

'She just finished telling everyone how dangerous the guy is, now she's asking people to come forward as witnesses. You ever heard anything so dumb?' De Garza looked over at Owen O'Brien and held out his upturned hands as he shrugged his shoulders. 'You see what I'm sayin: 'FBI agent'. All of a sudden we got the FBI sniffing our butts. It's like we're standing in a gas station pumping gasoline all over the forecourt and we got a lit cigarette in our mouth. Won't be too long before the whole fucking thing blows up in our faces. And what the hell is she doing reading the news anyway? Where's the guy with the wig, usually does it, what happened, he dead or something?'

Sly pulled the cigarette from his mouth and said through a cloud of smoke, 'He's sick. Got something wrong with his throat, means he can't talk. They done a piece on him earlier like it was a news item.'

'The way she says 'murder' makes it sound like something you get done in the beauty parlour,' interrupted De Garza.

'She didn't say 'murder': it's on the board behind her,' said Sly. 'They just suggesting those things to you to make you believe those two is guilty. Then when the cops catch them you've already convicted them in your head. Straight away you think the cops have done a good job and the world's a safer place.'

Hernando turned to O'Brien and raised his eyebrows.

'Sly survived fifteen years in Santa Martha so

297

he reckons he got it all figured out. Got these notions in his head, every time we watch the television or pick up a newspaper we're being manipulated . . . when in actual fact he's just a paranoid schizophrenic. You heard her say 'murder', yeah?'

Owen O'Brien shrugged. He wasn't really paying attention to what De Garza and his freaky 'cousin' Sly were saying: he was busy trying to figure out from the identikit photograph where he'd seen Finn O'Hanlon before. Hernando didn't wait for an answer, before continuing. 'All I'm saying is, she's way too light for the main headlines; she should stick to the fluff.'

'You want me to send a couple of the guys round and chop her fuckin head off for you?' said Sly.

Hernando laughed. 'What good's that gonna do?'

'Might improve her hairstyle,' said Sly, giggling like a five-year-old girl.

Owen O'Brien suddenly stood up from the sofa. 'Jesus fucking Christ!'

Sly was on his feet holding a Colt revolver in his hand like he'd done a magic trick. Hernando too: he'd slipped his hands under the desk and unclipped a small semi-automatic from a leather pouch concealed on the side panel of the drawer set. Neither of them looked too happy.

'What you jumping up so fast for, Mr O'Brien? You making Sly all nervous, you gonna end up with a bullet rattling around in your skull. You standing there so tight you nearly picked up that sofa with your ass. You listening to

298

me, my friend? You okay? You look like you seen a ghost.'

Owen O'Brien looked grave. 'I'm grand, Mr De Garza, just grand,' he said, his tone much less antagonistic than it had been just moments earlier. 'E. I. O'Leary appreciates everything you've done for us and sends his sincere apologies. I have half the money we owe you right here.' O'Brien lifted the small black holdall at his feet and placed it on the coffee table in front of him. 'The other half is thirty thousand feet over the Atlantic as we speak, on its way here. It'll be delivered to you first thing tomorrow morning if that's acceptable.' O'Brien was suddenly desperate to get out of there. 'I hope that's okay,' he concluded.

'Can't think there's ever been a time when receiving money isn't acceptable, Mr O'Brien,' replied Hernando. 'Why didn't you say you had it with you? We could have saved ourselves some unpleasantries. Tomorrow will be fine for the rest of it, as long as it's delivered no later than the close of play or I'll start shooting every fucking Irishman I see, on sight. Sly here'll show you out. Normally I'd get him to drive you wherever you want to go, but I think under the circumstances the less contact we have the better. You never know who's watching these days. You in a hotel?'

'The Radisson.'

'Not too far to walk,' said Hernando, dropping his head down like he was busy with something more important on the desk.

'I wondered if there was any chance — '

299

O'Brien started to say, but Sly interrupted him, 'No.'

O'Brien and Sly stared each other in the eye.

'No what? You don't even know what I'm going to say.'

'I don't give a fuck what you're going to say, your time's up. Mr De Garza is busy now. Can't you see?' Sly was already standing by the executive lift, beckoning O'Brien over.

The lift doors pinged open and Sly stood aside to let O'Brien past.

'I think maybe I'll take you in the rear . . . Sorry, *out* the rear,' said Sly, giving O'Brien another cheeky smirk: playing the court jester now for De Garza's amusement. O'Brien caught the half smile on Hernando De Garza's face as the lift doors slid shut.

The two men stood in silence, Sly with a grin on his face and O'Brien watching the illuminated numbers decreasing as the private lift descended towards the basement. Eventually there was a slight shudder and it came to a stop.

As the doors squeaked open O'Brien took a step forward then spun round quickly from the waist and delivered a thick left hook that caught Sly full on the face. His head snapped back and smacked against the mirrored wall with a loud crack, then he slid — semi-conscious — to the ground, leaving a thin smear of blood marking the length of his fall.

'That'll wipe the grin off your face, ya cheeky fucker,' said O'Brien as he leant over and pulled Sly's Colt from the shoulder holster concealed under his jacket. Sly let out a low groan.

'What was that? You'd like another one? Sure enough!' said O'Brien.

He held the Colt high above his head then swung it in a wide arc across Sly's face. 'I wasn't told anything about keeping *you* on-side.'

* * *

Owen O'Brien waited for the lights to change before crossing to the telephone kiosks on the other side of the busy junction. It was common practice around the world for law-enforcement agencies to bug kiosks in the immediate vicinity of well-known criminals' residences or places of work, so he'd walked a couple of blocks north from De Garza's building. He also wanted to make sure no one was following him and take a little time to think. The news item he'd just witnessed in De Garza's office had set his mind racing.

O'Brien fed some coins into the slot then listened for the familiar UK ring-tone.

Only when the correct code word was given would he start talking. If he didn't hear anything or the code word was wrong he'd hang up immediately and walk away. Usually the person at the other end would just listen, but O'Brien knew tonight would be different.

'Peace Brother.'

'The beginning of philosophy.'

O'Brien launched straight in.

'Slim?'

'Yeh.'

'You know who I am?'

'Of course!'

'I've just seen a dead person on the news.'

'Eh?'

'Sean McGuire is not dead, I'll say it again — not dead.'

'What the hell are you talking about?'

Owen had to talk fast before the money ran out.

'Everyone including the cops is looking for Finn O'Hanlon. It's all over the news here. But O'Hanlon is Sean McGuire.'

'Jesus Christ!'

'God knows how all this'll hit the ground, but I can guarantee there'll be blood enough to turn the Shannon red. We need insurance. Get McGuire's ma and the missus in detention as quick as possible and tell no one. Not a soul. I need to talk to The Farmer, but I want to do it in person. You're the only one who knows this information, Slim. If this leaks out before I get back you're dead: understand?'

'Understood,' replied Slim. 'D'you want the daughter too?'

'All of them.'

'Sean McGuire, Jesus, eh?' said Slim.

'Big fella?'

'What?'

'Put the kettle on, I'm coming home early.'

The line went dead as the coins tumbled into the belly of the telephone.

31

Órlaith had run out of ideas of who to phone. It was the fifth call she'd made: after this there was only one other person she could try.

The young girl on the other end of the line said, 'I'm sorry Mrs McGuire, I don't know. D'you want to speak to my ma again?'

'Don't worry, pet. Yes, put her on would you?'

There was a moment's silence while the young girl passed the phone to her mother.

'Sorry about that, Órlaith! Let us know what happens and be sure to call us if we can help. I'm sure she'll turn up. Have you tried Betty Devlin? Niamh's probably round there.'

'She's next on my list. Thanks anyway, Lucy. Sorry to have troubled you.'

'No trouble at all, hon. Keep us posted. I'll call you if I hear anything this end.'

Órlaith held down the black buttons on top of the phone for a few seconds before dialling again.

'Betty? It's me! You haven't seen our Niamh, have you? She's not come home. I just wondered if she's round there playing with Lisa?'

'She's not here, Órlaith, I'm sorry,' answered Betty Devlin. 'Hold on and I'll ask Lisa if she's seen her.'

Órlaith heard Betty shouting to her daughter,

303

and Lisa's small voice in the background, innocent, unaware of the impact her words would have as she replied. 'Yeah, she went in the car with the men. They said they would take her home.' Órlaith immediately felt the knot in her stomach tighten and had to concentrate hard not to throw up.

'Jesus! Órlaith, did you hear that?' asked Betty. Órlaith couldn't speak: she could barely breathe.

★　★　★

Just over forty miles away in Belfast, Angela Fitzpatrick was sitting in the back of a maroon-coloured Vauxhall Astra staring out of the window at what passed for normal life. Her hair was scraped back off her face and what little make-up she was wearing did nothing to disguise the fact that she looked drawn and tired. She'd just finished a long shift at the Royal Victoria Hospital on the Falls Road and had been looking forward to nipping into Shannon's Café for one of their famous home-made sausage sandwiches before heading home for a long hot soak and a few hours' sleep. She was hungry: wishing now she'd taken up the offer of lunch in the staff canteen.

The weedy guy in the driver's seat kept checking the rear-view mirror like he was expecting her to disappear.

The guy sitting next to her on the back seat with the handgun digging into her side didn't look like he needed to eat anything else for the rest of his life. He was known as Slim Jim McMahon and had a huge stomach bulging over his tautly stretched tri-colour snake belt. Her nurse's training had him down as a candidate for late-onset diabetes.

They were travelling south on the Lisburn Road past shops and bars she knew well. Today, however, they appeared alien to her, almost like she was seeing them for the first time. Even the people in the street seemed different. It reminded her of arriving in a foreign country and driving in from the airport: everything familiar, but somehow unrecognisable: her perceptions coloured by fear.

The situation she found herself in was linked with Danny McGuire, but she had no idea how, or in what way. For the first time since she had met him, Angela wished she had driven past the half-naked figure she'd found collapsed by the roadside.

'If we're going somewhere posh I'll have to go home first and change,' she said, trying her best to sound casual.

There was no response.

She had tried a few times to get a conversation going, but each time she had been ignored. Neither of the men had spoken a word to Angela since they'd grabbed her in the street and bundled her into the back of the car. 'If you're the taxi I ordered, you're heading in the wrong direction.'

The big guy with the gut gave her a sideways glance. 'If you don't keep your gobby mouth shut you'll get a punch in the fuckin jaw, all right? Keep it buttoned.'

Angela pressed her knees together to try to stop them trembling. She turned her face to peer out of the window, hoping that Slim Jim couldn't see the tears rolling down her cheek.

No one spoke again for the rest of the journey.

★ ★ ★

The telephone started to ring. Órlaith jerked her head up and snatched the receiver from its cradle.

'Hello.'

'Órlaith?'

'Jesus Christ! Where the hell are you?'

'Órlaith, I've got no time so just listen. You, Niamh and Ma need to get out of there. Don't take anything with you. Use the money Angela gave you to buy whatever you need, but get out of there now. Don't go to your sister's or your ma's, d'you hear me Órlaith? Nowhere anyone would think to look!'

'What the hell's going on?'

'Go to the hotel you had your honeymoon in. Go there and wait for me to call, but you have to go now. And tell no one, not a soul, d'you understand, Órlaith? Órlaith, are you there . . . *Órlaith?*'

'You're too late,' whispered Órlaith. 'They've got her, they've already got Niamh.'

On the other end of the phone she heard Danny cursing.

'And Eillean McGuigan called here yesterday,' continued Órlaith. 'Quig has been murdered.

That's Eamon Ò Ruairc and Quig McGuigan both murdered in one week.' Órlaith started screaming down the phone. *'What's going on? What the fuck is happening Danny? They've taken Niamh, for fucksake.'*

'I'm coming home, Órlaith, and I'm going to fix everything, okay? Just get yourself and Ma away from the house as quickly as possible . . . I'm going to fix it.'

★   ★   ★

The Vauxhall Astra making its way through the quiet housing development in the north of Newry took a sharp right and drove into the garage of a small semi-detached house. The house was painted the same 'council cream' as all the others and had nothing to distinguish it from every other two-up, two-down on the estate.

The skinny guy got out first and pulled the shuttered doors down behind them, plunging the garage into darkness. The car door flew open and Angela was dragged out and shoved towards the internal door connecting the garage to the house.

The skinny guy pushed her through into a dim, airless hallway that smelled of damp and decay. At the other end of the hall she could see the dark, distorted outline of two figures gesturing animatedly behind the mottled glass of the kitchen door. There was a heated argument taking place, but the conversation was too muted to hear clearly.

'Up here,' said the skinny guy, pointing to a steep set of stairs that led up to a half landing.

Slim Jim McMahon was standing behind her, digging the gun into the small of her back. 'She's to go in the same room as the other one,' he said.

The skinny guy nodded back at him. 'Sure enough.'

The bedroom walls were draped in a black fabric and the windows had been boarded over with the curtains still in place. From the outside it gave the impression that the curtains were drawn, but it was really just a makeshift prison cell. Aside from a single metal-framed chair placed in the centre, there was no other furniture in the room. The carpet around the chair was heavily stained and the air choked with a rotting smell that made Angela gag. When her eyes had fully adjusted to the darkness Angela noticed the young girl cowering silently in the corner of the room. 'Dear God,' she exclaimed. Angela recognised her straight away. 'You're Niamh, aren't you? I met you the other day with your ma.' The look of fear on the young girl's face made Angela instinctively reach out to her. 'Come on over here, love, you're all right. I won't let those animals lay a finger on you.'

*   *   *

Kathleen McGuire stood on the top stair, looking down at the crumpled figure of her daughter-in-law sitting at the foot of the stairs, weeping silently, her hands cupped over her face. An image flashed into Kathleen McGuire's

308

mind. She saw herself sitting in exactly the same position, years earlier, when she had heard the news of her son Sean's death. Kathleen knew instinctively that something terrible had happened.

'What's going on, Órlaith?'

Órlaith struggled to answer through her tears. 'Someone's taken her.'

Kathleen McGuire's knuckles whitened as her grip tightened on the banister.

'They've taken Niamh,' continued Órlaith. 'Danny called. We have to leave here right away.'

'We'd better get going then,' replied Kathleen.

★   ★   ★

Danny stood clutching a twenty-dollar bill in his hand, trying to attract the attention of the man serving coffee at the other end of the counter.

The 'Must-go-Jean' truck-stop café was quiet, but the guy was engaged in a conversation with a heavily tattooed truck driver who had pulled in off the road just in front of Danny. From the length of time it was taking to pour one coffee it was obvious the two knew each other. Neither of them seemed in much of a hurry.

Eventually the guy serving looked over his shoulder at Danny.

'Be right with you.'

Danny had to wait another few minutes while the truck driver's order was shouted through to the kitchen.

'Sorry for the delay! Sinner Joe was just telling me why he was late. Usually here exact same time every week. Never missed it yet. What can I get you?'

Danny held up the twenty. 'I just need some change for the phone.'

'Much d'you need?'

'The whole twenty if you can.'

The guy made a clicking noise in the side of his mouth. 'Be lucky to get you five, but I'll have a look.'

The guy moved over to the till and sprung the drawer open.

'This morning he's over an hour late so I'm thinking something must be wrong, maybe he's got the shits again or maybe he's been in an accident, but I'm wrong on both counts . . . Can do you three in quarters, that any good to you?'

'Whatever you have,' replied Danny, doing his best to stop himself from dragging the guy over the counter. He'd been waiting for nearly ten minutes already and the guy hadn't stopped talking once.

'If it's long-distance you can use the phone on the wall there and do a reverse charge. Sinner Joe says the tailback's got to be three or four miles long up on the 59. He's just after telling me he's late cause of the roadblocks. Sheriffs are stopping every goddamn vehicle on the road. Just do it to inconvenience the whole population, seems to me. Did the exact same thing a few years ago looking for a shipment of guns and didn't find a goddamn thing: not so much as a stray bullet. Too many ways to go other than the 59 if you're a smuggler. Upshot was they caught a lot of locals with weapons they wasn't supposed to have, and no permits. In the end they had to declare an amnesty cause no one was gonna vote the sheriff back in again if he was gonna start pushing for prosecution. What you gonna do?'

Danny looked up from the counter. He'd only been half listening.

The guy gave him a strange look. 'You want the quarters or you gonna use the phone on the wall?'

★   ★   ★

Someone was banging at the front door.

Órlaith stood frozen at the head of the stairs with a small holdall slung over her shoulder and a case filled with clothes hanging by her side. She cursed under her breath. She had spent nearly half an hour gathering some things together: clothes for Niamh, et cetera, but now, as the door rattled again, she wished she had done exactly what Danny had told her and left the house straight away.

Mrs McGuire was waiting for her in the kitchen downstairs.

'Kathleen!' whispered Órlaith as loudly as she dared. 'Kathleen!'

'What?'

'Head out the back and wait for me at the top of the lane.'

The banging stopped momentarily and Órlaith heard the flap on the letterbox being lifted. Both women stood still, barely daring to breathe.

After a few moments the banging started again.

311

Órlaith slowly made her way down the stairs, lifting the case one step at a time in front of her. She was just over halfway when the phone started ringing. The sudden noise startled her and caused her to lose hold of the case.

She watched helplessly as it tumbled down the remaining steps and crashed into the small table at the bottom of the stairs.

The flap lifted again. This time she could see eyes peering through the letterbox, staring straight at her.

'Off on a trip, Órlaith? Nice! Let us in, we'd like a wee word.'

Órlaith didn't answer. She descended the rest of the stairs as quickly as possible and grabbed the suitcase.

There was a loud thud. Whoever was outside was trying to kick the door in. Each blow ripped the screws holding the lock out a little further until eventually the door was ready to give.

They were shouting through the letterbox again.

'Be a shame to miss your daughter's funeral. C'mon, open the door.'

The telephone was still ringing.

Órlaith ran into the kitchen and grabbed a long carving knife from one of the drawers then headed back along the short hallway towards the front door. There was another loud crack as the lock finally gave way. But the door only opened three or four inches: it was held in place by a taut brass chain.

A hand appeared through the gap: the fingers fumbling around trying to free the chain from its holder.

Órlaith didn't hesitate. She raised the knife and plunged it as hard as she could into the back of the hand. There was a scream as the attacker tried to pull free, but the knife had driven all the way through. It was acting like a split pin: preventing the hand from being withdrawn. Every attempt caused the knife to cut deeper into the flesh.

Órlaith started kicking against the door and screaming at the top of her voice. 'Touch her and I'll kill every fucking one of you. Every . . . fucking . . . one.'

There was a loud splintering of wood and glass as the first shot was fired. A hole appeared halfway down the door followed quickly by another, then another just above it.

Órlaith turned and ran, leaving the phone still ringing.

★ ★ ★

'C'mon, pick up, for God's sake.'

Danny slammed the receiver against the cradle in frustration. A few seconds later he dialled the operator again. 'I'd like to make a reverse-charge call please . . . Northern Ireland . . . sure.' Danny read out the number and listened as the operator asked the person on the other end if they would accept the charges.

'Hold on, sir, and I'll put you through,' said the operator eventually.

'Hello?'

'Mrs Fitzpatrick, it's Danny here, I need to speak to Angela.'

313

'She's not here. She hasn't come back from work and I haven't heard from her. It's not like her at all. I was hoping that was her on the phone.'

Danny felt a familiar feeling in the pit of his stomach.

'I'm sure she'll be in touch,' he lied. 'If you just let her know I called.'

'If you talk to her first will you tell her to phone and let me know she's safe?'

'Sure enough.'

Danny hung up.

Someone was rounding up members of his family as an insurance policy. That could only mean one thing: they knew he hadn't killed Finn O'Hanlon. There was even the possibility they knew the reason why. But who could have told them?

And who would want Quig McGuigan dead?

It wasn't just the names that appeared on the list that were being targeted, but anyone who had handled the list. Danny stared blankly at the wall for a few moments then dialled another number.

'My name's Danny McGuire. Can you put me through to Mr De Garza?'

★ ★ ★

Sinner Joe watched the young man slam the receiver back on the wall and walk out of the café into the morning sunshine. The long slatted blind rattled noisily as the thin glass door closed with a bang behind him.

For a moment everything in 'Must-go-Jean's' was still.

314

Sinner Joe glanced sideways at the old guy serving behind the counter.

'You ever seen a grenade with the pin pulled out?' he asked.

The old guy shook his head. 'Can't rightly say I have.'

'Looks much the same on the outside as one with the pin still in,' continued Sinner Joe. 'Only difference being one of them is gonna make you cry out for your mommy.'

32

The rest area of 'Must-go-Jean's' was situated off Interstate 20/59 about fifteen miles east of Cottondale. A large area of trees had been cleared to accommodate the low-rise Fifties building with space enough for about thirty trucks, but the building company had run out of money to tarmac the parking lot and left it unfinished. Over the years the weight of the trucks and their trailers had compacted the earth into a light-brown, potholed dustbowl.

Danny crossed the uneven ground to where he had parked the Cadillac and opened the boot. Inside, Sean and Marie were lying side by side in a foetal position on the floor.

Sean sat up gasping for air.

'Jesus, Danny, what the hell was that all about? You were supposed to let us out when we reached the edge of town,' said Sean, looking around as he clambered out, 'not the edge of the eastern-bloody-seaboard. We were suffocating in there. Did you not hear us shouting?'

Marie climbed over the sill of the trunk and lowered herself stiffly onto the dusty expanse.

'Is Bush still the president?' she said without smiling.

Danny suddenly struck out and caught Sean

full on the side of the face with his clenched fist. The blow knocked him to the ground where he lay with his eyes closed.

Marie stood frozen with a look of shock on her face. It appeared as if Sean had been knocked unconscious, but just as she was about to go over to him he raised himself up on his elbows and spoke.

'Nice one, Wub. Not exactly how I'd imagined our reunion, but you never were blessed with the gift of the gab. I thought you'd have more to say than that, though.'

'I've got plenty more to say, don't you worry,' replied Danny.

'You been driving along getting yourself all wound up? That wee paranoid brain of yours running through everything that's happened to you in the last eight years and blaming it all on me?' Sean looked up at Marie and continued. 'Here's the extent of your typical Irishman's conversation. We do most of our talking with our fists. I'm going to stand up now, Wub, but I warn you, if you try that again I'll kick the shite out of you. And don't think cause you're my wee brother I'll take it handy.'

Danny had the Walther PPK in his hand, pointing it at Sean.

'And don't you think just cause you're my brother I won't blow your fucking head off,' he said. 'You're already dead so it won't make any difference as far as I can see. I don't care if you're the Thevshi or not. I don't care what you've done to me. That's not why I feel like putting a bullet in your brain right now. It's what you've done to your family, and what you've done to our ma.'

Sean shook his head. 'Jesus, put the gun away, Wub. If I stand up and get it off you I'll crack it over your bloody head. This is the second time tonight you've pointed that thing at me and it's beginning to piss me off. Use it or stick it up yer arse.'

They were staring each other out: Sean daring Danny to shoot.

'Go on then, you little fucker, either pull the trigger or put the bloody thing away.'

Marie felt helpless to intervene. The situation looked like it was about to explode and there was nothing she could do to stop it.

Danny held Sean's stare as he spoke.

'Delores?'

Marie looked at Danny blankly, then realised that although he was looking at Sean he was actually talking to her.

'It is Delores, isn't it?' he continued.

'No, Marie: Marie Bain,' she replied.

'Fair enough, Marie.' Danny held his hand out to shake hers. 'Danny McGuire.'

'I knew it wasn't Mr Leonard!' said Marie, almost triumphantly. 'That was the only bit you lied about.'

Marie was relieved that his attention seemed to be on her now and not shooting his brother. 'Your lying zone is to the right, did you know that? His I'm still not sure about,' she said, referring to Sean.

'It doesn't matter which way he's looking. Everything he says is a lie,' said Danny.

Sean had also raised his hand towards Marie.

'Sean McGuire. How you doing?' Marie took a step forward and shook his hand as well.

'Ah, the McGuire brothers, that explains a lot . . . I thought you looked familiar when I first saw you in the apartment,' she said, addressing Danny. 'So who the hell is Finn O'Hanlon?'

'Me,' replied Sean, 'but only for the last eight years. Mostly I was — and always have been — Sean McGuire.' Sean had a question too. 'Who the hell's Delores?'

'No one,' replied Marie. 'I'm not good under pressure, it was the first name that popped into my head.'

'Marie, would you do me a favour?' asked Danny. 'Would you go into the café and ask Sinner Joe if he's got room in his cabin for a few passengers?'

'Sinner Joe! Are you kidding?' replied Marie. 'There's a guy in there called Sinner Joe? He'll be the one wearing the sackcloth and ashes and beating himself with a switch?'

'You'll know who he is when you see him,' said Danny.

'Why would he want to give us a lift?' asked Marie.

'Five thousand dollars,' replied Danny. 'If he wants more, turn round and walk out.'

Marie didn't look too sure. 'Does Sinner Joe have a donkey and cart big enough to take us all?'

'Don't worry; I think you'll find him receptive. The guy's got some previous. Has a few interesting jail tats on his face. I'm pretty sure he knows the score.'

'Why don't you go and ask?'

'Sean and I have got some *talking* to do.'

'I'll go, but only if you'll let me take the gun. Don't want you boys shooting each other just for the fun of it . . . you know what brothers are like.'

Danny flipped the safety catch on and handed her the gun.

'You sure Sinner Joe is his real name?' she continued. 'Seems to me everybody round here's got a goddamn nom-de-guerre.' Marie tucked the gun behind her back and walked across the car park towards the entrance of 'Must-go-Jean's' café. She heard a faint scuffling noise behind her and the smack of flesh on flesh, but didn't turn round to see who had landed the first punch.

★ ★ ★

'If I'd known we were going to be this busy I'd have hired in some help. What can I get for you, young lady?' asked the old guy behind the counter as Marie entered the café.

Marie was standing looking at ten or so empty booths and a guy sitting on his own at the end of the counter finishing off a huge plate of fried food. The guy was in his late forties and had three teardrops tattooed on his right cheek that were surrounded by a face full of craters. His nose had been broken so many times it looked like it was no longer fit for purpose. He chewed everything with his mouth open and sounded like a pig with a bad cold. His hands were

320

covered in crude tattoos that had faded and blurred over time until they were barely distinguishable as anything other than dirty marks. She figured this must be him, but thought she'd better ask. 'Any of you gentlemen go by the name of Sinner Joe?'

The guy with the teardrops stopped eating and looked up from his plate. The older guy tipped his 'Birmingham Barons' baseball cap a little further back on his forehead and pulled on his cigarette. 'It ain't obvious to you?' he asked.

'It is, but I don't want to hurt anyone's feelings by asking the wrong guy.'

The man behind the counter wheezed out three small clouds of smoke as he laughed to himself. 'Well let's just say I'm already hurt. Always considered myself to have an angelic face, but just goes to show. Come over here and sit down, I'll get you a coffee. You want anything to eat?'

'No thanks,' replied Marie, 'coffee's fine.'

She walked over to the counter and pulled out a stool.

Sinner Joe's narrow eyes stared at her with suspicion. 'What d'you want, lady?'

Marie turned to face him. 'My friends and I were wondering if you had any space in your cabin.'

Sinner Joe took his time to answer. 'Where you heading?'

'Where you going?'

'Don't seem to me like it'd matter much. How many of you are there?'

'Three.'

The guy nodded to himself and repeated it like it was more than significant. 'Three, huh? They all as pretty as you?'

Something in the tarry gravel of his voice and the way he stared straight at her when he asked the question made the hairs on the back of Marie's neck stand on end.

'The other two are out in the lot beating each other to death so I doubt they'll be looking their best, but I guess it depends on what you call pretty.'

The old guy placed a chipped mug on the counter top in front of her and poured some coffee from a stainless-steel pot that he'd somehow managed to stain. 'You in the same party as the hothead came in to use the phone?'

'You could say.'

'Coffee with cream?'

'Milk, please, just a splash.'

'Sugar?'

'I'm fine, thanks.'

'You want my opinion he's running around with the safety off,' said Sinner Joe, like he'd been giving the situation some thought prior to Marie coming in. 'Presents himself as 'Mr Ordinary', but he got some cordite behind those eyes and acting like someone's just lit the blue touch-paper. They fighting over you?'

'No. From what I can gather it's because they're brothers and they're Irish. Who knows? They were hugging each other half an hour ago.'

Sinner Joe pushed his plate aside and flicked a cigarette from a soft pack of Camels. 'How'd you get here?' he asked.

'What d'you mean?'

'Did you walk, fly, drive? How'd you get to 'Must-go Jean's'?'

'Drove,' replied Marie.

'Your car busted? See, I'm wondering why you need a lift.' Sinner Joe didn't give her a chance to answer. 'Don't worry, I'm just riding you, lady. I don't give a damn how you got here. I'm more interested in calculating how much it's going to cost you to get away from here. What's your name?'

Marie didn't have to think this time. 'Delores.'

'And what are your friends called, 'Delores'?' He gave her name a little squeeze to let her know he didn't believe her, but he was happy to play along.

'Finn and Mr Leonard.'

'How much you got?'

'Three thousand.'

'Each. I'd say that's just about correct.'

'Three thousand in total,' said Marie.

Sinner Joe flicked his Zippo along his faded black jeans and lifted it to his mouth. He took one long draw on the cigarette and let the smoke slowly fill his lungs. When he spoke again, Marie was struck by how little of the smoke re-emerged.

'Delores, you need to tell Finn and Mr Leonard they gonna have to get a tow-truck, cause nine thou is as low as I can go.'

Marie took a sip of coffee and stood up. 'How much is the coffee?'

'Afraid it's a dollar,' replied the old guy behind the counter, with a frown. 'In case there's a next time, it's free if you order something to eat.'

Marie placed a ten-dollar bill on the counter

and headed for the door without waiting for the change.

She got as far as twisting the handle before Sinner Joe spoke again.

'I guess I could do it for three . . . but it's got to be cash: I don't accept cards or cheques. Gasoline is over and above.'

★   ★   ★

Danny was a slow burner. When he was younger he'd take a lot of pushing around before he'd react — then without warning, he'd explode. Every detail of every indiscretion, however minor, would be recalled and thrown back in a single angry outburst: he never forgot. If fists were flying, he would battle to the end even if it were obvious he wasn't going to win. Danny had no 'off' button. When he did snap — in Sean's experience — the best thing to do was get out of the way. Sean had no reason to believe that things were any different now — it was going to be a long and dirty scrap. He tried to stand up and was caught with a hard right hook that knocked him back to the ground.

'Now listen to me, you little fucker,' said Sean, trying his best to stay composed. 'I don't want to fight, all right? If you just calm yourself down then I'll answer any questions you want to throw at me. But if all you're after is a punch-up, then I'm not interested. That said, if you lay a hand on me again I'll rip you to shreds . . . understood?'

Danny's eyes were ablaze. There was so much

he wanted to say. His mother's breakdown, Órlaith's grief, Lep's death, the dozen or so lives Danny had taken in the mistaken belief that he was avenging his brother's death and now Angela's and Niamh's disappearance: these were the grim consequences of Sean's bogus 'murder'. There were so many questions, but in the end they boiled down to just one.

'What . . . the . . . hell . . . happened?'

Danny spat each word out like a bullet across the arid patch of earth.

Sean picked himself up slowly from the ground and slapped the dust from his trousers with the palm of his hands, not once losing eye contact with Danny.

'Well, if you stop throwing your goddamn fists around for a second I'll tell you.'

Every night for the past eight years Sean had rehearsed the words in his head; he had imagined this meeting so many times. But now that Danny was standing in front of him and he had to say them for real, it was suddenly much more difficult.

'Obviously you got my message. I haven't been able to get a hold of Lep so I wasn't sure if he'd passed it on. After two eejits tried to whack me in a bar I figured he must have told someone.'

'He did pass it on — but it cost him his life,' replied Danny.

Sean was visibly shaken by this news. 'Ah dear, God rest his soul.'

It was a while before he spoke again.

'I was working secretly for the IRA as an intelligence officer, gathering information on suspected informers mostly, but my main target was the Thevshi — 'The Ghost'. Every time it looked like I was getting close to discovering who the bastard was something would go wrong. My source would either disappear or get themselves murdered, or both. I was also doing a double-shuffle with the Special Branch at the time: low-impact shit. Feeding them just enough to make them think I was on their side. But all I was trying to do was find out who knew what, if anything, about 'The Ghost'. Then one day I was taken up to Castlereagh by my handler — a guy called Frank Thompson. He was there with a couple of other officers, but they were all as edgy as hell. Something was obviously going on, but I had no idea what. Halfway through the interview someone comes in and whispers something in Thompson's ear and the next thing they all disappear out the room, leaving me sitting there on my own: only they've left the door open. After about half an hour I'm still sitting there twiddling my thumbs, but I need to visit the gents'. So I wandered off down the corridor, did a piss and when I came out of the bog, there's cops running up and down the corridors looking for me. They dragged me back to the room and there's Thompson sitting waiting for me. Only now, the atmosphere is very different. 'Where the fuck have you been?' he says. 'For a pish,' says I. Then he starts in on me, asking me what I saw, did I overhear anything: coming on all aggressive now. I told him the only thing I'd seen was my dick and the only thing I'd heard was the toilet flushing. But something had him rattled. From that day onward it all changed. I could never get a hold of Frank and he wouldn't return my calls. Then I started getting the phone-calls threatening to kill me . . . threatening to kill Órlaith . . . even threatening to kill you.'

Danny didn't react. He stood there stony-faced and waited for Sean to continue.

'What stuck in my head — the bit I keep running over and over — is that Frank Thompson asked me at one point to give them more details about the operation we were planning, to bomb the Prime Minister when she was in Belfast. The thing is, I hadn't told him anything about that operation. There were only seven of us in the RA knew anything about it, so that narrowed my hunt for the Thevshi right down. It was a big op — top secret — the information could only have come from one of the other six. So whether he realised he'd made a slip-up, or whether 'The Ghost' was in Castlereagh at the same time as me, and Thompson thought I might have seen him when I went off to the toilet, I don't know. But when the death threats started I knew they were serious. I knew the only way out was to disappear. If I'd tried to take you, or Órlaith or Ma, we'd have all ended up dead. I had to disappear . . . but I also had to die.'

'Who were you reporting back to in the RA?' asked Danny.

'E. I. O'Leary.'

'Why didn't you tell him what was going on?'

'Because', replied Sean, 'he was one of the other six.'

327

★ ★ ★

The sight that greeted Marie on her return was not the one she had been expecting. The two men were leaning against the trunk of the car talking quietly to each other like they were making a plan. Danny had just handed a Sean small set of what looked like keys to a post-office box.

As she approached, Marie scanned their faces for signs of battle, but there didn't appear to be any.

'Have you boys kissed and made up?' she said.

'Sinner Joe not interested?' asked Sean.

'He wanted nine thousand dollars,' replied Marie.

'Did you tell him we only have five?' asked Sean.

'I told him we only have three.'

'What'd he say?'

'He's gone to the restroom to 'evac his back-pack' — his words not mine — then he's dusting down his chauffeur's cap and he'll meet us over by the blue-and-white Kenworth with the tandem axle: says we're lucky he ain't pulling a load or he wouldn't be able to help us. I just smiled like I knew what he was talking about. Says he'll take us wherever we want to go, but we got to pay extra for the fuel . . . ' she smiled half-heartedly before continuing ' . . . so, where d'you boys fancy?'

Danny pushed himself off the trunk and walked round to the driver's side of the car and opened the door. 'Sean is heading for the

328

nearest train station with Sinner Joe and you and I are going in the Cadillac to visit some pals back in Tuscaloosa.'

'Oh!' said Marie. 'Nothing turns out the way you expect it around here, does it?'

'D'you want to ride up front, or get back in the boot?'

33

Cochron Road, Newry, Wednesday,
late afternoon

Angela sat in the corner with her back pressed against the musty-smelling black drapes and cradled Niamh's tiny frame in her arms. The carpeted floor in front of them was covered with ominous black stains that glistened in the darkness and filled the room with a sickening aroma of stale blood and faeces. Someone had attempted to conceal the smell with disinfectant, but no amount of cleaning could ever neutralise the stench of death.

A door slammed in another part of the house. Seconds later Angela could hear someone making their way upstairs towards the room. The young girl's body tensed. Neither of them spoke as they sat staring at the door.

Niamh jumped when the lock turned with a sharp, metallic clunk. The handle twisted clockwise and the door swung open.

Standing in the doorway was the figure of a heavy-set man; behind him in the hall was the short skinny guy who had driven Angela to the house yesterday. Or was it the day before? Angela had lost all track of time.

'Take the young one downstairs and fix her something to eat, and get Slim to bring up the kettle,' said the big guy as he took a few steps into the room.

330

'Please don't. I don't want to go. Please,' sobbed Niamh.

Angela could feel her small hand gripping onto her arm as the skinny guy made his way over and tried to prise her off.

'Don't worry, you're going downstairs for a wee while so that I can have a few words with Angela here, in private,' said the big guy.

'Why don't you leave her be?' said Angela. 'The poor girl's petrified. Just say what you have to say then leave us alone.'

The skinny guy hesitated.

'It'll only take a few minutes, then she can come back up,' said the other one.

Angela watched Niamh's reluctant figure being dragged out of the room. Her tiny shoulders were hunched forward and her head bowed. There were tears streaming down her small face. It was as pitiful a sight as Angela had ever seen, and one she prayed she would never have to witness again.

When Niamh was out in the hall she glanced back and tried to smile, as if — in her own small way — she wanted to reassure Angela everything would be all right. It was a gesture so delicate and fragile that it made Angela's eyes sting.

The big guy slammed the door closed and turned the key in the lock.

'Take a seat . . . make yourself comfortable,' he said, nodding towards the metal-framed chair in the middle of the room.

'And sit amongst the piss and blood?' replied Angela, 'I don't think so.'

She raised herself up off the floor and stood in

the corner with her back to the wall.

'Fair enough! Makes no odds to me whether you're standing or sitting or doing a fucking headstand, outcome will still be the same,' he replied, making it sound like a threat.

'Outcome of what?' asked Angela. But the big guy ignored her question.

'Do you know who I am?' he asked.

'Should I?'

'Not necessarily, but maybe your boyfriend mentioned me.'

'My boyfriend?' Angela sounded surprised. 'I think you've got me mixed up with someone else. I don't have a boyfriend.'

'Is that a fact?' said the big guy, with a snort. 'Well why don't you take a wee seat anyway and we'll talk about the fuckin weather then. Either way, I'd like you to sit down.'

'I'd rather stand,' said Angela defiantly.

Without warning the big guy took a step towards her and punched her in the face. He weighed nearly two hundred pounds and put every ounce of his bulk behind the blow: no holding back. Angela's head snapped back and cracked against the wall. Instantly her legs gave way underneath her and she crumpled to the floor.

'Last time! Go and sit on the fucking chair,' he barked as he kicked her hard in the back of her ribs. 'Sit on the fucking chair. I'm not asking if you want to. I'm telling you. Sit in the fucking chair.'

Angela was badly dazed. She lay slumped on the floor staring up at the ceiling, and for a brief moment wondered what the strange thumping noise was she could hear pounding at the inside of her skull. She tried to get back on her feet, but for the moment was incapable of telling which way was up and which was down.

The guy looked like he was about to kick her again, but a knock at the door stopped him.

The fat guy — Slim Jim McMahon — pushed the door open and handed over a kettle and a tape recorder before leaving the room.

It required a lot of effort, but eventually Angela managed to get back on her feet. She felt nauseous, and had to lean against the wall to stop herself from toppling over.

The big guy plugged the kettle into the wall and switched it on.

'Are . . . you . . . making a cup of tea?' she mumbled incoherently.

'What?'

'Are you making tea?'

The big guy laughed like she'd made a joke. 'Aye, that's right . . . and you're the teabag. You don't mind if I record our conversation, to play back to your boyfriend,' he continued. 'When we do eventually catch up with him we'll probably need to have a wee chat with him as well. This is just to keep him focused.'

Angela stared back at him blankly. She couldn't think straight. One punch had done this to her.

'When . . . I've answered . . . your questions . . . can I leave?' she said falteringly over the dull burble of the kettle heating up.

'Depends.'

'On what?'

'How well we get on,' the guy replied. 'If I think it's going well, you can leave with a few bruises. If I think you're fucking me around, you'll leave in a wheelchair — but one way or the other you'll certainly get to leave.'

Angela didn't know how to respond. There was nothing veiled about this threat and its effect was immediate.

Her legs started to tremble involuntarily.

'Are those the two choices?' she asked.

'Who said it was a choice? It's a decision for me to make, not a choice for you.'

'I don't know who you think I am, or what you think I know, but I swear to God, you've got the wrong person. You can beat the shit out of me all you like . . . '

'I intend to,' he interrupted.

Angela continued, feeling oddly ashamed that she was close to tears, ' . . . but I still won't be able to tell you anything.'

He was moving towards her again.

'My name is Owen O'Brien. I'm 'the man' when it comes to getting information from people that might be useful to me, and the organisation I represent. Now, that wee slap I just gave you was to let you know that I'm not one for pissing about. Most people who have passed through here find it difficult to talk when they've had their teeth knocked out, or their noses broken, so if there's anything you feel you want to tell me, my advice would be to just come right out and say it. One other thing before we get started . . . ' O'Brien grabbed Angela by the hair and pulled her over to the centre of the

334

room. 'Sit in the fucking chair.'

He pushed her with such force that she fell backwards onto the chair and nearly tipped it over.

Angela was trying desperately to focus. She was staring at him trying to remember her nurse's training on how to deal with difficult patients. The guy was definitely psychotic: the smiles were gone and any pretence of friendliness dropped. She knew it didn't matter what she said, there was no placating a guy like O'Brien.

He was standing just in front of her with his arms folded across his chest. If she was quick enough she could kick out and catch him between the legs, but she didn't have the strength to sustain an all-out attack. As she gathered herself ready, O'Brien took a step backward and the opportunity was lost for the moment.

Angela had made a decision.

If he put his head anywhere within reach again she would grab him and gouge his fucking eyes out.

O'Brien was talking again.

'When did you last speak to your boyfriend?'

'Who?'

'Your boyfriend! When did you last speak to him?'

'I don't know who you mean.'

'Fair enough, if you want to play the dumb cunt that's fine, but don't think you're going to treat me like one.' O'Brien started shouting at her. 'Danny McGuire! When did you last hear from Danny McGuire, dumb cunt?'

'I saw him at the end of last week,' replied Angela.

'At the Mourne Arms — we know that. Then you went back to his place. I know you saw him, but that's not what I fucking asked. When did you last speak to him?'

How did O'Brien know they'd been to the Mourne Arms and how did he know that Angela and Danny had gone home together? Someone must have spotted them, or they had been followed.

'He called me the other night, but I don't know where from: he didn't say.'

'And did he mention anything about his brother, or say when his brother was coming home?' asked O'Brien.

Angela watched O'Brien pacing backwards and forwards.

'His brother is dead,' she said.

O'Brien stopped and smiled at her.

'You've just rendered yourself superfluous, you dumb bitch. It only took one question. One question and you fucked it.'

Angela felt she had regained enough strength to take O'Brien on, but she needed him to get close.

'It was two questions.'

O'Brien stared back at her. 'What?'

'It was two questions you asked, not one. ' "When did I last talk to Danny?' and 'Did he say anything about his brother?' Two questions! Who's the dumb bitch now?'

O'Brien stood gawking at Angela in disbelief.

'You think beating the shit out of women is something a smart person does?' She continued. 'Or kidnapping a seven-year-old girl? I've no idea what sort of voices you've got talking to you

336

in that tiny, retarded brain of yours, mister, but you're clearly fucking deranged. Sean McGuire's been dead for nearly ten years. My da — Joe Fitzpatrick — was a republican who was proud to fight for a cause that he believed in, but you are just a bloody animal. You're a disgrace to republicanism. You've hijacked it to justify behaving like a goddamn psychopath. That's all you are, a big, dumb psychopath. You can ask me what you like, but I'm not saying one more word, you prick.'

Angela watched O'Brien's face contort into a twisted sneer.

He advanced slowly towards her and leant forward.

Angela knew this might be the only opportunity she would get.

When his face was just inches away she reached up with her hands and dug her fingers into his face. She ripped and tore and tried to stab her thumb into his eyes: gouging as deeply as she could. O'Brien let out a yelp and quickly pulled away, easily breaking Angela's hold. She reached out and tried to grab him again, but he was too quick. He caught her by the wrist and bent her arm back, twisting it over her shoulder. Angela flipped round and lashed out again, but O'Brien caught her hard on the side of the face with the back of his hand, knocking her to the floor again. 'D'you think I'm fresh out of the wrapper, bitch? I saw that coming before you'd even thought it.'

O'Brien had blood pouring down his face where her nails had dug into the soft flesh of his

337

cheek, and his right eye had tears streaming from it. He towered over her, waiting for her to make a move. 'If you don't know that Danny McGuire's brother Sean is still alive, then obviously you are not in the loop,' he said, grabbing a handful of Angela's hair and yanking her to her feet. 'And if you're not in the loop, you're no good to any fucker. One question, two questions: who gives a shit? Either way you've landed yourself in a wheelchair — cunt.'

Angela tried to struggle free, but the more she twisted and turned the more force O'Brien applied.

When the blow came, Angela had no way of avoiding it. O'Brien suddenly tipped his head backward and — before she could turn away — butted her hard on the face. The loud cracking noise she heard was the sound of her nose breaking.

Angela let out a low moan and felt the warm blood gushing over her lips and dripping from her chin onto her blouse. She could taste the blood running down the back of her throat. O'Brien kept hold of her hair and started punching her repeatedly in the face with his large fists. There was nothing she could do to protect herself.

After several more loud cracks her body went limp.

★ ★ ★

She had no idea how long she had been unconscious, but she woke up with a start.

338

Something was causing an excruciating pain at the top of her thighs. Her instinct was to push back and get away from whatever it was, but her legs wouldn't move: she couldn't straighten them. They had been tied to the chair and her hands bound tightly behind her back. She opened her mouth and screamed until her throat crackled and croaked and no more sound would come.

Owen O'Brien was pouring a kettle of boiling water over her legs: starting at her crotch and moving slowly down her thighs and along her shins.

When he saw that her eyes were open he lifted the kettle up until it was directly over her head.

'In some respects, you should consider yourself lucky,' he said. 'You being a nurse and everything you'll understand how hard it is to cover burns with make-up. But lucky you: there's hardly any water left. When your boyfriend sees you next your face won't look too bad.'

Angela was taking short, sharp intakes of breath. She wanted to scream again, but the only noise she could make was a long lowing growl, like an injured animal.

Suddenly her head was on fire as the boiling water seared across her scalp and down over her forehead.

The pain was so intense that it caused Angela's bowels to open.

The last thing she heard was O'Brien laughing at her. 'Don't you be worrying yourself there, darlin, everyone who sits in that seat pisses themselves.'

339

34

The Moonshine War, Tuscaloosa, Wednesday, evening

'That's nice you come all the way from Ireland to visit your brother,' said Ardel.

'I didn't come to visit him, I came to kill him,' replied Danny.

Ardel looked across at him and raised his eyebrows. 'In that case I withdraw my previous statement.'

Hud's eyes almost met in the middle as he focused on the lit end of the expertly rolled three-skinner flaring brightly between his fingers. He held his breath momentarily to let the tetrahydrocannabinol take effect, then let out a long satisfied moan as he exhaled. 'Forget your troubles, c'mon, get happy,' he said with a grin before offering the joint across the table to Danny. 'Man, this greenery don't give you a hit, it clubs you to death. You want some?'

Danny shook his head: the last thing he needed right now was to take a trip to la-la land. There were too many angles to cover, too much to think about before he could make his next move. He needed to stay sharp.

'Man, you want to try this. It won't solve your problems,' continued Hud, 'but you get to go on vacation and leave them to fend for themselves for a while. Lock em in the fridge and let them

340

cool down while you're gone. Make you come at it from a different angle. You sittin there with your face all screwed up thinking way too much about the situation you is in. You is clouding your mind with all the bad things that *could* maybe happen rather than how you gonna make things turn the right way.'

Danny was only half listening, but a lot of what Hud said was true. He had been focusing too much on what could go wrong: not trusting his instincts. There was nothing he could do to help Angela or Niamh until he was back in Northern Ireland, and the only way to get back was to concentrate on what was happening here and now. With any luck Sean would be boarding a plane in the next hour or so using Danny's false passport. What Danny needed to ensure was that he could get on a plane as soon as possible too.

Hud offered the wrap to Marie. 'You?'

'I'm okay with this, thanks,' replied Marie, holding up a glass of water. Marie felt as though she'd been drinking non-stop over the past few days and despite the temptation had decided to take a break. If she was going to smoke a joint she might as well have some alcohol and she didn't want to do either. 'One day I'll have a go, but not today,' she continued.

'You never had a smoke before, Marie?' asked Ardel with his eyebrows raised.

'No! White wine and whiskey sours is about as dangerous as I get. Had a husband who smoked it all through college: came out dumber than he went in. Kinda put me off.'

'That's why me and Hud didn't go to college: we couldn't afford to get any dumber,' said Ardel, nodding his head like he was agreeing with her. 'When all this shit is past,' he continued, 'and we's seeing you in a less formal capacity, Hud an me will set you up with something nice and mellow . . . Why you smiling? We friends now, and once you are in the Ardel and Hud club you get all the benefits of being a member. Ain't no rules cept you got to be nice to us and in return we gonna look after you. Make sure no harm comes your way. Set you up with a few nice smokes: make them trips you won't want to end. You'll come out the other side like one of those Senseis from Japan or wherever: you'll come out a wiser chick than you went in. The beauty of this stuff, Marie, you can journey far and wide and never leave your favourite armchair, and cause you is a friend of Mr O'Hanlon-McGuire you get to travel for free.'

Marie was touched by Ardel's little speech. He might be stoned, but he looked like he meant it.

'Sounds good,' she replied.

They were seated round a table in the small back room of a bar on the outskirts of Tuscaloosa, just south of the Black Warrior River. 'The Moonshine War' belonged to a friend of Bulldog Jo's by the name of Jesse Ezekiel. She was a Mormon from Salt Lake City who'd given up on her faith. Once she'd tasted her first beer she turned her back on God and started enjoying herself, like she was trying to make up for what she called 'the lost years.' She drank anything and everything, turned to prostitution, and made enough money to buy herself a bar. She soon realised that if she was going to make a success of the venture she would have to quit drinking. Fifteen years later the Moonshine War was turning over enough to pay her bills, and let her travel to Europe once a year, where she would stay for a month.

It wasn't that Jesse didn't like the law: she just didn't have time for it. She had dirt on nearly all the city officials, including the Mayor of Tuscaloosa: over the years she'd slept with most of them. As long as she kept her nose clean she was left pretty much to her own devices. She got a permit and drinks licence every year without any inspections. Most of her clientele were ex-cons or hookers or dopeheads, but she still preferred them to the Mormon Elders. Even the most troubled of her patrons were more honest than anyone she'd ever met at church.

Jesse welcomed Ardel, Hud, Danny and Marie without asking any awkward questions. Told them they could go through the back for their meeting: even offered them a room upstairs if any of them needed somewhere to crash for a few days.

The room they were sitting in was directly behind the bar: the two areas connected by a doorway that had a plastic curtain of different-coloured strands hanging instead of a door. In the far corner there was a Western-style swing door leading down to the cellar and next to it a small rectangular window that was too high to see out of, and even on the brightest days

343

admitted no daylight. Dark wood strip panels covered the lower half of the walls and a bare light bulb dangled precariously from a thin piece of flex above the centre of the table, casting a faint forty-watt glow over the shiny painted surface of the upper part of the wall. The light — secured by a small brass hook screwed into the plaster ceiling — swung gently back and forth every time someone entered or exited the bar next door. It gave the uneasy sensation of being on a ship floating in a mild swell.

'You sure this is the best place to be?' asked Danny. 'I don't know my way around, but we seem to be a bit too close to the action here.' Danny had questioned the wisdom of staying in Tuscaloosa, but Ardel and Hud had persuaded him that this would be the last place the cops would look. Even though he wasn't convinced, Danny had no option — he needed their help.

'Mr O's bro, Jesse is sound. She been in all sorts of trouble herself, so she knows how to keep a clamp on it. Most of the cops in this city slept with most of the 'ladies' that drink in this bar, and most of them tell Jesse most everything that's goin on. If Jesse says it's all right to be here then it's all right. She ain't just got her finger on the pulse, man, she's the goddamn beating heart. Ain't nowhere safer in Alabama. We take a stretch towards a state line, they grab us easy. That's where they gonna be focusing their attention. We safer here than if we was the Federal Reserve and had the National Guard watchin our ass.'

Ardel scraped the overloaded ashtray towards

him and flicked a column of ash onto it, before turning back to Danny like he was ready to talk business now. 'Only problem we got, Mr O's bro, is the time it's going to take to get you a new passport. These guys I been telling you about are the best there is. The quality of the workmanship is outstanding, but outstanding can't be rushed.'

'How long did they say?' asked Danny.

'Quickest they can do is two days,' answered Ardel. 'They aware it's an emergency and they gonna work on it all the hours available, but if you want something that's gonna get you past immigration that's as quick as it's gonna be. They asked if there was anyone special you wanted to be — you know, like a particular name you wanted on the passport, but I said you wasn't too fussed so long as they did it quick and accurate, and they didn't give you a black dude's name or something dumb like that . . . You don't want to show up at the airport trying to pass yourself off as Leroy Smith, would that be right?'

Danny nodded.

'In the meantime,' continued Ardel, 'you welcome to hang out with us for the next forty-eight hours, but we's heading off on vacation till the party across the street from our shack has died down. We never seen so many cops in the one area at the same time. Didn't know there was that many cops in the whole of Alabama. Luckily the apartment in Cottondale ain't the only property we operate our business from, otherwise we'd have to close down, we losing so much revenue, cause ain't no one visiting. Made us realise we was the only draw

345

for miles around . . . should be on the tourist trail or something . . . you know, like on one of those maps tells you where the stars live or the best places to visit. We even thought about accompanying you back to Ireland: sit on the plane behind you like we don't know each other, but watchin out for your ass at the same time. We both carrying a few convictions, though, and the last thing we want to do is fuck up your chances of getting home. The cops got a big caravan parked round in the alley runs up the back of our building: looks like a spaceship. Gonna ask them to leave it behind so we can include it as part of a sightseeing trip for the tourists.'

Hud, who had been sitting quietly, started to laugh as Ardel tried to do an imitation of a bus-tour operator making an announcement.

' 'Over on our right, ladies and gentlemen, is the building where notorious criminal Vincent Lee Croll found himself on the wrong end of an M10 semi-automatic as he practised his sword-swallowing routine.' It's just what this area needs, man, is the tourist buck. The word is they only just moved his body down to the morgue.'

Hud was looking across the table at Danny. 'You got first-hand experience what he smelled like before he got punctured, you imagine how bad he smelling now?'

Danny looked up as the light bulb swayed from side to side.

Jesse suddenly pushed her way through the multi-coloured plastic curtain separating the small back room from the bar.

'What's up, Ardel?'

Ardel eased himself out from behind the table and gave Jesse a squeeze.

'What's up, Jesse?' replied Ardel. 'Man, you still looking good, girl. If we was alone I'd be picking you out of the line and asking you to come upstairs; we get some rhythm going.'

Jesse smiled. 'You so full of shit, Ardel.'

'I full of other stuff too, Jesse, needs some relief, you know what I'm saying . . . you okay?'

'Everything's cool,' replied Jesse. 'Got Bulldog on the phone says there's two FBI officers sitting at her bar talking about your man there.' Jesse nodded in Danny's direction. 'You want to come out and talk to her?' she asked Ardel.

'I'll go,' said Danny, getting up from his chair.

'Got some nice cold beer from a little microbrewery, gets its water direct from the Appalachian Mountains. Nice and refreshing. You want me to bring in a pitcher?' asked Jesse.

Marie was the first to answer. 'Yes please . . . and if you could throw in a sour for good measure that would be great. I've been sober for over two hours now. I think that's long enough.'

'Sure, babe,' replied Jesse. 'Anyone want anything else?'

'How d'you stop that goddamn light bulb swaying, Jesse? It's making me feel seasick,' said Ardel.

35

Jeff Kneller and his partner Joe Evelyn stood on the balcony of Finn O'Hanlon's apartment with their backs against the railings, looking into the scene of devastation. The walls were covered in ragged craters where the bullets had ruptured the plasterwork and there was glass and debris covering most of the floor. A CSI officer was standing in the kitchen area talking to two guys from the forensic team who were laughing about something. Vincent Lee Croll's remains had been bagged and removed from the scene, leaving behind a large area of dried blood over by the front door.

'You think there's a crime been committed here, Mr Evelyn?' asked Kneller, working the sarcasm.

'Several by the looks of it,' answered Evelyn.

'You figure it's the same guy that killed Conrado, did this?' asked Kneller.

'Probably.' Evelyn shrugged.

'I'd like to shake his hand rather than lock him up,' continued Kneller. 'The way I see it, he's done us a favour.'

Joe Evelyn nodded his agreement.

'Did you manage to use the phone?' asked Kneller.

'Got hit by a couple of rounds from an M10.

348

Looks like it's been in an automobile accident. The microphone's good as new, but the earphone bit is blown to shit: you can talk, but you can't listen. Only person you'd want to try calling on it would be your wife.'

'You feel like a beer?' asked Kneller wearily, leaning his elbows on the railings and making a mental note of the number of police vehicles parked in the street below.

'To start with, then maybe something a bit stronger,' replied Evelyn.

'How many police officers can you see in here?'

Evelyn turned to look at him. 'None, why?'

'There are six squad cars parked down there and I can't see one goddamn officer — what the hell they all doin? Let's head across to that bar on the corner and see if *they* got a phone we could use,' said Kneller.

The two FBI officers made their way carefully through the lounge, past the large patch of dried blood and out into the hallway. They walked down the dark communal stairs in silence, and held their breath as they headed through the stench of decay to the main entrance. Six uniformed officers were standing just inside the doorway chatting and having a smoke. They smiled and nodded as Kneller and Evelyn walked past. 'Careful you boys don't pop a hernia, all the strain you putting into investigating this crime.' Kneller couldn't help himself. 'The residents of Cottondale can sleep easy tonight knowing you boys are out there keeping them safe. Great job, keep it up,' he said, knowing he was being an ass.

'We're off duty, asshole,' replied one of the cops, just as Kneller and Evelyn reached the front door. Kneller smiled at Joe Evelyn and pressed the buzzer to release the door catch. 'You hear that, Joe? Did he just say they were off-duty assholes?'

Kneller didn't catch the reply, but the uniforms started laughing behind his back.

Outside on the street Joe Evelyn took several deep breaths to fill his lungs with clean air. 'The smell in there is so bad I feel like I should shower or something,' he said as they crossed the street towards Bulldog Jo's.

★   ★   ★

Kneller settled himself on a stool at the bar and ordered two Skeeter Bites while Evelyn used the phone on the wall to check in with 18th Street North: the FBI's headquarters in Birmingham, Alabama.

He was only gone a few minutes before he was back pulling up a chair alongside Kneller. 'We going to drive back up to Birmingham or find somewhere to stay?'

'Looks like this is turning out to be a big story,' answered Kneller, stifling a yawn. 'Let's find somewhere to camp for a few nights, I'd fall asleep if I was to get behind the wheel now,' he continued. 'What's the scoop from 18th Street?'

Joe Evelyn picked up the beer bottle from the bar and studied the label. 'Skeeter the only thing they got?'

350

Kneller had worked with Joe Evelyn for so long he could read him in Braille. He could tell things from the tone of Evelyn's voice or the expression on his face. 'C'mon, you've got that dumb look you get when you're trying to play it cool, but you got something you can't wait to blurt. What'd they say?'

Joe Evelyn made a quick scan of the bar before answering. Aside from a few late night drinkers and a couple of uniforms, the room was quiet. Bulldog Jo was standing at the other end of the bar reading a newspaper and didn't appear to be paying them any attention.

'Interesting development,' said Evelyn. 'The guy who lives, or lived, across the street — O'Hanlon — doesn't show up on any of our records. Got no National Security number, no papers whatsoever. Turns out he is a goddamn IRA terrorist on the run.'

'On the run from what?' asked Kneller.

'Who fucking cares? Real name's Sean McGuire. But, that's not the good bit — His brother arrived from Northern Ireland with a sack full of cash to try and buy some arms from your friend and mine . . . '

' . . . De Garza?' said Kneller, finishing Joe Evelyn's sentence for him. Kneller looked surprised.

Joe Evelyn nodded his head. 'Hernando De-goddamn-Garza! Can you believe that? But wait till you hear this . . . Danny McGuire — the brother — is also an assassin for the IRA with a contract to kill Finn O'Hanlon. Got drafted in after Conrado and Lee Croll screwed up the hit.'

351

'Danny McGuire has a contract to kill Finn O'Hanlon who is really Sean McGuire, who is really Danny McGuire's brother. *And* he's supposed to be doing a deal with De Garza? Jesus!' exclaimed Kneller. 'I'm going to find a house and move the family down here: we ain't going anywhere for a while. Looks like this is the big one,' he continued as he finished off his beer and placed the empty back on the counter: thinking now. 'Then again, it could be one of those gigs where everyone gets to screw the bride but the husband. You know what I'm saying? The kind of situation that starts off fucked up and no matter what you do or say, it stays that way. Anything else on the brother?'

'Danny McGuire is travelling on a passport under the name of 'Leonard'. Entered via Logan International in Boston about five days ago and made his way down from there,' replied Evelyn.

'To kill his own brother! What the fuck is that all about?'

' . . . and buy some heavy-duty weaponry from De Garza for his friends back home in Ireland.'

'How come we know all this if we haven't got a rap sheet on O'Hanlon? Why we suddenly so well informed?' asked Kneller.

Joe Evelyn was about to answer when he noticed Bulldog Jo hovering near the till directly opposite where they were sitting.

'You boys thirsty enough to try another?' she said, trying to cover.

'Sure,' replied Kneller. 'Same again, and a pack of smokes, don't care what brand.' He let it hang for a while before continuing, 'You got anywhere we can sit and have a private conversation?'

Bulldog Jo gave him a look that said 'Stop being an ass.' 'If you don't want anyone listening in then you can take your beers and drink them on the sidewalk so long as the po-lice don't see you, else they bust your ass for vagrancy . . . if that's no good then there's another bar, bout half-an-hour's drive from here, but chances are it'll be closed by the time you get there. Failing all that, you can sit right where you are and keep your goddamn voices down . . . is up to you.'

Jo put the beers down in front of the two men and turned to get the cigarettes from the display stand behind her.

'Maybe we'll ask the cops that bust us for vagrancy to step inside and check you got all the right permits. Could be a nightmare trying to run a bar if your licence got pulled over something stupid.' Evelyn said, talking to Jo's back.

Jo turned and placed the cigarettes down on the bar then smiled at the two FBI agents. 'You got maggots on your balls, or something? I didn't shoot no one. You want to have a beer and a smoke it's fine. You don't want anyone listening in, that's fine too . . . Don't have to bust my tits just cause I got ears. I'll be over there if you need anything else. Make sure you holler loud cause I's suddenly gone deaf.'

When Bulldog Jo had moved to the far end of the bar Joe Evelyn finished what he was going to say. 'We are 'so well informed' because you got a call. Someone called 18th Street and left you a

353

message. They mentioned the hit in McHales, they mentioned the Lakeshore Hotel, they mentioned O'Hanlon's flat in Cottondale: only thing they didn't mention was who they were, but they knew what they were talking about. Spoke with a thick Irish accent: had to repeat themselves a few times.'

Kneller picked up Joe Evelyn's pack of cigarettes from the bar. 'You mind if I have one of these?'

'I ain't your doctor,' replied Evelyn.

'So what do we call O'Hanlon now?' said Kneller with a scowl. 'We got to call him Sean McGuire? I kinda got used to calling him Finn O'Hanlon. Be weird to call him something else.'

Bulldog Jo leant across, picked the phone up from the bar and dialled. After about thirty seconds she said, 'Jesse, it's me. Let me speak to one of them?'

Eventually Danny came on the line.

'You just got a name-check, boy,' said Bulldog, whispering under her breath. 'They mentioned Finn and you and the fact you was travelling under an assumed name. Even said it: 'Mr Leonard'. They said you came in at Boston and you got some business with Hernando De Garza. These guys seem to know a whole load of shit.'

*   *   *

Danny didn't like what he was hearing. He had to get back to Ireland and he had to make sure Sean got back too. If the FBI knew about the

354

false name on the passport then the chances were high that Sean would be stopped before he got anywhere near a plane. He thanked Jo and replaced the receiver.

The smiles disappeared from Ardel and Hud's faces when Danny told them what Jo had said; Marie was staring anxiously at Danny.

Hud was the first to speak. 'Sounds to me like there's someone up a ladder with their ass hanging over your head, Mr O's bro. You getting shit on,' he said. 'I ain't being paranoid, but I hope you don't think it's any of our skinny black asses talked to the FBI. You in the Ardel and Hud club too and that means we take a vow of silence over anything that happens to be your business. We don't know even half that shit anyways.'

'Don't worry, I know that information didn't come from you,' replied Danny, pulling the Walther PPK from behind his jacket and placing it on the table in front of him. 'Where are you going to be in forty-eight hours? Where can I pick up the passport?'

'If it's okay with Jesse we was thinking of dropping it off here,' replied Hud. Jesse shrugged her shoulders. 'Don't bother me none,' she said.

'That's fine,' continued Danny. 'Marie, if you don't mind, would you let Jesse look after you till then? After that I'm going to — hopefully — make sure you can go back home and forget all this ever happened.'

'Where are you going?' asked Marie.

'Got a few things to sort out,' replied Danny. 'You guys fit to drive?' he asked Ardel and Hud.

'We fit to fly, man,' answered Hud. 'Don't know if we's fit to drive. Why don't you take the wheel and we'll give you directions. You need some back-up?'

'Maybe,' answered Danny as he handed his Walther over to Marie. 'Would you mind holding on to this for me till we get back?'

'Sure. Why not.' Marie took the gun and put it in her purse.

'You okay, Mr O's bro?' asked Ardel. 'You acting all distracted, like you got a plan coming together in your head.'

'I'll tell you on the way,' answered Danny. 'You coming?'

★ ★ ★

Kneller watched the guy with the beat-up face push through the entrance door and walk towards him. Something about his manner — the way he carried himself, or the look in his eyes — made Kneller instinctively reach inside his jacket and rest his hand on the safety clip looped over his revolver.

The guy pulled up a chair and sat between him and Joe Evelyn like he was late for the meeting. 'Can I help you, mister?' Kneller said, keeping his gaze fixed firmly on the guy's eyes.

'I'm hoping we can help each other. My name is Danny McGuire. I arrived at Boston International on Saturday travelling on a passport in the name of Leonard with a few jobs to do, but due to some unexpected turns of events I've had to change my plans.'

'Why are you telling us things we already know? You trying to prove you been listening in to our conversation?' Kneller threw a glance over at Bulldog Jo then asked, 'You carrying any form of weaponry, Danny?'

'No.'

'Mind if I check?'

Danny held his arms out to the side and said, 'Feel free.'

Kneller stayed in his seat.

'Aside from throwing you in cuffs and sticking you in jail for the next forty years, you mind me asking what other business you got here, Mr McGuire?' asked Joe Evelyn.

Danny didn't answer. He'd already worked out that Kneller was the one in charge so he would direct the conversation towards him. Kneller had the touch: calling him by his first name like they were already friends. Asking if he minded being searched — as though it mattered to him what Danny thought — then not bothering to search him, letting Danny know he was already prepared to take him at his word. Kneller knew how to play the game.

Jeff Kneller picked the pack of cigarettes off the bar and offered one to Danny.

'Don't smoke, thanks,' said Danny.

Kneller took his time lighting his cigarette before continuing. 'My name is Jeff Kneller and this is Special Agent Joe Evelyn. Now, I know we've only just met, Danny, but already you strike me as the sort of person who doesn't get into a situation without a way of getting out . . . would that be correct?'

Danny nodded. Ardel and Hud were parked in the alley that ran along the back of the building. If everything was going well Danny would go to the restroom and flick the lights on and off. If he didn't do that within ten minutes of him leaving the car they were to make their way round to the front and get ready to start shooting.

'Well, assuming you wouldn't have walked in here tonight if you didn't think you could walk right out again,' continued Kneller, 'we'd be happy to hear what you've got to say.'

'I want to do a deal,' said Danny, his voice steady: under control. 'The girl Marie Bain, she has nothing to do with any of this,' he continued. 'All she's guilty of is trying to survive a shitty situation that wasn't of her making. I want any charges against her dropped and a guarantee of immunity from prosecution.'

'Do you know where she is?' asked Kneller.

'Yes,' replied Danny.

'Is that it?'

Danny hesitated: he couldn't be one-hundred-per-cent sure the FBI knew his brother was attempting to leave the country. If they didn't know, he would be compromising Sean, but at this stage it was an all-or-nothing throw.

'My brother Sean is going to get on a plane in the next few hours using the passport in the name of Mr Leonard — he must be allowed to go unimpeded, with no alerts sent to the British authorities for at least seventy-two hours.'

'Maybe we could organise to give him a massage and get his dick sucked while he's waiting to board,' exclaimed Agent Evelyn.

358

'If you're volunteering that'd be grand,' said Danny, 'but I'm not sure you're his type.'

'You think cause you strolled in here to face us off, you've got big balls?' said Evelyn getting up from his chair. 'All it means — asshole — is we've got a bigger target to kick when we beat the shit out of you and throw you in jail.'

'And . . . anything else?' interrupted Kneller putting a hand between the two men and pushing Evelyn back into his seat.

'I want to leave too — same deal as my brother: no alerts for at least seventy-two hours.'

'You booked your ticket?'

'Yes.'

Evelyn sat there trying to stare Danny down, but Danny ignored him: he hadn't come to start a fight. His only objective was to buy enough time to get Sean out of the country and then leave as well. Kneller took a long drag on his cigarette and finished the last of his beer before he said anything else.

'So far the traffic's travelling in one direction, Danny, and as far as I can make out there are a couple of juggernauts packed with explosives heading our way that could cause a nasty pile-up and get us all burned. We got information says you're here to procure arms, and that you have a contract to murder someone. We also got your brother down for a fatal shooting in Tuscaloosa, and a murder right across the street here in Cottondale. Whichever way you cut it, you and your brother are looking at a major term indoors, with no chance of parole. If your lawyer advised you to come here and make this play, I hope he — or she — also told you the only way you're gonna win is if you're playing with a marked deck, or you got a royal flush, otherwise you made a bad call. What I'm getting at is this: what do we get out of it, except clearing up all the shit you're proposing to leave behind?'

Danny noticed Kneller's hand resting on the handle of the gun. Kneller was taking the situation in his stride, playing it cool — but Danny had him sussed. He knew Kneller would have no hesitation in drawing the weapon and shooting him dead if he made one wrong move.

'In return for everything I'm asking,' replied Danny, 'I'll give you enough on Hernando De Garza to guarantee he'll never come out of jail again.'

Kneller's face was like stone: it was difficult to read any sort of reaction, but he was taking his time to answer, which told Danny everything he needed to know. If it wasn't a possibility Kneller would have dismissed it straight away.

'Can I get you another couple of Skeeters?' said Danny as he nodded over to Bulldog Jo.

'Sure,' replied Kneller.

'You mind if I go to the restroom?' asked Danny. 'I need to signal my colleagues to tuck their guns back in their pants and head off home.'

'Go right ahead,' said Kneller.

36

Sherwood Avenue, Tuscaloosa, early hours
of Thursday

Danny drove north-east along Jack Warner
Parkway for a few miles looking for somewhere
to pull over. He eventually turned right into
Sherwood Avenue and drove to the top of the
hill, where he parked, making sure the car wasn't
visible from any of the houses he had passed on
the way.

Sherwood was a quiet cul-de-sac with only
four or five bungalows on one side of the street
and a patch of tall woodland on the other. There
were no street lamps. The only light came from
small electric storm lamps that swayed back and
forth in the picket-fenced porches.

It was 12.30 a.m. and all curtains were drawn.
Danny killed the engine and sat in silence for a
few moments, watching the road behind in his
rear-view mirror to make certain no one had
followed him. When he was sure he was alone,
Danny got out of the car and made his way
round to the boot. Inside was a dark-blue
checked duffel bag and a slim leather case that
measured roughly four feet in length, and
eighteen inches wide. Danny lifted out the
narrow case and locked the car.

The air was cool and fresh: a faint hint of
the river mixed in with the aroma of pine from

361

the adjacent trees. Danny crossed to the other side of the road and climbed over a low barrier into the shelter of the shrubs that were scattered in large clumps under the canopy of the trees. If anyone did happen to glance out of their window, Danny would be well hidden.

Following the line of the road he walked quickly back down the hill through the trees until he was standing on the corner of Sherwood and Jack Warner Parkway, making sure he would not be visible to any passing motorists.

At this time of night there was little traffic, but a faint rumbling sound in the distance made him stop. The long shadows of the trees swept along the road as a large freight truck passed — its headlamps blazing — on into the dark night.

The two-lane County Road 88 ran parallel with Jack Warner Parkway, separated by a flat central reservation of dried grass. When he was sure there was nothing else coming, Danny sprinted across and disappeared into the tall spindly pine trees that ran along the eastern banks of the Black Warrior River.

The ground underneath the sprawling canopy was covered with rotting leaves and fallen pine needles. It wasn't long before Danny was standing on the shore of the great river. Moonlight reflected off the slick black surface as the current pulled it silently along its wide, meandering course.

In the far distance the lights of a bridge twinkled through the darkness and danced around on the swirling surface of the water. On the western bank — about half a mile from where he was standing — there was the dim outline of a large shed or boathouse.

Danny took a few paces back and, using his bare hands, began to clear a patch of ground. He had only just started scraping away the leaf-cover when he heard something crashing through the branches of the tree overhead. There was a loud shrieking sound and he dived forward, fumbling for his gun. He realised with dismay that he had left it in the glove compartment.

Danny twisted round just in time to see a black, misshapen form splash into the river just yards from the shore. His heart was thumping hard. Whatever it was struggled and thrashed around battling for its life.

'Jesus Christ, scared the shit out of me,' he muttered as he got back to his feet.

A large black raven was being carried away by the current, its waterlogged wings unable to break free from the Black Warrior's icy grip.

After only a few minutes the sound of thrashing gradually diminished until — eventually — all that could be heard was the rush of the dark river. The Morrigan's return had been a brief one.

Danny looked up at the clear night sky and wondered if the raven's death was an omen. If everything was going to plan then Sean would soon be boarding a plane to fly back home. Danny would follow on as soon as possible and together they would sort out the mess. But what if the FBI had gone back on their word and Sean was now languishing in jail somewhere in Alabama?

He returned to clearing the patch of ground.

When he finished Danny placed the leather case he'd taken from the car in the shallow hole and covered it with leaves. Next he looked around for some reference points, then stood for a few moments to make sure he had them fixed in his mind. He then turned, and — following the course of the river — walked along its shore, counting in his head the exact number of steps he was taking. The length of his stride was slightly exaggerated and would give him only a rough estimate of the distance, but that was all Danny needed. He had only been walking for five minutes when he stopped and looked across to the other bank. Directly opposite was the boathouse: 720 paces, just under half a mile — perfect.

When Danny got back to the car it suddenly occurred to him that he had nowhere to stay the night.

37

*Lookout Mountain, Alabama, Thursday,
morning*

Hernando De Garza reached across and replaced
the antique telephone handset in its cradle, then
propped himself up against the plump duck-
down pillows on his bed. He stared thoughtfully
at the small, silk, mauve-coloured lampshades
hanging from the excessive chandelier in the
middle of the bedroom. His mansion house — 'nest-
ling at the foot of Lookout Mountain in seventeen
acres of secluded rolling hills and lush green
pastures' — had seven bedrooms in total: one for
every day of the week. Today Hernando was in
Thursday's: modelled on a French boudoir, with
rich silk-braided curtains, and a deep-purple velvet
bedspread that complemented the ornately carved
seventeenth-century, black-oak bedstead. All the
bedrooms were themed: the French Revolution,
the American Civil War, the Second World War,
et cetera. The idea would have been a bad one if
Hernando hadn't had the money to carry it off to
perfection. Every detail — the antiques, relics
and mementos — that filled each room were all
one-hundred-per-cent genuine.

The oval-shaped entrance hall to the property
was covered in grey Spanish marble and had two
long sweeping staircases on either side that led
to the first floor. A large mahogany breakfront

chiffonier sat against the back wall of the landing with an original Picasso hanging above it. The Picasso had belonged to Hernando's grand-mother and — as far as the art world was concerned — no longer existed. His grand-mother told the insurance company the painting had been destroyed after a house fire and claimed substantial compensation for its loss. De Garza didn't particularly like the painting, but he loved the story behind it, which was why it had such a prominent place at the head of the stairs. It made him wonder how many other priceless works of art had a catalogue listing that read 'Destroyed by fire'. If anyone ever asked, he would tell them it was a passable replica of the original.

'What's the matter? You been staring up at that light for nearly ten minutes now and you haven't said a word. You worried no one's going to show up to your party?' asked Sly.

'I couldn't give a shit about the party,' replied De Garza wearily. 'I still don't like the idea of having it on a boat, but it's too late to change that now.'

'What's wrong with a boat?'

'You kidding me? Once you're on you can't get off. You're stuck on the goddamn thing until the boat has gone all the way from one end of the river to the other and back again: with all those city officials, and local suits, drinking your booze and kissing your ass, and if you *do* want to get off, you gonna have to jump overboard and swim ashore. The Black Warrior River isn't where you go for a quick swim, it's where you go if you want to drown. Even the fish don't like it.'

'I thought you enjoyed having your ass kissed.'

De Garza smiled distractedly. 'I do, but you end up talking to someone whose breath smells of shit.'

'Order some breakfast. You ain't even been awake half an hour and you're coming across all cranky. I think maybe your blood sugar is low.'

'Have you called those fair-skinned, red-headed mongrels across the water yet to tell them their boy McGuire has finally been in touch?'

Sly was sitting on a matching mauve-leather armchair at the bottom of the bed, bent over, tying his shoelaces. 'Not yet. I was thinking we should set up the meeting, shoot the fucker in the head, and pocket the money. He obviously hasn't been in touch with back home or he would know we've already concluded the deal: technically the Stingers belong to him anyway. This makes me think he's operating on his own. If those Irish cocksuckers ask, we'll deny ever having heard from him. McGuire has $200,000 that he's supposed to hand over to us, but as far as his people back in Ireland are concerned he's still a no-show. They don't know where the hell he is — but we do.'

'I agree with you, but we have to be careful,' replied Hernando, pulling his silk dressing gown closed. 'It's not going to be that straightforward.'

Sly sat upright and looked across at De Garza. 'What d'you mean?'

'That was Mr Danny McGuire on the phone. He wants to change the meeting place.'

367

'Where to?' asked Sly.

'He didn't want to say over the phone,' replied De Garza, still staring up at the chandelier.

'What's wrong with the *Bama Belle*?'

'Nothing. He's still coming to the boat, but he said we can't discuss anything to do with the Stingers.'

Sly furrowed his brow. 'What the hell is he playing at?' He stood up and walked over to check his appearance in the gilt-edged mirror hanging over the white-marble Regency fireplace. 'Why the fuck not?'

'Because he's going to be wearing a wire supplied to him by the FBI.'

Sly stopped preening and turned to look at De Garza. 'McGuire told you that?'

'Yes,' he replied. 'What I can't figure out is why he would do that?'

'Do what . . . go to the FBI?'

'Well, yes, that as well, but what I'm saying is why — if he is working for them — why call to tell me?'

'Could be he's trying to beat a charge. If the only thing they've got on him is suspected arms dealing — but there ain't no arms dealing going on — then they gonna have to let him go.'

De Garza nodded his head, but still looked unconvinced. 'Could be that simple, but something about it is giving off a nasty smell.'

'How we supposed to set up another meet if he won't discuss it over the phone and he can't say anything tomorrow on the boat cause he's wearing a wire. He telepathic or some shit like that?' asked Sly.

'He said when he comes onto the boat he's going to shake my hand and slip me a piece of paper that has written on it where and when the meet can take place.'

'Shit . . . sounds like he's trying to bend you over and show you what his big Irish dick is for. We gonna show up and find a few hundred FBI officers been invited to the party too: be hiding in the bushes holding a big net they gonna throw over us and capture our asses. You're right, there's some bad aroma coming off this one.'

'We got friends in the Bureau owe us a few favours,' said De Garza. 'Let's give them a call and see if they know what is going on. And if McGuire does show up at the boat tomorrow we'll get a couple of our boys to follow him when he leaves: see where the asshole goes. But make sure you warn them they could be part of a convoy, with the goddamn FBI tailing their asses as well: they best not do anything stupid.'

'If he's going to write us a note, and the meet's not for a few hours, why don't we just send one of our guys ahead to check it out. If it looks like there's a posse of Feds gathering then we don't show,' said Sly.

De Garza nodded again. 'You look like a dumb shit, but you got a brain in that pert little butt of yours, Sly. Now, I got another question for you.'

'Yeah,' said Sly.

'D'you think those lampshades need cleaning?'

38

The outskirts of Tuscaloosa, Thursday morning

Danny lay on top of the faded quilted blanket, staring up at the ceiling. The air around him was warm and musty with an unpleasant undertone of stale perspiration. It was well after 2 a.m. when he'd finally checked into the roadside motel near Northport on the outskirts of Tuscaloosa. He'd collapsed onto the bed and slept soundly for nearly nine hours. He was still fully clothed.

Danny ran through his plan once more, to make sure he had covered all the angles. The only real problem he could see would be shaking off the FBI once he'd delivered the note to De Garza. Danny had told them about the meeting and insisted that he be left alone to get on with the job, but he knew they would be watching.

One other potential problem: after the meeting De Garza would almost certainly have him followed. Danny thought it over a little longer before deciding that it would be no more than a minor inconvenience.

After a long shower he sat down to an 'all-day breakfast' of bacon and eggs that was delivered to his room along with a large pot of steaming coffee. Danny felt better than he had in days. The swelling on his face had reduced significantly and the deep purple bruising around his

370

right eye had given way to a lighter, less noticeable buttery yellow. He recognised himself in the mirror again.

De Garza's reception was scheduled to start at 1 p.m. At two the boat on which it was being held was due to set sail, spending the rest of the afternoon meandering up to Holt Lock, where cars had been laid on to take his guests home. Danny looked at his watch. It was now 12.15: time to go.

Danny scanned the room to make sure he had all his belongings, then pulled the door closed behind him. He walked in the shade of the narrow wooded veranda, then crossed the parking lot to a low-rise building housing the small reception area of the motel.

The old guy behind the upright desk nodded as Danny pushed through the glass door. 'Afternoon! You sleep okay?'

'Grand, thank you,' replied Danny, pulling a thick wad of notes from his jeans. 'How much do I owe for the breakfast?'

'Be an extra five dollars if that's okay.'

Danny handed over a twenty-dollar bill. 'Keep the change. That's the best breakfast I've ever eaten.'

'Thank you, nice of you to show your appreciation,' said the old guy, lifting up an old wooden cash tray and sliding the twenty underneath. 'Pigs are local. Get them from my friend Farmer Lee: he does the eggs too. Don't go in for all that processed shit you get in the supermarkets.'

'Do you grow the coffee too?' asked Danny.

371

The old guy smiled. 'Nope, but I roasts and grinds it myself.'

'You don't have a bit of paper and a pen I could borrow?' asked Danny.

'Sure,' replied the old guy. 'You want Farmer Lee's number? You won't get him in. Always out eating in restaurants trying to convince them to take his produce. Calls it work!'

'No, I need to write a note.'

The old guy tore a leaf from the back of the check-in ledger and handed it to Danny along with a pen that had the name of the motel embossed along its side.

Danny wrote one word on the piece of lined paper and handed back the pen.

'You done already?' asked the old guy. 'It must've been an important word for you to need to write it down.'

'It's an address to remind someone where to meet me.'

'And they'll know where they're going just from one word?' asked the old guy.

Danny folded the piece of paper four times and put it in his back pocket.

'Sure they'll know,' he said.

★ ★ ★

Fifteen minutes later Danny's black Cadillac pulled off County Road 88 and freewheeled slowly for a few hundred yards down an easy incline to the end of Greensboro Avenue. The road led to a wide, open parking lot that was situated on the south shore of the Black Warrior

River. The lot was almost full, and a number of onlookers and local press had gathered in the small quayside area to its left, where the *Bama Belle* steamboat was moored.

Danny drove round until he spotted an empty space, then reversed the Cadillac in and switched off the engine.

The grounds surrounding the quay were dry and featureless and provided little cover: nowhere for the FBI to hide, at least. A few bare trees and scrawny laurel bushes were all that separated the car park from the river. Acting as a backdrop to the scorched, arid landscape was a bridge: the Lurleen B. Wallace Boulevard. The structure was a deep gash of concrete that spanned the Black Warrior River, and spoiled the clear blue sky beyond it.

Danny sat for a moment taking in the scene. Two patrol cars were parked near the entrance to the freeway he had just turned off, and there were a few uniformed officers watching over the small crowd. A steady stream of cars and taxis made their way down Greensboro Avenue and dropped their passengers close to the boat.

Five musicians wearing checked shirts with bow ties and dark, ill-fitting suits stood just to the left of the gangplank leading on to the boat. They played a mixture of Appalachian and bluegrass classics; all their faces showed little or no emotion, in sharp contrast to the sliding tones and up-tempo beat of the music. The banjo player picked out the melody of 'Omie Wise' accompanied by a fretted dulcimer, a mouth bow and two fiddlers. The music reminded

373

Danny of the ceilidhs he'd attended with Sean and his mum and dad, when he was a kid growing up in Newry. Even if you didn't like the music it was impossible to stop some part of your body from joining in with the rhythm.

At a table on the quayside, guests registered their names and were handed badges to wear on their lapels to identify themselves. Danny counted four security guards: two at the head of the gangplank and two standing on the boat scanning the passengers as they joined the rabble on board. Just behind them was a small, dark-haired guy shaking people's hands and welcoming them with a disingenuous smile. This — thought Danny — must be De Garza.

It was only when he got out of the car and looked behind him that Danny spotted the dull brown van sitting in a clearing a few hundred yards further along the river bank. He was pretty certain Jeff Kneller and Joe Evelyn would be in there. It crossed his mind to give them a wave, but he decided against it.

Danny checked the time. Five minutes to go before the boat was due to leave. He made his way through the parked cars, past the trees and down towards the crowd and security guards standing on the shore.

'You have to register over at the desk, sir,' said a guy who looked like a professional wrestler, wearing dark sunglasses and no expression on his face.

'I'm not here for the cruise,' replied Danny. 'I have a message for Mr De Garza. He's expecting me. Would you let him know I'm here?'

374

'What's the name?' asked the guy.

'Danny McGuire.'

The guy spoke into the mouthpiece of the headset he was wearing and waited for a reply. Over his shoulder Danny could see De Garza nodding and looking across. The message came back that he was allowed to go on board.

De Garza greeted him like an old friend. 'Mr McGuire, how nice to meet you at last.'

As they shook hands Danny pressed the folded piece of paper from the motel into De Garza's palm. He didn't acknowledge it, but quickly placed his hand inside his jacket pocket. 'Are you joining us for our little trip upriver?'

'Unfortunately I have a few things I need to take care of before I head home,' said Danny.

'Sure!' replied De Garza. 'Well, best not hang around: boat's just about to leave.'

The meeting was over.

'Fair enough,' said Danny.

As he turned to go De Garza caught him by the arm and pulled him back. 'I forgot to say: I had a conversation with one of my friends at 18th Street; you know it? Where the FBI got their place,' continued De Garza. 'He seemed to think there had been no authorisation for anyone to wear a wire: he'd never even heard of you — can you fucking believe that? The guy's a commander, so I'm sure he's got his facts straight.'

Danny realised he may have underestimated De Garza. 'They're trying to fly this one in under the radar,' he replied calmly: repeating what Kneller had told him earlier. 'So I'm not surprised no one else knows.'

'I discussed the situation with a few of my business associates and we all agreed that we were willing to take the risk. We also agreed that my partner should come with you just now and show you the merchandise you are interested in buying. At the same time you can prove to him that you have the necessary funds: makes things easier. It means when we meet later, we can simply do an exchange.'

This was not what Danny had in mind. He was expecting to be followed, but taking one of De Garza's men with him now would screw the whole thing up.

De Garza was talking again. 'The alternative is: we ram the big 'fuck-off tablet' down your throat and pray you don't choke to death. That was my preferred option, but I was persuaded otherwise.'

De Garza's face betrayed no emotion. Either he didn't believe Danny was wearing a wire, or he simply didn't care.

'If that's how you want to play it, Mr De Garza, that's fine,' replied Danny. 'The commander probably told you about the unmarked observation vehicle watching everything that's going on: it's the brown van you can see over my shoulder. Provided you're happy to have *them* tag along,' continued Danny, 'I'm happy for your man to come for the ride.'

De Garza looked along the shoreline to where Danny had indicated and saw the van parked in the clearing. There was a moment's hesitation before he said, 'You make my shit itch, Mr

McGuire. My head is telling me you're going to fuck things up for me, but in my heart I'm a gambler . . . so let's see how this one plays out.'

★ ★ ★

Jeff Kneller and Joe Evelyn were sitting in the back of the observation truck looking at black-and-white screens, trying to make sense of what they were watching. Danny McGuire had just finished a brief conversation with De Garza and was now walking back across the gangplank, accompanied by one of De Garza's men.

'Jesus, is that Sly Rivera trailing behind him?' exclaimed Joe Evelyn.

'Yeah!' replied Kneller.

'You think McGuire's aware what an asshole Rivera is?'

'Well, we're not in any position to warn him if he doesn't,' replied Kneller.

'How we supposed to prove anything when we can't hear a goddamn word they're saying to each other. They could be passing on baking tips, for all we know. This is not evidence, this is bullshit.'

'I get the feeling we're not going to need to hear anything,' replied Kneller.

Joe Evelyn picked up a dull grey handset and pressed it to his mouth.

'Fat-boy, you ready to go?'

The line crackled into life. 'All set!'

'Denny, you take the lead and let Fat-boy trail. Get ready to move out.'

Kneller tapped Joe on the elbow and pointed

377

at one of the screens.

'Look.'

Just as Sly Rivera and Danny reached the black Cadillac a taxi drew alongside them. Kneller and Evelyn watched a woman get out of the cab and join the two men by the car. There was a brief exchange between them, then Danny turned and pointed straight at the van.

'Jesus shit! What the fuck is he playing at?' exclaimed Joe Evelyn. 'That's Marie Bain,' he continued. 'What the hell is going on here? . . . Shit! . . . Why did we agree to this? We're sitting here like a couple of old men watching a strip-show. Let's get on the stage and start fucking someone. Aiding and abetting, attempting to pervert the course of justice, forgery, illegal entry to the USA, conspiracy to murder, associating with a known criminal: let's round the lot of them up and bust their asses. We've got enough to put all three of them away for the rest of their lives.'

'She's walking towards us,' said Kneller.

★   ★   ★

'You mind if I sit in the back?' asked Sly as he climbed into the car.

'You can sit on the fucking roof if you like, makes no difference to me,' replied Danny.

'Now now, Paleface, what you getting all testy about?' said Sly as he slid in behind the driver's seat. 'We going to be together for a few hours, then we going our separate ways, won't see each other ever again: make things a lot more pleasant if we's friends for that short time,' he continued. 'Now, what you got in mind: you want to see what you is buying, or we going to have a look at your finances first? This beautiful little Glock 17 I got pointing at your spine says we ought to go to where the money's at: make sure it's all there. Got a suppressor fitted so only thing those FBI men are going to see is your body jumping about, if I decide to start shooting. They ain't going to be able to hear the shots. You ready to go for a ride?'

'Sure,' replied Danny.

As the Cadillac pulled out of its parking space Danny checked his rear-view mirror and saw Marie disappearing into the back of the brown observation van. He also saw a light-grey Oldsmobile on the other side of the car park swing out of its space and fall in behind. Sly caught Danny looking in the mirror and glanced over his shoulder. 'Don't worry about the Oldsmobile, Paleface, that there is what I call my insurance man. Goes by the name of Bo-Bo. He's going to trundle along behind us and make sure I'm okay. Bo-Bo ain't too bright, but he's a good shot. Conversation ain't his thing. More a shooter than a rapper.'

* * *

By the time Danny had reached the top of the road another two cars had joined the convoy. This time he was sure the cars belonged to the FBI.

Danny waited at the intersection for a gap in

the traffic then drove across the central reservation and swung left onto Jack Warner Freeway. He checked his mirror again. There were definitely three cars following him: none of them making any real effort to conceal the fact.

'Have you and Bo-Bo got any ideas what to do about the Federal agents that are on our arse?'

'Don't you worry about them, Paleface. Soon as we is a little bit further up the road I'm going to give you some directions. Take you up a few dark Tuscaloosan alleyways. You do like I tell you and we'll be fine. Fed-free and back on route to the money in no time.'

A little way ahead a turquoise-blue Chevrolet Camaro and a white 78 Ford Mustang suddenly pulled out in front of Danny, causing him to brake hard.

'Man, you get some asshole drivers, don't you,' said Sly. 'I ought to shoot their fucking tyres out. Teach them a lesson.'

For the next half a mile or so the Camaro and the Mustang drove alongside each other, blocking the road and preventing anyone from overtaking.

'You think it's right they give inbreds a fucking licence? GO HOME AND FUCK YOUR SISTER YOU GODDAMN RETARD. GET THE HELL OUT OF THE WAY,' screamed Sly.

Eventually the Mustang pulled over and allowed Danny to accelerate past. But no sooner had he done so than the Mustang moved back and blocked the road again. Bo-Bo started flashing the Camaro to pull over and let him pass as well.

Danny tapped lightly on his brake pedal three times then pushed his foot hard on the accelerator. He glanced in his rear-view mirror again to see if the Mustang and the Camaro were keeping up. They were right on his tail. All three cars started to pull away from the queue of traffic that had built up behind them.

'Hey asshole, slow down, we just about to hang a right,' said Sly.

The Oldsmobile that Bo-Bo was driving had nearly caught up with the group when the Camaro and the Mustang suddenly slammed on their brakes. Danny heard the screeching of tyres and the sound of the Oldsmobile careering headlong into the back of the Mustang.

At precisely the same moment Danny stamped down on the brake pedal and simultaneously yanked the steering wheel hard to the left. The Cadillac's front end dipped violently and the car spun almost 180 degrees before shuddering to a halt. There was no time for Sly to brace himself. He tumbled across the back seat and slammed into the rear passenger door — the impact knocking the wind from his lungs and leaving him gasping for breath. His gun had fallen to the floor and slid under the passenger seat in front. As he made a grab for the Glock the rear passenger door flew open and Sly looked up to see Danny McGuire standing over him, pointing a Walther PPK directly at him.

'Fuck you, Paleface,' wheezed Sly.

Danny shot Sly Rivera four times. Double-tap to the head — double-tap to the chest — all at point-blank range. There was no need to check if

381

he was dead. He reached in and dragged the limp, lifeless body across the back seat and out onto the freeway.

Two men wearing black, full-face balaclavas suddenly emerged from the Camaro and Mustang, and started sprinting along the freeway towards the Cadillac. Both of them were armed with Ingram M10 sub-machine guns. Danny quickly climbed back into the driver's seat and turned the key in the ignition. But the car wouldn't start: the engine was flooded. He tried again, this time without touching the accelerator pedal. The starter motor whined in protest as it cranked over and over, but still didn't catch.

The two figures were nearly at the car.

Suddenly the engine caught, and a dark cloud of exhaust fumes blew out from behind the car. At the same moment the back doors flew open and Ardel and Hud clambered in. 'There's gristle and all kinds of shit on these seats, man,' said Ardel as he pulled the balaclava off over his head.

Danny floored the accelerator pedal and the Cadillac screeched off down the empty freeway.

'Didn't know you were bringing a passenger, Mr O's bro. What happened? He say something to upset you?'

'He called you two 'inbreds', because of the way you were driving,' replied Danny.

'Did he now?' said Ardel. 'Asshole got what was coming to him then.'

★ ★ ★

Bo-Bo limped from the wreckage of the Oldsmobile over to the sidewalk and sat down. He was badly dazed from the impact of his head striking the dashboard at over seventy miles an hour, and there was blood streaming down his face from a deep gash on his forehead. Through clouds of billowing smoke and radiator steam he could just make out Danny's Cadillac disappearing over the crest of the freeway's shimmering horizon.

The blast of a horn made Bo-Bo turn.

There was little the driver of the tanker truck carrying three thousand gallons of gasoline could do to stop the freightliner careering into the wreckage piled up on the freeway. He'd noticed too late that the traffic up ahead was at a standstill.

Bo-Bo lifted his arms in a pathetic attempt to shield his face from the searing heat of the explosion.

★ ★ ★

Hud turned to look back at the rising column of smoke on the freeway. 'Man, when you pull a stunt you go all out. We got fireworks and all kinds of shit thrown in.'

Ardel sat nodding in agreement, then a thought struck him. 'The owner of that Camaro is going to be pissed when he sees what happened to his car on the news.'

A few minutes later the Cadillac turned off County Road 88 and stopped on the corner of Sherwood Drive. Danny jumped out and Ardel

383

climbed over from the back seat to take his place.

'We're going to pick you up here in exactly twenty minutes, Mr O's bro,' said Hud, winding down the rear window. 'Did you get a can of gas?'

Danny nodded. 'It's in the boot.'

'The what?'

'The trunk,' said Danny.

'We'll be driving a G-series Chevy van: it's red. Be waiting for you right here once we torched the Cadillac. I'm glad we don't know what the hell you is up to: makes it more exciting.'

Danny watched them drive off, then sprinted across County Road 88 and Jack Warner Parkway, and disappeared into the tall pines on the other side of the road.

★   ★   ★

Word of the freeway pile-up had not yet reached the partygoers on board the *Bama Belle*. A sumptuous buffet with platters of Cajun shrimp and smoked crab and great salvers of barbecue ribs and locally caught fish were being passed round by serving staff, with the guests encouraged to fill their plates. Hernando De Garza was standing near the prow of the boat — holding a glass of Lynch Bages in one hand and a Cohiba in the other — making small talk with the Mayor of Tuscaloosa and his wife. The party had been organised to celebrate the signing of a contract between De Garza's construction

384

company and the Mayor's office to develop a large area of land next to the University of Tuscaloosa. There was never any doubt that De Garza would get the contract: not when he was paying close to $100,000 a year into the Mayor's personal bank account.

A few of the guests noticed the column of grey smoke rising from behind the trees that shielded the river from the freeway, but no one thought anything of it. When the Mayor started yet another story with 'Oh I must tell you this one, it's a scream,' De Garza considered stubbing his cigar out in the fat fucker's eye. As he stood there listening with a fixed grin on his face he suddenly remembered the piece of paper that Danny McGuire had passed to him. It was supposed to have the address of where they were going to meet written on it. De Garza switched his cigar to his other hand and pulled the folded scrap of paper from his jacket pocket and opened it out. As he stared at it his brow furrowed.

'Are you all right?' asked the Mayor, breaking off from his story.

De Garza stared back at him with a vacant expression.

There was only one word, written in block capitals.

'HELL.'

The shot — when it came — was like the sound of a champagne cork being popped. Those who turned round saw De Garza lurch forward and fall to the floor. The Mayor heard a strange whistling noise just before De Garza's throat exploded in front of him, spraying the Mayor and his wife with shattered fragments of spine and blood from his severed jugular vein. The high-velocity hollow-point would have sliced his head clean off had De Garza not shifted his weight on to his right foot a split second before the impact. The scrap of paper he had been holding fluttered from his hand and landed without causing a ripple on the cold black surface of the river. As the water soaked into the paper the ink started to separate from it. It danced and swirled in unison with a droplet of De Garza's blood as it drifted along with the current.

The shot had been fired from exactly 720 metres away — almost half a mile — and had killed him instantly.

★   ★   ★

'Friend says he can land you at a small airstrip close to New York, but you gonna have to make your own way in from there. It's only a single-engine crate, but it'll get you where you're going,' said Ardel. The bright-red G-series Chevrolet van was cruising along Rice Mine Road heading for Tuscaloosa's regional airport. 'Got a present for you, Mr O's bro,' said Hud, handing Danny a small brown envelope. 'Got your passports, your airline tickets and a card from me an Ardel wishing you a safe journey home.'

39

The aeroplane was on its final approach into Glasgow International Airport. In less than ten minutes Sean McGuire would be landing in Scotland. From there it was a short bus ride to the coastal town of Troon, then a ferry crossing that would take no more than a few hours.

The time had passed without incident. The hardest part of the journey so far had been the train ride from Birmingham, Alabama to New York's Penn station. The only option available to Sean had been to buy a seat in a coach. He was on the train for the best part of twenty-two hours and in that time had managed to get just a few hours of fitful sleep. The rest of the train ride was spent staring out of the window at the relentless American countryside.

But the last few days' travelling were nothing: his real journey home had taken over eight years. Now — as the plane's wheels screeched along the tarmac — Sean could feel a growing sense of unease.

There was so much he wanted to say to his mother and to his wife: things he needed to explain. He'd tried to document the years he'd spent away — and his reason for leaving — by writing a sort of diary: more a random series of notes than a fully formed explanation. But

387

rereading some of the passages on the long flight across the Atlantic had only highlighted how inadequate they were.

For the moment Sean had to put Órlaith and his mother to the back of his mind. Their reunion would have to wait.

There was some business to take care of first.

★　★　★

The small queue inside the terminal building moved quickly. When Sean got to the front he handed over his passport. The customs officer looked at the photograph then back at Sean.

'Is this supposed to be you?' he said with a broad Glaswegian accent.

'It's me before I discovered alcohol,' replied Sean with a slight shrug of his shoulders.

'You here for a visit or just passing through?'

'Heading home,' replied Sean, 'for a decent pint of Guinness.'

'Did you pack an umbrella?'

'It's not raining *again* is it?' said Sean, playing the game. 'You know that's why everyone in Ireland's name begins with 'Mac' . . . to remind you not to leave home without one.'

The officer smiled and handed back the passport. 'Safe home, Mr Leonard.'

'I hope so,' replied Sean.

★　★　★

Sean booked a room in the hotel next to the airport and after a few beers and a hot shower slept until the following morning. After a quick breakfast he caught a taxi to Troon on the west coast of Scotland. Four days after leaving Tuscaloosa, Sean found himself standing on the top deck of a P&O ferry being blasted by the wind and rain that swept and blustered across the heaving Irish Sea. The sight of the ragged green coast of Ireland standing proud of the water caught Sean unexpectedly in the back of his throat. The cold streams of rain running down his face could easily have been mistaken for tears.

Eventually the large ferry manoeuvred noisily into position alongside the quay at Larne until the lines could be thrown and the boat secured to the huge brass capstans on the quayside. The retaining door at the back of the boat slowly descended till it touched the concrete ramp leading on to the dock.

Cars started to appear from the bowels of the boat and passengers disembarked in straggly lines into the red-brick customs hall. The sight of soldiers in their combat greens — arms folded across their chests cradling sub-machine guns — reminded Sean that he was re-entering the war zone: the sobering reality was that the hardest part of the journey was still to come.

40

Frank Thompson walked across the compound
to where the black Saab 900 was parked and
crouched down. Force of habit made him check
underneath the car for explosives before getting
in. The Saab was sitting in the grounds of the
Castlereagh security complex surrounded by a
twelve-foot-high perimeter wall and protected by
heavily armed officers of the Royal Ulster Con-
stabulary. The chances of anyone being able to
plant a bomb in or around the vehicle were less than
zero, but there was always that nagging doubt.

He drove round to the front of the building
and waited for one of the sentries to open the
large reinforced gates that guarded the entrance
to the headquarters of Special Branch. The
four-storey red-brick building to his rear was in
two sections that sat almost end to end, with one
wing situated just behind the other and
connected by a short corridor on each level. It
looked like a bland, badly designed office block,
but the clearly visible fortifications and array of
aerials and transmitter masts gave some small
hint of its fearsome reputation.

The large steel gates swung open, allowing
Frank to pass through and out onto Alexander
Road. A hundred yards further on he stopped at

the junction with Ladas Drive and took a few moments to decide which route he should follow home tonight. As the head of Special Branch he was a target: he'd seen — with his own eyes — the 'wish-list' of political figures and serving officers of both the RUC and Special Branch whom the IRA wanted to assassinate. The name Frank Thompson was high up amongst some senior politicians.

Frank left the office at a different time every night, he never drove home the same way on two consecutive evenings and as an added precaution he and his fellow officers shared a pool of different vehicles so that even the car he was driving changed from one day to the next. All the cars were fairly basic models that had been modified with bulletproof glass and armour plating. The downside was that the extra weight made them unwieldy and difficult to drive, and because the engines had to be supercharged to cope with the extra load they would often run out of petrol.

Frank switched on the radio and tuned in to Larry Gogan on RTÉ 2fm, 'cominatcha.' The soaring vocals of Billy Mackenzie, lead singer of The Associates, came blasting out of the speakers. 'White car in Germany' — it made Frank smile. He'd far rather be driving a white car in Germany than a black Saab in Belfast. Frank turned the music up.

He was trying not to think about work. The prospect of sitting at home by the fire with a large glass of red in one hand and a book in the other had — just about — carried him through

391

the day. The break-in and subsequent removal of the files on republican informers — now referred to in the office as the 'tout rout list' — was having a far wider impact in the media than he had hoped. Every newspaper in Ireland — and most of the broadsheets on the mainland — had covered the story and all of them had an opinion. There were various theories as to who the perpetrators were, ranging from the loyalist UDA and UVF, to the republican IRA and INLA. The British government's tactics, of creating a smokescreen so dense that it was impossible to tell which way was up and which was down, had worked. In a war where even people fighting on the same side didn't trust each other — and prejudice was ingrained — it was very easy to manipulate the truth to suit whatever agenda most satisfied the politics of the day. Frank's job was to fan the flames whilst steering the interested parties away from the real story: that the British government had run out of money to finance the Informers' Protection Fund and it was therefore easier, and cheaper, to hand them over to the very people they were informing on to dispose of: expediency at its simplest and most cruel.

The effect in the short term would be to make Frank's job a lot more difficult. Informers were easily groomed. They all had a certain characteristic that made them want to keep talking, informing on their comrades, spying on their neighbours. They would justify their actions by saying it was for the greater good — they were trying to shorten the length of the conflict — but really they were in it for themselves. Insecure characters with massively inflated egos: most of them had nothing else going on in their lives. Informing gave them a sense of importance.

Not any more.

Frank pressed the lighter on the dashboard and fumbled in his jacket pocket for his cigarettes: he was back up to twenty a day already. He inhaled as much smoke as his lungs could take and frowned as he glanced down at the folder sitting to his left on the passenger seat. Sheena had looked apologetic when she'd handed it to him. Not because of its contents, but because it was too late in the day and Frank was on his way home. 'First-draft report on the four SAS personnel that were murdered out at that cottage. D'you want me say you'd already left?' she had asked. 'No. I'll take it with me and have a read at home,' Frank had replied. 'It's classified, sir: not supposed to leave the building.' Frank had given her one of his looks and said nothing more.

He'd scanned the report briefly as he made his way downstairs and out towards the car park. Only one thing made him stop. Danny McGuire's name was mentioned on several occasions as a possible suspect and Frank suddenly realised that this might be the reason McGuire had unexpectedly disappeared. The close-surveillance team that had been tracking his movements for weeks reported that McGuire had vanished into thin air.

Frank put Danny McGuire top of his 'wishlist.'

It was only when he pulled up at the traffic lights on the corner of Castlereagh Road and Knock Road fifteen minutes later that he first noticed the dark blue VW Golf three cars behind. Something in his subconscious had made him aware of the car just after he'd left the compound, but now he felt certain it posed a threat. When the lights changed to green, Frank cancelled his indicators and instead of turning right drove straight on. The Volkswagen did the same. Traffic at this time of night was heavy, so Frank made a detour round Shandon Park and up through the Tullycarnet estate, all the time watching the VW in his rear-view mirror. It could be a coincidence, but Frank's training told him that coincidences in his line of work usually resulted in someone getting killed. Frank checked the petrol gauge. There was just under a quarter of a tank left: enough to get home, but not enough to get himself out of trouble if he suddenly had to put his foot down.

'Bollocks,' said Frank quietly to himself. DI Holden was the last person to use the car and should have filled the tank: those were the rules.

Frank pulled his Beretta from the side holster under his jacket and placed it next to the light-brown folder on the passenger's seat. The only problem he could see was that he'd have to wind down the window, or get out of the vehicle, in order to return fire: the windows were bulletproof. One of his colleagues had forgotten; he'd made the mistake of trying to shoot through the glass. The only injuries sustained had been self-inflicted. A bullet from his own weapon had ricocheted round the car before embedding itself in his thigh.

Frank decided to head onto the Upper Newtonards Road. It, in turn, led to the Portaferry Road, which had a single carriageway that ran along the eastern shore of Strangford Lough. If he were being followed it would be obvious. Also — due to the amount of oncoming traffic on the narrow road — it would be more difficult for someone to drive alongside and take a shot at him.

All the cars were fitted with an open-line communication system that gave him direct contact with an operator back at Castlereagh. Frank wanted to be sure before he called it in.

Ten minutes later the car was still behind him. Frank had identified the driver as being a male in his early thirties and had also memorised the car's number plate. The traffic had started to thin out and the Portaferry Road was unusually quiet, but so far the guy had made no attempt to overtake. He'd also made no attempt to hide. He was either incompetent or — which now seemed more likely — a civilian on his way home from work. Frank picked up the small handset and pressed the talk button.

'Anyone there?'

The built-in speakers hissed and crackled briefly before someone spoke.

'Yes, sir, everything all right?'

Frank recognised the voice. 'Liz?'

'Yes, sir.'

'Can you do a plate check for me? Need it urgently.'

'Certainly, sir, pencil's ready.'

Frank read out the number plate.

'Be with you in less than a minute, sir,' said Liz.

There was more hissing then Liz spoke again.

'Car's registered to an address in Portaferry, Sir, do you want the details?'

'No. Thank you, Liz, that's all I need to know,' replied Frank.

'Anything else, sir?'

'If you see Sheena will you tell her to stop worrying, I'll have it back to her in the morning . . . She'll know what I mean.'

'Understood. Goodnight, sir.'

'I bloody hope so, Liz . . . Goodnight.'

The guy in the VW was on his way home. It *was* just a coincidence. Frank felt a sense of relief: the last thing he wanted to do was get involved in a gunfight.

He was only minutes from home and the notion of one glass of red had turned into a bottle of red and a small Cohiba.

Just to be sure, Frank drove past his turn-off and took the next right into Watermeade Avenue. A few seconds later the Volkswagen sped past and disappeared into the distance. Frank reversed back onto the main road. Just moments later he squeezed his car through the tall hedge that surrounded his property and rolled gently to a stop in his driveway.

He lived on his own in a rented pebble-dashed bungalow, on a quiet street near Greyabbey, at the bottom end of Strangford Lough. It was considered too dangerous for his wife and two kids to move over so they had stayed in their main home back in Highgate, north London. At least once a month he got to fly home for the weekend, but it wasn't ideal. At times like this he really missed having his family around. Most of the time he was too busy to think about them, but when he did, the sense of longing for some sort of normality would eat away at him.

Frank got out of the car and stood for a moment enjoying the fresh spring air. He hadn't eaten all day and his stomach was making noises.

He entered the kitchen through the back door and made straight for the fridge. After grating some cheese onto a slice of bread and sliding it under the grill he headed into the lounge to light the fire and choose a bottle of red from the small rack below the bookshelf. There wasn't a big selection, but all the wines were decent: he would rather spend his money on six good bottles than twelve mediocre ones. Frank walked back into the kitchen and pulled the piece of toast from under the grill and froze.

Suddenly the hunger was gone.

A corner of the piece of bread was missing. It looked like someone had taken a bite and put it back under the grill. Frank sensed a presence behind him.

'You're some cook, big fella.'

Even though it had been over eight years since Frank heard it last, there was no mistaking Sean McGuire's laid-back tone.

Frank slipped his hand inside his jacket and realised with alarm that his gun was still sitting on the passenger's seat of his car.

'You wouldn't have time to pull the trigger anyway, Frank, so I wouldn't worry too much,' said Sean.

Frank turned and saw Sean McGuire standing in the kitchen doorway pointing a semi-automatic at him. 'You look very well for someone who's been dead for eight years, Sean,' he said, managing to sound nonchalant.

'Thank you,' replied Sean. 'You still look like a prick after eight years, Frank.'

'Thank you.'

'You don't seem that surprised to see me,' said Sean.

'I heard a rumour about your miraculous recovery. I suppose — somehow — I've been expecting you, although admittedly not as a house guest.'

'Who'd you hear from?' asked Sean.

Frank hesitated before replying, well aware that the question was loaded. 'An old friend of yours.' He raised the unopened bottle of wine he was holding before continuing. 'Do you mind if I pop this, I've been gasping for a drink all day?'

'Crack on there! I'm not here to ruin your dinner. I've a few questions to ask and then I'll be on my way,' said Sean.

Frank took two glasses down from the shelf above the sink and a bottle opener from the drawer and moved over to the small kitchen table in the corner of the room. 'D'you want a glass?'

'Too much ground to cover. Got to keep my wits about me, so no thanks,' replied Sean.

Frank poured himself a large glass of Burgundy and took a sip. 'There are security

398

cameras inside and out, and panic buttons in every room: in less than two minutes I could have this place surrounded, you know that?'

'Good for you, Frank. But you're forgetting — as far as the law is concerned, I'm dead: got a certificate to prove it. You'd have a job getting me into court. Anyway, that's beside the point: I've no intention of harming you. I'm not here for revenge, Frank. I'm in Ireland to get my life back, not fuck it up all over again. The gun is a defensive measure, not an offensive one. I'll only use it if you try anything stupid.'

'How's your brother taking your resurrection?' asked Frank, taking a cigarette from a packet that had been left on the kitchen table from the previous evening. He took a second to light up before continuing. 'We haven't seen him around for a while. Did he come back with you, or is he still in the States?'

'You tell me, Frank . . . you fuckers seem to know it all anyway,' replied Sean.

'It looks like he murdered four SAS men before he left, did he tell you that? If he shows his face around here he's going to the H blocks for a very long time . . . if he makes it that far: you know what the SAS are like when it comes to getting their own back. They don't go in for that 'revenge is a dish best served cold' shite.'

'Aye, well, you'll have to talk to him about that — it's none of my business.'

Frank returned to the kitchen table and pulled one of the wooden chairs from underneath it before sitting down. His job now was mostly administrative: office-based. He was seldom — if ever — out in the field. It had been a long time since he'd had a gun pointed at him. He'd forgotten how unpleasant an experience it was: one he'd never quite got used to. The only comfort was that Sean McGuire was not a hothead. Frank had no doubt in his mind that Sean would shoot him if he had to, but he believed him when he said it wasn't the reason he was there.

'What's his name, Frank?' asked Sean.

'Whose?'

Sean didn't reply. He stood in the doorway in silence, waiting for Frank to answer the question.

'It's irrelevant now, anyway,' said Frank eventually. 'The British government, for reasons best known to themselves, decided to 'release' the details of all the informers working for us into your organisation's hands. Whoever has the list has the answers. Why don't you go and ask them?'

'I've narrowed it down to one of six people that could be the Thevshi,' said Sean. 'There were only six people in our 'organisation' — seven if you include myself — with access to the information about the plot to bomb the Prime Minister. It has to be one of them. That day you asked me about it in Castlereagh, there was no way you could have known unless one of the six had told you. That's the only mistake I think the Thevshi made. He came to you too early; before anyone else in the IRA had any idea what we were planning. I just need a name, then I'll be on my way.'

'As far as I'm concerned,' said Frank, 'the name is in the public domain now anyway. It's not worth me getting shot for. The problem is I can't pass on that information in person: goes against my training. Why don't you say the names out loud and I'll nod when you get to the winner.' Frank took another drink of wine. 'That way I won't have broken the Official Secrets Act, and I can go to bed with a clear conscience.'

It crossed Sean's mind that Frank Thompson might be stalling for time, but he decided to play along.

'Either one of the two Rogers brothers?' asked Sean.

Frank didn't move.

'Eamon Ò Ruairc?'

'Shot dead outside his house a few weeks ago . . . keep going.'

'Tim O'Neil?'

There was still no response from Frank Thompson, but Sean wasn't surprised: he'd been fairly certain it wasn't any of them.

That left just two names.

Over the years of Sean's self-imposed exile he had picked over various scenarios and incidents in his mind that all six of the men had been involved in. He'd run through each one time and again: examining every small detail, or coincidence, reaction or turn of phrase that had struck him at the time as odd or out of place. He was looking for a link or common denominator that would identify the informer that had become known as the Thevshi: 'The Ghost'.

He always came to the same conclusion: there were only six possibilities, and of that six there were only two that Sean had suspected all along.

401

'Owen O'Brien?'

The hint of a smile flashed across Frank's face. 'O'Brien is a murdering psychopath with a brain the size of a walnut, his mind doesn't retain information long enough to be able to pass it on to a third party. He would be useless as an informer. If you called him stupid you'd be gracing him with an intelligence he doesn't possess.'

There was only one other person it could be, but it didn't make sense.

'E. I. O'Leary?'

'You've had eight years to mull it over, Sean, and you've missed out number eight: the most obvious . . . ' Frank took his time refilling his glass. 'All that time! I'm surprised you haven't worked it out. That day you went walkabout in Castlereagh, the Thevshi was in the room next to you. He was convinced you'd seen him. Wanted us to kill you there and then . . . just shows you, eh? He couldn't believe his luck when you got yourself blown up, none of us could. We should have known you'd faked the whole thing. We even had the SAS telling us they had nothing to do with it, but we didn't believe them. Well done, you had us all fooled. Incidentally, the Prime Minister was in the building that day as well. If you'd had your wits about you, you could have had a crack at her too.'

The telephone sitting on the counter top next to the sink started to ring. Frank looked over at Sean. 'That's my office calling to check I'm all right. They'll be wondering why I haven't rung in yet,' he said. Then, by way of an explanation, 'It's to cover eventualities such as this. What should I tell them? If I don't answer they'll send a couple of officers round to check I'm all right.'

'Tell them there's a dead man in your kitchen eating your dinner, but he's just about to leave.'

Sean watched as Frank made his way over to the phone.

'Hello Sheena . . . yes, sorry about that! There's a ghost in my kitchen, but he assures me he's just about to leave . . . bugger took a bite out of my cheese and toast . . . I'm fine. No, really I am fine. Sorry I didn't check in, something came up. Yes, see you in the morning . . . wait! Before you go, you don't happen to have Lep McFarlane's file handy, do you? Would you mind, I just want to check the approximate time of death and which side of his head they put the bullet in. No, take your time, I'll hold.' Frank watched the expression on Sean's face change as the implication of what he was saying slowly sank in.

Frank covered the mouthpiece on the phone with his left hand. 'If you want your life back, Sean . . . gather up your family and get the fuck out of Northern Ireland. The Thevshi is dead . . . someone beat you to it.' Frank turned and glanced out of the kitchen window into the darkness and waited for Sheena to come back on the line. 'Thank you, Sheena, that's great. Don't worry, I'll bring the report back in the morning. Goodnight.'

When he turned round again, Sean McGuire was gone.

Frank stood for several minutes without moving, giving Sean enough time to make his getaway, then picked up the phone and punched in a number. The phone rang for several minutes before it was answered.

'He's back,' he said quietly into the mouthpiece. There was no response from the other end of the line.

'I've put him off your trail for the time being, but it won't take him long to figure out what's going on,' continued Frank in a sombre tone. 'This is a courtesy call for old times' sake, but from now on you're on your own: that's official. You'll have no further contact with us or from us, do you understand? Any monies that are owed will be sent to the usual address. I hope you live long enough to enjoy it.'

Frank replaced the handset and stood in silence for several minutes staring at the wall.

★   ★   ★

The following morning Frank Thompson cast a bleary eye over the uniform he was wearing. The Secretary of State for Northern Ireland was visiting the province later that day and Frank was due to brief him on — amongst other things — the rising number of deaths related to the names on the 'tout rout list'. It wasn't only the informers that were being systematically hunted down and murdered. Frank had finally been given access to the names of those suspected of carrying out the break-in at his offices in Castlereagh when the list was stolen. He was under strict instructions not to make any arrests: which, as circumstance would have it, was purely

404

academic now. In the last week all the men involved in the burglary had been murdered, including the security guard.

There was a clear-up operation going on and Frank was certain he knew who was behind it. The Thevshi was protecting himself: destroying anything or anyone that might compromise his identity.

As he headed for the kitchen door Frank glanced over at the debris from the night before sitting on the table. Two empty bottles of wine and a whisky glass with an inch of Laguvulin still in it reminded Frank of why he was feeling so rough.

Outside the day was clear and bright, and the sun was starting to make an impression on the early-morning mist. He thought of his wife back in London getting the kids ready for school and reminded himself to phone her to apologise for being drunk when he'd called at one in the morning to tell her he loved her. That in itself wasn't worth the apology: he meant every word of what he'd said — it was the fact that he kept repeating it. A drunk's rationale: the more you repeated it, the more it was true.

'Bugger me, it's not raining!' exclaimed Frank to himself as he pushed his car key into the passenger-side door. Sheena's brown folder lay unread on the seat with his Beretta — in full view — sitting on top.

'Sloppy, Thompson . . . sloppy!' he muttered.

Suddenly, a shock of adrenalin swamped his system.

It was too late to turn and run: too late to do

anything. Without thinking he'd twisted the key in the lock. The circuit was complete.

With his arms hanging limply by his side Frank raised his eyes to the heavens and thought of his wife and children.

'Fuck you, Thevshi,' he said.

Despite weighing nearly one and a half tonnes the black Saab lifted six or seven feet off the ground and lurched forward towards the cottage like a toy car being thrown at a wall.

A bright orange fireball rose high into the air and for a brief moment obscured the sun.

41

It took Sean nearly three hours to drive from Frank Thompson's house in Greyabbey to the border with the Irish Republic. The traffic was light, but he'd taken a detour to pick a few things up on the way: cash and ammunition from Danny's post-office box, and a passenger arriving off the ferry at Larne.

Just as he was approaching a large army checkpoint that blocked both carriageways of the main Dublin Road near Jonesborough, he turned off and started heading along Lower Newton Road. As he drove deeper into the countryside, the roads narrowed until eventually they were barely wider than the car. The Carewamean Road twisted and turned as it cut through the large patchwork of fields and overhanging hedgerows. Sean had to concentrate. It was a long time since he had made his way to the farmhouse in Carrick-broad, and even though he'd nearly always made the journey in the dark, the once familiar landmarks now had eight years of growth on them: nothing was quite as he remembered it. One wrong turn could have him driving around the Armagh countryside for the rest of the night.

Eventually he came to a T-junction he recognised and made a left turn. Sean switched off the car's headlights and drove for another half a mile or so in complete darkness until he came to a small iron gate. Beyond it was a footpath that led through a large ploughed field to the back of E. I. O'Leary's farm buildings. It was just after 10 p.m. and there were several lights on in the imposing main farmhouse. To the left, some fifty metres away from the main house, were several large barns, one of them clad in corrugated metal sheets. Sean knew this was where E. I. O'Leary hid his contraband and had his illegal drinking den. The back end of the barn was just metres away from the official border with the Republic of Ireland and had a network of tunnels burrowed under the large barbed-wire fence that separated the two countries. The tunnels were once used for smuggling, but now mainly as an escape route.

The moment Sean stepped out of the car, the intervening eight years seemed to vanish. It could have been a month, a week, or even an hour since he'd been here last. The farmhouse looked exactly the same; nothing had changed.

Sean felt the chill, damp air seeping through the light cotton jacket he was wearing. Marie had bought it for him in Tuscaloosa to replace the blood-stained leather jacket with the hole left by Vincent Lee Croll's bullet. If everything had gone according to plan, Marie would be sitting down with Kneller and Evelyn signing an affidavit proclaiming her innocence, and that would be the end of it for her.

Tuscaloosa already felt like another lifetime. But Sean was aware that this was not the first time Marie had been on his mind since he'd returned home. He thought of the night in the motel, when he'd almost slept with her. He'd registered the confusion on her face when he'd pulled away — then frozen her out. He'd played the look over and over again in his mind and it didn't make him feel good. But it had been obvious even then that he would need to go back to Northern Ireland, and — at some point — face Órlaith. The circumstances around his disappearance and the reason for leaving he could just about explain, but there was no way he could stand in front of Órlaith and tell her he was in love with another woman.

Sean wished he could have explained the situation to Marie before leaving: filled in the blanks for her. But the less she knew the safer she would be. The only thing he'd left her in no doubt about was the fact that he would return. No matter what happened in the next few days, his life in Ireland was over.

The sound of dogs barking and the distant clank of chains as they strained against their tethers brought Sean's attention back to the present. They may well have caught his scent as they sniffed at the cold easterly breeze whistling between the farm buildings.

Sean climbed over the tubular-metal gate and made his way across the muddy field. He didn't feel any need to disguise his approach. As well as the dogs and regular armed patrols, O'Leary had a sophisticated security system in place. He would have been able to track Sean's car from as far back as the main road. O'Leary would already know someone was coming.

When he was just a few yards from the back door of the main farmhouse, Sean heard a familiar metallic click and a voice from somewhere in the surrounding darkness.

'Keep your hands where I can see them and state your business, mister. If you know what damage a double-barrelled shotgun can do then you won't want to be making any sudden movements.'

The dogs tied to a fence post on the other side of the yard were growling menacingly, their muzzles curled up at the edge, baring their sharp teeth.

'I'm here to see O'Leary,' he replied calmly.

'Is that right! And do you have an appointment, or d'you think you can just wander in off the street any time you like?'

'Tell him Sean McGuire's here.'

There was a moment's silence before the man with the shotgun spoke again.

'Put your hands up against the wall there, Sean, spread your fingertips and spread your legs . . . you know the routine.'

Sean did what he was told and stood spread-eagled against the white roughcast wall while he was searched for weapons.

★　★　★

Minutes later he was led into a low room with dark oak beams running in parallel strips along the length of its ceiling. E. I. O'Leary was standing with his back to a large blazing fire: his arms wide open like he was expecting the two of

410

them to embrace. Before he'd even said a word Sean could tell E.I. had a drink in him.

'Well, if I wasn't seeing it with my own eyes I'd never have believed it,' said O'Leary. 'Easter's been and gone, big fella. The resurrection thing is old news. The Son of God beat you to it. What do I call you? Is it Sean, or Lazarus . . . or Finn O'Hanlon?' E.I. continued. 'Please tell me it's not the Thevshi . . . Though to be honest with you Sean, everything is so fucked up these days, nothing would surprise me. Can I get you a drink?' E.I. moved over to a large, ornate Georgian drinks cabinet that looked out of place in the rustic farmhouse. He pulled out a bottle of whiskey. 'A wee Bushmills to warm you up? It's Black Label.'

'I can't stay,' replied Sean. 'Got a few things I need to sort out, but thanks anyway.'

'Your ma must be delighted. She took your 'passing' bad. Wouldn't let us anywhere near your funeral, so I've no idea if you got a good send-off. I tell you Sean, if I looked as good as you after eight years buried, I'd think about giving the death thing a go. But here, if you're in such a hurry let's not fuck about. What are you doing sneaking round a man's back yard in the dark? Are you looking to get yourself killed for real? What do you want?'

'Whose idea was it to take the wee one and the Fitzpatrick girl?'

E.I. turned and gave Sean the stare.

'Watch your tone, big fella.'

Sean heard the threat in E.I.'s voice, but he didn't care. He kept O'Leary fixed in his gaze.

411

E.I. grinned. 'Come on, let's not get off on the wrong foot. The kidnappings were certainly not my idea, if that's what you're suggesting,' he continued, 'although in the light of recent events I'm beginning to think it wasn't such a bad move. Your Danny is causing us a major fucking headache. I got a call in the middle of the night to say that a business associate of ours, Hernando De Garza, has been hit: long-range sniper shot, one bullet, nearly ripped his head from his body. Now whose modus operandi does that sound like to you? God only knows what the implications are for us if it turns out Danny was the triggerman. He's got the SAS after his arse too. They seem to think your brother whacked four of their comrades, and if all that isn't bad enough, he's still cutting about with $200,000 of *our* money that he was supposed to hand over to De Garza. Not to mention the money we paid him — in advance — to show *you* the door marked 'exit'. So, let's just say, the IRA would like to have a word in his ear too. For what it's worth, I think taking the wee one was a mistake: overstepped the mark. But you know what Owen O'Brien's like when he gets that look in his eyes, there's no stopping the stupid big fucker. By all accounts he went after yer ma and Órlaith too, but they've done a runner. Smart!'

'Where are the girls?' asked Sean.

'Where's our $200,000?'

Sean wanted to grab the whiskey bottle from E.I.'s hand and smack it over his head, but for the moment he simply turned and headed for the door.

'Here's the deal,' said E.I. as Sean reached for the door handle. 'I've known you and your family for a long time. Whatever happened to you eight years ago we can set aside for the moment. Right now I don't give a shit why you disappeared. One day, maybe, we'll sit down, crack open a bottle and you can tell me the whole story, but for now let's just say it's good to have you back. As far as De Garza goes, I know Danny will have his own version of events and I'm willing to sit down and listen: take him at his word. I know he's as straight as they come. Money is not what drives your brother. He may not be a member, but he's a believer, I know that. You guarantee the $200,000's safe return and I'll give you my word no harm will come to the wee one, or to Danny.'

Sean stood by the door with his back to E.I.

'Unfortunately,' continued O'Leary, 'I can't give you the same assurances as far as the Fitzpatrick girl is concerned. I'm still not sure what went wrong, but the word on the street is she had a pretty rough first interview with O'Brien. Shame really! Turns out I knew her father: he was a good republican man. Anyway, what d'you say, have we got a deal?'

Sean looked back at E.I. with no expression on his face and said, 'I'll see what I can do,' as he headed out the door.

★　★　★

Sean wiped his feet along the grass verge to get rid of the mud from his shoes, then climbed back into the car and pulled the door closed.

The Thevshi had haunted Sean for almost a decade now. The question over his identity had eaten away at his subconscious ever since he'd left Ireland in forfeit of any chance of a normal life. But Frank Thompson was right: it was now irrelevant. He was certain Thompson was trying to throw him off the scent by implying that Lep was 'The Ghost', but Lep had been inactive for as long as Sean had — over eight years — and never had access at a high enough level for him to pass on any useful information to the security forces.

That left the same two names as before: Owen O'Brien and E. I. O'Leary.

Sean turned the key in the ignition and waited a few moments for the warm air to start flowing through from the engine. He opened the glove compartment and pulled out two Heckler & Koch P7s, dropped the clips out of both handles and checked they were loaded. He laid one on the seat beside him and put the other back in the glove compartment, then reached over and pulled a long black coat off the back seat. Underneath the coat lay an AR15 semiautomatic assault rifle and on the floor, just in front, a plastic shopping bag with five thirty-round STANAG magazines. He slid one of the magazines home until it clicked and locked in place, then wound down the window. All he had to do now was wait for his brother.

The passenger he'd picked up from the ferry port at Larne was his brother Danny, who had lain under a coat on the back seat — hidden from view for the rest of the journey to O'Leary's.

When they'd arrived at the farm Danny had waited for Sean to cross the field before slipping out of the car, unseen.

Sean checked his watch. Another two minutes and he'd open fire at the farmhouse.

★ ★ ★

E. I. O'Leary stood staring into the fire. He had a lot on his mind.

Over the years he had come to put more and more trust in Owen O'Brien, but now there were serious doubts creeping in; maybe there was more to him than met the eye. It was O'Brien who had first come to him with the revelation that Finn O'Hanlon was the Thevshi. He claimed to have picked up a scent coming out of Dundalk. Lep McFarlane had been overheard shouting his mouth off in the Emerald Bar that he was about to make a comeback and clear his name. He was drunk. By the time O'Brien arrived at the pub, McFarlane had disappeared, but not before telling anyone who'd listen about his contact with Finn O'Hanlon. O'Brien must have seized the opportunity to pass him off as the Thevshi, but sending Danny McGuire over to kill him had screwed up the plan. No one — not even Danny himself — could have guessed at O'Hanlon's real identity.

The more E.I. thought it through, the more the story fell into place. Owen O'Brien had organised the break-in at Castlereagh: the whole

415

operation had been under his command. He had kept the list of informers that Special Branch had 'supplied' to them close to his chest. Anyone associated with the break-in — or who had seen the contents of the list — had been murdered. Maybe O'Brien's name was on the list as well and that was why he didn't want anyone else to see it?

It would explain why he was so diligent in his role as head of internal security for the IRA. If a tout was becoming a problem for the Special Branch they could pass the details on to O'Brien and have the problem eliminated. In the event that O'Brien was spotted talking to the security forces he could haul the accuser in for questioning, charge them with being an informer and execute them without raising any suspicions: it was always his word against theirs. A reciprocal arrangement that worked well for both parties!

E. I. O'Leary had come to a decision. Whether O'Brien was the Thevshi or not didn't matter now: he was out of control and had to die. Danny McGuire — because of his actions in Tuscaloosa — had become too much of a liability, and he too had to die. In order to prevent any reprisals Sean McGuire would also get the bullet.

He would make it clear — to whoever was dumb enough to ask — that Sean McGuire *was* the Thevshi, and that way avoid any embarrassing questions regarding the length of time O'Brien was able to carry on informing without raising suspicions. It would also save having to make reparations to the families of those who had been wrongfully accused and murdered by O'Brien. The Thevshi would be dead. De Garza's associates would be satisfied that the IRA had acted swiftly to eliminate De Garza's assassin and a valuable link to the supply of arms would hopefully remain intact. It was a good plan.

This was the reason O'Leary was the head of the organisation: he could see the bigger picture and he wasn't afraid to make difficult decisions. No problem was so big that a few simple executions couldn't put it straight.

It was getting late, but he could at least make a few phone calls and set the wheels in motion. After that he might take the dogs for a walk.

E.I. left the lounge and made his way down the short corridor and into his study. He placed his glass of whiskey on the large oak desk and lifted the receiver before sitting down. He didn't know why, but he suddenly felt uneasy. Something was wrong. Instinct or intuition made him slide his hand under the desk and unclip his revolver.

The dogs had stopped barking.

* * *

Sean chose a lighted window and waited a few moments to make sure there was no one moving around inside. He didn't want to hit someone by mistake. When he was sure, he lifted the AR15 and fired two short bursts, then chose another window and fired again. A few seconds later there were figures running around the yard, their

417

outlines silhouetted against the white walls of the farmhouse.

E.I. looked up from his desk. The sound of the upstairs window crashing to the floor made him start. He jumped up from behind the desk with the revolver in his hand and ran into the hallway. 'Seamus, Brendan, are you there?' he shouted down the small corridor. 'What the hell is going on?' But there was no reply. More gunfire and another window shattered. He could hear his men outside shouting to one another. E.I. ran back into his office and pulled the corner of the paisley-patterned rug aside, then lifted the heavy latch on the trapdoor and descended into the underground tunnel, letting the trapdoor fall closed behind him.

As he squeezed his way along the narrow passage the trapdoor suddenly flew open again. E.I. tried to twist round, but the confines of the tunnel and his large bulk made it almost impossible. He finally managed to turn enough to aim his revolver, but there was nothing to shoot at. The air around him filled with smoke as he fired off a couple of warning shots.

O'Leary shouted over his shoulder, 'You've picked the wrong man to fuck with,' but again, there was no reply.

Something dropped onto the ground with a dull thud and the trapdoor slammed shut. E.I. twisted sideways to allow more light from the string of worker-lamps hanging overhead to illuminate the floor. As he strained to see what the object was, he suddenly recoiled.

'Holy Mother of God!'

★ ★ ★

Sean watched the silhouetted figure sprinting across the field towards the car. There were muzzle-flashes from various locations round the farmhouse and bullets whistling overhead. He raised the AR15 and pointed it out of the window, fixing the crosshairs of the sight on the advancing figure; when it was less than twenty yards away Sean fired a short burst either side, then slid the rifle back under the coat on the back seat. A few moments later the passenger door flew open and Danny climbed in.

'Jesus, you nearly took me down there, big fella. What were you firing at me for?'

'If I'd been aiming at you, you wouldn't be sitting here now,' replied Sean. 'I was making sure O'Leary's men kept their heads down.'

Suddenly there was a loud bang and the window behind the driver's seat shattered.

'What are you waiting for?' said Danny, trying to catch his breath.

Sean crunched the gearstick and the car sped off along the narrow lane.

'How'd it go?' asked Sean.

'Fine!'

'What did O'Leary say?'

'He never said a thing,' answered Danny.

'What did you say to him?' asked Sean.

'I never said a thing,' replied Danny. 'I left him talking to a hand grenade.'

42

Slim Jim McMahon took a couple of faltering steps onto the wet pavement at the front of the Bridge Bar and stopped to light a cigarette. He cupped his hands together to shield the fragile flame from being extinguished by the cold easterly wind. It took several attempts, but eventually the cigarette glowed fiery orange and a cloud of smoke swirled and twisted into the night sky. Slim stood impatiently with his head bowed against the stiff breeze and waited for a car to splash its way along the road.

He was about to cross North Street when he caught sight of a figure withdrawing into the grimy shadows of the building opposite.

Slim's brow creased to a frown. It was just before midnight. He had been drinking Guinness for nearly five hours and was willing to accept that he'd had too much to drink: his inebriated mind could be playing tricks on him. But he knew instinctively that what he had seen had nothing to do with the alcohol.

Slim's eyes narrowed, trying to detect further movement. But apart from a line of parked cars on either side, the street appeared to be empty. Slim decided to go back into the bar and put a call in to O'Brien: tell him what he'd seen . . . the rumours were true. Sean McGuire was back from the dead.

As he turned there was a flash of steel that reflected the glow from the street lamps. Slim felt a sharp stabbing pain at the top of his stomach. The blow appeared to come from nowhere. There was another bright orange flash and another stabbing pain. Before he could react or retaliate, a knife was rammed home for a third time, penetrating just below his ribcage and puncturing his left lung. Slim reeled backward and stumbled with the handle of an eight-inch 'Black Bear' combat knife protruding from his dark overcoat. He reached his arms out and tried to twist round to break his fall, but the speed and ferocity of the attack had taken him off guard; his reactions were too slow. Slim hit the ground hard, his nose and forehead striking the solid pavement with a sickening thud. He tried to stand up, but the sole of a boot stamped down on the side of his face, pinning his head to the ground, making it impossible for him to move.

'Do you know where your abdominal aorta is, big fella?' said a quiet, familiar voice.

'Fuck you,' Slim spluttered.

'The amount of blood you've got pumping out your stomach I'd say I've scored a direct hit. Blood in your mouth too, that means I got your lung. Bull's eye on both counts! Tell me where the girls are and I'll call an ambulance, but you'd better hurry up, you could drown before it gets here. Simple question: where are the girls?'

Slim Jim McMahon was already gasping for breath, the short, sharp inhalations making an unpleasant gurgling noise in his throat.

421

Everything was happening too quickly.

His left lung had already started to fill with fluid. That, in combination with the rapid blood loss and lack of oxygen, was making him feel nauseous and confused.

On the other side of the street the figure he had noticed earlier emerged from the darkness and stood staring across at him. No question this time; Slim definitely recognised him. 'It *is* Sean McGuire,' he said, answering his own question.

'He's waiting for me to give him the nod,' said the figure standing over him. 'If I do, he'll go into that telephone box over there and dial 999. But the longer you leave it the less chance you've got. The choice is yours: priest or paramedic? Where are the girls, Slim?'

McMahon was dying. His breathing was becoming increasingly noisy and laboured.

'Cochron Road, near St Joseph's,' he replied, spluttering out the words. 'I told that fucker O'Brien it was wrong. And I tell you, I played no part in what happened to the Fitzpatrick girl.'

Slim felt the pressure on his skull suddenly ease.

He tried to sit up, but the effort made the pain in his stomach worse and started a coughing fit that had him writhing around on the wet ground, moaning in agony.

A shadow passed over his face and he could feel a presence close by, but in the dim light it was impossible to make out anything other than a hazy silhouette.

'I had nothing to do with it,' he repeated, sounding increasingly desperate.

Slim could feel the figure's warm breath on the side of his face. A voice, barely raised above a whisper, said, 'You were there.'

Slim Jim McMahon was disorientated. The figure appeared to float away from him: hovering just inches above the ground like a spectre as it travelled silently across the street to join Sean McGuire on the other side. It didn't stop, nor did it turn as it moved away.

Danny and Sean McGuire walked together for less than twenty yards, then climbed into a car. There was never any intention of an ambulance being called.

The blood gurgled in Slim's throat as he rolled over and swallowed his last breath.

★   ★   ★

Fifteen minutes later, Sean scaled the slatted wooden fence at the end of the rear garden of a small semi-detached house in Cochron Road and dropped silently onto the overgrown lawn. There was a light on in the kitchen. Three men sat round a table drinking beer from cans and smoking cigarettes, but there was no sign of Angela or Niamh.

As Sean edged closer to the rear of the house he recognised them. Chip O'Shea: a ratty little prick with rotting teeth and a permanent sneer. Marky-Mark McGuigan, who rode shotgun for O'Brien, and the big man himself, sitting at the head of the table scowling at the hand of poker Chip had just dealt him. He was positioned at the far end of the kitchen closest to the door and was partially obscured by the other two.

Sean hadn't seen any of them for almost ten years, but aside from slightly heavier-set faces and less hair they all looked exactly the same.

He had a clear line of fire to McGuigan and O'Shea, but O'Brien was more difficult.

There was no clear plan. All Sean had to do was wait for something to happen: that's what Danny had said as the two had parted company.

He didn't have to wait long. Suddenly all three men stood up. O'Brien reached behind his back and pulled a handgun from his belt. The skinny guy, O'Shea, picked up an Armalite from underneath the table and was already on his way out of the room with Marky-Mark following close behind, a shotgun clamped across his chest.

Sean raised the assault rifle to his shoulder and took aim.

On the other side of the building, outside the front door, stood Danny with his finger on the doorbell. He wasn't going to release it until someone answered.

In his left hand he held a Heckler & Koch P7 with a suppressor fitted: the small round end of which was pressed firmly against the spyhole situated two-thirds of the way up the door.

He heard a voice from inside. 'Who is it?' asked Chip O'Shea.

'The bogey man,' replied Danny.

Danny counted three seconds for Chip to put his eye up to the door and fired a single shot through the spyhole.

From the far end of the hall Owen O'Brien saw a jet of blood spraying out of the back of

424

Chip O'Shea's head before his skinny frame slumped slightly and collapsed limply to the floor.

* * *

Outside in the garden Sean squeezed off two short bursts. The kitchen window shattered and O'Brien saw Marky-Mark's body suddenly lift three or four inches off the ground and fly backwards against the kitchen wall. Half of his face was missing and there was a stream of blood pumping steadily from a cluster of bullet holes in the middle of his chest.

There was a loud rapping noise next to O'Brien and a cluster of ragged holes suddenly appeared in the door frame just above his right shoulder. Splinters of sharp wood lacerated the side of his face. He lurched to the side and tumbled out of the kitchen.

O'Brien's instinct was to run. He considered heading out through the garage, but there was no way of knowing who, or how many, were involved in the attack: it was too risky. His best option was to get the girl.

* * *

The garden was now in total darkness. Sean was sure he'd taken down Marky-Mark with his first burst of fire, but he couldn't be sure if he'd been killed outright. He made his way over to the kitchen window and climbed onto a waste pipe. Marky-Mark's body lay still on the kitchen floor.

Sean hauled himself onto the ledge and swung his legs over the sink, then dropped onto the linoleum-covered floor. As he cleared the doorway he saw O'Shea's body lying at the other end of the hall.

Suddenly there was movement upstairs and the sound of a young girl screaming. Outside, Danny could hear the screams too. He stood back and emptied a full clip into the front door, then started kicking.

Sean made his way quickly down the hall. 'Wait up, Danny, wait up, it's me, I'm inside,' he said with an urgent whisper.

Sean bent down, dragged Chip O'Shea's limp torso clear of the door and yanked it open. There were a few more muffled screams then the house fell silent. Danny dropped the clip out of the bottom of his gun and reloaded. 'You keep me covered till I get to the landing, then I'll cover you,' said Danny.

Sean knew what his brother was doing. The first person onto the stairs was the most likely to get shot. Danny was volunteering to be that person.

Sean shook his head. 'I'm going first.'

Before Danny had a chance to argue, Sean was already at the foot of the stairs. With his AR15 pressed firmly to his shoulder Sean cautiously made his way up to the first landing. After checking that there was no one on the floor above, he gestured to Danny to join him. Sean then edged up the next flight of stairs until he was standing outside the door of a bedroom on the upper landing. There were two other doors

426

leading off: all of them closed. Sean tried the first handle. It wasn't locked.

Danny was squatting on the step just below him, with his back against the banister — his gun pointed at the bedroom door. When he gave the nod, Sean twisted the handle and pushed. The door swung open and crashed noisily against the wall inside the room.

The men stood stock-still and waited, listening.

An uneasy silence returned to the house. Sean moved first, slipping sideways into the darkened room. The stench of urine, dried faeces and vomit was overwhelming. He immediately put his hand up to cover his mouth and nose. Danny was right behind him, standing in the doorway, peering into the gloom: unaware that this was where Angela had been just a few days earlier. The windows were boarded up and all the furniture had been removed except for a single solitary chair that sat in the middle of the floor. Sean knew instantly what the room was used for. If he'd learned anything from his years away it was that he no longer wanted anything to do with this life. If he survived the next few days, he was getting out and never coming back.

A muffled thumping noise from overhead made them both turn back to the hallway. The hatch leading to the attic was open: the hole cut in the ceiling was much larger than normal.

'O'Brien's trying to get next door through the roof space,' said Danny, as he climbed onto the banister and tried to hoist himself up into the dark void.

There was a sudden flash of light from

somewhere deep inside the attic and the wooden rafter just above Danny's head made a loud cracking noise as a bullet from O'Brien's gun burst through it. Danny ducked out of the line of fire, but lost his footing on the banister and fell heavily onto the floor of the landing.

Sean quickly pulled him up. 'You okay?'

'Fine,' replied Danny. 'O'Brien's in the roof space of the other house.'

'I'll head out the front and see if I can get in next door,' said Sean, already on the move. 'You stay here in case he doubles back.'

But Danny had no intention of staying anywhere: he was already balancing on the banister, reaching up to try again. He grabbed hold of the ceiling joists that ran along the inside of the trapdoor and heaved himself up into the darkness.

★ ★ ★

O'Brien had wrapped some tape round the girl's mouth to try and shut her up, but she was still hysterical, writhing around, making it difficult to move quickly. It would be much easier just to shoot the little bitch in the head. He considered it for a second, but right now she was more valuable alive. Once he was clear of the house he'd rethink.

The IRA owned both properties and had knocked through the dividing wall in the attic to provide an escape route in case the security forces raided either of the houses. But some arsehole had padlocked the attic door in the

428

other house shut. O'Brien stamped down heavily on the flimsy hardboard panel with his foot, but it didn't budge.

There was a movement to his right. He glanced over and saw Danny McGuire's head poking through the open hatch in the roof space next door. O'Brien fired one round, but it was impossible to tell if he'd hit him or not. Two more shots at the metal plate that secured the padlock in place, and the trapdoor dropped open.

He only had one full clip — twelve bullets in total — after that he was out. The rest of his shots had to count.

★   ★   ★

The first-floor landing next door was in darkness and the air smelled damp and fusty. Moments later O'Brien was climbing down the foldaway ladders with Niamh slumped over his shoulder like a rag doll.

Just as he reached the head of the stairs, there was a burst of automatic gunfire and the front door flew open. He pulled Niamh round in front of him and pressed his gun roughly into her temple. She flinched and started struggling again, but he simply squeezed more tightly, crushing the air out of her until she stopped.

O'Brien had nowhere to go, but that didn't matter. He had the girl.

He glanced quickly from side to side; first at the hatch in the ceiling, then down to the hallway below. He was pumped: ready for anything. 'Life or death: who gives a fuck?' he thought.

★ ★ ★

A narrow opening in the middle of the brick wall was all that separated the two buildings. There were three large white box-shaped objects sitting in a row under the ridge of the roof. Danny made his way carefully over the ceiling joists towards the crude doorway. As he got closer he realised that what he thought were boxes were actually large larder freezers. This explained why the trapdoor to the attic was much wider than normal. It must have been enlarged to accommodate their bulk. It was a curious thing to do: who would want such large freezers in their attic? He edged his way over and lifted the lid of the one nearest to him. As it opened, the freezer light came on, illuminating the surrounding attic space with a dull, eerie glow.

The sight that greeted Danny as he peered inside made his stomach turn. The freezer was full of body parts. Laid up like lumps of meat: butchered to make them fit the confined space. Stored here to prevent them from spoiling and causing a stench, until such time as they could be disposed of more permanently. A piece of arm cut from the elbow joint was clearly visible through a thin layer of white frost. But worst of all, a head shorn at the neck: the face partially covered by long matted strips of hair and caked with dried blood; the drawn, colourless skin stretched tight over its skull.

Danny stared at the head in horror, unable to break away. Suddenly every muscle in his body contracted in the same instant, as a terrible realisation left him struggling to catch his breath.

He recognised the face.

Danny reeled back, slamming the lid closed behind him, and crawled backwards until he hit a wall, forcing him to stop. Why had he opened the lid? What had made him do it?

He started to retch.

Danny could hear voices from next door and Sean calling out his name, but he couldn't answer.

The image of the raven battling for its life in the Black Warrior River flashed through Danny's mind, and he wondered if that was the moment Angela had died.

It had been an omen — not for Sean, but for his Angel.

He'd broken his promise to take care of her.

★ ★ ★

As Sean made his way along the hallway O'Brien appeared on the landing at the top of the first flight of stairs with Niamh clamped to his chest and a gun digging into her temple.

'Leave the girl be, O'Brien, she's got nothing to do with this,' said Sean.

He was weighing up the possibility of taking a shot. But Niamh was covering most of O'Brien's torso and she was moving around too much: it would be far too risky.

'A dead man talking: that's quite an act you've

431

got, Sean,' said O'Brien. 'I bet you're wishing you'd stayed dead now, eh?'

'Being a tout not enough for you any more, Owen, you have to abduct wee girls as well?'

'Shut your mouth and drop your weapon on the floor.'

Sean knew that if he didn't do what he was told then O'Brien would simply pull the trigger and Niamh would be dead. If he did do what O'Brien asked him, then Danny would be the only hope left of getting out alive.

'Drop it on the floor and kick it towards me,' repeated O'Brien.

Sean had no choice. He bent forward and tossed the AR15 on the floor out of reach.

'Tell your brother to throw his weapon down and come out of the attic with his hands where I can see them.'

Sean was out of options. While O'Brien had the girl there was nothing he or Danny could do, but as soon as his brother gave up his weapon O'Brien would shoot them all and walk away: of that, there was no doubt.

Sean shouted to his brother, but there was no reply.

He tried again.

'Danny!'

O'Brien had his eyes fixed on the opening in the ceiling at the far end of the hall.

'I want you down out of that attic in ten seconds or I'm going to put a big fucking hole in this wee girl's head,' shouted O'Brien. 'Drop your gun onto the floor and get your arse down here. No fucking about now, all right?'

When O'Brien looked back at Sean he saw that he had taken a step closer to the bottom of the stairs. 'Got a notion to rush me, big fella?'

O'Brien fired a single shot that hit Sean on the bottom of his thigh, just above his knee. The force of the impact made his leg buckle underneath him and Sean dropped to the floor.

'I'm not fucking around, Danny,' continued O'Brien. 'Out of the attic now or I'll kill the two of them. Your brother's already down. You've got ten seconds before I shoot again, only this time I'll be aiming for his fucking skull.'

O'Brien started counting.

'Ten . . . nine . . . eight . . . seven . . . '

When he got to 'three' there was a hard metallic sound as Danny's gun clattered down the attic steps and onto the floor.

A few seconds later Danny emerged from the hatch and slowly made his way down the ladders, until he was standing less than three yards from O'Brien with his hands hanging loosely by his side.

Niamh started writhing around, but once again O'Brien tightened his grip and squeezed her until she could no longer move.

Danny could see the fear in his young niece's eyes. 'Don't you worry about a thing, darlin, okay? Everything is going to be all right,' he said, trying to reassure her.

'Yeah, don't you worry there, darlin,' repeated O'Brien. 'Everything is fucking great. You'll all be together, very soon. Might be a bit cold for you, but don't you worry, darlin, okay!'

Danny knew exactly what O'Brien was referring to, but he wasn't going to give him the

433

satisfaction of acknowledging it. His face betrayed no emotion.

The sound of Sean's laboured breathing could be heard coming from downstairs.

'You okay, Sean?' shouted Danny.

'Fine,' came the reply. 'Copped one in the leg, but I'm fine.'

Danny looked straight at Niamh. 'Do you remember the trick I taught you when we used to do our dummy fighting?'

Niamh looked puzzled for a second, then gave a slight nod.

'Shut your mouth, McGuire,' said O'Brien, sensing that Danny was up to something.

'You have been found guilty of treason against the republican cause and sentenced to death,' continued Danny, shifting his gaze from Niamh to O'Brien. 'I'm here to carry out the will of the Republican Army council and execute you.'

O'Brien stared back in disbelief. 'And people think *I'm* off my fucking nut. You take the biscuit, big fella. You're not even a fucking member of the RA.'

'I was given a job to do and I'm here to do it,' replied Danny. 'Let the girl go,' he said, keeping his tone steady and resolute.

'Maybe you hadn't noticed, fuckwit. I'm the one with the gun,' replied O'Brien. 'Look,' he said, relishing the moment as he pointed the pistol downstairs and fired another round into Sean.

Danny heard an agonised groan from Sean as the bullet tore a strip of flesh from his arm.

'You're fucked, Danny boy. Once I've killed

your brother, and shot this wee girl in the head, I'm going to kill you. Then it's off to the pub for a pint. I don't know what I'm looking forward to the most: watching your face as I kill *them*, or watching *your* face as you die. Or will it be the look on people's faces when I tell them that you were the Thevshi all along? I'll tell them you squealed like a stuck pig when you realised you'd been found out. What a result! O'Leary is going to lap this up like a cur at a desert well. It's been fucking with his mind for years who 'The Ghost' could be. Too easy, shitehawk, too easy! Couldn't have worked out better if I'd planned it myself.'

'O'Leary's dead,' said Danny.

O'Brien hesitated momentarily, a brief flash of doubt crossing his eyes. 'Aye right?'

'E. I. O'Leary, Slim Jim, everyone connected with the kidnapping of that wee girl there and the death of Angela Fitzpatrick.'

'Aye, well, that was unfortunate! She wasn't quite up to the pressure. I meant to give her back to you disfigured, like, but the hot water proved a bit too much for her. Shame really: nice girl. *She* was a squealer too. Got it on tape if you fancy a listen.'

'You're next,' said Danny.

'Come on, McGuire . . . any time you like,' said Owen O'Brien disdainfully. 'Come'n have a go.'

★ ★ ★

All this time Niamh had kept her gaze fixed firmly on Danny, waiting for the signal.

435

When it came it was almost imperceptible: a slight movement of the eyes, nothing more, but she caught it.

Niamh's body suddenly went limp in O'Brien's arms. Although she was small in stature, her body weight was enough to tip him forward momentarily. It was a move Danny had taught her when they used to play-fight. Drop your body in a limp feint to pull your opponent off-balance then tense and strike.

In the same instant Danny raised his arm in a small, but powerful upward movement and flicked his hand forward. A black-handled knife left his grip and spun through the air in silence, delivering the blade point-first deep into Owen O'Brien's right eye.

O'Brien let out a high-pitched squeal and stumbled backwards, clawing at his eye socket, then he suddenly pitched forward, his arms flailing wildly, grabbing for the girl. But Niamh was too quick. She ducked out of reach and started down the stairs.

Sean was up on his feet waiting for her, his face wracked with pain.

'Get her outside,' shouted Danny, as Niamh disappeared from view.

Danny took a step forward and swung his right leg in a high arc. The heel of his shoe struck O'Brien on the side of his face and knocked him sideways to the ground, but as he fell O'Brien managed to twist himself round and squeeze the trigger of his gun, firing wildly in all directions. Bullets smashed into the walls and ceiling.

Danny ducked out of the way as one whistled

dangerously overhead. In the same movement, he flicked his foot forward again and managed to kick the weapon from O'Brien's grasp.

O'Brien screamed wildly and lashed out. In his frenzy he managed to grab hold of Danny's leg and start to pull him off balance. He tried to kick his way free, but O'Brien's grip was like a vice. Suddenly Danny pitched forward, cracking his head on the top of the banister as he fell to the floor.

In an instant O'Brien was on top of him with his knee digging painfully into Danny's chest, forcing the breath from his lungs: his big, rough hands wrapped tightly round Danny's throat, choking his airways.

Danny struggled desperately to tip O'Brien off by raising his stomach off the floor and twisting back and forth, but O'Brien's weight and the lack of oxygen made it impossible. He threw punches at his face, but O'Brien's arms were splayed out at the elbows, blocking anything from landing with any force.

Danny was rapidly losing his strength. He could feel his arms becoming heavy and limp. He was starting to lose consciousness.

Nearby, a small voice shouted something indiscernible.

He saw O'Brien turn his head and felt the pressure on his neck ease slightly. Suddenly there was a deafening boom and O'Brien's face appeared to explode in front of him.

Danny coughed and spluttered as the air rushed to fill his lungs. He tried to sit up, but his strength had not yet returned. O'Brien's

437

headless body lay jerking and convulsing on the floor beside him, no longer any threat.

Danny turned his head, searching for the source of the noise, and saw Niamh on the landing below: her face taut with fear, her expression grim, as she took her finger off the trigger then lowered the AR15 gently to the floor.

She started to cry.

43

The reflections of bright orange street lamps slipped silently over the windscreen of the VW Polo as it picked its way through the quiet streets of Newry. In the back of the car sat a small girl, curled in a tight ball, staring out of the window with an unfocused gaze.

The expression on the driver's face was grave, as he glanced round at his brother, sitting with his arms wrapped, like a protective shield, round the young girl's shoulders. His brother's face was pale and bloodless: covered in sweat.

No one spoke for the entire journey.

★　★　★

At around 2 a.m. Father Anthony heard a knock at the door. He was sitting by the open coffin of one of his parishioners, keeping vigil over her body. He carefully placed his tea cup on the floor underneath his chair and made his way over to the large vestry door.

Sean McGuire's cadaverous frame stood hunched in the doorway. Father Anthony offered his hand as support and led Sean through the vestry and along the short corridor towards his kitchen. Danny followed closely behind with

439

Niamh clinging to him, her arms wrapped tightly round his neck.

'Anyone we know, Father?' asked Danny as he passed the coffin.

'No! One of the invisibles! Her husband died a few years ago and she has no family over here to mourn her passing, but a great woman nonetheless. A fighter. Used her wit and humour to fight her battles, not guns and fists,' said the priest pointedly. 'But you're not here for a lecture. Does anyone want anything to drink? Doctor Campbell's on his way; should be here any minute.'

'Tea would be grand, Father,' replied Danny. 'I'm sorry to put you through this, but we didn't know where else to go.'

Father Anthony waved his hand dismissively and said, 'I'm not doing this for you, Danny, I'm doing it for your mother.'

Sean lifted his head and spoke in a quiet voice. 'All the same, we appreciate it, Father.'

The priest gave Sean a look. 'I spoke at your last funeral, Sean, and I don't intend to do the same at your next one. I can't think of another occasion when I've had to minister to someone I've already buried, but these are strange times. As far as I can make out it doesn't mention anything in the Bible about it being wrong — or a sin — to help a dead man. In fact I would argue that is the very tenet of the bloody thing anyway: looking after the dead . . . ' He paused for a second and smiled ruefully. 'In particular, the ones that have come back to life.'

44

Marie's apartment, Tuscaloosa, Friday

Marie tipped two heaped spoonfuls of freshly ground coffee into a pot and filled it almost to the brim with boiling water. 'How do you take it?'

'Black, please,' answered Jeff Kneller through a hacking cough. 'Who did you get to represent you?' he continued eventually. 'I hope you didn't plump for that idiot the court were going to appoint: Geraldine Fitz, she's a bloody nightmare.'

Marie bit her lip as she handed Kneller a steaming mug of coffee. 'Went for Mr Larsson. He seems okay, but his summary took longer to read than it did for me to live through the actual events.'

'Yeah, he does go on a bit, but once he gets going he's very good; covers all the angles,' replied Kneller.

Her living room was now clear of all the boxes; most of their contents were packed away in drawers and cupboards. But despite her best efforts to make it feel more homely, the apartment felt strangely empty.

She was smartly dressed, but wishing she'd opted for casual.

Jeff Kneller sat awkwardly on the sofa — it was too low down for a guy wearing a suit, and

441

the whites of his shins were showing above his faded black socks.

'You sure I shouldn't have my lawyer present for this meeting?' asked Marie.

'This is an 'after hours' visit: I'm not on duty, more of a social call.'

Kneller looked uncomfortable without the support of his partner.

'Are you going out?' he asked.

Marie smiled. 'No. I have this strange need to look respectable whenever I'm around a grown-up. I thought the suit would make me look more . . . organised.'

She was hoping he would smile back and make her feel that she wasn't quite as dumb as she sounded, but Kneller just nodded.

'Got a couple of questions I'd like to ask, then I'll leave you to enjoy the rest of your evening.'

'*Sounds* official,' said Marie. 'Where's your boyfriend?'

Kneller knew she was referring to his partner, Joe Evelyn, but he didn't take the bait. 'Where's yours?' he replied.

'Is that one of the questions?'

'I promise you, this is just to satisfy my own curiosity. If you feel uncomfortable with what I'm asking, don't answer. I want to spend my retirement in peaceful contemplation, not worrying over unsolved mysteries or wondering which — if any — of the bad guys are still out there lurking in the shadows. Besides, it doesn't look like you'll need a lawyer at all. The only solid piece of evidence we had on you was the letter you wrote to Finn O'Hanlon . . . ' Kneller

442

looked embarrassed as he finished the sentence. ' . . . and that's been misplaced.'

'Misplaced?' said Marie.

Kneller gave a slight shrug. 'No one knows where it is. The asshole whose job it was to file it put it down somewhere, but can't remember where. It may still turn up, but we can't go to a prosecutor and say, 'We have evidence, but do you mind waiting till we find it again?' A simple case of ineptitude, but one that works in your favour.'

Marie was surprised at how candid Kneller was being with her, but she kept her thoughts to herself. 'Are you old enough to retire?' she asked.

'By rights I should have another nine years to serve, but ill health doesn't come with an age limit, and I cut a deal with my doctor. Which reminds me: d'you mind if I smoke?'

Marie shook her head. 'Only if I can have one too.'

Kneller pulled out a packet of Marlboros and offered them to Marie before taking one himself. 'Don't suppose you have a light?' he asked.

Marie took his cigarette from him and crossed over to the hob. She lit hers first then pushed the tip of Kneller's cigarette against hers and lit it too.

'What d'you want to know?' she asked, blowing a small cloud of smoke out across the room.

'Is Sean McGuire/Finn O'Hanlon — or whatever he likes to call himself — still in the country?'

'No.'

'Do you know where he is?'

Marie shrugged her shoulders. 'I think he's gone back to Ireland, but I've no idea where.'

'Did he kill De Garza?'

Marie looked surprised. She'd seen the news reports. It was a huge story, making not only the local news, but the national as well.

Everybody had a theory as to who had organised the hit on De Garza — the guy had a lot of enemies — but it had never once crossed her mind that Sean was somehow involved. 'I'm pretty sure not.'

'His brother?'

Marie shrugged again. 'I honestly don't know.'

'Did you know that Finn O'Hanlon was his assumed name: that he was living here under a false passport and his name was Sean McGuire?'

'I didn't know that from the off, but I did find out later,' said Marie.

'He used to be involved with the IRA and at one point was being groomed for the leadership.'

'That I didn't know,' answered Marie truthfully.

'We've had some preliminary contact with the British authorities and the one thing that none of us can work out is why they sent his brother over to assassinate him?' Kneller sounded like he was asking her a question.

'I have no idea. Everything happened so fast, like an avalanche of events, but at no point did we all sit round a table and discuss why we were all present, in these circumstances, at that moment in time, y'know what I mean? The only thing I would say is that Danny seemed more surprised to see Sean than Sean was to see

Danny. In a weird way it was almost as if Sean was expecting it to be his brother.'

'And the night you were over at O'Hanlon/ Sean McGuire's apartment collecting his *belongings*, that was the first time you'd come across Ardel and Hud.'

'A few weeks ago I'd never heard of *any* of them. If that asshole Conrado hadn't come into my place of work and started shooting the place up like he was at a goddamn fairground, then I would be sitting here in my pyjamas watching the news wondering who all these fucked-up people were and how they ended up getting involved in so much shit. I'm one of life's observers, Jeff, I'm not a participant. I shouldn't be standing here in my own apartment, with a goddamn suit on — cast in one of the leading roles.'

Kneller nodded quietly to himself for a few moments. He seemed to have made his mind up about something.

'Culo Conrado was an asshole, Vincent Lee Croll was an asshole and Hernando De Garza was twenty different sorts of asshole rolled into one. There's no one in my department mourning their loss. Whoever terminated those suckers did us a favour as far as I'm concerned. The trouble with people like De Garza is, he was very influential. You can't shoot an asshole as big as that and not expect to get covered in shit. His murder has created a power vacuum that's going to cause an explosion, with shock waves that will destroy a lot of people. There will be certain colleagues of his looking for revenge and others who are glad to see the back of him and hoping to fill his shoes. Now, it makes no odds to me if they want to fight it out amongst themselves, but my worry is that if we prosecute *you* for aiding and abetting Sean McGuire — the man who shot Cola Conrado — then the newshounds will get their teeth into it and make the connection between Conrado and De Garza. If that happens you are going to be linked — however tenuously — to De Garza's death. Chances are you're going to have some very nasty people knocking on your door. And *they* won't be here for a coffee and a smoke.'

Marie's expression was grave. She was standing with her back against the kitchen worktop, but she needed to sit down. She wondered if Kneller could see that her legs were trembling under her black gabardine slacks. 'Why are you telling me this?'

'I'm here to deliver a warning. I'm not trying to scare you, just give you the information and let you make up your own mind. There's a very strong possibility that all the charges against you will be dropped now. To my mind that's the right decision. I believe you when you say you were an innocent in all this. That's not to say you didn't go along with what was happening, but you're not a criminal. If I were you I'd take the opportunity to go away for a while, certainly move to a different address, better still get out of the state. The press still have a lot of questions and if you're not here to answer them, there's not much they can do.'

'I've just finished unpacking,' said Marie.

'You still got the boxes?'

Marie smiled. 'Threw the last of them out this morning, would you believe?'

'Go buy some more,' said Kneller.

Marie held up the coffee pot. 'You want a top-up?'

'No, I'm good.'

'Can I ask you a few questions?'

'Sure.'

'What'll happen to Ardel and Hud?'

'Who knows!' answered Kneller. 'They've disappeared. If they know what's good for them they'll stay disappeared. There's already a big prize fund on the heads of anyone involved with De Garza's murder and Sly Rivera's. And from what I can gather, Ardel and Hud are in the frame for causing the pile-up on the freeway.'

'Shame. They were nice boys,' said Marie.

Kneller placed his coffee mug on the low table in front of the sofa and stood up. 'I have to go. Don't take too long to make up your mind.'

'Does your partner Joe Evelyn know you're here?' asked Marie.

'No,' replied Kneller.

'Should I tell my lawyer about our conversation?'

'No.'

Marie held the front door open and put her hand out to shake Kneller's as he walked into the hallway. He looked at it for a second as if it was an odd thing to do, then reached out and took hold of it. His grip was firm and he held on to her for a few seconds longer then she was expecting.

'You take care,' he said, looking straight into her eyes.

'You too . . . I hope you have a long and peaceful retirement.'

Kneller gave her a wry smile as he finally let go.

'It'll be peaceful, but it won't be very long.'

Marie closed the door behind him then secured both of the dead bolts and turned the key before pulling the handle to make sure the door was firmly locked.

She listened a few moments for the sounds of Kneller's footsteps heading for the elevator, but the hallway outside was silent. Maybe he had already left.

Truth was she'd never really liked the apartment anyway. She'd only taken it on until she could save enough money for a deposit on a small house further out of town. First thing she'd do was change out of the bloody trouser suit then — after she'd fixed herself a large sour — head down to the trash and see if her boxes were still there.

Suddenly her letter box flipped open, making her jump. An envelope dropped on to the floor just by her feet. Straight away she picked it up and tore it open.

Marie froze.

There were footsteps moving quickly away from her front door. Someone was outside in the corridor.

Marie strained to listen then relaxed again as she heard the call-bell for the elevator ping.

The envelope contained a sheet of white

foolscap covered with handwriting that she recognised instantly. Marie stared at the piece of paper and smiled. It was the note that she had written to Finn: the note that 'some asshole' in the FBI had 'misplaced'.

Marie bent down to the letterbox and lifted the flap. 'Thank you, Mr Kneller,' she shouted. Then added, 'For your ineptitude.'

There was no way of knowing if Kneller heard her as the elevator doors closed behind him, but she hoped he had.

45

Cushendun, Northern Ireland's north-east coast, Saturday, morning

The small peninsular island was dotted with large granite boulders that eventually merged into a cluster of craggy rock pools before dipping into the cold clear waters lapping around its edges. The tiny outcrop was covered in gorse and heather, and jutted into the Irish Sea at the far end of a long, arching spine of alabaster-coloured sand.

At the opposite end of the beach sat the village of Cushendun, built round the mouth of the River Dun. Two granite-block quays faced each other on either side of a small inlet that harboured a number of fishing boats, pleasure craft and dinghies, Sail ropes snapped against their metal masts and gulls floated and hovered overhead, squawking as the boats swayed back and forth — clunking together in the gentle offshore breeze. The south bank of the quayside was lined with a terrace of white houses once used for fishermen, but now largely owned or rented by holidaymakers.

There was a two-storey hotel near the high street with a seaward view from the second floor that — on a clear day — stretched all the way over to the Mull of Kintyre in Scotland. The hotel also overlooked the north-bank quayside which was triangular in shape and used mostly as a visitors' car park. It had a two-foot-high stone wall that framed its circumference and separated the car park from the sandy beach beyond.

The holiday season wasn't yet under way, so the car park was empty, apart from a few vehicles belonging to the locals. The village had a post office that doubled as a convenience store, a pub, a café and a tourist information bureau that stocked Celtic souvenirs. There were no roadblocks, or army patrols or sectarian graffiti on any of the village's walls. The Troubles affecting the rest of Northern Ireland had left Cushendun to its own devices. Even the local police officer — despite having the authority to carry a firearm — left his weapon locked in the station's gun cabinet when he went out on patrol.

Many years ago this was where Órlaith and Sean had spent their honeymoon.

★　★　★

It was early. The only sign of habitation was the two distant figures picking their way through granite boulders and gorse at the northernmost point of the bay. The rising sun cast their shadows long over the dewy tufts of grass.

Órlaith jumped the final few feet onto the sandy beach and stood waiting for Kathleen McGuire to join her.

She regretted coming here to hide. The carefree memories of her past were being pushed to one side and replaced with less happy ones. It had been five days since Órlaith and Mrs

451

McGuire had checked into the hotel. There was still no word from Danny, and no news of what had happened to Niamh.

Órlaith looked pale and drawn. Her skin was as dry as the sand she was standing on and almost the same colour. Even the thin lines around her eyes and mouth seemed to have deepened in the last few days.

Kathleen McGuire on the other hand had lived with the consequences of the Troubles for so long that, for her, little had changed. Since the death of her husband, followed by her son's murder, pain and anguish had become so familiar to her that they were now part of who she was. Every day was the same battle: a struggle to keep herself sane.

She had given up all hope of ever finding peace, but she was no longer at war.

Kathleen had always liked Órlaith. She had been good for Sean. She had watched her son mellow and mature under Órlaith's influence. Órlaith had her head screwed on and she could play Sean like a fiddle.

Intellectually she was more than his match. She'd studied politics and Irish history at Queen's University in Belfast and could put across a convincing argument in favour of a political settlement to the Troubles as opposed to an armed struggle.

Sean and Órlaith would argue long into the night about the best approach to take. Philosophically they were in agreement, but the means each of them would employ to reach the goal were at opposite ends of the spectrum. At the heart of their relationship was their ability to see each other's point of view. They respected each other's opinion and that's why they had worked so well as a couple.

Over the last few days Kathleen had found herself opening up to Órlaith in a way that she hadn't done with anyone since Sean had been murdered. Perversely the situation they now found themselves in had been good for their relationship. It had brought them closer together. They shared a common tragedy: Órlaith had lost her husband, Kathleen her son.

Both of them prayed that Niamh's name would not also be added to the list.

The two women made their way across the sand in silence. They had spent every night since their arrival talking over the events of the past week, trying to piece a narrative together out of what little information they had.

The conclusion they had come to at the end of every evening was the same: none of it made any sense and there was almost no point in trying to explain what happened.

Suddenly Órlaith reached out and grabbed Kathleen by the hand, pulling her to a stop.

The unexpected movement startled her. She turned quickly and saw the look of apprehension on Órlaith's face.

'Are you all right?' she asked.

Órlaith gripped her hand even more tightly and stared straight ahead of her. 'Look,' she replied.

Her voice was so quiet against the noise of waves breaking along the shoreline that Kathleen strained to hear what she said. 'What's wrong?' she asked again.

Órlaith nodded in the direction of the car park and repeated herself.

'Look.'

Kathleen followed Órlaith's gaze along the beach.

Two men were walking towards them.

Without saying another word, Órlaith let go of Kathleen's hand and started running across the sand towards the men.

Kathleen stood watching in confusion: rooted to the spot.

One of the men was limping quite badly and was using the other's shoulder to support him as he struggled over the loose sand. His head was bowed forward as though he was ashamed to show his face. The other man was holding a young girl in his arms and was walking slowly to provide a steady prop for his injured companion. Kathleen watched the young girl wriggle free from the man's arms and run to meet Órlaith, who scooped her up and held her in a tight embrace.

It was only then she realised that the young girl was her grand-daughter Niamh and the man carrying Niamh was her son Danny. She had barely recognised him at first. He looked so much older than when she'd last seen him: life had scarred his face, the boyish looks gone for ever. She watched as Órlaith exchanged words with Danny and the other man, their conversation swallowed up by the wind.

Suddenly Órlaith collapsed to her knees and had to be helped back to her feet. Kathleen looked on as the other man reached out and held Órlaith to him, her head buried in his shoulder.

454

Eventually Kathleen saw Órlaith lift her head and turn, the expression on her face imploring Kathleen to join the small group.

But Kathleen didn't move. She knew instinctively that it was for them to come to her; not the other way round.

A few moments later Danny and the other man left Órlaith — with Niamh standing by her side — and continued along the beach.

As they drew closer the man leaning on Danny's shoulder raised his eyes and stared at her, seemingly uncertain what to do next. His face was pale and drawn, and full of sadness.

'I'm so sorry, Ma . . . ' he said as he reached her.

But Kathleen held her finger to her lips.

'Shh. You don't have to say it, son. I've always known.'

She slowly struck her clenched fist against the middle of her chest and continued, 'In here . . . I've always known.'

In her dreams she knew exactly what to say: she had lived this moment many times, but never dared to hope that one day it might come true. But standing there now, with her son Sean in front of her, Kathleen found that she could no longer speak: the words were choked back by her quiet, gentle sobs.

The tears she'd held locked in her heart for eight years tumbled freely down her face.

Sean took the final few steps towards his mother and accepted her embrace. The long journey home was finally at an end.

46

The outskirts of Newry, Sunday

Sean and Danny decided to take the country lanes around the back of Camlough on their way to Newry. Most of the main routes in and out of the small town had army roadblocks. A random 'stop-and-search' was the last thing they needed.

The headlines on the car radio carried the news of Frank Thompson's murder. The report focused mainly on the links between the head of intelligence's death and those of E. I. O'Leary and Owen O'Brien. Almost the entire programme was given over to this one story.

Danny sat stony-faced as the commentary revealed that several — as yet unidentified — bodies had been recovered from the attic of a building in Cochron Road where O'Brien's corpse had been discovered. It also mentioned that one of the big newspapers had received a phone call late the night before, alleging that Owen O'Brien was the notorious informant known as the Thevshi.

A massive security operation was under way with the security forces issuing a warning that there were bound to be major repercussions over the deaths. They appealed for anyone with any information to come forward, and urged the caller who had contacted the newspaper to get back in touch in order to substantiate their claims regarding O'Brien.

Sean gave a wry smile. 'Just as well we're leaving, eh?'

The day was milder than usual for the time of year and several times on the journey Danny had to squint against the sunlight streaming in through the car window. They had spent the previous night with Órlaith, Niamh, and their mother in the hotel at Cushendun, talking into the small hours about nothing in particular.

There was so much to be discussed, but they all seemed to recognise that the deeper conversations concerning what had happened would come at a later date. For now they were happy to be in each other's company.

The hotel owner served them drinks until closing time, then left them the keys of the bar and told them to keep a tab: they could settle up with him in the morning.

Órlaith had gone to her room first, taking Niamh — who had been asleep for hours — with her. Kathleen McGuire stayed on for one more drink, then held both boys in a tight embrace for several minutes before retiring to her room. Danny and Sean had sat on in silence and finished their drinks, then Danny helped Sean upstairs and into bed.

The only awkwardness had been between Sean and Órlaith: they were like strangers meeting for the first time.

Órlaith had loved Sean once, but he had died, she'd grieved, and emotionally she had moved on. It had been a long and difficult process to get to where she was now and — to his credit — Sean seemed to have recognised that she was a different person now. At one point during the evening whilst Danny was talking to his mother, Sean had leant across and whispered to her, 'Do you think we can still be friends?' Órlaith knew exactly what he was saying: it was impossible to go back. She was unable to disguise the sadness in her eyes as she nodded in reply. But if she was being honest, the sadness was tinged with a sense of relief. It was exactly what she had wanted to say to him.

For a number of reasons she'd also decided not to tell Sean that he was Niamh's father. Uppermost in her mind was an overriding instinct to protect her daughter from any further harm or emotional upset. It was obvious from what Sean had been saying that — ultimately — he was planning to go back to the States. Gaining a father who was already making plans to leave would be too much for Niamh to bear: it was in no one's best interest.

In the morning the family had breakfasted together, then Sean and Danny set off for Newry to pick up the girls' passports from their mother's house.

It had been decided during the course of their conversations the previous evening — even before they'd heard the news reports — that staying in Northern Ireland was no longer an option for any of them.

★ ★ ★

Back in the car, Sean reached across and retuned the radio to a music channel. David Bowie was singing 'Wild-Eyed Boy' from *Freecloud*. 'It's good to hear some decent music for a change,' he said, looking round at Danny. 'All they play in Tuscaloosa is bloody Country and Western or bluegrass. Not that they're shit, but it does your head in after a while . . . Are you all right, our lad? You haven't said a word for the past ten minutes.' asked Sean.

'I want to go in and visit Angela's ma, Mrs Fitzpatrick, before we head off.'

'Is that wise?' asked Sean. 'The RUC are out in force. Could cause us a few problems.'

'The least I can do is pay my respects in person.'

'It's up to you, our lad.'

⋆　⋆　⋆

The first he was aware that anything was wrong was when the car started swerving from side to side. Danny struggled briefly to keep it travelling in a straight line before the car suddenly slewed off to one side and crashed into a deep ditch that ran along the edge of the narrow road.

They came to a shuddering halt with the car resting on its side at a ninety-degree angle: the front and rear offside wheels spinning in mid-air and steam billowing from the engine.

Sean was slumped against the passenger door with his head pressed against the roof of the car and blood oozing from a cut above his right eye.

Luckily Danny had been wearing his seatbelt otherwise he would have landed on top of him. Instead he was clinging on to the steering wheel and trying to manoeuvre himself into a position where he could wind down the window and escape.

'Jesus, Danny, what the hell happened there?'

'God only knows, I think the front tyre blew.'

'We need to get out your side.'

'You okay?' asked Danny.

'Fine! Got a crack on the head, but I'm fine. C'mon, let's get out.'

Danny braced his legs against the steering column while he unclipped his seat belt, then clamped his arms on the side of the car and pulled himself clear.

He jumped down onto the rough tarmac, then turned to help Sean. As he reached in to take hold of his brother's arm, he caught a movement on the hillside just a few hundred metres over to his left.

There was a muzzle flash.

Sean's head was just above the level of the car door when the first bullet whistled past and caught Danny on the shoulder.

The impact spun his body backwards and sent him crashing to the ground.

Sean ducked back inside. Another round pierced the roof and buried itself in the padding of the driver's seat — closely followed by another, then another.

Sean shouted to Danny, 'Are you hit?'

The roof exploded just above his head.

'Fuckers got me in the shoulder,' replied Danny. 'The front tyre's in shreds: they must have shot it out.'

'Where's your gun?'

'Nine mil's in the glove box,' replied Danny. 'Armalite's in the back.'

'Any movement out there?'

'Up on the hill to the left, but I've no idea how many.'

'I'm going to throw you out the Armalite. Tell me when you're set up, and see if you can keep the bastards' heads down. I need to get out of here. You ready? Here it comes.'

The instant Sean pushed the AR15 assault rifle up out of the window he heard several more rounds cracking off the hillside.

Another three holes appeared in the car roof.

'Have you got it?'

'Yeah!'

'On the count of three?'

'Go for it!' replied Danny.

'One . . . two . . . three.'

Danny stood up with the assault rifle clamped to his injured shoulder and sprayed several short bursts into the hillside.

Almost immediately there was a return of fire from not one, but two locations — three hundred metres separating them.

Danny retaliated, this time alternating between the two areas.

Sean was already out of the window and scrambling across the door. He was nearly over the edge of the car when a bullet punched his leg out from underneath him. A searing hot pain surged up the middle of his calf. 'Bastard,' he screamed as he crumpled onto the ground next to Danny. 'Ya fucker!'

His calf muscle had a six-inch tear running

lengthways along it.

'Is it bad?' asked Danny.

Sean shook his head. 'Nah! Stings like fuck, but I've had worse playing football.'

'You reckon we could make it across that field?'

'Probably . . . '

'But?'

'But, there's no glory in running away. They're never going to write a rebel song about two brothers that jumped over a hedge and crawled away.'

Sean and Danny exchanged a look.

'We are in the shit, are we not?' asked Sean. 'If there are two snipers up on the hill, there's bound to be another one at the bottom of the field behind just waiting for us to come leaping over that hedge. And then there's the fucker that shot out our tyres. He'll be along in a minute as well. These SAS guys give good ambush.'

'We could split up, take a flank each, see how far we get down the field,' said Danny. 'Take at least one of them in a pincer movement.'

'I'm not crawling anywhere,' replied Sean.

'Nah, neither am I,' said Danny. ' . . . Listen!'

'What?'

'What's that noise?' asked Danny.

A low rumbling noise like a peal of rolling thunder growled in the distance.

'Here, you take the pistol and I'll have this,' said Sean, reaching over to take the Armalite from Danny. 'They've got back-up. Shitehawks have called in a chopper.'

'Ah well,' sighed Danny, 'that's the end of that then, eh?'

'No option but to take the fuckers on, eh?'

'Aye, it looks like it,' replied Danny. 'Remember that night at Cailleach Berra Lough?'

'Jesus! Talk about random! What the hell's that got to do with anything?'

'I never thanked you for saving my life.'

Sean thought for a second then said, 'You've got it all wrong, Wub. It wasn't me saved you. I was too scared to go on the ice. It was Lep ran on and grabbed you.'

'You sure?'

'Positive. That ice was thinner than a sheet of cling film.'

Danny looked up at the cloudless sky and sighed. 'Ah, well . . . thank you, Lep.'

'You know, the worst part of those years I spent in America was not having you there. I missed you like crazy, our lad. I wish we had a wee bit longer.'

'Sure, you've nothing to worry about, Sean: we'll be together for the rest of our lives,' said Danny, looking over at his brother.

Another thought struck him. 'What does Wub stand for?'

'What made you think of that?'

'Because I've never known.'

The helicopter was getting closer, drowning out their voices.

'Wee ugly bastard,' shouted Sean over the din.

Danny smiled.

Sean cocked the Armalite and stood up. 'You coming?'

Danny raised himself off the ground and stood beside his brother.

They walked out from behind the car together and took it in turns to fire into the hillside and up at the approaching dark-green military helicopter.

Suddenly the air around them was filled with the rasp and crack of gunfire.

The ground they were standing on disintegrated and crumbled and seemed to vanish beneath their feet as the two men disappeared behind a fine mist of blood, dried earth and smoke.

Their bodies buckled and bucked as the bullets ripped and tore at their flesh.

When they fell they landed side by side in the ditch at the front of the upturned car.

Sean lay staring blindly at the clear blue sky overhead, his eye sockets filled with blood.

The shooting had finally stopped.

Through the stillness he could hear the echo of a woman's voice calling to him.

★ ★ ★

Two young boys raced each other across the sands of Cushendun towards their parents, who were standing together at the head of the bay.

Sean could see his father waiting to sweep the winner up into his open arms. He tried even harder to catch his brother, who was just a few paces in front.

But as they approached the finish line, Sean noticed Danny starting to tire. Rather than push past and overtake him — which he could easily

464

have done — Sean held back so that his brother could still win the race.

He stood and smiled at Danny's whoops and screams as his dad spun him high through the air.

★   ★   ★

Sean reached out and fumbled beside him, searching for his brother's hand. Using what little strength he had left, Sean pulled Danny closer.

'You'll be all right, our lad, don't you worry now,' he said as he kissed his brother on the forehead for the last time.

Epilogue

Niagara Falls, New York

Two days later at 11 a.m., a woman entered a small bank in Niagara Falls on the east coast of the United States and opened a deposit account using a false passport and social security number. She told the bank clerk she was moving to the area and the money was the proceeds from the sale of her house back home. The clerk didn't even look up when she handed over nearly $200,000 in cash. The transaction took less than ten minutes.

He only asked one question: 'Do I spell 'Marie' with or without an 'e', Mrs O'Hanlon?'

Marie slipped the deposit receipt in her purse and crossed the busy main street, heading for the small coffee shop on the corner of the cross-roads. She ordered a tall latte and sat by the window watching the passers-by with distracted interest. Sean's flight was due to arrive at Niagara Falls International Airport later that afternoon, so she had some time to kill.

She had no reason to doubt he would be on the plane.

We do hope that you have enjoyed reading this large print book.

Did you know that all of our titles are available for purchase?

We publish a wide range of high quality large print books including:
Romances, Mysteries, Classics
General Fiction
Non Fiction and Westerns

Special interest titles available in large print are:
The Little Oxford Dictionary
Music Book
Song Book
Hymn Book
Service Book

Also available from us courtesy of Oxford University Press:
Young Readers' Dictionary
(large print edition)
Young Readers' Thesaurus
(large print edition)

For further information or a free brochure, please contact us at:
Ulverscroft Large Print Books Ltd.,
The Green, Bradgate Road, Anstey,
Leicester, LE7 7FU, England.
Tel: (00 44) **0116 236 4325**
Fax: (00 44) **0116 234 0205**

INTO THE DARKEST CORNER

Elizabeth Haynes

Catherine has been enjoying the single life long enough to know a great catch when she sees one. Gorgeous, charismatic, spontaneous — Lee seems almost too good to be true. And her friends clearly agree, as each in turn falls under his spell. But Lee's erratic and sometime controlling behaviour makes Catherine feel increasingly isolated. Driven into the darkest corner of her world, and trusting no one, she plans a meticulous escape. Four years later, and struggling to overcome her demons, Catherine dares to believe she might be safe from harm. Until one phone call changes everything.